$4—

D0048893

DATE DUE

MI SAGA
5

Fic
MoR
2028O4

GILBERT MORRIS
✫
Out of the Whirlwind

Tyndale House Publishers, Inc.
Wheaton, Illinois

Library of Congress Cataloging-in-Publication Data

Morris, Gilbert.
       Out of the whirlwind / Gilbert Morris.
          p.   cm. — (The Appomattox saga; 5)
       ISBN 0-8423-1658-2 (SC)
        1. United States—History—Civil War, 1861–1865—Fiction.   2. Man-
woman relationships—United States—Fiction.   I. Title.
II. Series: Morris, Gilbert.   Appomattox saga; 5.
PS3563.08742O92   1994
813'.54—dc20   93-35507

Printed in the United States of America
99 98 97 96 95 94
 9   8   7   6   5   4   3   2

To David and Audrey Coleman.
God has blessed Johnnie and me
with many fine friends.
You two have been a blessing
to us both!

EDITOR'S NOTE

The Quakers are well known for their unique speech patterns, particularly their use of *thee* in place of *you*. This is especially true among the old-line Quakers. However, as with any tradition, we found that younger generations tend to use the two terms more or less interchangeably, depending upon circumstance and audience. We have attempted to adhere to this pattern in *Out of the Whirlwind,* making the old-line Quaker characters consistent in their use of *thee,* while the younger and more prominent characters will at times replace *thee* with the more common *you*.

CONTENTS

Part One: The Spinster and the Prodigal

1. *A Gentleman Caller—At Last!* 3
2. *Two Kisses* 17
3. *Good-bye to Love* 31
4. *"I Won't Have a Husband"* 47
5. *The Return of Burke Rocklin* 59
6. *A Rapid Promotion* 73
7. *A-Courtin' He Would Go!* 87
8. *The Battle* 99

Part Two: The Patient and the Nurse

9. *Grace Comes to Washington* 115
10. *Mysterious Patient* 129
11. *The Awakening* 145
12. *"Thee Has a Man of Thy Own!"* 159
13. *A Sleigh Ride* 173
14. *An Unexpected Visitor* 185
15. *"A Wife Ought to Know"* 199
16. *Into the Valley of Death* 211

Part Three: The Prisoner and the Bride

17. *Captain Clay Finds a Man* 223
18. *"I Remember You!"* 237

19. *Two Visitors for Burke* 251
20. *Desperate Journey* 265
21. *The Verdict* 279
22. *"Give Love a Chance!"* 291
23. *Witness for the Defense* 303
24. *The Oregon Trail* 313

GENEALOGY OF

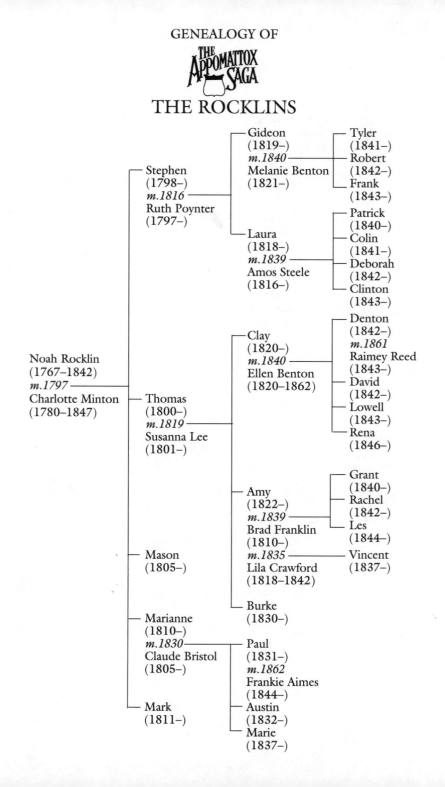

THE APPOMATTOX SAGA

THE ROCKLINS

Noah Rocklin
(1767–1842)
m.1797
Charlotte Minton
(1780–1847)

- **Stephen**
  (1798–)
  m.1816
  Ruth Poynter
  (1797–)
  - **Gideon**
    (1819–)
    m.1840
    Melanie Benton
    (1821–)
    - Tyler (1841–)
    - Robert (1842–)
    - Frank (1843–)
  - **Laura**
    (1818–)
    m.1839
    Amos Steele
    (1816–)
    - Patrick (1840–)
    - Colin (1841–)
    - Deborah (1842–)
    - Clinton (1843–)

- **Thomas**
  (1800–)
  m.1819
  Susanna Lee
  (1801–)
  - **Clay**
    (1820–)
    m.1840
    Ellen Benton
    (1820–1862)
    - Denton (1842–) *m.1861* Raimey Reed (1843–)
    - David (1842–)
    - Lowell (1843–)
    - Rena (1846–)
  - **Amy**
    (1822–)
    m.1839
    Brad Franklin
    (1810–)
    m.1835
    Lila Crawford
    (1818–1842)
    - Grant (1840–)
    - Rachel (1842–)
    - Les (1844–)
    - Vincent (1837–)
  - **Burke**
    (1830–)

- **Mason**
  (1805–)

- **Marianne**
  (1810–)
  m.1830
  Claude Bristol
  (1805–)
  - **Paul**
    (1831–)
    m.1862
    Frankie Aimes
    (1844–)
  - **Austin**
    (1832–)
  - **Marie**
    (1837–)

- **Mark**
  (1811–)

THE YANCYS

Buford Yancy
(1807–)
m.1829 ————————
Mattie Satterfield
(1813–1851)

— Royal
(1832–)
— Melora
(1834–)
— Zack
(1836–)
— Cora
(1837–)
— Lonnie
(1843–)
— Bobby
(1844–)
— Rose
(1845–)
— Josh
(1847–)
— Martha
(1849–)
— Toby
(1851–)

PART ONE
The Spinster and the Prodigal

CHAPTER ONE
A Gentleman Caller—At Last!

★

MARCH 1862

When Clyde Dortch appeared at the home of Amos Swenson with a bouquet of flowers in his hand, Swenson at once assumed that the young man had come to court his younger daughter, Prudence. "Come in, Friend Dortch," Swenson said, stepping back. "Thee has come calling on Prudence, I take it?"

Clyde Dortch, a trim young man of twenty-eight with crisp, curly auburn hair and bright brown eyes, stepped inside, but surprised the older man by saying, "Why no, sir, I'm calling on Miss Grace."

If Dortch had announced that he had come to burn the house down, Amos Swenson could not have been more taken aback.

"Grace? Thee is calling on Grace?"

"Yes, sir," Dortch said, seeming to enjoy the older man's confusion. "I should have asked your permission first, but I'm doing that right now."

Amos Swenson, at the age of sixty-nine, was broken in health but not in mind; he was still a sharp man. He knew every acre of his fine farm in detail, and his careful and judicious use of hired hands enabled him to keep it as up-to-date as any farm in Pennsylvania.

In Amos's youth, he had been a very tall man, but age and sickness had broken him down so that he was bent and stooped. His white hair was still full and thick, and his face wore the patient look of a chronically ill man. He was never sullen or resentful—he was too fine a Christian for that! Yet one could often see the pain he suffered reflected in his mild eyes. Now he fixed his light blue eyes on the young man as he quickly rearranged his thoughts.

After Amos's wife had died, he had never remarried. Thankfully, he had been gifted with enough wisdom to raise five girls, guiding three of them through courtship into successful marriages. With those three, it had not been a matter of enticing suitors, but of sorting through the numerous young men who cluttered up the house. It would be the same with his youngest daughter, Prudence, for at the age of seventeen, her youthful beauty was already drawing attention.

But Grace . . . ah, Grace was another proposition entirely.

Swenson became aware that Dortch was waiting for his response and said at once, "Well, come into the parlor, Friend Dortch." Turning, he led the young man into the parlor, then said, "I'll fetch Grace." He hesitated, then attempted to probe the mystery of Dortch's sudden appearance. "Is she expecting thee?"

"I don't think so, Friend Swenson." Dortch was wearing a Sunday meeting suit of brown wool, which fit him superbly. He was a fine dresser—which made some of the old-line Quakers suspicious of him. However, he managed to stay away from the more colorful items of dress and was the envy of most of the young men of his acquaintance—not to mention the young ladies. "It just came to me that I'd like to pay a call on her," Dortch added and smiled, exposing perfect white teeth. "Perhaps with the idea of seeing if she'd be receptive to my calling on a regular basis."

Swenson blinked with surprise. This was serious! Among the Friends, calling on a young woman "on a regular basis" was tantamount to an engagement! At the very least, it was a statement that a young man was prepared to advance toward the state of matrimony.

"There's a new tract from that evangelist named Finney you might like to read," Swenson said quickly. "It may take Grace a few minutes to freshen up."

"Oh, tell her not to hurry, sir!" Dortch picked up the tract and settled himself firmly on the horsehair sofa. "I'll just see what the minister has to say." He began reading the tract, but as soon as Swenson left the room, he tossed it on the table beside him, then got up and wandered around the room. Had anyone looked in upon him at that moment, they would have noted that Dortch had the air of a man who'd made up his mind to do something difficult and was set to do whatever was necessary to accomplish the task.

Swenson hurried out to the barn and found his eldest daughter forking hay out of the loft so that it fell to the floor in a great shimmering flow.

"Grace, come down!"

Grace Swenson paused and looked down at her father, who seemed strangely agitated. His hair was wild due to his running his hands through it—a sign that he was disturbed, the young woman knew. At once she tossed the hand-carved wooden fork aside and came down the ladder. She was wearing a pair of men's trousers, a plaid shirt that had been her father's, and a pair of heavy work shoes that had seen much service. It was her usual costume when she did the heavy chores outside the house, and usually her father paid no attention. Now, however, he eyed her with dismay.

"Grace, get thee inside and put on something fitting."

Grace stared at him sharply. "What's wrong, Father?"

Amos Swenson shook his head, and there was wonder and hope in his blue eyes such as Grace had not seen for some time.

"It is Clyde Dortch," he said with a trace of excitement. "He has come calling."

"Oh." Grace understood at once—or thought she did.

5

"Well, didn't thee tell him that Prudence is visiting over with the Williamsons?"

"No, Grace, thee doesn't understand!" Suddenly Swenson took a deep breath, for a sharp pain had come to him. He had felt it before, this pain. It made him feel fragile, like hollow glass about to shatter. Generally, he had come to expect it, but now it came without warning, shooting into him, leaving him feeling a sick gray emptiness within, like a hole had cut clean through his body. He looked down to hide the pain on his face from Grace, waited until he could speak firmly, then said, "It is thee he has come to call on, not Prudence."

The announcement, he saw, was almost as much a shock to his daughter as it had been to him. She stared at him uncomprehendingly for a moment, then licked her lips. "To call on me, Father?"

"Yes. Thee had better go clean up and put on a fitting dress."

Grace dropped her gaze to hide the confusion she knew must be showing on her face. As she struggled with her emotions, her father studied her with compassion and love. This daughter had always been his favorite, though he'd kept it hidden from her and from her sisters—or tried to.

She's like me, he thought, noting the tall, erect figure and the solid features. *All the others looked like Martha—but Grace is like me.* The other girls had been small and dark, like their mother. Grace alone had his height and Scandinavian ruddiness and blond hair. *It would have been better if she'd looked like the others,* he thought with a stab of regret.

Yet as he kept his gaze on her, he could not keep down the surge of pride that came to him. He'd wanted sons, of course. When none came, he'd learned to love his daughters well enough, but it was Grace who had been most like a son—perhaps because she was so much stronger than the others, or perhaps because she seemed to have gotten that part of his blood that loved the land and the animals. While the other girls had been playing with dolls, Grace had been right at her father's heels as he plowed or fed the stock. By the time she turned thirteen she had become the equal of almost any hired man, making up in enthusiasm for what she lacked in physical strength.

After Martha Swenson had died, during Prudence's birth, it had been Grace who'd kept the house together. *Shouldn't have let her do it,* Swenson thought suddenly. *She should have been spending that time seeing young men and that sort of thing. Instead, she was taking care of the others.*

His thoughts were interrupted when she looked up and said briefly, "I'll go change clothes."

"Put on thy blue dress," her father said, a smile coming to his thin, pale lips. "I've always been partial to that one."

"All right, Father."

Grace turned and, as she left, her father said, "It would do thee no harm to use a little of that rice powder Prudence is so fond of."

But she shook her head, saying, "That would not go well with the Friends, would it, Father? A preacher decorating her face with powder?"

"It never hurt a woman to make herself look well, Daughter," Swenson retorted. He had never gotten accustomed to the fact that his daughter was a Quaker preacher. He himself was a faithful Friend, but it somehow never ceased to give him some sort of shock when she stood up to preach at meeting. Shaking his head, he went back to the parlor to entertain the young man.

Grace left the barn, thinking not of her unexpected caller but of how poorly her father looked. He had failed badly since the spell he'd had the previous summer. It took all the strength he had, she knew, just to get out of bed some days. A stab of fear shot through her, and she lifted a short prayer as she crossed the barnyard and stepped into the house. *Lord, look to my father. Let him have strength for this day.*

She had developed the habit of offering short prayers as she went about her work. No one had taught her this, but she was a woman who thought much about God, and it was as natural as breathing for her to speak to him, sharing with him her thoughts, wishes, and fears.

Once in her room, it didn't take her long to get ready for her first suitor. She washed her face and hands at the washstand, using the heavy china basin, then turned to the pegs that held her clothing. Most of her dresses were gray or black or dark brown. She frowned. They worked very well for Meeting Time . . . but were not at all what a woman would wear to please a man!

She regarded the dark blue dress her father had mentioned, the only silk dress she'd ever owned. She'd worn it only twice since her father had almost forced her to buy it on one of their rare trips to Philadelphia. Both times she had worn it to please him rather than out of vanity.

Slipping into a pair of cotton stockings and pulling a heavy, stiff petticoat over her head, she took the blue dress from the peg. For a moment she stood there, running her work-roughened fingers over the smooth material, then pulled it on. She tied the sash and picked up a comb and brush, but catching her reflection in the small oval mirror, she studied herself.

She saw reflected there a woman of twenty-six years, who was tall and strongly built. The blue dress set off her figure well, for she was not fat—simply robust and more statuesque than her sisters. While a stranger viewing her would consider her fine indeed to look at, she turned from her own reflection with a regretful shake of her head. Her ideas of feminine beauty came from her sisters, all of whom were petite and slender as their mother had been—so much so that Grace had always felt outsized and awkward when she stood beside them.

She had her father's broad, well-shaped face, with a broad mouth and large eyes. But again, she had come to believe that her features were coarse and masculine. Had she been an only child—or at least been blessed with handsome brothers instead of petite, beautiful sisters—she would not have reached the age of twenty-six without having had a suitor.

Not that Grace was homely. Far from it! But her facial structure was *strong,* rather than delicate, and she was labeled plain and out of scale when weighed against the feminine prettiness of her four younger sisters. It was something that she had accepted when she was in her early teens, and others had sensed this in her. Particularly her sisters. It was not uncommon for one of these fair ladies to remark publicly, "Oh, Grace isn't interested in young men." And, with the callousness of pretty young women who are told too often just how pretty they are, they spoke more freely in the privacy of the home. Such statements as "It's a good thing Grace is so taken up with religion and being a preacher, because as plain as she is, she'd have a hard time catching a good man" were painfully common.

Now, as Grace examined herself in the mirror, she wondered what it would be like to have a home and a husband. For the greatest irony of her situation was that, in acting as a mother to her sisters, she had developed a maternal side to her character that none of the other girls possessed.

Maybe a little of that rice powder wouldn't hurt. The thought flashed through her mind and for an instant she was tempted to go to Prudence's chest and take out the small china case in which her sister kept the cosmetic. But almost instantly, she rebelled against the impulse, saying under her breath: "Grace Swenson, thee needs no man who has to be caught by dust on a woman's face!"

She drew the comb through her long blonde hair, then tied it quickly back and left the room. As she approached the parlor, she heard Dortch talking with her father, and she stopped abruptly. Standing in the hall, she had the absurd impulse to turn and flee—to run into the barn and hide, or rush along the path beside the brook in the woods. She was a sensitive young woman, far more so than most people knew, and her lack of knowledge of men made her anxious and vulnerable in a situation such as this.

9

Quakers were not known for parties or dances, but they had, over the years, established a highly developed system of courtship. Since her teenage years, Grace had dreaded such things as she was about to face. The other girls had lived for the encounters with boys, it seemed to her, but she had only memories of shame and humiliation in such situations. She had grown tall during adolescence, so that the boys of her own age were shorter than she, and this made her feel like some kind of giantess. A feeling that the boys only confirmed by their avoidance of her, and the girls only made worse by their pitying glances. Gradually Grace had managed to assume the role of sponsor at such affairs, serving the food and doing the other small chores that kept her busy—and enabled her to avoid the embarrassment of sitting alone with no young man coming to talk to her.

In all her twenty-six years, no young man had ever come to call. And now that one had, she was possessed of a terror wondering what she would say to him! She had listened to the laughing talk of young couples and was certain she could never achieve such a teasing tone or such lightness of spirit.

Grace closed her eyes. *Lord, I feel so—so helpless. Help me to talk to this man!* Then, opening her eyes and clenching her teeth, she entered the parlor.

"Ah, here thee is, Miss Grace!" Dortch stood up at once, and a smile exposed his fine teeth. "Your father and I were about to get into a controversy."

"No! No!" Grace's father shook his head with alarm. "That would not do—not at all!"

Grace said, "It's good to see thee, Friend Dortch, but I think you'll find it hard to have an argument with my father." She smiled fondly at her father, adding, "He's not much for contention."

"Oh, I was only joking," Dortch said quickly. "We were just discussing this man, Charles Finney, and his 'new measures.'"

Swenson said quickly, "I'll leave Grace to defend Mr.

Finney. She's quite taken with him." He got up, nodded, and left the room.

Dortch smiled ruefully at the woman who stood regarding him, saying, "I know better than to argue religion with a preacher, Miss Grace. And the truth is, I don't really understand what it is Finney's doing that's caused all the controversy. I wish you'd explain it to me."

Relief washed over Grace. This was something she could talk about! *Thank you, Lord!*

"Why, I'm no authority, Friend Dortch," she said. "I don't know what it is about Rev. Finney that's caused all the controversy, but I *have* studied Rev. Finney's teaching closely."

"Fine!" Dortch exclaimed. "Why don't we sit down and thee can try to explain it to a rather thickheaded layman." He indicated the narrow couch and, when Grace sat down, he joined her. Grace tried to forget that this was the couch the girls called "The Courting Couch" for obvious reasons. When two adults sat together, they were very close. She licked her lips nervously and began talking.

"Well, Mr. Finney teaches that the new birth is necessary for everyone who comes into the world . . . ," Grace began, and for the next half hour she explained Finney's "new measures" and some of the controversy that they had occasioned.

Dortch listened carefully—or seemed to. He kept his eyes fixed on Grace, asking an occasional question. He was not a tall man, being of no more than average height, so that his eyes were on a level with those of the woman next to him. "So Mr. Finney says that revivals of religion are 'harvests'? Is that it?" he asked. "And you don't quite agree with that?"

Grace was beginning to have a difficult time concentrating on theology. The narrow couch worked very well as long as the occupants sat straight up and faced the front, as if they were sitting in a wagon seat. But Clyde Dortch and Grace were forced to turn slightly so that they could face each

11

other—and in the process, Dortch's knee had come to press against Grace's knee.

The intimacy of the contact brought a slight flush to Grace's cheeks, but Dortch didn't seem to notice. As they continued to talk, however, the pressure of his knee grew more pronounced, and his right shoulder somehow began to press on her left.

Don't be a fool! Grace told herself when the thought came into her mind that she was allowing the man too much liberty. *You've got to get over this foolishness!*

Nevertheless, she said abruptly, "Friend Dortch, I baked yesterday. Would thee like some pecan pie and a glass of milk?"

"That would be fine," Dortch responded, his teeth gleaming. "The best part of our socials are your pies and cakes, Miss Grace."

The compliment caused a rosy flush to touch Grace's cheeks, and she grew flustered. "Oh, there are better cooks than I am!" she murmured, getting to her feet.

"Now that's your opinion, Miss Grace, but it's not valid," Dortch responded. "Everybody knows you're the best in the whole community at making pies."

Grace was pleased at his praise, and when he ate two thick wedges of the pecan pie, she said, "Would thee like to take some home, Friend Dortch? I still bake for six after all this time."

"That would be a treat for a lonely bachelor," Dortch said, then added with a winsome smile, "but I can think of one thing I'd like even better than the pie."

"Why, what's that, Friend Dortch?"

"That we agree to call each other by names, not titles." Dortch made a slight face, adding, "Don't you think 'Friend Dortch' sounds too formal? Couldn't it just be Clyde and Grace?"

"I—I don't see why not," Grace said slowly.

Noticing the hesitation in her voice, Dortch said quickly,

"I don't want to be presumptuous or forward, Grace, but—well, the truth is, I've admired thee for a long time."

This admission drew a glance of astonishment from Grace. For some time, Clyde Dortch had been one of the most eligible bachelors in the Quaker community. His family was not prosperous, but their farm was better than average. Hiram Dortch, Clyde's father, had suffered a stroke two years earlier and was an invalid, so it was Clyde's older brother, Daniel, who was now in charge. The Dortches were good Quakers—though a little too prone to slightly radical doctrine than the more conservative element of the fellowship liked.

Still, Clyde was handsome and stood to own at least half the farm one day. He was a fine musician, too, which made him a popular addition to the social life of the community. Grace well knew that Dortch liked the company of women, but she also knew he had never singled out any one girl for special attention. She recalled he had had some trouble with a few of the other young men whose sweethearts showed too much attention to him. Grace's sister Dove had once said, "Clyde likes women, but he likes taking them away from other men too well."

Grace thought about that fleetingly, but his compliment silenced her concerns—though not before she had a quick flash of memory of a time when James Thomson had beaten Clyde thoroughly for trying to take Hannah Toler from him.

"I didn't know you ever thought about me," Grace said finally.

"Oh, for a long time," Dortch said quickly. Then he shrugged and grinned ruefully. "But I never said anything."

"Why not . . . , Clyde?" The use of his first name was difficult for Grace. "Was it so hard?"

"Oh, I think it's because you're a preacher," Clyde said thoughtfully. "That scares fellows off, you know."

"I suppose so."

"Sure it does! I mean, how's a fellow supposed to *act* when a girl is a preacher?"

Grace stared at him. "Couldn't thee act just like thee does with other young women?"

"And if I did," Dortch asked quickly, his eyes gleaming, "what would you do?" He suddenly reached forward and took her hand, holding it tightly. "For example, it's not unusual for a fellow to hold a girl's hand like this. Do you mind, Grace?"

The suddenness of his action caught Grace off guard, and her first impulse was to jerk her hand back.

But that would prove he was right!

"No-o-o . . . I don't think I mind." She spoke slowly. With great daring, she pressed his hand—then color rushed to her cheeks. She laughed awkwardly and pulled her hand back. "I'll put your pie in a covered dish," she said and got to her feet.

When Clyde left, he smiled at her, saying, "I'd like to come by some evening. Your father said he wouldn't mind."

Grace said, "Why yes, Clyde. Why don't you come for dinner tomorrow?"

"I'll be here!" Dortch looked at her and asked, "Will you wear that blue dress?"

Grace nodded and smiled at him. "I might even put on some of Prudence's rice powder."

"Don't do that, Grace!" Dortch said quickly. "That's only for girls who need it. You have the most beautiful complexion I've ever seen!"

Grace watched as he mounted his gray mare and rode away. Slowly she made her way back to the kitchen and washed up the dishes.

I didn't make a fool of myself, she thought. *He's really very nice . . . if only he were a bit taller.* Then she scolded herself for her foolish wish.

"Did thee have a good visit with the young man?"

Grace was so preoccupied with her thoughts that her father's voice startled her. She turned quickly to face him, saying awkwardly, "Oh yes. It was nice."

"Fine-looking young man."

Something in her father's tone made Grace look at him. "Well, I asked him to come to dinner tomorrow. Is that all right, Father?"

"Of course, Daughter. Be nice to have him."

Grace felt very awkward, which was unusual for her, for she and her father were great friends. "Father, I—I let him hold my hand."

Swenson smiled. "Did thee now?"

"Yes. Do you think that was wrong?"

"No, I don't," Swenson said firmly. "I held your mother's hand before we were married."

The admission made Grace smile. She had a wry sense of humor that few ever saw, and it came out now. "Sit down and drink some milk," she ordered. "And thee can tell me how to trap a man."

"Oh, now—!"

"I can't ask anyone else, can I?" Grace poured a glass of milk and set it before him, then sat down and put her chin on her hand. Now that the ordeal was over, she was feeling light and happy. "Come now, give me some counsel. Shall I order some French perfume from Philadelphia? Or maybe one of those dresses with a bustle on the back?"

"Daughter! Thee would get read out of the meeting!"

Grace broke into laughter at the horrified look on her father's face. "I can see myself rigged out like that! Wouldn't it be something to see, though? My going to preach in a thing like that?"

Swenson suddenly laughed with her. "Might do us good. Nobody would go to sleep, would they?" He took a sip of the milk, then shook his head and grew silent. Finally he said, "I wish thee could marry and have children." He looked at her, asking, "Has thee thought of that?"

Grace sobered at once. "When I was younger. Not for a long time."

Her confession seemed to hurt Swenson. He knew his illness was serious and that he would not live very long— though he had never mentioned this to his family. "I wish I

15

could go back," he said heavily. "I made a mistake letting thee work so hard."

"I don't want thee to think that, Father!" Grace spoke almost sharply and went to stand behind him. Leaning over, she put her arms around him and placed her cheek next to his. "God will take care of me—and of thee."

She could feel the thinness of his frame and knew a moment of fear as the thought of losing him came to her. She held him tightly, whispering, "Don't thee mind about me! I'm choosy about my men! Until I find one as good and loving as the one right here in this chair, I'll not have him!"

Swenson's eyes filled with tears, and he reached up and held her hands. *Good Lord in heaven—keep this lamb safe as the apple of your eye!*

CHAPTER TWO
Two Kisses

✦

Among the Quakers, affairs such as courtship move very slowly. One wag put it, "If you enjoy watching the movements of major icebergs, you'll enjoy watching the courtship of Quakers."

As for Grace, she was not at all disturbed that Clyde Dortch had little to show for the fact that he had come to take dinner with the Swensons twice a week for two months—little, that is, besides the slight bulge around his middle. She was not by nature a hasty young woman, and she was prepared to cook twice a week for ten more months before the next stage of courtship began.

Truthfully, she was enjoying the mild sensation that the courtship had stirred in the small, tranquil world of the Friends. For the first time in her life she was aware that people were staring at her, watching with interest as she moved through the rites of passage! Always before it had been one of her sisters, though Grace had never resented their moments of glory—if a Quaker courtship could be so labeled.

The community had long ago, she realized, grown accustomed to the notion that their lady preacher would remain in single bliss, taking care of her father and serving as an aging aunt for the offspring of her sisters. It was a role that they could understand and approve. They loved ritual and the even tenor of habit, these Quakers, and Grace Swenson had been neatly identified, labeled, and consigned to a certain slot.

Now the tall young woman had astounded them all by stepping outside the classification into which they had locked her, and it set her little world—and in particular a Mrs. Lula Belle Gatz—to buzzing. One of the Friends had said of Lula Belle Gatz, "She's got a tongue long enough to sit in the living room and lick the skillet in the kitchen!" While this might have proven anatomically impossible for the lady, metaphorically, she lived up to the reputation!

Sister Gatz, in truth, had too little to do at home—her children being all grown and mostly beyond her "arrangings"—so she moved from house to house, from quilting to quilting, discussing the affairs of others. She was at heart a kindly woman—a Dorcas, who was always the first to help when trouble came. She was so assiduous in this sort of thing, that folks in the community swore it was always, "First Lula Belle, then the doctor, then the undertaker!" Once, when Mary Rochard sickened and died with record speed, Sister Gatz arrived *after* the doctor and the undertaker had come and gone. It grieved her so greatly that she became almost ill over her delinquency, but she found solace in rearranging the funeral plans made by the family.

When she presented herself at the front door of the Swenson home bearing a quilt as a wedding gift, both Grace and her father knew that it would be an expensive gift. And they were not mistaken, for with the quilt came a host of warnings, suggestions, and searching questions about the match.

"She's settling in for a long visit, Grace," Amos said gloomily. "I don't think I feel up to it. That woman is worse than a case of grippe!"

Grace laughed at the gloomy comparison. "Go lie down, Father. Don't come out until I come for thee," she said. In truth, she was worried about her father. He seemed to have grown weaker for the past two months, and she spent much time fixing foods he would eat.

"That might not come for a day or two," Amos sighed. "Sister Gatz is a fine woman, but gives away too much advice."

After she got her father off for his nap, Grace squared her shoulders, put a smile on her lips, and marched in to take her medicine. It proved to be a long, rather bitter dose. She sat in her rocker knitting socks as the older woman spent two hours running down a rather vivid list of dangers that a young couple could expect to begin no later than ten minutes after they were married. Sister Gatz was an angular woman, in shape as well as in mind, with a hungry-looking face set in sharp planes and a pair of piercing black eyes.

As she drew breath to begin another chapter in her remarks, she happened to glance out the window. The words shut down momentarily, and her mouth drew into a small round *O*. "Isn't that young Prudence with Clyde?" she demanded, turning an accusing look upon Grace.

Grace glanced up from her knitting, looked out the window, and nodded. "Yes, Sister Gatz. Prudence needed to go over to Riverton to fetch some material for my dress. Gelt's Store didn't have anything suitable."

The *O* of Sister Gatz's mouth drew down to form an inverted *U*. "I'd think thee would want to go choose thy own material, Sister Swenson."

"Oh, the new calf is due, and I'm expecting some trouble with the birthing. And Prudence has a better eye for dress material than I have."

"Humph!" Sister Gatz formed this monosyllabic expression by snorting through her long nose. It was an odd sound, but one the lady used effectively to express doubt, disgust, or displeasure. She stared out the window, observing the couple as Clyde helped Prudence out of the buggy, noting the ease with which he lifted her up and set her down. The two were laughing—a most inappropriate activity in

Sister Gatz's mind, for she was always suspicious when a young man and a young woman laughed together.

"Humph!" she echoed, and when the pair came into the parlor, she carefully examined Prudence's rosy complexion and bright eyes. Then she fixed her sharp gaze on Dortch, noting the pleased look on his face. Though she dared not use a third *humph*—even she recognized this would be overly critical—she did sit straighter, and she nodded only slightly when Dortch said, "Good afternoon, Sister Gatz. Has thee had a good visit with Grace?"

"We've had an edifying time."

"Oh, Grace!" Prudence's dark blue eyes were sparkling, and she looked fresh and pretty in a simple, well-fitted, tan dress. "The circus was in town! We saw an elephant, didn't we, Clyde?"

"Yes, we did." He came over and sat down in the oak rocker. He was looking handsome and dapper in a gray suit and his flat-crowned hat, which he left on his head as was the fashion of Quakers. He looked pleased and happy, and there was a satisfied look on his handsome face as he laughed. "Does thee know what I thought when I saw the beast, Grace?"

"I can't imagine."

"I thought, *There is no such animal as that!*"

Prudence giggled suddenly, adding, "The great beast stopped right in front of us and put his—his nose out for something to eat. It was so scary, Grace! But Clyde wasn't a bit afraid of him. He just laughed and gave the creature the last of my sandwich!"

Clyde became aware of Sister Gatz's scowl and said quickly, "I wish thee had been there, Grace. I thought we might go back tomorrow and see the circus."

"Oh, can I go?" Prudence demanded. "The sign on the side of one of the wagons said there was an 'Ethiopian Eccentricity.' I can't imagine what that is!"

"Nothing that thee should be seeing, I'm sure, Sister

Prudence!" With that phrase, Sister Gatz firmly settled the question of a trip to the circus!

Prudence glared at the woman and would have argued, but Dortch said quickly, "Prudence, why don't you show Grace the material?"

Grace put aside her knitting and soon she and Prudence were examining the fine white silk Prudence had found—but the beautiful material pleased Sister Gatz even less than the idea of an Ethiopian Eccentricity. "I don't recall ever seeing one of our young women wearing such finery," she sniffed. Getting to her feet, she looked at Dortch, then at Prudence, and then at the glistening silk in Grace's hands.

"Humph!" she snorted. "I'll take my leave of thee."

When she was safely out of hearing, Clyde winked wickedly at the two women, then bowed in the direction of the door. "Thee could not have taken anything from me that I would be more willing to give," he said mockingly. Prudence giggled, but Grace shook her head.

"She's a very unhappy woman," Grace said.

Prudence removed her bonnet and shook her mass of dark curls in a careless manner. She had little patience with the ways of older people and said sharply, "She's too nosy and a terrible gossip." Then she dismissed the old woman from her mind. "I couldn't find any ribbon that I liked. I'm going to change, and then Clyde and I are going to Ellen Dorsey's and see if she has any."

Clyde said suddenly, "Grace, you come and we'll look at the ribbon."

Grace looked at him with a slight surprise. "Why—all right, Clyde. But Prudence will have to make the final decision." She rose and moved to get her cloak and bonnet, pausing long enough to stop and give her younger sister an affectionate pat on the shoulder. "I'll just tell Father where we're going."

"Oh, I'll stay home if thee is going," Prudence said. "It doesn't take two to pick out a ribbon!"

She spoke sharply, causing Grace to stare after her sister as she flounced out of the room without another word. But Grace was accustomed to Prudence's sudden mood changes, and she said only, "I'm ready, Clyde."

When they got to the buggy Dortch attempted to help Grace into the wagon, but she was unaccustomed to such attention and pulled herself into the seat with a quick ease that left him standing there, looking slightly foolish. Grace saw the displeasure in his eyes and thought, *I've got to learn to wait—to let him help me.*

When they pulled up in front of the dressmaker's shop, she forced herself to wait as Clyde stepped out of the buggy and came to her side. She took his hand and stepped out, smiling at him. He was a well-built man, but not tall, and though he did his best to hide it from Grace, it touched his vanity that she was able to look him squarely in the eye. He forced a smile to his lips. "Let's go get some ice cream after we get the ribbon, Grace."

"All right."

They shared a pleasant time. Grace examined every ribbon that Ellen Dorsey had, but in the end could only say, "Thee and Prudence will have to decide."

"Why, thee has a good eye for color, Sister Grace," Mrs. Dorsey said, a little impatiently. She was an attractive widow of thirty-five who supported her three children by her needle. She had followed the courtship of the young couple before her avidly—as had practically every other member of the community. Now as she stood there with ribbons draped over her arm, she studied the young pair, then frowned slightly as if something seemed not quite right to her. Carefully she said, "Prudence came to talk to me about the dress, but thee needs to come in so we can decide on it."

Grace agreed, but when she and Clyde left the dressmaker's shop, Mrs. Dorsey went next door at once, where she told her neighbor of the visit. Shaking her head, she said with asperity, "Sister Grace had better give more attention to this wedding. Why, her sister Prudence acts as though *she's* the one getting married!"

Blissfully unaware of the currents of speculation around her, Grace enjoyed the afternoon, especially the visit to the ice cream parlor, where she ate two helpings of ice cream. Afterward she walked along the streets of the small town with Dortch, speaking to those they passed. She remembered to let Dortch help her into the buggy, and when they got back to the farm, she said, "I've got to get supper ready, Clyde. Why doesn't thee sit and talk to Father while thee waits?"

"All right, Grace." When they reached the house, however, Amos Swenson was napping. So Clyde sat in the parlor for a time, reading a week-old paper, then grew restless. He wandered outside to stroll around the farm, admiring the sturdy stone barn and the smaller outbuildings. The stock were all sleek and healthy, the fences all tightly knit, the fields all laid out in a carefully planned design. He spoke to the two hired men, Jed Satterfield and Benny George, discussing the state of the crops and the animals. Both men, Dortch knew, were hard workers who did a good job of handling the work Swenson could no longer do himself.

Satterfield, a tall, gangling man of thirty, gave Dortch a careful look, then said, "Guess you won't be needing one of us when you and Sister Grace get married."

"Oh, there'll be plenty of work for three men, Jed," Dortch said quickly. "I've got some new ideas that'll be taking up a lot of my time, so thee and Benny can count on staying on."

As Dortch wandered away from the barn, he decided to head for the pasture to look over the cattle grazing by the creek. As he walked, a sensation of satisfaction came over him. He had been unhappy at home since his father's stroke. His older brother had little of Clyde's lighthearted approach to life. In direct contrast to Clyde, Daniel was heavy in body and mind, caring little for anything except his religion and the farm. He put in long, hard days and expected everyone else to do the same.

Clyde, however, did not hold with such a strict outlook

on life, and hard feelings had developed between the two brothers. Mrs. Dortch had spoiled her younger son, and her husband had been swayed by her so that he had not curbed Clyde's careless ways. As long as Mr. Dortch had been in charge, he had let Clyde slide by with his work—but now Clyde's father was helpless, and Daniel had laid his iron hand to everything on the farm. Especially Clyde. The tension had become so intense that Daniel had finally said, "If thee wants to be a gentleman of leisure, thee will have to find another place to do it, Brother Clyde!"

Now, walking about the Swenson farm, breathing air that was fresh as wine, Clyde smiled to himself. "Indeed, Brother Daniel, thee was right," he muttered with some satisfaction as he considered what his days would hold after his marriage to Grace. He strolled along the pathway that led to the lower pasture, enjoying himself immensely. He was not a man to think much of the future, but as he walked along and counted the fat cows dotting the landscape, he thought of how pleasant it would be to escape Daniel's harsh demands. Here, things would be different! A man wouldn't have to kill himself working, not with two good hands like Benny and Jed!

He thought suddenly of Grace and shook his head in an involuntary gesture. She was a fine girl, of course—just not very exciting. *Never thought I'd wind up marrying a preacher,* he thought, a wry smile on his full lips. *She's no beauty—but she'll take care of a husband well enough.* He thought of the good food and the other advantages of being master of this fine farm and shrugged slightly. *A man can't have everything, I guess. Besides, Grace will never give me any trouble. She's too glad to get a husband for that!*

Suddenly, Clyde heard his name called. He looked up to see Prudence standing beside the creek, waving at him. Immediately his mood lightened, and he hurried across the field to her. "What are you doing out here, Prudence?"

"Picking flowers." She motioned toward a basket lying on the ground beside the creek, filled with yellow, blue, and red wildflowers. She was wearing a thin white cotton dress, and the beauty of her figure startled Dortch. She caught his expression, understood it for what it was, and smiled. "Did thee have a good time in town," she asked demurely.

Dortch shrugged carelessly. "I guess so. Grace said that thee would have to help pick out the ribbons."

"What else did thee do?"

"Oh, we got some ice cream." Dortch made a slight gesture of depreciation. "It wasn't a thrilling trip, I guess." He smiled at her, his teeth white against his skin. "Not nearly as much fun as seeing an elephant."

The memory of their visit to Riverton lit Prudence's face. "Oh, that was fun, wasn't it, Clyde! I'd give anything if we could go see the actual show!"

Prudence may not have known what an attractive picture she made as she stood there looking up at him. She was petite, small, and well formed—and very pretty. It did something for Dortch's vanity to have her look up at him as she was, her eyes bright with excitement. It made him feel much taller, and he suddenly found himself saying, "I'd like to take thee there, Prudence—" then he caught himself and added quickly, "but of course, that wouldn't look good."

"Oh, *pooh!* I get absolutely *sick* of having to care about what people think!"

"Prudence!"

She shook her head angrily, her curls bouncing about in a most appealing manner. "Well, I don't care if that shocks thee. Sometimes I think I'm in a jail or something. A girl can't even *smile* at a young man without those—those old *vultures* starting to gossip!" She looked up at Clyde, her lips drawn into a pout. "There! Now thee will think I'm a brazen hussy, won't thee?"

Clyde laughed suddenly. "No, I won't, because I feel exactly the same way most of the time." This was true, for Clyde's religion was not terribly deep. He was the most liberal of liberal Quakers and had often wished he was an Episcopalian so that he could have a little breathing room.

As a rule, he kept this heresy to himself, but now that Prudence had spoken so frankly, he felt secure enough to agree.

"I'm not much of a Quaker, I guess," he said ruefully. "I just can't see anything wrong with having a little fun. After all, there's dancing and singing in the Bible, isn't there?"

Prudence nodded at once. "Yes, there is, but can thee imagine what Father would say if we went to a dance?" Her eyes gleamed wickedly, and she giggled. "We'd be read out of meeting!"

"Well, I don't much care," Clyde grinned. "We could have some fun—and then we could repent and get back in."

"Oh, Clyde, that's just awful!" Prudence tried to look shocked, but her amusement won out. "Come on, thee can help me pick some flowers. We'll decide what wicked thing we'll do to get put out of the meeting . . ."

For the next hour, Clyde Dortch had one of the most enjoyable times of his life. He liked sprightly young women and had not known that this youngest Swenson girl was so lively and clever. The two of them wandered over the fields, picking flowers from time to time, but mostly talking and laughing.

By the time they got back to the creek, the sun was turning the water red with afternoon beams. They stood there admiring it until Clyde said, "I guess we'd better get to supper." Regret was heavy in his voice. He turned to the girl standing close beside him. "This has been nice, Prue. We'll have to pick flowers more often together."

Prudence stood before him and suddenly gave voice to a thought that had been lurking inside her for some time. "Clyde, you're so *different* from Grace. How will thee ever—?" When Prudence broke off uncertainly, Clyde understood what she was trying to say.

"How will Grace and I get along?"

"Well—she's so *religious!*"

"And I'm not." Dortch nodded slowly. He had thought of this at length, but had arrived at no good answers. He was honest enough to admit his faults and knew that he would be cheating Grace Swenson out of what every man should bring to a marriage—an honest love. He'd fought this battle out, however, and justified his course by telling himself that since Grace wasn't likely to get any sort of a husband other than him, he was actually doing her a service. Even so, he was realistic enough to understand that he would not be entirely happy in their relationship. He had been trying to blot this out of his mind by telling himself that it would be an *easy* life and that he would be relieved from the drudgery of work that he was now doomed to.

Now, though, as he looked down into Prudence's sweet face, he suddenly became serious. The sun in the west cast shadows on his clean-cut features, and he spoke quietly and honestly—something he hadn't done much of lately! "I'll be giving Grace something," he said quietly. "She'll have a husband—and that is something she never thought to have."

Prudence was a quick girl. She read into Dortch's words what lay beneath them. "But what about *thee*, Clyde?" With an impulsive gesture, she moved closer to him and put her hand on his arm. Looking up into his eyes, she whispered, "What will thee get?"

Dortch looked down at Prudence and said evenly, "Most people say I'm getting a good farm out of it."

But Prudence, to his relief, didn't even answer that. Her features softened and she whispered, "Thee will be a lonesome man, Clyde." There was an air of sadness about her as she spoke. "And that's not right—because thee is a man who needs loving and fun."

As Prudence stood looking up at him with such an air of sweetness and concern, Clyde suddenly was acutely aware of her youth and beauty. He had thought of her as a pretty girl who would grow up someday . . . but now, in the silence of the evening air, as she looked up at him with her lips slightly parted, he knew that she was already a woman.

Almost without meaning to, he moved to put his arms

27

around her and let his lips fall on hers. She was soft and yielding, and he felt the pressure of her arms around his neck. Her embrace stirred him as nothing else had ever done. And he was aware that she was stirred as well, for she clung to him, holding him fast.

Finally she pulled away, and her voice was unsteady as she said, "Clyde—we shouldn't—!"

"No, I guess not," he said huskily.

She saw that he was half ashamed of kissing her, and it was part of Prudence's charm that she knew how to make people feel better. She gave him a dimpled smile and said in a bright voice, "Well, that's one kiss Grace won't get!"

Clyde could not refrain from smiling. "Someday you're going to keep a man hopping, Prudence. The man thee gets will never know exactly what thee is going to say or do next."

Struggling to conceal the tumult Clyde's kiss had stirred in her, she said, "It's good for a man to be teased. Keeps him on his toes." She picked up the basket of flowers, then said, "Come on, I'll race thee to the house!"

They returned just as Grace came out on the porch. "I was coming to call you two for supper." Her eyes fell on the flowers, and she smiled. "Put them in the blue vase, Prudence. They'll look nice on the table."

"Clyde helped me," Prudence said quickly. She smiled, adding, "He's a good flower picker." She left and went to look for the vase, and Clyde said quickly, "Didn't mean to stay out so long, Grace."

"Oh, I'm glad you and Prudence had some time together," Grace said at once. "She gets lonely out here sometimes. Thee'll be good company for her after we're married."

Clyde had the grace to look uncomfortable, and that night at supper he was quieter than usual. The talk came, as it always did, to the war between the states. They were all saddened by it, for Quakers, who were opposed to all violence, were particularly grieved over a civil war.

"I don't think it will last long," Clyde remarked. "The

Rebels whipped us so badly at Bull Run that people won't stand for going on with the campaign."

"I don't think that's the way it will go," Amos disagreed. "The Union was beaten in that battle, but the people want slavery outlawed. And they don't want the Union broken up by secession. No, this new president won't let it drop. It'll be a long war, I'm afraid."

Clyde prepared to leave shortly after supper. "Got to get an early start in the morning," he said, excusing himself. Grace went with him out on the porch, where he turned and said, "It was a fine supper, Grace."

"I'm glad thee enjoyed it, Clyde."

Dortch had a sudden thought and moved closer to Grace. She looked at him with quick apprehension in her eyes—he intended to kiss her. He had done so only twice thus far, and both times had been rather perfunctory affairs.

But this time he took her in his arms and pulled her close—so that she felt the pressure of his arms and the beating of his heart beneath her palms where they rested on his chest—and the intimacy of the contact frightened her. Still, as he sought her lips, she submitted, for she knew this was part of courtship—or so she had been told. She had heard girls laughing and joking about being kissed and had never been able to join in.

Clyde's lips were hard and demanding, and something about the way his hands touched her only increased her fear. Instinctively she pushed him away, though with more force than she intended. Dortch stared at her, something in his face that she could not read.

"Forgive me, Grace," he said briefly. His tone was clipped and terse, but he tried to smile. "I'll see thee tomorrow."

As Dortch wheeled abruptly and walked to his horse, Grace clasped her hands together tightly. She opened her mouth to call out, to say something that would take the sting from her abrupt rejection, but no words came. Finally as he mounted and spurred his horse into a run she called out.

"Clyde—!"

But he was gone, and she stood there in the warm darkness, her cheeks burning, thinking of what had happened. Tears burned at her eyes unexpectedly, and she brushed them away impatiently. She was a warmhearted young woman, and she had been sure that when this time of her life came—the time when she agreed to marry a man— she would be able to respond to her beloved's caress. But all she had felt with Dortch was fear . . . and repulsion.

There must be something wrong with me. Turning, she moved back into the house, her heart heavy and her mind troubled.

When her father saw her face, he asked quickly, "Did thee and the young man have a quarrel?"

"No, Father," she said, but there was no happiness in her face, and as she left to go to her room, Swenson watched her carefully. He knew she was more afraid of marriage than looking forward to it. Finally, he shook his head, muttering, "There's no way I can help her with this thing." He moved slowly to blow out the lamp, then turned and went to his room where he lay awake for a long time thinking of many things.

CHAPTER THREE
Good-bye to Love

Spring had come, and the days when the sun was sharp and bright and full became more common. The sun settled westward, seeming to melt into a bed of gold flame as it touched the faraway mountains, and the air became warmer with breezes coming out of the south, smelling of pleasant weather.

Amos Swenson knew his land as well as he knew himself. He well understood that in another few months' time, winter would crouch on the rim of the horizon, ready in one day or night to come over the land turning it black and bitter, shriveling every living thing exposed to it. But it was for this violent change of seasons that Amos loved this land—a land that was full of goodness, like a smiling and beautiful woman whose lavish warmth and generosity sprang from those same strongly primitive sources that could make her cruel.

Yet it was not just the changing of the seasons that Amos felt as the days began to lengthen. No, he knew that he himself was beginning to fade. He measured his strength carefully, grieving at times as he thought of the vigor of his youth, but he felt no fear at leaving this life behind. For him it was like stepping over from a dangerous and difficult place into a place filled with kindness and light.

His only regret was leaving his daughters.

One evening he sat on his front porch, wrapped in a light blanket against the breath of the cool night air, studying the stars. They glittered overhead like cold fire—tiny points of light that never failed to draw his interest and admiration.

Grace came out, looked down at him, then sat down in the swing. Following his gaze upward to the brightly lit heavens, she asked, "How many are there, do you suppose?"

"Someday I'll ask the Good Lord to let me count them." Almost he added, "And it won't be a long wait until that day," but he caught himself, coughing slightly to cover his near slip.

Grace looked at him quickly. "It's too cool out here. Let's go in the house, Father."

"Nothing in there like that." Amos smiled, waving at the spangled heavens. "'The heavens declare the glory of God, and the firmament showeth his handiwork.'"

Grace looked upward again, but her mind was on her father. He was failing rapidly, and the doctor could do nothing. "Don't let yourself hope too much, Grace," the doctor said quietly to her in private. "His heart is very weak. He could go at any moment."

A thickness came to her throat as she thought of losing her father, and she dropped her eyes from the stars to look across the porch at him. He had been an anchor in her life ever since she was a little girl, and the thought of being alone stirred a sharp pain in her breast.

She sat there trying to turn her thoughts away from loss, and his quiet voice broke the silence. "Has thee made up thy mind about the wedding, Daughter?"

"Sometime soon," Grace said evasively.

Swenson was not a persistent man, but there was an urgency in his thin voice as he said, "It would please me if thee made the date soon."

Grace looked up, startled—this was as close as her father had come to mentioning his death. Filled with confusion, she could not answer, and he added, "It would be a comfort to me, Grace, to know you were provided for."

"I don't want thee to worry about me," she said quickly. She sought some reassurance that would give him comfort and said finally, "Thee has taught me how to run this farm. It's paid for, and there's good help in Jed and Benny. I am well taken care of."

Silence seemed to fall all about them as they sat there. Grace could hear the ticking of the big clock in the hall, and even at that moment it chimed seven times—a mellow sound that faded slowly away.

"We are God's children, Grace," Amos said slowly. He'd been thinking about his departure, and now he decided that it was time to discuss it with this tall daughter of his. "We've not talked about it, but I'll not be here long." Grace made a small sound, and her father got up and went to sit beside her on the swing. He took her hand and held it in both of his, saying nothing until she grew still.

"We're not like people tied to the earth, are we?" he asked. "We're pilgrims, looking for a city not built with hands. And when I leave, I'll see my dear mother and father and my brothers. And my beloved Martha. And one day, thee and thy sisters will come, and then all the others. It'll be one family, Grace—the family of God, all together! That's a thought I've clung to for years, and it's more real now than ever."

"But I'll be all alone!"

"No! No!" Amos said quickly. "Thee will have the Lord Jesus! 'I will never leave thee, nor forsake thee,' he said. Remember that?"

"Oh yes, but it's hard!"

Swenson squeezed her hand, wishing he didn't have to continue—but he was a wise man and knew that certain things had to be discussed. "Let me tell thee what must be done. . . ."

Grace sat there as he spoke of his funeral and where he wanted to be laid at rest. He mentioned that he'd seen

Lawyer Simms and that all was in order. "The farm is left to thee," he said. "Thy married sisters have husbands to care for them. I can depend on thee to take care of Prudence until she marries." He hesitated slightly then nodded. "When thee marries Clyde, that will make a difference as far as the farm is concerned."

Grace sensed some doubt in her father's voice. "How is that, Father?"

Swenson stroked his chin, considering what he must say. It was not a simple matter, and he had prayed much over it. "Clyde is not a settled man, Grace." He held up his hand quickly as if to ward off her protest. "That's not to say I'm opposed to him as thy husband. But he's not had his own place to run, has he?"

"N-no," Grace agreed haltingly. "But he's a good farmer!"

"I do not doubt this, but it is one thing to know how to plow and another to keep a place going. Think of how many times we've seen young men who couldn't manage that. Some of them were just too young, and others were just the kind who can't build."

"And you think Clyde is one such as those?"

"I think he needs time to mature. That's why I'm leaving the farm in thy name, and I'm asking thee to let it stay that way for two years. By that time, the young man will either have proven himself—or he will need more time."

Grace thought of what he was saying, then shook her head. "I don't know if Clyde will agree. Isn't the man supposed to be the head of the family? He might be shamed at such a thing."

"Pride is a dangerous thing, Grace. It's the sin through which the angels fell."

When Grace didn't respond to this, Amos added gently, "I've prayed much about this. The Lord has given me a Scripture." This often occurred with Amos Swenson, and Grace had learned to trust such things. Since her youth she had seen her father wait on the Lord in times of need, meditating on the Scripture until some portion of it fixed itself on his mind.

"What is the word?" she asked.

"It's a verse from the third chapter of Lamentations." Amos nodded. "'It is good for a man that he bear the yoke in his youth.'" He sat there silently, the creaking of the swing making a faint noise, then added, "I believe it is God's will that thee should wait until Clyde proves himself before handing over the farm to him."

Grace was troubled, but it never occurred to her to dispute her father. "I'll tell him right away."

"No, that is my place," Swenson said at once. "It is but a small matter, if he will have it so." He hesitated, then asked again, "Will the wedding be soon?"

Grace nodded slowly, knowing that her father wished to see her safely married before he died.

"Yes, Father," she said quietly. "I'll speak with Clyde. It'll be very soon."

Summer came to Pennsylvania overnight, it seemed. With the wedding drawing ever nearer, this should have been a happy, exciting time for Grace. Instead, it was a time of tension, for her father grew no better. He spent long hours in bed. When he did rise and make his way around the house, it was with the careful steps of the confirmed invalid. More and more, Grace stayed close to the house, leaving the outside work for Jed and Benny, not wanting to be far from her father's side.

The plans for the wedding were made, but she felt little of the joy she had always believed such an occasion would bring her. Rather, she felt queer stirrings at the thought of what lay ahead. She had seen less of Clyde than she'd expected, for as the date of their marriage grew closer, he seemed to be more and more taken up with other things. Grace felt that she was the cause of some of this, for she had refused to go with him on more than one occasion, pleading as an excuse that she had to stay close to her father.

More than once she had suggested that he take Prudence to accompany him. After a brief resistance, he would agree. One time Prudence, who hated to miss any sort of activity, had said, "It's you who should be going with Clyde, Grace."

But Grace had smiled, saying, "I'm a better nurse than you are, Prudence. Go on and have a good time. I know it gets lonesome for you around the farm."

One of Grace's good friends, Charity Blankenship, came often to visit with her. The two women were the same age and had been close since childhood. Charity, who was married and had one child, a boy named Caleb, was a cheerful young woman. She had found great happiness in her marriage and with her lot in life.

One afternoon Charity drove her buggy up to the front door and brought her three-year-old Caleb into the kitchen. Grace put him at once on a high stool and proceeded to stuff sugar cookies into his mouth as though he were a young bird. She loved children, and as Charity rambled on about what she'd been doing, Grace listened quietly.

Finally the two women sat down at the table to hot, spicy sassafras tea. Almost at once Charity asked, "Well, how does it feel to be nearly married, Grace?"

"Oh, fine," Grace said at once.

Something in her tone drew the other woman's attention, and she laid a sharp glance on her friend. "Thee doesn't sound as happy as I'd like," she murmured. "Not having some last minute fears, are you?"

Grace shrugged uncomfortably, then came up with a small smile. "I suppose most women do, don't they?"

"I don't know about other women. *I* didn't have any."

"You're different, Charity. You and Tom were made for each other."

Charity sipped her tea, then said carefully, "I think it's pretty common for women—and men, too—to have some doubts. It's a big thing, getting married. Aside from choosing to serve God, it's the biggest decision any of us ever make."

"That's true, isn't it? It's for the rest of our life." Grace's smooth face usually reflected a peace that most people admired, but she was agitated now. "If thee makes a mistake in marriage, there's no way to go back and erase it and start over."

"Grace, aren't you certain about Clyde? I've heard you talk about how we can know God's will so often. Don't you have any inner light on getting married?"

"I—thought so," Grace nodded. "But lately I've been wondering if it might not have been something *I* wanted instead of something God has planned." She leaned forward, shaking her head with doubt. "Father wants me to be married, and I've always leaned on him for counsel. But lately I've thought his sickness has influenced him. He wants so much to see me safe before—," she broke off abruptly. "In case something happens to him," she finished. Then she frowned and laughed shortly. "And it's sort of a last chance for me, Charity."

"You don't know that, Grace!"

"No? Hasn't thee noticed there isn't a group of young men lined up to court me? Clyde's the only one—and I can't risk missing out on marriage and having a family!"

Charity yearned to help her friend, but she didn't know what to say. Finally she gave it up, saying, "Well, I'm sure thee and Clyde will be happy."

"I'm trusting we will."

"Where's Prudence? I wanted to talk to her a little about the plans for the wedding."

"We needed some things from town, so she and Clyde rode in to get them." Almost defensively she said, "I would have gone, but Father's having a bad spell and he seems to be comfortable only when I'm here."

"Oh, that's too bad, Grace." Charity studied her friend and seemed about to say something, then apparently changed her mind. With a sigh she said, "Well, this time next week thee will be an old married woman like me. Then you'll have a little Caleb to take care of. It'll be nice when we can get together with our children and our husbands, won't it, Grace?"

"Oh yes!" The thought brightened Grace's eyes, and she seemed to brush away the cares that had been weighing her down. By the time Charity left, she felt much better and went to check on her father. He was asleep, but half an hour later he came into the kitchen and sat down.

"How about some fresh milk?" Grace said with a smile. She had been trying everything she could think of to get food into him, and she insisted that he eat one of her cookies and drink some milk.

He nibbled dutifully at the cookie, but obviously had no appetite. "Was that someone come to visit?" he asked. His voice was rusty—as though from lack of use—and his eyes were dim with the pain that never seemed to leave him.

"Yes, Charity came by," Grace said with a nod. "She wanted to talk about the wedding plans."

Amos looked out the window, swallowed a sip of milk, then asked, "Prudence and Clyde not back yet?"

"Not yet. They had quite a few errands." Grace came to sit closer to him on the deacon's bench. "How does thee feel?"

"I can't complain."

Grace put her hand on his and whispered, "Thee never does."

The two sat there quietly, letting the old clock tick away the seconds. It was a gift they had, this ability to sit and say nothing while drawing strength from each other. It was the Quaker gift of inner peace, of silence, and as the time ran on, neither of them felt the need to say anything.

Finally Grace moved her head. "I think I hear them." Getting up, she went to the window and looked across the yard. "Yes, it's them." She watched as the wagon drew up, and as Clyde jumped to the ground then moved quickly to lift Prudence to the ground. He put his hands on her sides and lifted her slight weight as though she were a child.

Too bad he'll never be able to lift me like that, Grace

thought. *He can't help it if he's small, and I can't help it if I'm large.*

As she watched the two laughing together about something, Grace realized sadly that she didn't have her sister's light air and feminine mannerisms. She had thought of this before, but there was no way she could change herself. *I can't be the kind of wife Prudence would be—but I can make him good food and give him comfort in his home.*

Somehow that didn't seem like much, but it was all Grace could think of, and she forced herself to smile as the two entered the kitchen with their arms full of bundles.

"It looks like thee bought the store out," Grace smiled, helping to unload the boxes. "It took a long time."

Prudence turned to face Grace at once, saying, "It takes time to buy things for a wedding party!"

Her sister's sharp tone surprised Grace. "Why, of course, Prudence," she said at once. "I wasn't scolding."

Clyde said quickly, "It was my fault it took so long, Grace. I was hungry, so we went to the restaurant and had some pie and coffee."

"Was it as good as my pie?" Grace asked, trying to lighten the moment. Prudence had been so quick to offend lately.

"No one makes pies as good as thee, Grace," Clyde said. He went outside to get the other boxes. When he returned, he smiled at Amos. "How does thee feel, sir?"

"Oh, very well, Clyde," Amos nodded. "The Lord is good."

"Stay and have supper, Clyde," Grace said.

But Dortch seemed troubled. "No, I thank thee. I have things to do at home." He said his good-byes, then left the kitchen.

"Clyde seems upset," Amos observed. "What's the matter with him, Prudence?"

"Why, nothing that I know of, Father," Prudence said. She looked pale and tired and turned at once to go to her room, saying, "I'll come and help with supper in a bit, Grace."

There was silence for a few moments, then Amos sighed. "I'm a little worried about Prudence. She's been touchy lately." He looked over the table, which was now filled with supplies for the wedding party. "Didn't take all this when Martha and I got married. Sometimes I think it'd be better if young couples just went back to the simpler ways."

"Thee is just stingy," Grace teased him. "Thee would like to save the money thee must spend on thy daughter's wedding." She came to stand beside him and brushed a lock of lank white hair from his forehead. "Thee has certainly spent thy share on marrying daughters off!"

Swenson reached up and caught her hand. He held it gently, noting how round and strong it was, then said, "I never was so happy to see any of thy sisters married as I am to see thee married, Grace."

He could not see her face, so he missed the expression of doubt that tightened her features. "I know," she whispered. "It will be soon, Father. Then your ugly duckling will be safely married." She ignored his protests at the name she gave herself and held his head tightly to her breast in a protective gesture.

"Oh, you look beautiful, Grace!"

Charity stood back and gazed with admiration at Grace, surprised at the way the white silk wedding dress brought a pristine beauty to her friend. The dress was simple, as befitted a Quaker bride. The bodice was decorated with embroidery around the high neckline, and the only color was the silver lace that the dressmaker had added at the neck and cuffs. The skirt fell to the floor, barely touching the fine white calf slippers, and with every motion the tall woman made, it shimmered like compressed light.

Grace turned to stare into the mirror, and she gasped at the effect. "It—it's the most beautiful dress I've ever seen, Charity!"

Charity was filled with admiration. "It must be nice to be tall," she said with a sigh. "I'm so short and stubby that everything I put on makes me look like a *keg!* Thee looks like a—a *queen* or a princess!"

Grace laughed, "Oh, come now, Charity—!"

"I mean it, Grace," Charity said fervently.

She turned to look at herself again. "I—I hope Clyde likes it."

"He'd have to be *blind* not to love you in that dress," Charity said emphatically. For the next few minutes, she stayed and talked with Grace, then said, "I guess the night before a girl's wedding, there's bound to be a few butterflies in the stomach. But after tomorrow, you'll be fine."

Grace tried to smile, but after Charity left, she found her hands trembling as she removed the dress and hung it up. She put on a robe and left her room, going to the kitchen. It was late afternoon, and the sky was gray and threatening. She stood at the window, staring out at the grass and trees, which would gladly soak up the impending rain, and wished that it were all over.

A noise behind her caused Grace to turn, and she found Prudence standing in the doorway. "The dress fits fine," Grace said. "I thought you might come and help me try it on."

"I . . . meant to," Prudence said with a slight hesitation. "But I wasn't feeling too well."

"Oh? What's wrong, Prudence? Not flu coming on I hope?"

"No, just a headache."

"Well, thee go lie down and I'll fix supper."

"No, I'm all right now," Prudence said. She looked tired, and Grace thought that the preparations for the wedding might have been too much for her. But Prudence insisted, "Go sit with Father while I fix supper."

"If you don't mind, I'd like to."

Grace found her father in the parlor reading his Bible. She sat with him until suppertime, listening as he read slowly but with enjoyment. Finally they went in to eat, and his appetite seemed somewhat better. "I'm looking forward to the wedding," he said after the meal. "Everybody in the community will be there to wish thee well."

Grace dreaded being the object of so much attention, but said nothing. It was Prudence who broke the silence. "I think I'll go to bed early."

Grace went to her, put her arm around her and said, "I've let thee do too much. After the wedding, I want thee to rest up. We can take a trip to Riverton. It'll be good for us to spend more time together."

"That would be . . . nice." Prudence held her head down, but when she looked up, both Grace and her father saw that there were tears in her eyes. She started to speak, but seemed to change her mind and left abruptly.

"That's strange," Amos murmured.

"She's worn herself out," Grace said. "She needs to be around young people more."

After Grace washed the dishes, she saw that her father was very tired. "I think we all need to go to bed early," she said. When he agreed, she gave him his medicine and, when he was in bed, kissed him, saying, "Good night. Tomorrow thee will have a new son-in-law."

"And thee will be a wife."

Grace left him and went to bed at once. She was tired, but it took some time for her to go to sleep. Finally she drifted off into a fitful slumber, awakening several times during the night. She dreamed short, unhappy dreams, and when morning finally arrived, she got up more drawn and weary than she'd been when she had gone to bed.

Pulling on her robe, she moved out of her room and down the hall toward the kitchen. She went at once to the stove and built a fire, then moved to the cabinet to get coffee.

As she reached for the heavy white coffee jar, she noticed an envelope leaning against it. She blinked with surprise when she saw her name on the front of the envelope, in Prudence's handwriting. Puzzled, she opened the envelope and took out the single page inside. She began to read—and at once her face lost all color. The room seemed to tilt under her feet and her stomach knotted up.

> Grace,
>
> I know thee will hate me, but I can't help myself. I love Clyde, and he loves me. We are going away to be married. We have been so unhappy and could not find a way to tell thee. Take care of Father and try not to hate me too much.
>
> Prudence

Grace closed her eyes and for a moment swayed slightly as the words seemed to burn into her soul. She had never fainted before, but felt she must be perilously close to doing so at that moment. She became nauseated, and unconsciously crumpling the note into a ball, she walked across the room and opened the door, then stepped outside.

The fresh, cool morning air did nothing to wash away the sickness that seemed to choke her. Her legs began to tremble, and she reached out and grasped one of the posts that held up the roof. Clinging to it until her hands ached with strain, she pressed her brow against the round surface and began to weep. Her body shook with great sobs, and she could not muffle the sound that disturbed the quietness of the morning.

Rip, the old sheepdog, came up to the porch and stared at the sobbing woman uneasily. He climbed the steps and timidly put his nose against Grace's hip. Startled, Grace stopped weeping and looked down. "Oh, Rip!" she cried and sank beside the dog, hugging him and holding back the tears. Rip wiggled, trying to lick her face, then put his huge paw on Grace's leg and whined sadly.

Finally Grace arose, patted the dog, then turned and walked back into the kitchen. She washed her face at the sink, dried her face, and then stood for one moment, thinking of what had to be done.

The wedding would have to be canceled—and she would

have to bear the brunt of the reaction . . . the shame of being cast off and of having a sister who had proved to be totally untrue. She knew that from this time forward, men and women would stare after her and whisper things as she passed.

Suddenly a great bitterness began to grow within her—and at once she knew her danger. Falling on her knees, she prayed, "Oh, God, forgive me for my thoughts! Let me not be a bitter woman! I pray for my sister . . . and—and for Clyde, too! Bless them and let me never harbor hatred for them. I forgive them . . . as you forgave me when I was but a sinner. . . ."

For some time she knelt there, praying, opening her heart to God in sorrow and repentance. Finally, she slowly rose to her feet. Once again there were tears on her cheeks, and she carefully washed them away, then soaked her face with a cold cloth, pressing away as much as she could of the marks of strain.

I'll have to stay close to Father, she thought. *He'll blame himself for agreeing to the marriage. I'll have to make him understand that it's not his fault.*

She turned and filled the kettle, then put it on the stove and moved about the room, making preparation for breakfast, praying constantly. *It's not the end of the world,* she thought. *I have Father to take care of. I have work on the farm. I have my church—and I have Jesus.*

By the time she'd poured the scalding water into the coffeepot, then drank two cups, she was ready. She poured hot coffee into her father's mug, added milk and sugar the way he liked it, then turned toward his room. She knew he would be awake, for she always brought him his coffee at this early hour. As she carried the cup, she took some pride in the fact that her hands were steady and her face was calm.

As she came to his door and reached for the knob, she prayed one quick prayer that the news would not upset him too much. Pain shot through her again, and she leaned her head against the door, praying for strength. When at last she lifted her head, there was resolve in her eyes.

I'll never be a wife. This is the time that I say good-bye to love. From now on, I'll have God's love—and that will be far sweeter than any man's love!

Then she turned the knob and entered the room. When her father greeted her, she said, "Father, take your coffee. We have to have a talk."

CHAPTER FOUR
"I Won't Have a Husband"

★

"I'm afraid he's going, Sister Grace." Dr. Wells' round face was filled with compassion, for he knew how attached Grace Swenson was to her father. He'd watched her carefully some time earlier, when she'd gone through an experience that would have devastated most young women, and had been impressed with how well she'd borne the deception of her sister and Clyde Dortch.

The doctor was not himself a man of faith—he leaned more in the direction of agnosticism—but he'd told his wife, "That oldest Swenson girl, she's got grit enough for ten men! Most girls would have been ruined by what happened to her, but Grace has kept her head up high. If I ever became any kind of a Christian I guess I'd like to look into the Quaker brand!"

Grace was aware of Dr. Wells' scrutiny. She had grown to respect him during the last few months, for he had been kind and honest. Now she looked at him and nodded. "Is it time to call in the family, Doctor?"

"I think that would be best." He hesitated, then added, "I wish there was more that I could do, Miss Swenson. I really do."

"Thee has been so good to my father . . . and to me, Dr. Wells," Grace said, smiling at him warmly. "No doctor in the world could have been more attentive. But it's time for my father to go meet his God, and we must all accept that."

Wells dropped his head, stared at the floor for a long moment, then lifted his gaze to meet her honest blue eyes. "I admire your faith. Your father, he's the kind of Christian I didn't think existed. The way he's faced this illness—and is facing death—makes me think I've been a little hasty in forming my beliefs." Then, as if he was afraid he'd revealed too much, the stubby physician cleared his throat and said in a businesslike tone, "I'll stay close by for the next few days. Call me anytime."

"God bless thee, Dr. Wells." Grace showed him to the door, then moved back to the bedroom. Her father's eyes opened as she sat down beside him, and she asked, "Can I get thee something, Father?"

"Yes . . . call the girls."

Grace whispered, "All right. I'll send for them right away." She left the room and found the two hands splitting wood. "Father's sinking," she said at once. "We have to get the girls here."

"Aw, that's too bad, Miss Grace!" Jed Satterfield shook his head. He was very fond of Amos Swenson, and sadness came to his face. "You want me to go fetch them?"

"Thee go tell Martha and Dove. Benny, thee please take word to Sarah and . . . Prudence."

Benny and Jed exchanged a quick glance. Prudence had not been to see her father since she had left with Clyde Dortch. Word had come that they had returned and were staying at the Dortch farm. "All right, Miss Grace." Benny nodded agreement for both men. "We'll be right fast about it."

"It's good to have you both," Grace said. "I don't see how we could have gotten by without the two of you." She turned and walked quickly into the house, and the two men went to saddle up for their errands.

"If it was me," Benny said as he clapped a bridle into the mouth of a gray stallion, "I'd not have the woman on the place, sister or no!"

"Well, it *ain't* you, so jist do whut Miss Grace tells you to!" Jed Satterfield's disagreement with the shorter man was more out of habit than anything else, for truly he felt exactly the same way as Benny. He slapped a saddle on a roan mare and, as he drew the cinches tight, muttered under his breath, "Don't see how them two could have the unmitigated gall to come back after whut they done to Miss Grace!"

"What you mumbling about?" Benny demanded as he swung into the saddle.

"Nothing! Now git on your way and don't take all day about it!"

"Wasn't plannin' on no pleasure ride, thank you!" Benny George drove his heels into the sides of the stallion and shot out of the barn. He rode hard until he came to the farm belonging to Nick Sanderson, Sarah's husband. Sarah met Benny at the door, and he pulled his hat off to say haltingly, "Miss Sarah—Miss Grace sent me to tell you, you'd better come quick."

"How is he, Benny?"

"Well, Miss Grace said for you to hurry up, please."

"We'll go at once."

Benny nodded, went back to his horse, and rode off toward the Dortch farm. When he came into the front yard and dismounted, Mrs. Dortch, Clyde's mother, came out of the house. "Got to see Miss Prudence, Miz Dortch," Benny said briefly.

The woman stared at him, then nodded. "I'll fetch her." She stepped into the house and went upstairs, where she found Prudence sitting listlessly beside her bed. "One of your father's hired hands just come in. Wants to see thee."

Prudence looked up quickly, fear in her eyes. "It must be my father!" She leaped up and ran down the stairs. Rushing outside, she looked up at Benny.

"Is it Father?" she whispered.

"Yes, ma'am, it is," Benny nodded without expression.

Prudence's face flushed under his accusing stare. "Did— who asked you to come for me?"

"Miss Grace." Having delivered his message, Benny turned to pull himself back into the saddle. He added curtly, "She allowed you'd better hurry." He kicked the stallion's flanks and the horse shot out, sending mud flying from his hooves.

Prudence stood watching him go, then turned and slowly made her way back into the house. Mrs. Dortch came to ask, "Thy father is going?"

"Yes," Prudence whispered, then she hugged herself and said, "I'll go tell Clyde."

"He's working with Daniel over to the south meadow, burning stumps." Mrs. Dortch was a thin woman, worn down with the constant care of her invalid husband. She had not been unkind to Prudence when Clyde had showed up with her, tired and hungry, but there had been little she could do to shield the couple from her older son's hard ways. Daniel had allowed them to stay, but insisted that they both work hard for their keep. As Prudence walked out of the house, Mrs. Dortch asked, "Do you think Clyde will go to thy place with thee?"

Prudence could only say, "It's my father—we've got to go."

She walked the mile and a quarter to the south meadow, and as she drew near, both men stopped work. "It's my father, Clyde," she said. "He's dying."

Clyde was thinner than he had been, for Daniel had driven him hard. He was wearing a pair of worn overalls, and his hands were blistered. He stared at Prudence with lackluster eyes, asking, "Did he send for us?"

"Yes. And we'd better hurry."

Clyde bit his lip nervously. His marriage had been a hard thing, for when their money had run out, there was no place to go but back to the home place. He'd worked harder than ever, with no pay and little prospect of any. He'd grown to hate his brother Daniel, but had no options other than to continue on as he was. And if there was one thing Clyde Dortch hated, it was feeling helpless.

"Wouldn't think thee would want to go back and face them," Daniel grunted to his brother. "Best let her go and thee stay here."

Clyde glared at him, then threw down his axe. "We'll be back when we see how things are," he announced defiantly. He well knew that Daniel would begrudge him every moment he was away. The anger that rose in him gave him the impetus he needed to go back and face Grace and her father.

Daniel Dortch glared at the pair. "Better be careful. It's only my generosity puts food in your stomachs and a roof over your heads!"

"Come on, Prue," Clyde said shortly. He ignored his brother, and when they were out of earshot, said, "I—don't feel good about going back to your place."

Prudence shook her head. "I know. But we've got to do it."

When they reached the barn, Clyde hitched up the team while Prudence went inside to gather up some clothes. She came out as he drove up, and he held the horses steady while she tossed the bag inside and climbed up to sit beside him.

"I'm ready, Clyde," she said quietly, and he spoke to the horses, sending them out of the yard at a fast clip. They rode without speaking for half an hour, and finally Prudence asked, "What will Daniel say when he finds you've taken his team and buggy?"

"I don't care *what* he says!"

"We'll—have to come back," Prudence said, shaking her head. "There's no place else for us to go."

A hot answer rose to Clyde's lips, but the bitter truth of her words silenced him. As they moved along down the rutted road, he wondered how he'd ever gotten himself into such a predicament. Truth was, he thought about little else these days, but the more he considered it, the less he understood.

I could have had an easy life, he thought bitterly. *Grace may not look like much—but that doesn't seem to matter now.* He wanted to blame Prudence, but there was enough honesty left in him to know she had not been at fault—not completely. *We were both crazy,* he concluded. *She's a pretty, lively woman, and I wanted her, just like she wanted me. But if we had it to do over—!*

When they were within sight of the house, Prudence said, "Oh, Clyde, how can we face them?"

Shaking his head, Clyde said doggedly, "They sent for us. Maybe it won't be so bad." He halted the buggy, then got down and went around to help Prudence step to the ground. They turned, and when they reached the porch, the door opened.

Grace came outside and met them, her expression calm. She walked right up to Prudence and embraced her, and Prudence gave a small cry and clung to her fiercely. Grace's lips were broad and maternal as she held the sobbing girl. She turned to meet Clyde's eyes, but he dropped his head to stare at the ground.

"I'm glad you've come," Grace said, including both of them in her welcome. "Come inside. The others should be here soon."

"How is father?" Prudence asked as they entered the foyer.

"Very weak, I'm afraid. He's been asking for thee."

When the two women turned to go to the sick man's room, Clyde remained where he was. When Grace turned to him with an inquiring look, he said tersely, "He won't want to see me."

"Yes, he's been asking for thee, too," Grace said.

Clyde stared at her for a moment, then nodded. "All right then, if he wants me."

When they entered the room, Amos looked up and smiled faintly. He whispered, "My children . . . come to me!" Sarah and her husband quietly left the room to give the newcomers some time alone with the dying man.

Prudence ran, weeping wildly, to fall on her knees and into the arms of her father. Swenson held her, patted her with one hand, then looked up and held out his other hand to Clyde, who took it awkwardly.

Quietly, Grace returned to the kitchen. She was putting a roast in the oven when she heard the bedroom door close, and she turned to face Prudence and Clyde as they entered. Prudence's face was swollen and Clyde looked terrible. He said hoarsely, "He . . . forgave us both, Grace." He swallowed and his voice dropped to a whisper. "Got no right to ask, but we treated you shamefully, Grace. How thee must hate us!"

Grace went to them at once, shaking her head. "No, Clyde. I don't hate thee. It would have been easy to fall into that, but God has delivered me from it. He's given me a love for you both. Please, let us speak of it no more."

Prudence began to weep again, and Clyde's face was pale as paste. It took some time for Grace to convince them that she harbored no malice toward them, but before too long, the pair had gained some control.

Dove and Martha arrived later, and the house grew busy with the activity of the three girls' small children. Grace thought it well that there was so much to do, for it gave Prudence no time to linger in embarrassment. Grace was certain that her sisters had talked with their husbands, for all three of Clyde's brothers-in-law said nothing of the circumstances of his marriage. There was, to be sure, some distance between the newlyweds and the others, but Grace did all she could to show affection for them. This did much to assure the others, and by evening when they sat down for dinner, Clyde and Prudence were able to join in the conversation to some extent.

Afterward, Martha helped Grace with the dishes. With the closeness that sisters share, she felt able to ask cautiously, "Thee feels no anger toward Prudence and Clyde?"

"I did, Martha, but God has taken it from me."

Martha smiled and gave Grace a sudden hug. "Only thee could forgive so completely!"

Grace shook off the praise, saying, "They've had a very hard time, Martha. Prudence is miserable, and so is Clyde."

Martha nodded. "I think living with Daniel Dortch could have that effect. He's a hard man."

The two women talked quietly, and it did Grace good to share a little of what was in her heart with her sister. Afterward, she found beds for everyone, but when they retired, she went to sit beside her father. He seemed quiet enough, but about one o'clock, Grace woke up from where she'd been dozing to find him seeming to gasp for air.

At once she knew that it was the end and ran to knock on the door of a bedroom, calling out, "Martha, Father's very bad! Get the others and come quickly!"

She ran back to her father and did what she could to relieve his discomfort. When Martha and her husband, Lige, rushed in, Grace said, "Lige, would thee send Jed for Dr. Wells?"

"Right away!"

But even as her brother-in-law rushed away, Grace knew that the doctor would be too late. By the time the others had gathered and Lige returned to report that Jed was on his way, Amos Swenson was almost gone.

"Can't we do something, Grace?" Dove whispered.

"He's in God's hands, Dove."

The room was silent except for the harsh gasping breaths of the dying man. As Grace gently wiped the clammy sweat from her father's brow, he opened his eyes and looked at her.

"Father . . . does thee know me?"

"Yes." Amos seemed to grow stronger. His eyes went around the room and his breathing grew easier. "I've asked the Lord . . . for time to say a farewell to you—"

None of the family ever forgot the next half hour. Amos spoke to every one of them, telling how each one had blessed him in his life, assuring them all of his love for them. As he spoke to Prudence and Clyde, both were ashen-faced, but he smiled and held their hands, saying, "You two have had a bad beginning, but God is merciful. Obey him and submit to his love, and he will keep you in his care."

Then, finally, after he had spoken to all the others, he

looked at Grace. Fighting her tears, she went to him. "Come closer," he whispered, and when Grace put her head very close to his face, he laid his hands upon her head. "Thee has been the delight of my life, Daughter," he whispered. "The Lord has chosen thee to serve him in a special manner. Thee will be alone, but not alone, for the good Lord will be at thy side always. Thee will have great sorrow, but God will turn thy mourning into joy."

Hot tears filled Grace's eyes and flowed down her face, and he finally said, so faintly that only she heard his words: "Thee has been my crown and my joy on this earth, Grace. I will tell thy mother . . . how like . . . thee are . . . to her—"

He smiled faintly, drew a deep breath, and looked around the room, saying clearly, "God watch over you!" And then he closed his eyes—and how well he endured his going forth!

When Lawyer Simms read the will to the family, there were no surprises. Swenson had talked to all his daughters prior to his passing, explaining that he was dividing his cash assets equally among the four married sisters. The farm was left to Grace, and Martha spoke for all of them when she said, "It's a fair settlement. Father was wise."

After the reading of the will, Martha, Sarah, and Dove all left with their families. Grace asked Prudence to stay and help her clean the house. As they worked, Grace drew her sister out skillfully, listening carefully as she talked about their life at the Dortch house. Prudence tried to be cheerful, but Grace knew she was miserable.

Finally, when the house was cleaned, Clyde came in to say that the buggy was hitched up. His mouth was tight, and Prudence knew he was dreading the return to his father's farm. "Can't we take our share of the money and go away, Clyde?" she asked timidly.

"I think we'd better," he said grimly.

Grace said suddenly, "I want to talk to you both. Come and sit down." She fixed coffee, and when they were seated, she said simply, "I want you to stay here."

Clyde blinked with astonishment. "Stay here? On the farm?"

"Yes," Grace nodded. "I know thee is unhappy working for thy brother, Clyde."

"That's true enough," Clyde acknowledged. He glanced at Prudence, whose eyes were suddenly alive with hope.

"Oh, Clyde, could we?"

Clyde licked his lips, seeming to struggle with a thought. Finally he said in a halting fashion, "Why, Grace, I can't deny that would be good for us, but what about for thee? People would talk."

Grace shook her head. "No, they won't talk."

Clyde said stubbornly, "Thee has a better opinion of people than I have. Why, I can hear Mrs. Gatz babbling now, about how strange it is that thee would take in the people who betrayed thee—"

"We've agreed to forget that, Clyde," Grace said, breaking in. "I spoke with Father about this, and he was pleased. A bride needs her own house—" Grace smiled at Prudence—"and I would like to have you both here."

Clyde swallowed hard, then glanced at Prudence. He knew she was miserable at his father's house, as much as he was himself. With a sigh that was both from relief and apprehension, he finally said, "If thee will have us, we'll be grateful, Grace."

"Good, that's settled!" Grace nodded. "Now, Clyde, thee go tell thy people and bring thy things back."

It was a happy day for Prudence, and for the next month she radiated joy. Clyde, too, was so relieved to be out from under the iron control of Daniel that he threw himself into the work on the farm with all his might.

The three of them got along well after the strangeness of the situation wore off. Grace stayed alone much of the time, riding her mare through the solitude of the woods. Watching her, Prudence thought she seemed withdrawn. "Why is Grace so—so distant?" she finally asked Clyde.

"Got to be a little uncomfortable for her, Prue." He

shrugged. "I know she's forgiven us, but she can't have *forgotten* what we did."

"I don't think she's angry with us," Prudence disagreed. "She's unhappy about something."

"Don't go pestering her, Prue," Clyde said quickly. "Likely she misses thy father. They were very close."

Clyde was right in that respect. The loss of her father had left Grace with little intimate companionship. She rode often to visit Martha, but even spending time with her sister could not fill the gap left by Amos's death. Grace was regular in her church duties, even more devoted to good works, but still everyone noticed that she was not as lively as she had been.

Then, to make matters worse, a problem arose about the management of the farm. Clyde wanted to do more than simple chores. For the first time in his life he was ready to take hold of something, but he had nothing of his own to take hold of. Jed and Benny quickly discovered that Clyde had no authority, and both of them felt they knew the farm better than he, which was true enough. This resulted in Clyde feeling useless and out of place.

Prudence saw Clyde's restlessness and spoke of it to Grace. "It's just that he needs some responsibility, Grace. Can't thee let him do more?"

Grace agreed to think about it and in less than a week she came in from a long ride. She found Clyde putting up a fence and called out, "Clyde, come to the house!"

Clyde followed her, and when Prudence met them, Grace said, "I've been seeking guidance from the Lord." She smiled at Prudence. "I fear thee has noticed I've been a little distant lately. Well, my answer just came." She removed her bonnet and shook her hair loose, her blue eyes bright. "It came suddenly," she said in wonder.

"What is it, Grace?" Prudence asked.

Grace hung her bonnet on a peg, then turned to face them. "I'm leaving the farm for a while."

"Leaving here?" Prudence asked, giving Clyde a glance of surprise. "Why—where will thee go, Grace?"

"I'm going to Washington," Grace said.

"The capital?" Clyde asked. "What in the world for?"

"The papers are full of stories about the wounded soldiers," Grace said. "The hospitals are filled with them—and there are not enough nurses." When she saw the astonishment in their faces, she nodded, "I am against war—but it's God's commandment to take care of the sick and helpless. Now, sit down and I'll tell you the rest. . . ."

When they had sat at the table, she went on. "Clyde, thee will be manager of the farm. Thee must make all the decisions as if it were thy farm. I may be gone for years, until the war is over, I suppose. Whatever profits come from the farm we will share equally. Does this suit thee?"

Clyde stared at Grace, wonder in his face. "Suit me? Why, I'd be a fool if such a thing didn't please me!"

The conference lasted long, and Grace was happy to see what a difference the new situation made to her sister and brother-in-law. They were ecstatic, and she was hopeful that Clyde would throw off his old careless ways and find satisfaction and fulfillment in his new responsibilities.

She herself was anxious to leave. Now that she felt she knew God's direction, she longed to be gone. "I want to leave as soon as possible," she said finally. "We'll draw up the agreement and take it to the lawyer tomorrow. Then I'll leave."

"So soon?" Prudence exclaimed in surprise.

"I must be about my Father's business." Grace smiled.

Two days later Clyde and Prudence drove her to the train station. She kissed them both, boarded, and, as the train pulled out, waved at them through the window.

As the train wound its way along the narrow gauge tracks, she felt a burden lift from her heart.

I won't have a husband, she thought, *but I'll be serving God!*

CHAPTER FIVE
The Return of Burke Rocklin

★

JULY 1862

The black walnut of Ellen Rocklin's casket had been sanded and polished until it glowed with a rich warmth. The two oil lamps—one stationed at the head of the coffin and the other at the foot—shed their amber glow over the room, somewhat dispelling the predawn darkness.

The gleam of the yellow lamplight highlighted Clay Rocklin's face as he sat loosely in a leather-covered sofa across the room. He was a big man, darkly handsome with black hair and strong features. He wore the uniform of a sergeant in the Confederate army.

As the silence of the house seemed to close around him, he let his dark eyes gaze at the casket, thinking of the woman who lay within. She had been his wife for over twenty years—every single one of which had been stormy. He thought of the early years of their marriage, but even those had not been happy. Ellen had known that Clay had married her while loving her cousin Melanie. This knowledge had embittered her, creating a hardness in her heart that only grew worse as the years went by—a hardness that inspired sarcasm, resentment, and criticism; a hardness that left no room for real love.

Shaking his head, Clay rose and went to stand over the

59

casket, pain evident on the sharp planes of his face. *If I hadn't abandoned her and the children,* he thought bitterly, *she might have been different.*

Tormented by his love for Melanie, who was married to his cousin Gideon, Clay had left Ellen after only a few years of marriage. He thought of his years of wandering, of the time he spent working and living on a slave ship. Those had been bitter and hard years for him, but he knew it had been even harder on his family. While he had been running from one empty endeavor to another, Ellen had stayed at Gracefield with their children—and before long had become a promiscuous woman. When Clay had finally returned to his home and his family, he found little welcome. Now, looking at Ellen's still face, Clay admitted to himself that Ellen's life-style had been, at least in part, his fault. *Should have stayed here for Ellen . . . for us and for the children!*

The pain in Clay's eyes deepened at the thought of his children. They were all grown now, or almost so. Dent and David, the twins, and Lowell, their younger brother, were men. Clay and Ellen's only daughter, Rena, was on the verge of young womanhood. At the thought of Rena, Clay's stern face relaxed into smoother lines. Although the boys had not forgiven him upon his return—though he had had hopes that they would do so someday—Rena had received him almost at once. She had been so starved for love, especially for a father's love, that it had been simple to win her confidence.

Clay pulled his eyes away from the casket, thinking of his return from the years of wandering. It had been difficult, asking his family to forgive him. Dent had been the hardest of all, but now the two of them had come closer together and Clay's hopes had been realized. David and Lowell had been much readier to accept him, as had his father and mother.

But Ellen—!

Bitter memories came to Clay as he stood there in the gloomy room, memories of how Ellen had changed so greatly during his absence that he scarcely knew her when he returned. She'd become a hard woman and had lost most of her prettiness in her pursuit of pleasure. Even when Clay had become a Christian and begun to live a life of sincere faith, Ellen had not softened at all—and she'd had affair after affair since he'd returned home. Then came the accident that had made her a hopeless invalid, bound to a wheelchair. . . .

Clay desperately tried to convince himself that he'd done all he could to make her life as comfortable as possible, but he'd been gone—serving with the Richmond Grays—most of the time. He'd known that Ellen's mind, as well as her body, had been affected by her injury, but none of them, he thought bitterly, had known how seriously her mind had warped.

"Well, we know now how bad off she was." Clay's whisper seemed very loud to his own ears. He started as though the suddenness of it might disturb someone, but the only one who could possibly have heard him would never hear again. Clay whirled and walked over to the door at the end of the large room, opened it, and stepped outside.

The summer nighttime sky was lit up by a large moon and millions of glittering stars. He took a deep breath, relieved to be out of the room, and tried to pray. Far off he heard the cry of a foxhound, shrill and clear, and subconsciously noted that the dog was on the scent.

Standing in the shadow of the overhanging balcony, he ran his eyes over the grounds of Gracefield. He'd been away from this place for so many years—and now would be away for many more, he feared. After the Confederate victory of Bull Run some zealots had insisted that the Yankees would never come back. But they had—over 100,000 of them under the command of Gen. George McClellan.

Shaking off the memories, he half-turned to go back in when a movement caught his eye. It was only a shadow, but as he watched, he saw that it was a man. Clay grew alert, then relaxed. Perhaps it was one of the slaves.

But which of them would be out at three in the morning?

The figure moved across the yard, and Clay stepped out on the grass, walking to the corner of the house. Peering around, he saw the man approach the steps that led to the west entrance of Gracefield. Something about the way the intruder moved made Clay suspicious, and he moved forward quietly, his feet making no sound on the tender grass as he avoided the oyster-shell drive.

Clay had no gun, so he came up behind the figure so close that he could grapple with him if necessary. He could see only that the man was very tall, and without warning, Clay reached out and grabbed the intruder by the arm, saying abruptly, "Who are you, and what—!"

He got no further, for the man had suddenly whirled with a catlike motion, striking out with a hard fist that caught Clay on the temple. Lights seemed to explode in Clay's head, but he managed to retain his grasp on the man's arm. He threw his arms around the man, butting him in the face with his head. The blow drew a sharp gasp of pain from his antagonist, but the man did not go down. Clay could feel his opponent's strength as they struggled, and he hung on determinedly, pinioning the man's arms until his head cleared.

When he could think straight, Clay quickly stepped back, ducked a hard right, and threw a hard left to the man's body, following it with a thundering right to his chin. The blow drove his man backwards, and Clay went in at once, but was caught by an unexpected blow in the mouth. Once more he tried to close with the big man.

The two of them struggled, falling into a flower bed, grunting and straining. They fought free of the bed, stood up, and suddenly the man got a good look at his adversary.

"Clay—!"

Clay stopped short and peered suspiciously at the face of the man who stood in front of him. A pale silver bar of moonlight suddenly illuminated the man's features, and Clay cried out in shock.

"Burke!" Pure astonishment ran through him, which

almost immediately became anger. "Burke, what in blazes are you doing sneaking around the house? A man can get shot for that!"

Burke Rocklin glared at his older brother—then burst into laughter. "What are *you* doing, jumping a man like that? I'd have shot you for sure if I'd had a gun." He touched his forehead, then looked at his finger and said petulantly, "You've cut me up, blast you, Clay!"

Beginning to hurt from the blows he'd taken, Clay said roughly, "Come on inside."

The two men entered the house and went at once to the kitchen. Clay poured some water from a pitcher into a basin, thinking with some irritation that it was typical of Burke to arrive home after a year's absence in such a fashion. Finding a cloth, he dipped it into the water and rinsed his face, wincing from the bruise on his mouth. He washed his hands, noting that he'd scraped his right knuckles, then washed the basin and filled it with fresh water.

"Here," he grunted, handing it to his brother. "Clean up, and then we'll talk."

"All right. Is there anything to eat?"

As Burke cleaned his face, Clay prowled through the cabinets, finding some biscuits. Then he located a large bowl of pinto beans still warm inside the oven. He set a jar of milk and a glass on the table and found the remains of a raisin pie in the pie safe. As he pulled the meal together, he studied his brother surreptitiously.

Burke, at the age of thirty-two, was ten years younger than Clay. He had always looked up to Clay, but the difference in their ages—and Clay's years of absence—had kept them from being close.

Burke's the same as he always was, Clay thought as he sat down and watched him eat ravenously. *Still wild as a hawk! But he looks as good as ever.* He thought of Burke's willful temper and the many scrapes he'd gotten himself into, some of them fairly serious. Clay himself had been fairly wild as a young man, and Burke's temper and daredevil ways seemed a mirror of Clay's younger years.

He looks no older now than he did when he was twenty, Clay thought. He let his eyes run over the tall form, all six feet three inches, and saw that Burke was still wiry and strong. With a wry smile, Clay remembered how his younger brother had despaired of ever reaching six feet in height. But when he hit his late teens, Burke suddenly "shot up like a sprout dying for the light of day," as his father had put it, and soon towered over most men.

Lifting his gaze, Clay studied the lean face, so much like his own in some ways. Dark eyes, so dark that the pupils were almost invisible, could sparkle or glare from under heavy black brows. The fine features were crowned with the blackest possible thick hair—Burke had always had hair that was the envy of men and of women. Heavy and glossy black with just a slight curl, he wore it long, and now it was hanging down almost to his collar. His face, which had tended to roundness when he was younger, was now hard and lean. His high cheekbones and fine broad forehead gave him a pleasing appearance, as did his broad mouth—which was shaded by a neat mustache—and strong chin, complete with the cleft that marked most of the Rocklin men.

Clay noted the worn coat and frayed trousers and said, "You didn't come home prosperous, I take it?"

Burke bit off a chunk of biscuit, chewed it with relish, then grinned. "Nope. Haven't got a cent."

Clay was annoyed. "Fine, just what we need around here. A broken-down gentleman." His words, he saw, had no effect on Burke. But that came as no surprise, for this younger brother of his—though he adored his older brother—had paid no attention to the advice of anyone since he was fifteen years old. "What happened to the scheme you wrote about?"

"Scheme?"

"The plan that was going to make you rich," Clay said sarcastically. "The big real estate deal in Mobile."

"Oh, that!" Burke waved the half-eaten biscuit with an airy gesture. "I sold out and went to Haiti. Lots of opportunity down there."

"Oh?" Clay raised one heavy eyebrow. "And what happened in Haiti?"

Burke sopped the bean soup with the last morsel of biscuit, popped it into his mouth, then washed it down with the rest of the milk. He ignored Clay as he pulled the pie toward him, cut off a bit with the edge of his fork, and tasted it. "That's good pie," he said with a nod. "I sure have missed Dorrie's pies!" Closing his eyes, he chewed thoughtfully on the pie, swallowed it, then shrugged. "There was a fancy gambler down there named Ace Donlin. I thought I could take him. Planned to come home and build me a mansion down the road from this place."

"And—?"

A trace of disgust showed in Burke's dark eyes. "I guess Donlin will be building the mansion." He pushed the pie around with his fork, then said, "So here I am, back to sponge off the folks again." When Clay said nothing, he shoved the plate back with irritation. "Like you said, Clay, you need another useless wastrel around."

Clay eyed Burke sharply, then frowned. "You know how things are, Burke. With this war on and no market for cotton, things are pretty thin."

"I know, I know!" Burke shrugged his shoulders and then let them sag. He looked across the table, and Clay saw the corners of his lips draw up. Burke had a perverse sense of humor, sometimes aimed at his own foibles. His dark eyes gleamed, and he said, "But I have a plan, Brother. A plan that will keep me from being a parasite on my beloved family."

"Have I heard this one before?" Clay grinned in spite of himself. It was difficult to stay mad at this rascal of a brother!

"No, this one is brand-new, and it doesn't involve fast horses or gambling in any form."

"That'll be different!"

Burke leaned back and studied Clay carefully. "I don't know why I never thought of it before, Clay. It's so simple!" He paused for effect, then put his hands out, palms up. "I'm going to marry a rich woman!"

Clay laughed out loud. "Aren't you the man who's always run from a wedding ring as if it were a rattlesnake? I don't believe it!"

"I'm getting mellow, Clay," Burke answered, his humor fading as quickly as it had come. "Time for me to settle down. But to what?"

"I thought you got a piece of paper from the university saying you were an engineer."

"No money in that, not unless you own a big company." Burke shook his head. "I'd have to start as a junior clerk, carrying a chain for an eighteen-year-old boy!"

Clay could not believe his brother was serious about this scheme. "Got the girl picked out? No doubt you can charm some poor young thing into falling in love with you. You never had any trouble with *that!* But rich girls are likely to have parents who'd like their son-in-law to have more than the clothes on his back."

"I can charm the girl's mama—and the papa, too."

Clay stared at his brother's smooth face. "I never know when you're joking, Burke."

"I'm serious about this," Burke replied. His mouth drew tight and he nodded adamantly. "I'll make a good husband, Clay. Got most of my foolishness behind me. And I've gotten to where I know plantations. All I need is a beautiful girl—an only child, preferably—with rather *elderly* parents. They'll be worried about what happens to their little girl when they're gone, and I'll be there to take care of her. That makes sense, doesn't it?"

"You only left one thing out, Burke. For every rich girl, there's about fifty poor young men standing in line to 'help' her manage her money."

"Competition never bothered me." Burke took another

bite of the pie. "Now tell me, what's going on around here? I haven't got a letter for weeks."

"Ellen died last Thursday," Clay answered simply.

Burke blinked and stopped chewing. Quickly he swallowed the bite, then said quietly, "I'm sorry, Clay." The words seemed inadequate, and he asked, "What was it?"

Clay hesitated, not knowing how much of the tragic story of Ellen's death he should reveal. The bare truth was that Ellen, her mind affected by her physical problem, had fallen into a jealous rage, convincing herself that Clay and Melora Yancy were having an affair. Nursing the suspicion until it became a certainty in her mind, Ellen had finally sent word for Melora to meet her at an abandoned sawmill, deep in the woods. When Melora arrived, Ellen had pulled out a pistol and tried to kill her. The shot had only grazed Melora's neck, but it had startled the horses attached to Ellen's buggy, causing them to bolt. Unable to hold on to the seat, Ellen was thrown down an incline and critically injured. Melora had gone at once for help, but by the time they got Ellen back home and under a doctor's care, it was obvious that she was dying.

All this ran through Clay's mind as he faced his brother's sympathy, but he said only, "She was thrown from her buggy in an accident, Burke. She lived only a day."

Burke dropped his eyes, ashamed of his light talk. "I wish you'd told me earlier, Clay. I wouldn't have acted such a fool."

"It's all right, Burke," Clay answered reassuringly. "In a way, Ellen's better off."

"Better off?" Burke looked up with surprise in his dark eyes. "What do you mean?"

"You can imagine how miserable she'd be, confined to a wheelchair," Clay said slowly. "Now she's free from those restrictions. And just before she died, Melora was able to help her in a wonderful way—she led Ellen to faith in Jesus." Clay rubbed the bruise on his jaw absently. "I think the last hours of Ellen's life were the only ones that held any joy for her."

Not being a man of faith, Burke wanted to argue with this. But he knew his brother's stand on God, so instead he merely asked, "How are the children taking it?"

Clay thought about the question for a long moment. "Better than I expected." He shuddered, then said, "The funeral is tomorrow. Sorry to spoil your homecoming, Burke."

Burke Rocklin was not a man to show his feelings much, but now compassion was on his face. Although he had idolized his older brother, they had never been very close because of their age difference. But he knew enough about him to realize the suffering that Clay had gone through. He sat there, trying to think of something fitting to say, but could not manage it.

Seeing Burke's embarrassment, Clay stood up. "Go get some sleep, Burke. We'll talk more later."

Burke mumbled a good night, pushed back his chair, and left. Clay returned to the parlor, going to stand beside the casket. He looked down on Ellen's still, white face. Knowing that the next day would be filled with emotional turmoil and tension—as most funerals were—he reached out and touched her hair.

"Good-bye, Ellen," he whispered. "I wish I'd done better by you!"

Then he went to the chair and sat down, waiting for the sunrise.

The funeral was held in the white church three miles from Gracefield. The sanctuary was filled—every pew was packed. Clay had chosen ten o'clock in the morning for the service, knowing that the church would be sweltering if it were held at the customary hour of two in the afternoon.

Clay sat silently between Dent and Rena, with Lowell and David flanking them. Many uncles and aunts were there, along with cousins. Many of the men wore Confederate uniforms, several of them officers.

Clay heard little of the sermon. He was thinking of Rena most of all. He glanced at her from time to time, noting the pallor of her cheeks. He gently took her hand when he saw she was trembling, and she grasped it hard, looking up at him for reassurance. Her eyes were brimming with tears, and Clay was glad he was there. *She's going to need a lot of love,* he thought. *And I won't be here to give it to her.* That was the way of a war. It tore men away when they were needed most. Unlike most Southerners, Clay didn't believe in the Cause. He hated slavery with a passion, but he had chosen to stay with his state and his family rather than join the Union forces. And then his love for his sons had compelled him to join them in the Confederate army . . .

He looked more than once at his father, Thomas, and saw that the sickness that had plagued him for the past two years had made an old man out of him. Thomas Rocklin had been a fine-looking man for many years, but now he was stooped, and his legs trembled as he walked. His cheeks were pallid, his hair thin and gray. Clay glanced at his mother, Susanna, thinking, *She looks more like his daughter than his wife!* His mother's auburn hair was sprinkled with silver, but she retained much of the beauty of her youth. She caught his glance, and compassion came to her eyes as she nodded slightly at him.

Finally the service ended, and the visitors were permitted to pass by the coffin before the family did, for one last glimpse of the dead woman. When all but the family were outside, Clay stood up along with the others. He waited until all had passed by, then said, "Come, children. We'll say good-bye together."

The boys went first, Dent and David, the twins, then Lowell, the youngest. Clay took Rena's arm and the two of them came to join the boys. Clay felt Rena tremble and held her tightly. "She's happy now," he said quietly. "I thank our God that she found Jesus." Rena began to weep, and Clay felt tears of grief sting his own eyes. He knew that if Ellen had gone out to meet her God unprepared, he would have been stricken for the rest of his life.

They turned and left, going outside to the open grave just south of the church. The crowd made a circle, with the family in close. The minister read the Scripture, then prayed a brief prayer . . . and it was over.

All except the worst part—for Clay, at least. For now was when the family must stand and receive people's condolences.

Clay stood there, his face tight, saying to each person, "Thank you—" but the faces were a blur, and he longed for it to be over.

And then it was Melora who was standing in front of him, holding one of his hands and one of Rena's. She was wearing black, and her eyes were filled with peace as she said, "God is on his throne, isn't he?" She moved forward and embraced Rena, whispering, "We must help each other now, Rena!"

"Yes!" Rena held Melora fast, clinging to her for a long moment. "Will—will I see you, Melora?" she asked as she drew back.

"Yes, Rena," Melora said. Then she extended her hand to Clay. When he took it, she said quietly, "God be with you and give you peace, Clay."

Clay nodded, his lips dry. He had loved this woman for years—as she had loved him—but they had been faithful to God and to Clay's marriage. Despite Ellen's suspicions, Clay and Melora had never been more than dear friends. "You were a blessing to Ellen, Melora," he said now. "Thank you for helping her."

Melora turned, not unaware of the glances she received from some standing nearby. She made no sign that she noticed, but she knew that she and Clay would be the target of many eyes in the future. Gossip had been rampant about them for a long time, but Melora had never shown any anger toward those who were unkind. There was a rare sweetness in her that stemmed from her desire and determination to honor her Lord. She had fallen in love with Clay Rocklin when she was a mere child. From that first affection, she had found love growing, and by the time she was a mature woman, she knew that there was no other man in the world for her. Even so, she and Clay had long ago faced up to the sad truth that they could never share more than friendship and respect. Clay had a wife, and for both of them, that settled the matter. Neither she nor Clay would dishonor their God—or their love—by breaking his wedding vows to Ellen.

Not that Melora had lacked for suitors. She was a beautiful woman, and several men had sought her company. Her most persistent suitor had been Jeremiah Irons, the fine young pastor who had joined the Confederate army. Jeremiah had finally won Melora's consent to marry a year and a half ago—shortly before he was killed in battle. Now, at the age of twenty-seven, she was still single.

As Melora turned away, making her way to the wagon where her father, Buford, waited for her, she saw the concern in his greenish eyes. "Are you ready to go home, Melora?" he asked.

"Ready, Pa."

Melora mounted the seat beside him as her brothers and sisters scrambled into the back of the wagon. For them, Melora was more of a mother, for after the death of their real mother, she had practically raised them.

As the wagon pulled away, Burke stood off to one side, watching the drama. He had been aware for years of the hopeless love between his brother and Melora Yancy. He had beaten one man into insensibility for speaking of the pair in public, and his skill with a dueling pistol had shut the mouths of others.

Now he saw that Clay was holding his daughter, Rena, closely—but his eyes followed Melora as the wagon moved out of the churchyard.

"Too bad for Clay," Burke muttered. He respected few

women. In his opinion, most were deceiving creatures without much honor who wanted husbands and would play any game to get one. But two women he did respect were his mother—and Melora Yancy.

Burke knew there *were* other women like his mother and Melora and some of his aunts, but they were few and far between—a thought which made his self-assigned duty of finding a wealthy wife less than enjoyable. He knew he would have to make concessions to assure his future, but the thought of living with a devious woman for the rest of his life—no matter how attractive her money might be—left a sour taste in his mouth. He moved to help his father into the buggy, but his thoughts were on what lay ahead for him.

Not the war; Burke was no patriot. He was not incensed by slavery as was Clay, yet he did believe the leadership of the South had led them into a deadly war that they would lose.

As he rode back to Gracefield, he thought of the plan he'd explained to Clay and mused, *It's got to be that way, I guess. What else am I fit to do but be some kind of kept husband?* A thin feeling of self-disgust ran through him, but he clamped his lips tightly together and settled down in the carriage, thinking of what would come in the next few weeks.

CHAPTER SIX
A Rapid Promotion

The smoke of the fighting, which would be called the Seven Days' Battles, still hung over Richmond. The campaign was made up of a series of battles fought outside the capital, and it was Robert E. Lee's genius that staved off defeat for the newborn Confederacy.

Gen. Joseph Johnston had been in command of the Confederate forces as the Federals' Peninsular Campaign started, but had been wounded at Seven Pines, and President Jefferson Davis had appointed Gen. Lee as commander. That would prove to be the best decision Davis ever made as president. Lee had attacked the Federals so audaciously that McClellan had been driven off and forced to retire back to the safety of Washington.

The Seven Days' Battles rocked both North and South, for neither side had been prepared for the enormous losses they would sustain. The Union forces suffered almost sixteen thousand killed, wounded, captured, or missing. The Confederates lost approximately twenty thousand men.

The Richmond Grays, in which three of the Rocklins served, were devastated by the Seven Days' Battles. When Lt. Dent Rocklin, along with his father and brother, went back to camp immediately following his mother's funeral, he found that half of the officers had already been killed or wounded so badly that they would be out of action for months. His own platoon had lost over forty percent—*and the fighting was still going on!* This meant he would have to train privates to become corporals and corporals to become sergeants, as well as commandeer whatever recruits he could manage to get his hands on. Unlike the Northern adversary, the South had scant few replacements for those who fell. All Lincoln had to do was issue a call, and he would have fifty thousand new recruits to fill the federal ranks. But when a Southern soldier died, he left a gap that, often, no one could be found to fill. So the ranks grew thin, and those who were left had to fight harder on less supplies and energy than ever before.

After the Seven Days' Battles, Richmond was like a swimmer who had exhausted himself. The city had not been invaded as McClellan (and the North) had promised, but the herculean effort expended by Lee and the army in repelling the Army of the Potomac had drained the people terribly.

The small towns just to the northeast of Richmond marked the bloody battles. Mechanicsville, Gaines' Mill, Savage's Station, Malvern Hill . . . these tiny hamlets that most people had never heard of soon became household words all over the country. Many a parent or a wife wept over one of these names as the news came that their sons and husbands slept forever in one of the obscure towns beside the Chickahominy River.

The Peace party in the North began sounding its cry: "Stop the War," and Abraham Lincoln padded for long hours in the White House each night, his homely face furrowed with care. When his secretary of war asked him if he could keep the North to the task of defending the Union, he said, "I knew an old fellow back home in Illinois. He kept dogs, bought and sold them. But there was one old dog he never would sell. Wasn't much of a dog to look at, and I asked him once why he wouldn't sell him. 'Abe,' he said to me, 'That ol' dog ain't much to look at, and I got dogs that's faster—but that ol' dog—you can't beat him on a cold scent!' I guess I'm like that old dog; I'm not much to look at, but I know how to hold on, and that's what I'm going to do until the Union is secure!"

McClellan's army went slinking away, whipped again, as they had been at Bull Run—but it had not been their fault that they had lost. They had fought as bravely and with as much determination as the Confederates. What had whipped them was their commander's lack of will. George McClellan was a fine commander, right up until a battle came. He could train troops and whip an army into shape and give it heart better than any man in the North. And he proved that he was an expert soldier by the manner in which he conducted his retreat from Richmond: orderly and with almost no losses.

But the man lacked nerve. When it came time to send men in large numbers to their deaths, he simply could not do it. He would prove this again and again. Lincoln could have done it, but he was not a general. It wasn't until the North found a man who *could* do this—a small, nondescript man named U. S. Grant—that the North would overcome the smaller armies of the Confederacy. When Lincoln finally found Grant and put him in charge, he received complaints about the man's drinking. In response, the president said adamantly, "I can't spare this man; he *fights!*"

So the Army of the Potomac—those who didn't remain forever in Southern soil, at any rate—went home. When they arrived, there were no parades with flags flying and people cheering. All the North, it seemed, wore black arm bands in memory of high-spirited young soldiers who had marched away a few weeks earlier, shouting "On to Richmond!"— but who now would march no more.

As soon as the fighting was over, Dent sought out his father. "How are you?" he asked Clay at once.

"Fine, Lieutenant," Clay said, using the formal term as he always did when they were in uniform. When Clay had joined the army to be near Lowell, he'd told his son Denton, "You'll have to be harder on Lowell and me than on any of the others. If you don't you'll be accused of favoritism." And Dent had acted on this, giving all the hard jobs to his father and brother. "How's Raimey?" Clay asked, aware that she hadn't been at the funeral.

A smile crossed Dent's face. He'd married Raimey Reed, a lovely girl from a wealthy family, nearly a year ago. It had been a stormy and bizarre romance, complicated by the fact that Raimey was blind. Dent had been terribly wounded in battle, his handsome face scarred by a saber, and it had been the determination of the blind girl that had led him out of self-pity into trust in God. The journey from there to love had been short, and Dent thanked God again, as he often did, for his wife and the joy they shared. He grinned at his father. "Well, Sergeant, she's doing quite well. In fact, I have news for you. You're going to be a grandfather."

"Dent!" Clay forgot the differences in rank at once. He beamed at his son, saying, "That's wonderful! I always wanted to be a fussy old grandpa!"

Dent kept smiling. "You look like a mighty spry grandpa to me, but Raimey and I are happy." He shook his head saying, "As much as I'd like to talk about it more, that the colonel wants to see you."

"Me? What does Col. Benton want with me?"

"You'll have to ask him, Sergeant. Come along."

Clay turned and followed his son toward the large Sibley tent used by the colonel. The two entered, and Dent said to the officer, who had his back to the entrance, "Here's Sgt. Rocklin, sir."

Col. Benton turned, and there was a smile on his face. "Sergeant, you did a fine job in the battles!" he said with excitement. "The men looked to you for leadership, and you provided it."

Clay thought sorrowfully of the men of his company who would fight no more. After the campaign, he'd helped clear the battlefields of the dead and wounded, and it sickened him to think of it.

He shrugged. "It was all pretty hot and heavy, Colonel. I guess none of us had a lot of time to meditate on what to do." The weariness on his face was plain. The battles, right on the heels of his wife's funeral, had taken their toll.

"That's as may be," Benton said quickly. "But we're just getting started. The Yankees will be back, and we've got to get ready for them."

"Yes, sir, they'll be back," Clay agreed. "And we lost a lot of good men."

"We did indeed." The colonel nodded sadly. "And their places have to be filled." He tugged at his mustache, winked at Dent, then said, "So from now on, you'll be *Lieutenant* Rocklin, in charge of your platoon." Col. Benton watched the stunned expression on Clay's face and let out a long laugh. "Well, I've surprised you this time, haven't I?"

Clay glanced at Dent, who was grinning broadly. "Yes, sir, you have. I never thought I'd be an officer."

Benton laughed, exposing white teeth. "When we lost Lt. Simms, I knew you'd be the man to take his place. Clay, you're a natural leader, and I need you badly. Tell you what, why don't you go into town, get a uniform, then take a few days off." He hesitated, then nodded. "You've had a hard time the last few days, and the new recruits won't be in until later in the week. Lieutenant, go get yourself a flashy uniform. Go home and show off, then come back." He hesitated, then said quietly, "I want your father to see you. He'll be very proud."

"Yes, I think he will, sir." Clay nodded, saluted, and left the tent.

As soon as he was gone, Dent said, "That's a relief, Colonel. The rest of us are doing the best we can, but my father—he's one of those natural soldiers. Don't know what it is, but some men can get others to follow them, and some can't."

Col. Benton nodded absently. "Yes, I think you're right.

We'd better look out, Lieutenant, or he'll be commanding both of us!"

Burke had breakfast with his parents out on the veranda. He'd gotten up late, having noticed that his father seldom rose early. His mother had come to wake him. When he'd answered her knock with a muffled, "Come in," she'd entered and crossed the room to open the shade.

Burke had sat up, blinded by the bright yellow beams. He peered at her, then grinned sleepily. "Mother, you didn't bring my breakfast."

"I'll bring a stick, just like I used to, if you aren't out of that bed and down to breakfast in fifteen minutes!" she responded tartly.

Susanna Lee Rocklin tried to look fierce, but it was a failure. Her blue-green eyes glowed as she smiled at Burke. *I can no more be angry with him now than I could when he was a little boy,* she thought. *And Lord help me, he's finer looking than ever! All his hard living hasn't coarsened him, thank God!* But she said only, "You've loafed long enough, Burke. Come to breakfast, and after I've fed you, I'll put you to work."

"All right, Mother."

His answer was so meek and so unlike him, that Susanna peered at him intently. "Butter wouldn't melt in your mouth, now, would it, Burke Rocklin! What scheme are you hatching up?"

"Me? Why, nothing!"

"Humph!" Susanna snorted. "I know you! Now get dressed and come to breakfast." She hurried out of the room, going at once to the kitchen, where she found Dorrie cooking biscuits. "Make some extra, Dorrie," she said. "You know how Burke loves your biscuits."

Dorrie considered herself the mistress of Gracefield, for she had been in charge of the house for years. Tall, heavy, and of a rich chocolate complexion, she was bossy—and loyal to the Rocklins above all things except God. "Yas, I

knows about dat," she grunted. She was most partial to
Burke, a weakness she tried hard—but unsuccessfully—to
hide. "But I got more to do den fix biscuits for dat worthless
man!"

Susanna knew Dorrie well. "He's shamelessly handsome,
Dorrie. No wonder women fall into his arms." She laughed,
saying, "But he still loves you the best! He told me so last
night."

"I guess he do!" Dorrie snorted indignantly. "Doan see
none of *them* fixin' him pies and biscuits!" She slapped a pan
of biscuits into the oven and wiped her hands on her apron.
"Whut he gonna' do now, Miss Susanna?"

Susanna shook her head. "I really don't know, Dorrie.
He's not a boy any longer. He's got to find his way."

"You don't reckon he'll join the army with Marse Clay
and Marse Lowell?"

"He hasn't said what he's going to do. But he doesn't
have any money, so he'll have to either go to work or go into
the army."

"Plenty of work round heah," Dorrie commented flatly,
but both women knew it was unlikely that Burke would
throw himself into the grueling work of running a planta-
tion. Dorrie's face assumed a heavy look, and she shook her
head dolefully, "Dat boy, he need a good dose of *religion*—
dat's whut'll fix him up! He gots to find the Lord."

"I think that's right, Dorrie," Susanna said with a nod.
The two women worked on the breakfast, and thirty minutes later, Susanna and Thomas were sitting at the table on
the veranda waiting for Burke.

Thomas was pale, and Susanna knew he was in pain.
"Have some milk, dear," she urged.

"Where's Burke?" Thomas demanded. "Thought he was
supposed to be here and eat with us?" He looked up even as
he spoke, for Burke entered and sat down. "Good afternoon, Mr. Rocklin," Thomas said sarcastically. "I hope we
haven't gotten you up too early?"

"Why, this is the most civilized time to have breakfast,"

Burke said with a cocky grin. But his eyes were serious as he asked, "How are you, sir?"

"I feel about as bad as I look! Which is saying a lot."

"Sorry to hear that." Burke had been shocked at how much his father had aged in the year he'd been gone. The illness had eaten away at him, and he'd had to work at concealing how concerned he was. He'd learned quickly that his father didn't like conversations or comments about his health, so he said, "You're looking fine, Mother—," but he broke off as Dorrie came in with a silver tray piled high with food. "Now *here's* the real woman in my life!" He got to his feet, took the tray from Dorrie and set it down, then turned to give her a huge hug. "I thought about you every day I was gone, Dorrie," he said fervently.

Dorrie fought to keep the grin from her face as she struggled to get out of his grasp. "You thought about yo' stomach, dats whut you thought 'bout!" she muttered. "Lemme go, you hear me?"

But Burke held her tightly and, reaching into his pocket, pulled out a silver coin. Taking her hand, he pressed it into her palm. "That's for you to buy yourself a pretty with. Come and show it to me when you get it."

Dorrie grasped the coin and did her best to look harsh. She went away mumbling something about "A fool and his money is soon parted—"

"Didn't know you came home a wealthy man, Burke," Thomas said with his eyebrows lifted. "I may have to ask you for a loan."

"Certainly, sir," Burke nodded. "Just give me a few days to get my affairs in order, and I think I can accommodate you. Now, let's eat this fine breakfast . . ."

It was a pleasant meal, for Thomas and Susanna always enjoyed Burke's company. Though Thomas often spoke to his younger son in a seemingly harsh manner, Burke and his mother both knew it was not because the father disliked the son. Rather, it seemed to be Thomas's only way of showing concern. All the years that Clay had been gone, it had been

Burke, the younger son, who'd sat in his place. And he had become a support to his parents during that time. Oh, he'd been a wild young man, but he was never vicious or careless with his family. When Clay had come back, he'd left abruptly saying only that he needed to see the world. He'd done this before, but for shorter trips. This was the longest time he'd been gone, and his parents had missed him.

Burke noted that his father picked at his food, and he saw how concerned his mother was. He was not unaware that in the early days of their marriage, Thomas Rocklin had given his wife some difficulty. He'd had a wild streak in him—a fact that made Burke smile when his father now reprimanded him for being "wild." In fact, when their sons began to behave badly, Susanna had feared for them, worried that they would find little guidance or correction in her husband. But time had cured Thomas of his vices, and he'd become more of a husband to Susanna, and a father to his sons.

We've been through a lot of changes in the last few years, this family of mine, Burke thought as he watched his parents. He remembered something his mother once had told him: "Your father's always felt inferior—especially where his brother Stephen is concerned." Stephen Rocklin had moved to the North, where he'd become a successful factory owner. Thomas spoke of him from time to time, and always with an air of respect . . . and regret that he himself had not done so well. Burke pursed his lips. He could understand that feeling of regret—far too well.

The three sat there for a long time, and finally Thomas asked, "What are your plans, Burke?"

Burke answered lightly. "I think I'll become rich, healthy, and good-looking—which is better than being poor, sick, and ugly."

But his father was not to be put off. "Will you go into the army with your brother?"

Burke grew serious at once. "No, sir, I don't plan to do that."

"I didn't think you would," Thomas sighed. He believed

in the Cause and was proud of the fact that one son wore the Confederate uniform. But he knew Burke was not happy with the war, for the two of them had argued about it before. "Will you stay here and help with the work?"

Burke said evasively, "I don't know, sir. I have one idea, but it's very vague. Let me have a few weeks. I'll do what I can around here while I'm waiting. Will that be all right?"

"It'll have to be, I suppose." After a pause, Thomas started to speak again, then lifted his head and narrowed his eyes. "Who is that riding up?"

"Why, I believe it's Denton!" Susanna said, noting the uniform. She got to her feet at once. "I wonder why he's come? I hope nothing's wrong with Raimey."

The three of them waited, and then they heard boots on the pine boards—but when the officer entered, all three of them spoke out with astonishment, for it was Clay, not Dent, who entered.

"Well, here I am, in all my glory!" Clay laughed at the surprise on their faces. "Don't blame you for being shocked," he said, coming over to hug his mother. "They're really scraping the bottom of the barrel this time!"

He shook hands with his father and with Burke, then sat down and began to eat, explaining his promotion.

Thomas listened avidly, and when he finally said, "I'm very proud of you, Clay! Very proud indeed!" there was a quiver in his voice and a mistiness in his eye.

Clay couldn't speak himself, for he knew too well the grief he'd brought into his father's life, and it made him very happy to do something to redeem himself.

"How long can you stay?" Susanna asked.

"Just a few days. I want to take Rena camping."

"Good. She needs you, Clay," Susanna said.

After breakfast, Burke pulled his brother aside. "Going into Richmond to start my campaign." He grinned. "Hope I do as well as you, Brother."

"Burke, you're not serious about that fool notion to marry a rich girl?"

"I'm as serious as a man can get," Burke insisted. He fished into his pocket, came out with a small box, and opened it up. A flash of light caught at the diamond ring inside. "Already got the engagement ring," he said fondly. "All that's left of a big bust." He put the ring away, then said, "I sold my horse yesterday, to Tom McKeever. Got enough out of him for a fancy set of clothes and some courtin' money." His white teeth gleamed as he grinned widely. "I'm off, Clay. Wish me luck."

Clay shook his head sadly. "I wish you *sense,* Burke. There's no happiness in what you're trying to do."

"No sermons!" Burke punched Clay on the arm lightly. "Congratulations, General! Father is proud as punch—and so am I!" He sauntered out the door, and as Clay looked out the window to watch his brother ride out toward Richmond, there was a heaviness in him.

Headed for a big fall, he thought sadly, then turned to find Rena.

Melora was swimming in the creek, enjoying the coolness of the water after the long hours she'd spent under the blazing July sun. She kept her shift on, for visitors sometimes came and hunters often crossed their land.

She floated on the surface close to the shore, watching the tiny transparent bodies of the minnows as they hung motionless in the clear water. A movement caught her eye, and she turned to see a V-shaped ripple—a water snake, she knew instantly—and got to her feet at once. It was, she saw, a harmless snake, not a moccasin, so she released her breath.

At that moment, she heard a faint cry that sounded like her name. She waded quickly to the bank and hurriedly pulled her dress over her head. "I'm over here," she called, slipping into her shoes. She thought it was Josh, her fifteen-year-old brother, coming to fetch her for supper, so she sat in the sun, drying her hair with the towel she'd brought. When she heard his footsteps, she said, "I'm almost ready,

Josh." Then, when she got no answer, she turned—and saw Clay standing there.

"Mister Clay!" Jumping to her feet, she stood stock still, taking in the new uniform. *He still doesn't know how handsome he is,* she thought, but said, "Congratulations, Lt. Rocklin. You look very dashing."

Clay laughed with some embarrassment. Walking toward her, he said, "How are you, Melora?"

"I'm very well." Melora studied his face and was relieved to see that the awful strain that had marked him after Ellen's death was now gone. She knew him almost as well as he knew himself, even better at times. "Come and sit down, Clay. Tell me about your promotion."

The two of them sat down, and as the water gurgled nearby, Melora picked up her comb and ran it through her hair, listening as Clay told her the story. When that was done, he told her about Burke, expressing his fears. There was nothing he kept from her, but he knew she'd never reveal a word of it.

Finally he said, "Rena told me how you'd asked her to come and spend the day. It was good of you." Clay's face grew heavy. He picked up a flat stone and skipped it across the water. "She needs someone, Melora. She looks as though she's almost a woman, but she's still a child in many ways."

As Melora shared her insights about his daughter, Clay glanced at her and smiled, watching her as she spoke of Rena. He knew she was unaware what a beautiful sight she was. Her height, her father's green eyes, and her mother's black hair all made a fetching combination.

They talked of Rena for a long time, then Melora put her comb down and looked at Clay.

Clay laughed as her look brought a sudden memory to him. "I remember when I was sick and stayed at your house. You fed me soup and acted so very businesslike about your patient. You must have been about six years old."

Melora nodded. "And I remember how you promised to

bring me books, and how excited I was when you carried out that promise. Our whole family has grown up on those books, Clay. I read them to Toby and Martha still. And Josh and Father listen, pretending that they're not."

"Is *Pilgrim's Progress* still your favorite?"

"Yes. I love the part when Christian slays that dragon!"

Clay grew still and his eyes clouded. "I remember when I went off to the Mexican War. I rode out here and told you I'd slay a dragon for you." He thought of all the wasted years that had followed, and pain filled his eyes. "I've made such a mess of things, Melora!"

She could not stand to see him hurt. Tossing down the comb, she rose and came to sit beside him. She took his hand and held it in both of hers. "You're not to think that!" she said fiercely. "Since you let God take over your life, you've become a wonderful father. And you were a faithful husband to Ellen. I want you to be glad for that," she said, her eyes enormous. "Most men would have abandoned her when she got so sick. But you never gave her a cross word!"

Clay studied Melora's face for a few moments, drawing strength from the feel of her soft hands. The love and respect he saw in her eyes touched him deeply, and slowly he put his arm around her and drew her close. She came trustingly. Her lips were soft and warm under his, and he could feel the beat of her heart as he held her.

Melora was not afraid, for she knew that Clay's honor was as firm as rock. As she leaned against him, savoring his taste and touch, she was reminded again that she longed for the love she would find only in this man.

Finally she drew back, her cheeks flushed and her eyes shining. She reached up to gently touch Clay's dear face, and when she spoke, her voice was not quite steady. "I'm sure Pa and the others are wondering where we've got to. They've already waited for supper so I could come swim for a bit." She got to her feet and picked up her comb and towel, glancing at Clay with a mischievous light in her eyes. "I must admit you amaze me, Mister Clay," she said, once again using the childhood name she'd given him. "In all the years I've known you, you've *never* come to our house when it wasn't mealtime!"

"I'm a slave to my stomach," he answered, laughing. He stood and took her hand, and she paused to look up at him. "Melora, you're the finest and most beautiful woman I've ever known." His voice, too, was unsteady with emotion.

Melora stared at him, then said, "Thank you, Clay." She hesitated, then went on, "You know people will still talk about us, even though Ellen is gone?"

"Let them talk!"

She smiled at his defiance, but shook her head. "You and I could bear it, Clay. But what about Rena? We can't let her be hurt."

Clay groaned, "Oh, Melora, what are we to do? I love you, I want to be with you . . . but there is still so much to keep us apart. Rena is only a part of it. I've got to go back to the war, and it may be years before I return!"

"Clay, never take counsel of your fears," Melora whispered. "You've been faithful. God never forgets faith. We'll wait." She nodded firmly and her eyes glowed with confidence. "And we'll see what God will do with us."

Clay gazed down at her, a faint smile on his lips. "All right, Melora."

Then they turned and made their way back to the house, smiling at each other when Rena came to greet them, happiness on her face.

"Oh, Daddy!" she cried, her young face lit up with excitement. "Come and see the new pigs!"

CHAPTER SEVEN
A-Courtin'
He Would Go!

★

Having spent all his life in the high society of Virginia planters, Burke Rocklin knew the available young ladies as well as he knew the bloodlines of the state's racing horses. But he had been gone for a year, and it took a little time to be certain how the lineup had changed—who had gotten married, who were the new arrivals, and who had risen from the middle class to the top of the social world through the riches of an industrious father.

It took only one session with Loren Delchamp, an old friend, to get all that together. Delchamp, the younger son of a rich planter from Lynchburg, was one of the first men Burke encountered after making his preparations for a siege. He'd bought a new suit and a new pair of boots, then ensconced himself in a nice room at the Majestic Hotel. When he had discovered that Delchamp was in that same hotel, he had considered it a stroke of good fortune.

The two had gone to eat at the hotel restaurant to talk over old times. Delchamp, a rather slight man of Burke's age, was very glad to see him. As they ate heartily and drank their wine, he spoke freely of the past year. "The worst thing, Burke," he complained, "is that the women have gone *crazy* over uniforms! Never saw anything like it!" He tossed off a glass of wine, filled his glass, and announced with disgust,

"Society is gone to Hades in a bucket! At every dance, the women practically swoon over some bumpkin who was pushing a plow before he joined up. Nowadays, unless a man's wearing brass buttons and a saber, he might as well stay home!"

"Always that way during a war." Burke nodded wisely. He sipped his wine and asked casually, "What about Annabelle Symington? She still the belle of the ball?"

"Oh, my word! She married Phil Townsend right before the battle at Bull Run! Poor Phil lost a leg there, but he's set, I suppose. The Symingtons take care of him very well."

Burke crossed one name off his mental list and for the next half hour skillfully plied Delchamp. Finally he had three names that he would use to plan his campaign, then his eyes grew sharp when Loren said, "There is a new star on the firmament, Burke. Family rich as Croesus."

"Ugly as an anvil, I suppose?" Burke shrugged.

"Ugly! Not a bit of it!" Loren insisted. "Good-looking wench named Belinda King. Her father owns four or five garment factories." He drained his glass, then gave Burke a sour look. "I made a try for her, but the competition was too hot." He grinned as a thought came to him. "Now there's something that would be a challenge to your talents, Burke!"

"Always liked a challenge," Burke murmured.

"I'd like to see you win her away from that big snob she runs with." Delchamp filled his glass again, drank it down, then said, "An old friend of yours."

"Who?"

"Chad Barnes."

At the name, Burke's eyes narrowed. Barnes, the son of a wealthy planter in the next county, had courted the same girl as Burke for a time, and it had turned out to be a rather nasty business. Angry words had been spoken, and if it had not been for the intervention of friends, a duel would have been fought.

"My old friend Chad, eh?"

"That interests you, doesn't it?" Delchamp grinned at his friend. "There's a ball tomorrow night in the Armory. I could introduce you to Belinda. It might be fun for you. She's a toothsome wench—and I'd like to see Barnes get left at the post!"

"Sounds like it might be fun," Burke said as he nodded. His eyes were half hooded, and as Delchamp talked on, he thought of what might come of the thing. He despised Chad Barnes—if he could steal the girl from him, so much the better. Finally he said, "Let's take in that ball tomorrow, Loren."

Delchamp grinned and winked broadly. "I'll bet you do the scoundrel in, Burke! You could always handle women!"

Burke and Delchamp spent the evening wandering around the streets of Richmond, then went back to the Majestic. They said good night, but agreed to meet at six the next evening. For a long time that night Burke lay awake thinking of his future, but it seemed rather bleak. Gracefield was not going to make any money until the war was over, not with England being blockaded from reaching Confederate ports by Federal warships. And if the Yankees won the war, *nobody* would have a dime, that much was clear to him.

Only chance I have, he thought just before falling asleep, *is to marry some girl who's got money. Then get it out of farms and plantations—out of everything here in the South. Buy land or a business in the Far West, even in the North if necessary!*

He did little the next day but stay in his room and read. At six he met Loren, and the two of them had supper, then proceeded to the Armory. The place was crowded, mostly by officers, for many units were stationed in Richmond. As for the women, there were plenty! "Looks like every woman in this part of the state is here," Burke murmured to Loren as they stepped inside the huge ballroom.

"All out for a bit of fun," Delchamp said, nodding. He gazed around with satisfaction. "They've done the old place up, haven't they?"

"Yes. It's pretty plush," Burke agreed. Chandeliers threw

their glittering lights over the crowd below, and the reds, greens, blues, and whites of the women's gowns added splashes of color. The brass buttons of uniforms glittered as dancers moved across the floor to the music of the excellent band. The noise was terrific, for everyone seemed to be talking at the top of their lungs.

Suddenly Delchamp nudged Burke. "There she is! Belinda King. The one in the blue dress dancing with the major."

Burke saw her at once and was impressed. She was petite, very pretty, and blessed with long blonde hair that hung down her back. At the moment she was smiling up at her partner, revealing two charming dimples. "Not bad," he said. "Let's move in so you can introduce me."

They maneuvered themselves so that when the dance was over, they were directly in the path of the pair. Loren appeared to be surprised as he said, "Oh, Miss King! How nice to see you!"

"Hello, Loren."

Belinda King and her partner would have moved on, but Loren said quickly, "I don't think you've met Burke Rocklin, have you? He's been out of town on business for some time."

Burke smiled and stepped forward. Before she could protest, he took her hand and bent over it with a graceful movement. He kissed it lightly and said in a low voice, "I'm charmed, Miss King."

Belinda King was accustomed to fine-looking men, but this man before her was exceptional. He was tall, dressed in excellent clothing, and was handsome almost to a fault. His dark eyes were somehow magnetic, and when he said, "May I have this dance, Miss King?" she found herself in his arms without quite knowing how it happened.

"Really, Mr. Rocklin," she protested mildly, "this is Lt. Baxter's dance."

"Well, we all have our disappointments in life." Burke smiled down at her. "I've discovered that what's bad for some is good for others. The lieutenant's misfortune is my good fortune."

He was, Belinda discovered, the best dancer she'd ever had for a partner. He made her feel as though she was floating weightlessly along and, at the same time, complimented her on her dancing skills. She was accustomed to being sought after—perhaps too accustomed, for she had grown weary of all the pretty compliments and accommodating young bucks who sought to please and win her. But as she gazed up into Burke Rocklin's eyes, she became aware that he looked down at her with a smile that was charming, but somewhat removed—as though he was letting her know that while he was glad she was dancing with him, he would not have been terribly upset had she refused! Her eyes widened at the realization that here was a man with a definite streak of independence—and the challenge that this presented her drew her more than all the pretty prose others had written, paying homage to her eyes or her delicate beauty.

When the dance was over, he was halfway through a story that amused her, so she allowed him to take her to the refreshment table. Then, drinks in hand, they moved to the section of the dance floor set apart for talk.

They sat out two dances, so amused was she by his conversation, and the third was just beginning, when they were interrupted.

"I believe this is our dance, Belinda?"

"Oh, dear!" Belinda rose at once, flustered. "I'm so sorry, Chad! I forgot." She looked at the two men, then said, "Chad, this is—"

"I know Mr. Rocklin," Barnes broke in stiffly. His nod toward Burke was brief, and he held his hand out to Belinda. "Shall we dance?"

"Yes, of course." Belinda smiled at Burke. "I'll see you later, Mr. Rocklin."

"Yes, you will, Miss King!"

As Barnes swept Belinda King out onto the crowded floor, she said, "You were rude to the gentleman, Chad."

"Burke Rocklin is no gentleman, Belinda!"

"Oh? He *looks* like a gentleman."

It was at this point that Chad Barnes made his big mistake. If he had shrugged off her questions, Belinda would have probably let the matter alone, but Barnes was a demanding man, accustomed to having his own way. "Belinda," he said sternly, "he's no good! I forbid you to dance with him or to have anything to do with him!"

Demanding, Chad Barnes was. Prudent, he was not. Immediately he saw that he had made his demands at the wrong place, at the wrong time, and to the wrong woman. Belinda's face darkened with fury and she stared at him, saying in a cold voice, "I beg your pardon, *Mister* Barnes, but I will see anyone I please! You're not my father to forbid me from doing anything!"

Quickly Chad tried to regain control of the situation. He softened his voice to sound concerned. "But—he's no good, Belinda! And you have your reputation to think of."

How many young girls have heard those words: *He's no good?* And how many have been swayed by them? Forbidden fruit always looks more delicious than the ordinary, easily available variety. Cap that with the suggestion that one's reputation could be so easily destroyed merely by association with one tall, handsome, undeniably charming man . . .

"I will thank you, sir, to tend to your own affairs," Belinda remarked stiffly as the dance came to an end. "And I will attend to mine." Her words were timed perfectly, so that she pulled away from Barnes just as the music ended, and no one around them was aware anything was amiss. No one except Barnes, Belinda . . . and Burke Rocklin, who had watched the whole thing with increasing amusement and satisfaction. He'd been almost sure Barnes would try something heavy-handed, such as forbidding the girl from seeing him. Burke smiled. If he had judged Belinda King correctly, he was certain that the one way to ensure she would pursue a man was to forbid her from being near him!

Apparently that was the case, for Belinda made it her business to dance with Burke Rocklin twice more, and when Barnes objected, she was so incensed that she agreed to go for a carriage ride with Rocklin the following afternoon.

"I don't know how you do it, Burke," Loren Delchamp sighed as the pair arrived at the Majestic after the ball. "But you never miss with a woman."

Burke knew that the campaign had just begun, but he was content with it so far. "Tell me about the girl's family, Loren," he insisted. Loren loved to talk, so for the next hour he told Burke all he knew and all he'd heard about Belinda's parents. When the two parted, Burke knew how to handle Mr. and Mrs. King. Neither of them would welcome a penniless son-in-law, but there were ways to conceal that fact. The one thing in Burke's favor was that Cyrus King was a self-made man. He'd been a fatherless boy and had pulled himself up by his bootstraps. Now that he had money, he wanted prestige. Both he and his wife wanted a marriage for their daughter that would pull them up in the social world of Virginia.

And there was Burke's chance. The Rocklins were not the Lees or the Hugers, but they *were* high in that world. Still, other young men, such as Chad Barnes, had both a good family *and* money. Burke frowned momentarily.

My only chance is to dazzle the girl, he thought. *She's spoiled rotten, I'd suppose, and if she chooses me, she'll have me or drive her people crazy.*

He smiled as he crawled into bed. "Well then, Burke, old boy, your duty is clear. You've got to make her fall for you!"

By the end of the third week of his courtship, Burke knew that he was in danger of losing it all. He'd pursued Belinda using every trick he knew, and she was swayed by it. But he was coming perilously close to the end of his funds, and she still was not willing to choose him.

It all came down to the fact that he was not in uniform.

Burke saw at once that Belinda was caught in the war fever that held Richmond. Everything centered around the war, and any able-bodied young man not wearing a uniform was suspect.

Belinda had inquired more than once as to his plans regarding enlistment, but her comments had *assumed* that he would serve sooner or later. "Which branch do you think you'll choose, Burke?" That was her way of putting it, and Burke was too wily to say that he had no intention of serving in *any* branch! Rather, he would simply sidestep the issue.

Finally a crisis came when Chad Barnes enlisted as an officer in the cavalry. He made a splendid picture in his new uniform, and Burke could sense Belinda slipping away from him.

Got to find an answer or I'm a dead duck! he thought desperately. But though he searched for a way to gain the woman, nothing seemed to work.

He was almost ready to admit defeat on the day that he accompanied Belinda to a tea held at her parent's home. When he arrived, he saw nothing but uniforms and was filled with despair. He moved around the room with Belinda, feeling very much out of the whole thing.

Suddenly Belinda whispered, "Look, Burke! There's Gen. Lee!"

Burke looked across the room and was favorably impressed with Gen. Lee. A fine-looking man, Lee wore only the simplest of uniforms. Belinda drew Burke with her as she pressed closer to hear what the general was saying.

"Yes, there will be other battles, sir, but I trust we'll be able to move out and meet the enemy a little farther away from Richmond than in the last battle."

Someone asked Lee what he needed most in the way of soldiers, and he mentioned several needs, then added thoughtfully, "It may sound strange, but in my thinking, we need engineers worse than anything else. Of course, being an engineer myself I may be biased."

Burke was seized by a sudden thought and he spoke up almost without thinking. "Pardon me, Gen. Lee. My name is Burke Rocklin. I'm an engineer myself, but I wasn't aware that the need for one with my skills was so great."

At once Lee asked about his training, and after listening carefully as Burke mentioned his background, his eyes grew brighter. "Why, you could be a great help, Mr. Rocklin!" he exclaimed. "As a matter of fact, I could use you on my own staff for the next three or four months."

Instantly Burke said, "I'd count it an honor to serve under you, Gen. Lee. Would it be possible for me to serve a short term that would give me time to prove myself?"

"Certainly, Mr. Rocklin," Lee said, nodding. He turned to the officer standing beside him. "Maj. Turner, would you go into this with Mr. Rocklin? I think we could brevet him as a first lieutenant for three months. By the end of that time, we'll know a little more about his place with our staff."

"Of course, Gen. Lee."

"Thank you, General," Burke said. "I'll serve the Cause as best I can."

"No man can do more than that, Mr. Rocklin," Lee said with a smile.

Belinda was beside herself with happiness. When she got Burke to one side, she suddenly reached up and kissed him. "Oh, I'm so proud of you, Burke! And to serve on Gen. Lee's staff!"

"It comes as quite a shock," Burke said slowly. He'd jumped into the thing on impulse, but now was wondering if he'd done the smart thing. Then he looked at Belinda beaming up at him and thought, *It's only for three months— and engineers don't fight in battles.* He held Belinda close and said, "A man needs a woman when he goes off to war, sweetheart."

"Does he, Burke?"

"Yes!" He kissed her then, and her response told him clearly that she was his. "I love you, Belinda," he whispered.

"I want more than anything else to marry you. Will you have me?"

"Oh, Burke—yes! I'll marry you!" She kissed him again, then said, "Come on, we have to tell my parents!"

That evening when Burke went back to the hotel, he was an engaged man. Belinda's parents were taken aback, but agreed to an engagement. They had insisted that the couple wait until Burke's short-term service was up, and Burke had nodded solemnly. "Yes, sir, that would be wise, and I thank you for your counsel."

Loren Delchamp was filled with admiration. "By George, you pulled it off!" he exclaimed jubilantly. "I knew you could do it! Now your worries are over. Her father's got enough money to burn a wet mule!"

Loren's reaction came as no surprise to Burke. Clay's reaction, on the other hand, was not what he expected.

"You'll be miserable, Burke!" Clay said when Burke told him the news. "You don't love her, and she's only infatuated with you. That's not enough for a happy marriage."

"It's enough for me, Clay," Burke shot back angrily. "Mother and Father don't have any objections, so why should you?"

"They don't know why you're marrying the girl," Clay responded. "Tell them the truth and then see how they react."

Burke grew more angry, but Clay held his ground. "You're making a mistake about the marriage and about the army. I know you don't have any patriotism. You don't belong in either one!"

"I've got as much patriotism as you, Brother!" Burke said at once. "You've said this war was a mistake from the first, yet here you stand, a lieutenant in the army."

"And I'll stay in the army until it's over," Clay said. "When I joined, I did so with every intention of serving to the best of my ability. You only joined to impress Belinda King. After your three months are done, you'll marry her and never serve another day."

The truth of this stung Burke, and he said angrily, "Well, you can keep out of it, Clay. I'm marrying Belinda, and that's final!"

Clay watched his brother storm away, wishing he could talk to his parents about the whole mess. But he knew he could not tell them any of this. Instead, he shared it with Melora. "He's going to make the biggest mistake in his whole life," he said to her. She had come to spend the day with Rena, and Clay had taken her to one side to talk.

Melora listened quietly, then shook her head. "You can't do any more, Clay," she said. "Burke has got his mind made up. But we must pray for him. A great deal can happen in three months. Let's join in prayer and ask God to keep Burke from going wrong."

"All right," Clay said heavily. He came up with a smile, saying, "I always bring all my troubles to you, Melora."

She reached up and touched his face gently, saying, "Who else would you take them to, Clay?"

CHAPTER EIGHT
The Battle

The first three weeks of Burke Rocklin's military career were splendid. He invested the last of his cash in a dashing uniform and escorted Belinda King to one social event after another. They became the most admired couple on the Richmond social scene, and despite the fact that Burke had never even smelled the smoke of battle, great things were predicted for him.

His military duties were not difficult. He reported each morning to headquarters, where he sat in on meetings with his commanding officer, Lt. Col. Jeremy Gilmer, Lee's chief of engineers. They were a small group, and Burke found himself well able to keep up the few tasks that came his way. Col. Gilmer, a hard-driving man of forty, was amiable enough, but demanding. He spent some time with Burke, sounding out his ability, and seemed satisfied. "We'll have need of you in the field soon enough, Lt. Rocklin." He nodded. He'd kept Burke after the main meeting to go over some figures with him, and the two of them were now having coffee in the small office.

"When do you expect the action to begin, Colonel?" Burke asked. He had hopes that it might be several months, but was disappointed to hear Gilmer's reply.

"Oh, those Bluebellies haven't given up on taking Richmond," he said with a shrug. "Lincoln has gotten pretty sick of McClellan, so he's replaced him with another commander." He sipped his coffee and shook his head. "Fellow called John Pope. Gen. Lee can't stand the man. As a matter of fact, he's the *only* man I've ever heard Lee speak against publicly."

"Why is that, I wonder?"

"Oh, the man's a braggart, and you know how modest Gen. Lee is. Pope made a windbag of a speech to his troops when Lincoln appointed him. Said things like, 'I come to you from the West, where we have always seen the backs of our enemies, and I presume I've been sent here to teach you how to soldier.' You can imagine how *that* went over with his men! Then he told a reporter his headquarters would be in his saddle." Gilmer suddenly hooted with laughter, adding, "Gen. Lee said the man didn't know his headquarters from his hindquarters."

Burke joined in the laughter, saying, "Man sounds like a fool."

"I hope so, Lieutenant," Gilmer said, nodding fervently. "We need every bit of help we can get, and it would be nice to have a fool in charge of the Army of the Potomac."

"Maybe they'll give up and go home," Burke mused. "They lost a lot of men in the Seven Days'."

"So did we," Gilmer answered. "Half the houses in Richmond have wounded men in them from that battle. Can't build hospitals fast enough to take care of our own men, and we have a host of wounded Federals as well." He drank the last of his coffee and shrugged. "I expect we'll be busy pretty soon. Gen. Lee's plotting something. He won't let Pope come any closer to Richmond than he has to. So don't wander off too far. You may be needed pretty urgently."

"Yes, sir," Burke said with a nod. He saluted and left the office. All day he worked on maps that showed the area around Richmond, then at five o'clock he left and went to meet Belinda. The Kings lived in a large brick house on the outskirts of Richmond, and Belinda's father was at home when Burke arrived.

"Glad to see you, Burke," Cyrus King said, greeting him with a handshake. "Come in, come in, and let's have a talk while that girl of mine gets ready."

Burke followed King into an opulent library, where he was offered wine and a cigar, which he accepted. "Now, tell me about what's going on in this war, my boy," the older man said, settling himself in a large chair as Burke spoke of the War Department's strategy. King listened avidly and was rather irritated when Belinda entered. "I never have any time with this young man," he grumbled. "Where are you hauling him off to now?"

"We're going to an engagement party, Father," Belinda smiled. She was wearing a beautiful dress made of pink silk with light blue ribbons on the bodice. Her fine blonde hair hung down over her shoulders, and she looked very pretty indeed. "It's Mary Lou Allen and Luke Hoakly. We'll be late, I think."

"You always are," her father grumbled as she kissed him. "Come and see me sometime when we can talk longer, Burke."

"Yes, sir, I'll do that."

When they were in the carriage, Burke said thoughtfully, "I like your father very much, and your mother as well."

"I'm glad, Burke," Belinda said with a smile. "They're very fond of you."

"Funny, I've heard so many stories about in-laws that I've always dreaded the thought of them." He put his arm around her and drew her close. "Now I'm getting the most beautiful girl in the world and a set of nice in-laws in the bargain!" He kissed her, and she clung to him. "I wish we could get married now, before I have to leave," he whispered. She was a beautiful girl, and though she was spoiled, Burke was surprised to realize that he'd become fond of her. He wanted nothing to go wrong with his plans and wished she'd agree to marry him at once.

"No, we can't do that, much as I'd like to, Burke," Belinda answered. "Three months isn't too long to wait, and it's all my parents asked of you."

"I know, but I love you so much it's hard to wait!"

Burke had told other women he'd loved them, but not once had it been the truth. Nor was it the truth this time. Now as the carriage moved down the streets and he held Belinda tightly in his arms, he wondered about himself. *Have I become an utter scoundrel? This girl loves me—or thinks she does. But I don't love her, probably never will love any woman.* He glanced at her and knew a sudden stab of remorse. *She'll never have to know I don't really love her. I'm a pretty good actor. Still, she's not getting much in the way of a husband. I guess some men just aren't capable of real love—and I'm one of those unlucky fellows!*

They arrived at the house, went inside, and enjoyed the party. The house was filled with young people, soldiers, and pretty girls. The only distraction was a clash Burke had with Chad Barnes. It came late in the evening, just as Burke and Belinda were preparing to leave, and it caught them both off guard.

Earlier, Barnes had come across the floor to confront the pair, and it was obvious that he was angry. He tried to conceal it, but Burke had learned enough about men to recognize the small signs. *He's spoiling for trouble,* Burke thought and was on his guard instantly.

Barnes was a big man, as tall as Burke and much heavier. He had a blunt, ruddy face and a pair of light blue eyes that dominated his face. Almost at once he began making remarks that verged on insult, but Burke was determined to ignore the man. He was rather proud of himself and said so to Belinda when he got her alone.

"Barnes is looking for trouble, but I've managed to keep my temper." He grinned at her and nodded. "I must be getting senile. When I was younger I'd have called him out for less than he's done tonight."

"Oh, don't do that, Burke!" Belinda's eyes widened with

alarm, and she put her hand on his chest with an imploring gesture. "Don't fight with him!"

"All right, but I think we'd better leave early. I don't need to be tempted any more than I have been."

Burke managed to stay away from Barnes for the rest of the evening, and it was only when he was helping Belinda on with her coat that the trouble came. He felt a hand on his shoulder and was abruptly turned around. His temper flared when he saw that it was Barnes, and he said, "Keep your hands off me, Barnes!"

"You're touchy, aren't you, Rocklin?" Barnes ruddy face was flushed with drink, and he sneered at Burke. "You might have Belinda fooled, but you're not fooling me!"

"Chad, you're drunk!" Belinda whispered. "Come on, Burke—"

But Barnes reached out and grabbed Burke's arm. "Think I don't know what you're up to? You're a woman chaser, Rocklin. Always were!" Barnes looked around at the faces of the guests and lifted his voice, "Why, when he was after Maureen Bailey—"

A sudden crack across the face cut off Barnes's words, and he stood there gaping with shock at Burke, who said, "You're no gentleman, Barnes. I won't have you mention a lady's name in public."

A shocked silence fell on the room, and Barnes's face drained. He touched his cheek, then said in a voice filled with fury, "My friends will call on you, Rocklin!"

Burke said clearly, "You know army regulations forbid dueling, Barnes. Your friends can save themselves the trouble."

"Coward!"

"You know my record better than that." Burke would have turned and escorted Belinda from the room, but at that moment Barnes completely lost control. He drew back his massive fist and threw a tremendous blow at Burke's head.

Burke had seen the flash of movement and drew back just in time to avoid the blow. Off balance, Barnes fell against his opponent, but Burke gave him a hard push, saying, "You're drunk, Barnes! Go home and sleep it off."

The push sent Barnes reeling back, but when he caught his balance, his eyes burned with drunken rage. "If you won't fight with a gun, you'll fight with your fists!"

Several men came at once, trying to pull Barnes away, but he shook them off. "There's no regulation about a fistfight, Rocklin. Now come outside—or are you yellow clear through?"

Burke stared at the big man and knew there was no way he was going to get out of a fight. If he refused, he'd be branded a coward by everybody in Richmond. He said tersely, "If you have to have a fight, Barnes, I'll give you one."

"Come outside!" Barnes cried out. "I'm going to open you up and let the yellow run out so everyone can see what you are!"

Burke turned to Belinda. "You know this isn't of my doing, but I'll have to fight him."

"Oh, Burke! Be careful!" Belinda cried. "He's so strong!" But Rocklin noted that her eyes were glistening with the thrill of the affair, and he knew that she was not entirely sorry to be fought over. Struggling to hide his disgust, he turned and moved away from her.

Women are all alike—wanting men to fight over them like dogs!

Barnes was waiting for him in a courtyard, the yellow light of the lanterns gleaming in his eyes. He stripped off his coat and threw it to the ground. As soon as Burke had done the same, he uttered a hoarse curse and threw himself across the flagstones.

Burke caught the full fury of the rush and was driven back against some of the men who'd made a circle around the pair. He had misjudged the speed of the big man and took several painful blows to the chest and stomach as a result. Gasping with pain, he twisted free and stepped around so that he was away from Barnes.

Got to stay away from him and wear him down, then take him out bit by bit. He's too strong for me to fight head on!

Barnes came at him again, but this time Burke sidestepped and, as the big man stumbled, drove two hard blows to his face. The blows made a sharp, meaty sound, and a mutter went up from the circle of men. But if the blows hurt Barnes, he didn't show it. Blood ran down from the corner of his mouth and he came in more slowly, but he was still danger- ous. He had big legs and arms and hulking shoulders. His eyes glittered as he followed Burke over the rough flag- stones. "Stand still and fight!" he grated, then without warning threw himself forward, aiming a tremendous blow at Burke's face.

If it had landed, Burke would have had his face smashed, but he managed to parry with his left, so that his opponent's fist only grazed his temple. There was nothing to do then but survive the blows that Barnes rained on him, and Burke took most of them on his forearms and his shoulders. They hurt and he knew he'd be black and blue, but he rode out the storm grimly, waiting his chance.

The eyes of the spectators glittered by the lights of the lanterns. They were like wolves gathered in a circle to watch a fight to the death, and the same faces that had seemed so cultured in the drawing room a few moments earlier were now cruel and predatory, for the men seemed to have reverted to some ancient strain of blood that craved action and violence.

Burke was bleeding now, his face cut by the massive blows of Barnes's fists. His ribs ached, and he suspected that one of them might be cracked. Most of the men in the circle, he realized dimly, thought he was whipped. But he had forced himself to wait and watch—and now he saw what he'd been waiting for: a slowness in the big man's movements and a rasp in his breathing.

Burke waited one more second as Barnes dropped his heavy arms and gasped for breath, then he moved. He shot forward and drove a thundering right into the mouth of the winded man, driving him backward. Following him fiercely, Burke hit his enemy in the pit of the stomach with as hard a punch as he'd ever thrown. The blow struck Barnes right below that spot where the nerves are bunched, just below the rib cage—and that punch proved a disaster for the big man!

His arms dropped and his eyes glazed. Burke knew what that was like, for he'd been stopped in the same fashion. A hard blow in that spot robs a man of everything—he can't breath or move or think, but is totally helpless.

With almost any other man, Burke would have called off the fight, but he knew with Barnes that doing so could be fatal. So he moved ahead, determined to put Barnes down, which he managed to do only after striking him in the jaw repeatedly. The man sank to the flagstones, his mouth open, his arms pawing helplessly. He tried to get up, but his legs didn't seem to support him.

"That's enough—!" Burke said, grabbing for breath. "Stay away from me, Barnes, or you'll get worse!" He walked over to pick up his coat, and as he left he felt the hands of the men on his shoulders and heard their voices congratulating him. *If Barnes had won, they'd be saying the same things to him,* he thought bitterly. He found Belinda waiting and knew she'd watched from the window. "Come on, let's go," he said almost harshly.

When they were in the carriage, she leaned toward him and touched his wounded face. "Oh, my dear, he hurt you!"

Burke let her murmur her little endearments, but was aware that she was not nearly so upset as she pretended. *She knows this will be all over Richmond,* he thought wearily. *Well, let her have her little triumph. I guess she's giving me enough to make up for a few bruises!*

Burke was correct in assuming that the fight would furnish delectable fare for the gossip mills of Richmond. He was disgusted with himself and with Barnes, but he realized it added glitter to his "reputation" and so made no protests.

His fellow officers ragged him a little, but were mostly supportive. Col. Gilmer, however, said sourly, "Better save some of that energy for *real* fighting, Lieutenant."

"It wasn't of my choosing, sir," Burke protested.

"Well, this fight that's coming up isn't of *my* choosing," Gilmer shot back. "If you've got time to roll around in a brawl, I guess you don't have enough work to do. I'll see to it that you have."

The colonel was faithful to his word, and for the next few days Burke was forced to stay late. Belinda pouted, but Burke pointed out that it was the price he had to pay for fighting over her. Belinda found this a satisfactory reason and said, "Well, you must get free next Wednesday. We've got an invitation to dine at the Chesnuts, and President and Mrs. Davis will be there!"

Burke never made it to that engagement. He was greeted on Wednesday morning by Col. Gilmer who said, "Pack your gear, Lieutenant. We're moving out."

Burke stared at him blankly for one instant, then inquired, "Where will we be going, sir?"

"You'll know when we get there!" Gilmer snapped. Then he mitigated his reply. "Didn't mean to bite your head off, Rocklin, but we've got to move fast. All I can say now is that Gen. Lee's going to meet John Pope, and we've got to do some engineering for him in a hurry!"

"Will I have time to say any farewells, Colonel?"

"We're leaving in two hours, but you'll need that time to get your gear and help us load the equipment. Write your apologies and send a runner."

Hastily Burke wrote notes to Belinda and to his parents, explaining his sudden departure. The one to Belinda he dispatched by a corporal, and the one to his parents he was able to deliver himself into Clay's hands.

He found his older brother drilling his platoon, and after calling him to one side, he said, "I've got orders to leave right away. Will you see that Father gets this note?"

Clay took the envelope but said, "I'll have to send it out, Burke. We're moving out ourselves."

"What's happening, Clay?"

"Going to whip Johnnie Pope, I guess." Clay studied his younger brother, then said thoughtfully, "We've had differences, Burke, but let's not be angry with each other now."

Burke was surprised but glad. "Sure, Clay!" He clapped his hand on Clay's shoulder, saying, "We Black Rocklins have to stick together."

"That's right." Clay smiled. "Keep your head down, you hear?"

"Can't shoot a man who's born to hang, can they, now?" Burke grinned and then left, saying only, "After this is over, we'll have some time to go hunting, OK?"

"God go with you, Burke," Clay muttered under his breath as he watched Burke's tall form march away. Then he turned to his men, calling out, "All right, men, let's sharpen those lines!"

Waco Smith came to Clay later, after drill was over, and asked, "We goin' to see the Bluebellies, Lieutenant?" Smith, a Texan who'd been with Clay at Bull Run, still carried a .44 in a holster on his hip, the same one he carried when he'd been a Texas Ranger. He was a lean man with light green eyes and sharp features. He was utterly dependable and fearless to a fault.

"I think that sums up our situation, Sergeant," Clay said with a nod. "The men ready?"

"Got to be." Waco bit off a huge bite of tobacco, tucked it into his cheek, then nodded. "You watch out for yourself, Clay," he warned, forgetting protocol for a moment. "I don't want to have to go to all the trouble of breaking in a new lieutenant."

"I'll do my best, Waco. And you show a little sense. Don't try to whip the Yankees all by yourself like you did at Malvern Hill!" Clay's eyes were moody, and he added with a sad tone, "This is going to be a long war, so take care of yourself." Waco winked at him and walked away, but both of them were aware that there was no way for a man to "take care of himself" when the bullets started flying.

The only people who have a very clear idea of what a battle is like are generals. Robert E. Lee and Stonewall Jackson understood the entire scope of what was taking place on August 29, 1862, at the Battle of Second Manassas, but infantrymen knew only their small portion of it.

Lee and Jackson planned a masterful campaign, one of the most daring in U.S. military history. Faced with superior numbers, Lee did an astonishing thing: He divided his small army into *two smaller* armies! This violated every rule of tactics in every military history book, but Robert E. Lee was an inveterate gambler.

Acting on instinct, Lee sent Stonewall Jackson around Pope's army, while he himself stayed in place and convinced the nervous Pope that the Confederate commander had his whole force with him. It would not have worked if Lee had not had Jackson, for no other general on either side could have accomplished such a march.

When Jackson was in place, he struck Pope's forces from the rear—and the Federal commander went to pieces. He lost his head, and he lost the Battle of Second Manassas.

But all of this was unknown to most of the soldiers who fought the battle. They only were aware of their little area and fought and died for a small field, never knowing why it was so important to have the field.

Clay's company fought its way across a small creek and held a much larger Union force to a standstill. And while neither Clay nor his men knew it, their holding action had been the means for giving Jackson time to get into position to strike Pope's army. Clay lost twelve men and grieved over them as if they were his own sons. He was relieved to see that Lowell and Dent came through safely, but was worried about Burke. He knew the engineers had been sent to bridge a small river and prayed that Burke had not been hurt.

But even as Clay prayed, Burke lay unconscious. He and

his fellow engineers had been caught up in an unexpected skirmish over the bridge. Two full regiments of Federals moved on the bridges, and Lee sent some of his best troops to stop the Northern troops from advancing. It had been one of those terrible battles, such as Shiloh, where ground was taken, lost, and taken again. Every man in a Confederate uniform was pressed into service, including cooks and engineers. Burke found himself lying on the ground, firing a musket at the men in the long blue lines who charged again and again.

Finally the colonel came down the line, screaming, "Get ready! We're going to drive 'em back! Get ready to charge!"

Burke's mouth was dry as he came to his feet. He had a musket with a bayonet fixed, and when the gray line moved forward, he found himself screaming with the rest. He had only one thought: to get to the line of trees where musket fire winked like evil red eyes.

But he never made it.

The Federals had gotten some artillery in place, and the shells cut the advancing Confederate line to pieces. Those who lived through the artillery fire were met by yelling Yankees who emerged from the trees in large numbers.

Burke shot one soldier, noting that he was no more than sixteen years old. He felt a pang of grief, then was suddenly trapped in a fierce mêlée and began clubbing with his musket as the blue-clad men rushed toward the position. He was striking furiously when a thunderous sound came from overhead, and Burke Rocklin's world suddenly exploded into a million points of pain—and a fathomless darkness.

The shell that burst over Burke Rocklin and the men around him killed dozens of men and wounded many others. Reb and Yank lay intermingled, most of them killed instantly. The Confederates retreated, but some of them stopped beside the tangled bodies long enough to rob the dead. One of them bent over a still form and, seeing the bloody face, assumed he was dead. He looked at his own bare feet, then pulled off the injured man's boots. Then he noted the fancy gold ring—the Rocklin family ring—and tugged at it until it came off. Slipping the ring on his own finger, the man looked fearfully around, then quickly stripped the uniform from the inert body, whispering, "I can sell this back in Richmond. Be worth a heap of money!"

But the scavenger never made it to Richmond. He made it only as far as the point where a shell from one of the Union batteries caught him. It destroyed his torso, mangling his upper body and head beyond recognition. The sergeant who led the burial squad found the tattered coat of Burke Rocklin still clutched in the corpse's hand. After looking at the papers inside one of the coat pockets, he said, "We'll take this one back with us. There's a lieutenant named Rocklin in the Richmond Grays."

After the battle, Dent and Clay came to identify the body. Both of them were sick when they saw the mangled body. Clay stooped and took the ring from the dead man's finger.

"Sergeant, I want to send my brother back to Richmond. Is there a coffin available?"

"Pine one, sir."

"Put him in it. I'll see to the transportation," Dent said. He shook his head, adding, "This will just about kill the folks."

Clay didn't even have the words to answer. He turned away, sick at heart, blaming himself for not having been more of a brother to Burke.

"I'll see if the colonel will let me go home, if it's all right with you, Dent?"

"Of course. I wish I could go, too."

Two days later Clay stood at his brother's graveside. The service had been simple and brief. From where he stood Clay could see the raw earth still mounded on Ellen's grave. He stood there, tears in his eyes, and then turned away to comfort his parents, who had taken the news of Burke's death very badly.

Had he been able, Burke would have done all he could to let his family know he was not in the coffin that was lowered into the earth. But he was far from able. He was unconscious, lying on a bed in a military hospital . . . in Washington.

When he'd been found in the midst of the Union dead, the stretcher-bearers had assumed that he was a Union soldier. The Confederates commonly robbed the dead for boots and clothing, so the stretcher-bearer had said, "This one's alive, but the Rebs stripped him. Put one of them jackets on him, Maxie. If we get him to field hospital, I reckon he won't die."

The man had been correct in his reckoning. Burke Rocklin had not died. The doctors had removed the shrapnel from his neck and back, had sewed up the cuts on his face, and then had sent him in an ambulance train that was headed back to Washington. But though he was alive, he did not regain consciousness. Even when he received better care and improved physically, he lay as still as a dead man.

One of the doctors said, "Must be ruined in the head. Physically he's healing, but his mind is gone. May as well put him in Ward K."

Ward K, where Burke currently lay, was the ward for men who did nothing but stare at the walls. Like zombies, they ate and moved, but they never spoke. None of the doctors knew what to do for these men. Usually, one by one, they were eventually sent back to their homes, most of them to live the rest of their lives in attics or a spare bedroom, kept out of sight—buried, though not in the ground.

"Poor man!" One of the women who came to visit at the hospital stopped in at Ward K and looked down at Burke. Pity was in her eyes as she reached down and touched his pale, still face.

Her voice shaking with unshed tears for all she had seen, she whispered what many had thought, but not allowed themselves to say: "It would have been a mercy if he'd died. Anything is better than this!"

PART TWO
The Patient and the Nurse

CHAPTER NINE
Grace Comes to Washington

★

From the time Burke fell on the battlefield, he knew nothing, which perhaps was a blessing!

The process of transporting sick and wounded men from the field of Manassas to the hospitals in Washington was as much a torture as anything that had ever taken place in the dungeon of a medieval castle. Wounded soldiers generally reached the haven only after a long delirium of agony and neglect. Most bore the gashes of canister or grape, the rent of shell splinters, or the neat hole that marked the entrance of the shattering minié ball. Frequently soldiers underwent crude amputations at the front, where field surgeons ruthlessly lopped off arms and legs, which they tossed into piles that sometimes rose man-high about the bloody operation tables.

Hungry, thirsty, and untended, the wounded at last reached a place where they were fed and washed and cared for. But the trip to Washington by road was a nightmare! While ambulances were meant to be a humane innovation, the frail two-wheeled vehicles used to transport injured soldiers tended to crack at the first strain, and their rocking motion was unbearable to suffering men. The cumbersome four-wheeled ambulances, which required four horses to pull them, were more comfortable, but for men with fresh amputations, with faces shot away, or with lead in breast or belly, being jostled, bumped, and jolted over rutted Virginia roads was excruciating.

The journey by rail was shorter, but men were closely packed on the floors, either on straw or on bare boards. Or, if they were on the flatcars, they were exposed to the blazing sun or to wind and rain.

Some of the wounded were transported by ship, but there were no lights, no figures at the rails, no stir of notice or greeting when they arrived. The injured men lay on the decks, in cabins and the saloons, or even on the stairs and gangway. Men screamed or moaned as they were unloaded, and the ghost ship then moved on to make way for another similarly loaded vessel.

By the autumn of 1862 Washington had been transformed into the vast base hospital of the Army of the Potomac. Clusters of white buildings and tents had changed the aspect of the city and its surrounding hills. Practically every construction job marked a huge new hospital. The rectangular pavilions of the new Judiciary Square Hospital replaced the old E Street Infirmary. Stanton Hospital was another modern institution, and opposite it, on Minnesota Row, the former mansions of Douglas, Breckinridge, and Rice now constituted Douglas Hospital. Lincoln and Emory hospitals were being constructed on the plain to the east of the Capitol. Near the Smithsonian, beside the open sewer of the canal, lay the clean parallel sheds of the great Armory Square Hospital. On the distant heights, long one-story buildings, lavishly whitewashed and encircled by huts and tents, seemed to bloom like monstrous flowers in the soft Washington light.

On Independence Day of that year the church bells had not been rung because of the suffering men who lay below them. The seizure of the churches had begun in June, and soon congregations of Union sympathizers were vying with one another in an effort to offer their buildings to the War Department. Carpets, cushions, and hymnbooks were packed away. Carpenters covered the pews with scantling, laid floors on top, and stowed pulpits and other furniture underneath. Wagonloads of furniture, drugs, and utensils were delivered, and the flag of the Union was run up as wardmasters, nurses, orderlies, cooks, and stewards arrived. Soon, ambulances were stopping at the church doors, followed, last of all, by the surgeons with their knives and saws and dirty little sponges.

In the patent office, thousands of beds were installed, and at night, like some new exhibit of ghastliness, waxy faces lay in rows between the shining glass cabinets filled with curiosities, foreign presents, and models of inventions. The nurses' heels clicked on the marble floor, and over all lay the heavy smell of putrefaction and death.

A stranger wandering about the city at this time might think he could find his way by using the low, pale masses of hospitals as landmarks—but many hospitals could only be recognized upon closer inspection. Sick and wounded men lay in hotels and warehouses, in schools and seminaries, in private houses, and in the lodges of fraternal orders.

Yet when the wounded from Pope's campaign began to arrive, it was discovered all too quickly that there still was not room enough to accommodate the injured. At last the Capitol itself was temporarily requisitioned, and two thousand cots were placed in the halls of the House and Senate, in the corridors, and in the Rotunda.

Sad to say, even after the wounded reached the army hospitals, they still were miserable. The unsuitability of churches and public buildings as hospitals was evident, but renovated barracks were even worse. In addition to filthy grounds, they were dark and badly ventilated, and the administration of the hospitals left much to be desired; corrupt cooks and stewards, inexperienced nurses, and careless and incompetent surgeons were all too common.

It was into this setting of misery, pain, and death that Grace Swenson was plunged as she stepped off her train holding a small suitcase and filled with both determination and trepidation. She stood there in the center of the rushing masses of people, jostled by a host of soldiers and civilians, confused and uncertain. Making her way to the ticket counter, she asked the round-faced agent, "Please, can thee tell me how to get to the hospital?"

"Which one?"

"Why—any of them, I suppose," Grace answered. "I've come to help nurse the soldiers."

The agent peered at her intently, then scratched his balding dome. "Well, you better go to the War Department, I reckon. They'll put you right, miss." He motioned vaguely toward the large double doors to his left. "Get a carriage outside them doors and tell the driver to take you to the War Department."

"Thank you."

Grace followed his instructions, finding a number of cabs vying for her business. "Goin' downtown, missus?" a tall, rawboned cabbie asked, maneuvering his competitors deftly aside.

"I need to go to the War Department."

"Ah, step right in, missus! Have you there in two shakes of a duck's tail!"

Grace settled herself in the carriage, and as the cab rattled over the cobblestone streets, she stared at the city of Washington. The main thoroughfare of the city was four miles long and one hundred and sixty feet wide. The Capitol, with its unfinished dome topped by a huge crane and encircled by scaffolding, blocked the straight line of Pennsylvania Avenue, which led eastward from the expanding Treasury Building and the Executive Mansion, as the White House was called.

Within minutes, a terrible odor hit her like a blow, and she finally asked the driver, "What's that awful smell?"

"Oh, that's the canal, missus." He shrugged. Glancing at the huge ditch that paralleled the road, she saw that it was a fetid bayou filled with floating dead cats and all kinds of putridity. It literally reeked with pestilential odors that nearly gagged Grace! *We do better than this in Pennsylvania,* she thought grimly.

Finally the driver pulled the taxi to a stop and nodded toward a huge building to his right. "That's the War Department, missus."

Grace descended and paid her fare, then turned and walked toward the building. Stepping inside, she found it swarming with officers of all grades. She timidly asked for the medical department, and after being sent to several wrong offices, she finally found a short major with a kindly face who listened carefully to her story.

"It's Miss Dix you'll want to see, miss."

"Miss Dix?"

"Yes, ma'am. Miss Dorothea L. Dix, to be exact." A humorous light touched the man's gray eyes, and he added quickly, "And I'd be certain to stress the word *Miss* if I were you. She's a maiden lady and doesn't like to be taken for a married woman."

"I'll be careful, Major," Grace answered. "But who *is* she exactly?"

"Her title is 'superintendent of women nurses,'" he answered, leaning back in his chair. "She's rather famous in her home state of Massachusetts for her public work. She's devoted her life to aiding paupers, prisoners, and lunatics. Been able to do a lot about the terrible conditions in almshouses and jails and insane asylums. Last June she was appointed to take over the women who are coming to nurse the wounded. And she's done a fine job, too! Let me have my corporal take you to her. Her office isn't in this building."

He called a lanky corporal, instructed him to take Grace to Miss Dix's office, then wished her luck. "Thank you, Major." Grace smiled. "Thee has been very kind."

"I wish you luck, Miss Swenson, but I doubt you'll be working for Miss Dix."

Grace was startled. "But—why not?"

The major hesitated, then said, "Well, to be frank, you're

119

just too attractive." Seeing her blink of surprise, he explained, "Miss Dix considers all persons under thirty disqualified for nursing. A friend of mine who works in her department said that an applicant must be plain almost to repulsion in dress. I think Miss Dix doesn't want attractive women because they might cause trouble with the men."

Grace was too surprised to answer for a moment, then took heart. "I'll still see her, Major. Thank thee for the warning."

She left the building, and the corporal took her to a smaller edifice where a private informed her that Miss Dix's offices were on the second floor. Climbing the stairs, she entered the office with the sign outside that read: Miss Dorothea L. Dix, Superintendent.

Stepping inside, she found an older woman sitting at a desk writing in a ledger. "I'd like to see Miss Dix, please," Grace said.

The woman looked up and studied her. "May I ask the nature of your business?"

"I've come to help nurse the soldiers."

The woman stared at her, then shrugged. "I'll see if Miss Dix has time to see you." She rose and disappeared into the inner office. When she came out, she said curtly, "You may go in."

"Thank you."

When Grace was inside, she closed the door and walked across the room to stand in front of the desk where a woman looked up at her. "What is your name?" she asked at once.

"Grace Swenson, Miss Dix."

Miss Dix put down her pen and stood to her feet. She was a small woman with a knot of hair that seemed too heavy for the gentle head set on a long neck. Her mouth and her chin were firm, and her blue-gray eyes were sharp. "I understand you want to join the nursing staff."

"Yes, Miss Dix."

"Why?"

The abrupt monosyllable took Grace off guard. She stared

at the smaller woman and tried to explain. "I—I believe the Lord has told me to do this work," she finally said simply.

A curious light appeared in the eyes of Miss Dix. "What church do you attend?" she asked.

"I am a Friend."

"A Quaker?"

"Yes, people call us that."

Miss Dix seemed interested. She examined Grace more carefully, then said, "I don't accept young handsome women in my service, Miss Swenson. It's too distracting for the men."

Grace was prepared for this, for she had been thinking how she might answer it. "I may be young, Miss Dix, but I'm not considered handsome. I have sisters who are very attractive, so I know that I'm quite plain."

Miss Dix cocked her head to one side, caught by Grace's words. She was favorably impressed by the young woman, but was careful not to let that show in her expression. "Just as well that you think so," she said quietly. She fell silent, then said, "Sit down, Miss Swenson." When they were both seated, she said, "Tell me about yourself."

Grace spoke quickly, giving Miss Dix her background. When she was finished, the older woman asked directly, "Why aren't you married?"

"I—was asked only once, Miss Dix. It didn't work out." She looked directly in the superintendent's eyes, adding, "I don't think I shall ever marry."

Miss Dix nodded, considering her words.

Though Dorothea Dix was sixty years old, there was something formidable in this fragile and consecrated woman. In a time when men were unaccustomed to having their work interfered with by women, she had come sweeping through the wards like an avenging angel and was soon detested by the medical profession. Under the pressure of her multifarious and unsystematized duties, she grew overwrought, lost her self-control, and involved herself in quarrels. Though she often was in the right, she too rarely showed the graces of tolerance and tact, which won her many opponents and few supporters.

Despite all this, she had brought cleanliness and order to the wards, which had too long been chaotic and filthy. She would stay at her post without a leave of absence throughout the entire war—small and frail, but as unmovable as the Rock of Gibraltar!

"Miss Swenson," she finally said slowly. "I need nurses badly—but I screen applicants very strictly. And I may as well say that my first impulse is to refuse you."

"Oh, Miss Dix!" Grace spoke up quickly, anxiety in her eyes. "Please—give me a chance! I'm strong and willing to work. I nursed my father for years, and I know that God wants me to do this."

As the young woman spoke, Miss Dix listened carefully. In her determination to do everything herself, she had eventually buried herself in a maze of details—which was wearing her down terribly. Her authority was ill defined and conflicted with that of the surgeons, most of whom didn't approve of her or her female nurses. She feared that putting this young woman to work—who *was* attractive, despite her modesty!—could create problems in her department.

Grace, aware of Miss Dix's hesitation, finally said, "Miss Dix, I'd like to be as effective as I can, and serving under thee would be best. But if thee doesn't want me, I'll find someplace else to serve. Even if it's for only one man in a private home."

Miss Dix quickly made her decision. "Miss Swenson, I'm going to admit you to my staff on a trial basis. If you would like to come for two weeks, we'll see how it works out. At the end of that time, I'll make a final decision. That's the best I can do at this time."

"Oh, I thank thee, Miss Dix!" A radiant glow touched Grace's cheeks, and she smiled shyly. "I'll do my very best for thee and for the patients."

"I'm sure you will, Miss Swenson." Miss Dix rose and came to offer her hand. "Now, I'm going to put you under our sternest supervisor, Miss Agnes Dalton." A slight smile came to her lips, and she added, "You may not last the full two weeks. Miss Dalton is a hard worker and very demanding of the nurses who serve under her. Where do you live?"

"I don't have a place, Miss Dix. I just got off the train and came straight here."

"You may have trouble finding a place. The city is packed."

"God will help me."

"I trust he will. Be at the Armory Square Hospital at seven in the morning. I'll introduce you to Miss Dalton."

"I'll be there, Miss Dix!"

Grace left the building happy, feeling as though a burden had lifted. She was going to be a nurse! As she walked along the paths she thanked God for his provision, then turned her thoughts to finding a place to stay.

This proved to be more of a problem than she had expected, for Miss Dix had been right. Washington was packed with soldiers, government clerks, families of wounded men. Grace trudged from one rooming house to another, finding nothing.

Finally it was a cab driver who proved to be her salvation. He was an older man, in his late sixties with white hair and arthritic fingers—but his blue eyes were sharp, and after he had taken her to three boarding houses, he spoke up. "Miss, it's a bad time to be looking for a room."

"Yes, I can see that." Grace looked at him suddenly, asking, "Does thee know any place where I might stay?"

"Well now, I know of a place. But it's not very fine."

"Oh, I'm not looking for a fine place!"

"Ah? Well now, I know of a widow woman named Mrs. Johnson. She lost her husband at Bull Run. Has two children and is havin' a hard time of it. If you'd think of sharing a room with the daughter—?"

"Oh yes, that would be fine! Could we go there now?"

"Yes, miss. My name is Ryan Callihan. And what might you be called?"

"I'm Grace Swenson, and I've just come from Pennsylvania to be a nurse."

By the time Callihan had pulled up in front of a tiny frame house on the outskirts of Washington, he'd gotten most of Grace's story. Stepping down, he tied the horses, then said, "Come along, and we'll see."

Mrs. Ida Johnson was a large woman of forty. She had dark red hair and still bore traces of an earlier beauty, but sadness had marked her. "Why, I don't know, Miss Swenson," she said slowly after the cab driver had told her their mission. "I could use the money, but I've never had a boarder."

"I need a place very badly, Mrs. Johnson," Grace said quickly. "I don't think I'd be here much. I suspect I'll be working long hours. And I'd be willing to pay whatever thee might ask."

"Well . . . you'd have to share a room with my daughter Lettie."

"I'm sure we'd get along. I have four younger sisters," she said with a smile. "I get along well with young girls."

"I suppose we can try it out," Mrs. Johnson said.

"Now that's fine!" Callihan smiled. "Let me get your bag." When he brought it in, he said, "It's a long drive to the hospital. I'll be goin' into town at six ever mornin', Miss Grace. I live right down the way. You be ready and I'll pick you up."

"God reward thee, Mr. Callihan," Grace said at once. She smiled and put out her hand. When he took it, she said, "I've heard of people who were helped by angels unawares. Thee wouldn't be one of those by any chance?"

Callihan stared at her, rather shocked. Finally a smile came to his lips, and he shook his head. "I've been called lots of things, Miss Grace, but nobody never called me an angel before!" He laughed silently, turning at the door to say, "Six sharp, Miss Grace."

"I'll be waiting, Mr. Callihan."

"Come this way and I'll show you the room, Miss Swenson." Grace followed Mrs. Johnson to the small bedroom, which contained one bed and a smattering of furniture. Mrs. Johnson left her, and she lay down for half an hour, tired from her trip and the tension. She awakened when she heard the door close. Sitting up, she saw a young girl who was staring at her, and came to her feet. "I'm Grace Swenson. And I suppose thy name is Lettie?"

"Yes." Lettie Johnson was sixteen years old and very shy. She was not a pretty girl, but her brown hair was well cared for and her blue dress was in style.

Grace smiled gently at the girl. "Does thee mind too much, Lettie, sharing thy room with me?"

Lettie shook her head. "I don't mind," she said, then added, "I work, so I'm not here much anyway."

"Where does thee work, Lettie?"

By the time Mrs. Johnson called that supper was ready, Grace and Lettie were well acquainted. Grace's long years with younger sisters made this easy for her, and Lettie was charmed by the idea of having a nurse for a roommate.

When they went to the small dining room, Mrs. Johnson said, "Miss Swenson, this is my son, William."

Grace smiled at the ten-year-old, who had his mother's red hair and many freckles. "I'm glad to meet thee, William."

The boy stared at her curiously, but only nodded. When his mother set the last bowl of food on the table and sat down, she looked nervously toward Grace. "We don't ask a blessing, but I suppose you do?"

"I'd like to." Grace smiled, then asked a simple blessing. As she began to eat hungrily, she found the food was good—well prepared and tasty—and she complimented Mrs. Johnson. "Thee is a fine cook!"

The two women began to talk about cooking, and finally William demanded, "Why do you talk funny?"

"William!" Lettie said sharply. "Don't be so impolite!"

Grace laughed aloud, saying, "It's all right, Lettie. I'm used to it." She turned to the boy saying, "I'm what people

125

call a Quaker, William. Our people have ways that are different. We use *thee* and *thy* because that's what the Bible uses." Grace felt it wise to give a few details about the Friends to her new acquaintances.

When she was finished, Mrs. Johnson asked, "You don't believe in war?"

"No. We feel it's wrong to kill."

"Well, it ain't wrong to kill the derned ol' Rebels!" Willie said angrily. "They killed my pa, and when I get big enough, I'm goin' to be a soldier! Then I'll show 'em!"

Mrs. Johnson said sharply, "William, be quiet!"

"Well, I am!"

The room was quiet, and Grace finally said, "I don't know much about the war. God told me to come and take care of the wounded soldiers. That's a good thing to do, doesn't thee think so, William?"

The boy watched her stubbornly. "If they're our soldiers—but not the Rebels!"

Grace was shocked at the hatred in the boy's face, but she could see that it was no time to discuss the matter. "Well, there are no wounded Rebels here."

"Oh yes, Miss Swenson," Mrs. Johnson spoke up. "There are quite a few, I understand." Bitterness touched her lips, and she said, "They killed my husband—so I don't care if they all die!"

Grace was even more distressed to see that Mrs. Johnson was filled with bitterness. *Not hard to see where William gets his terrible hatred from,* she thought. But tactfully she said, "I'll be tending our own Union soldiers." Then she changed the subject, and the meal ended pleasantly.

That night when she and Lettie went to their bedroom, Grace knew that the girl was watching her carefully. "I always read a chapter in Psalms then say a prayer at night, Lettie," she said. "Could we do it together?"

"I guess so."

Grace chose Psalm 56. When she had finished reading it out loud, she bowed her head and prayed. She felt a burden

126

for the Johnsons and prayed for each of them by name. When she was finished, she looked up to see that there were tears on Lettie's cheeks. Grace was touched and said, "Thee must pray for me, Lettie. I am a little frightened of my new job."

Lettie gave her a startled look. "Me? I can't pray!"

"Oh, God would love for thee to pray, Lettie," Grace insisted. "He loves us all so much. Thee can just pray in thy heart. Just say, 'God, help Miss Grace be a fine nurse!'"

Lettie licked her lips and lay back on her pillow. "All right," she said finally. "I'll do it."

"Good! And I'll pray for thee, too."

Grace blew out the lamp and got into bed. "Good night, Lettie. And I thank God for giving me a brand new younger sister. Now I have five!"

Lettie lay there stiffly, for she was not an outgoing girl and this woman seemed particularly strange in her ways and talk. But finally she whispered, "Good night, Miss Swenson."

"Just Grace. We're sisters now, Lettie and Grace."

Another silence, then . . . "Good night, Grace!"

CHAPTER TEN
Mysterious Patient

★

"Well, Miss Dix, I suppose you've been forced to change your policy."

Brig. Gen. William Alexander Hammond, the surgeon general of the United States, smiled down at Miss Dix fondly. He was a big man of only thirty-four, dark and powerful. A beard and mustache covered the lower part of his heavy, intelligent face, and with his strong physique and personality, he seemed to fill every room he entered.

Miss Dix stared at him, bewildered by his remark. He'd come on one of his periodic visits, and the two of them had gone over the Armory Square Hospital thoroughly.

"Why—I don't know, sir," Miss Dix said. "Which policy have I changed?"

Hammond nodded toward the tall, strong-looking nurse who was carefully moving a patient whose legs were heavily bandaged. "Why, everyone knows you won't have good-looking young nurses." He smiled, then added, "But that young woman certainly comes in the category of good-looking."

Miss Dix flushed slightly, but lifted her head in a belligerent gesture. "I haven't changed my policy at all, Dr. Hammond, but it is a foolish person who adheres blindly to a rule. Miss Swenson is an exception."

Hammond's dark eyes grew interested. "How is she exceptional?"

"She's a very serious young woman," Miss Dix said at once. "Most young women's minds are filled with thoughts of courtship and marriage, but this young lady thinks only of service." She watched the little tableau, noting how carefully the nurse eased the wounded man over to his side so that she could slide the soiled sheets out from under him, and how she spoke to him quietly the whole time. And she noted as well the expression on the face of the wounded man.

"Her name is Grace Swenson," Miss Dix said without taking her eyes from her young worker. "I'd like for you to meet her."

"Has she been with you long?"

"Not nearly as long as I'd like." Miss Dix's thin lips turned upward slightly in a rare smile. "Watch your behavior, General. Miss Swenson is a clergyman."

"A preacher?" Hammond's heavy brows shot upward in an involuntary fashion. "She doesn't look like any preacher I ever saw!"

"She is, though—a Quaker. Come along, General." She led the large officer to stand beside the bed, saying, "Nurse Swenson?"

The surgeon general watched as the young woman, dressed in gray except for the white bonnet on her head, helped the wounded man lie down. She was very deliberate, finishing the chore at hand before turning around to say, "Yes, Miss Dix?"

"I want you to meet someone. This is William Hammond, the surgeon general."

"I'm happy to meet thee, sir."

Hammond bowed slightly, saying, "My pleasure, Miss Swenson." He was favorably impressed with the young woman's calm demeanor. He was an astute student of people and studied faces carefully. He perceived in a glance that she was very tall, and he noted the strength in her feminine figure. He found her rather squarish face and fine complexion most pleasing to look at, and her light blue eyes held the direct stare that he was accustomed to finding only in men. Her blonde hair was tied up, but was obviously fine as silk, and he felt sure it would have fallen well below her waist if it were loose.

"Miss Dix tells me you're a clergyman, Miss Swenson," Hammond said. "That must be very handy when dealing with the men."

"Many of them do need spiritual healing as well as physical care," Grace said quietly. "But then, most of us need that, don't we, Doctor?"

Miss Dix had been almost intimidated by Hammond's strong personality, and it secretly pleased her to see the tall officer taken aback by Grace's straightforward manner—and by her question.

"Why—I must agree with that," Hammond stammered. He rubbed his whiskers, then said with a nod, "Yes, it is so. But do any of the men resent your preaching to them? I mean, they're a bit of a captive audience."

"Some of them are a little resentful," Grace admitted. "But I never force my beliefs on them. After all, Jesus never forced himself on anyone, did he, Doctor?"

"I—don't believe he did," Hammond said, then hastened to add, "but I'm not a Bible scholar."

Grace gave him a slow smile. "Thee does not need to be a scholar to love God, Doctor. The only thing Jesus seeks is a hungry heart. Has thee ever felt him knocking at thy door?"

Hammond was a tough man; he had risen to the top of his profession by sheer force of will and, as surgeon general, often found himself doing battle with Stanton, the secretary of war—a dragon who had burned many a man! So it was most disconcerting to find himself feeling almost sheepish before this young woman! Mustering his wits, he tried to bully his way out of the situation, acutely aware that Miss Dix was enjoying his discomfort. "I've not made up my mind about religion," he said gruffly. "I'm an agnostic." He caught the smile that touched the young nurse's wide lips and demanded, "What's so amusing about that, Nurse Swenson?"

Grace regarded the large man calmly—and he was somewhat put off to realize she was not in the least intimidated. "Why, it amuses me to hear thee, Doctor." She shook her head, and there was a strange mixture of gentleness and firmness in her that the general found both charming and challenging. "Thee would not say so about any other area of thy life. An agnostic says, 'I am ignorant; I don't know.' But thee would never say that of thy career, nor would thee let one of thy fellow doctors say that about his medical skill, would thee?"

"Well, no, but—"

"And we would agree that since a man's body is only here for a brief time, but his soul is forever, it can't be wise to ignore the one who made them both. So thee must seek God, Doctor, with as much eagerness and dedication as thee has sought success in thy profession."

Hammond stood before the two women silently. He wanted to lash out, to tell her to stop meddling in his private life—but somehow he could not. He had been struggling spiritually in his own life for the past year, and the young woman had put her finger on that very problem. He was a sensitive man, and though he had known many hypocrites, he had seen enough sincere Christians to make him aware that something of what they had was what he needed in his own life.

Now he said with some embarrassment, "We're keeping you from your work, Nurse Swenson."

"My work is serving God, Doctor," Grace said sweetly but with a glint of humor in her eyes. "It doesn't matter what form that takes, bandaging a wound or bearing witness of the love of Jesus to the surgeon general."

Hammond suddenly was filled with a desire to get away. "Ah yes . . . well, Miss Dix, shall we move on?" When he had made his escape out of the ward, he turned abruptly, demanding, "Is she like that all the time?"

Miss Dix's smile grew broader. "She was the same with me, General. I think she'd be the same with President Lincoln."

Hammond shook his head, admiration coming into his expression. "Well, she's different from any of the other clergymen I've met. And you say she's a good nurse?"

"The finest I've had, and I've had some fine ones. She'd taken care of a sick father before she came so she knew some things already. Not about wounds, of course, but she's very bright and catches on quickly." Miss Dix sighed and shook her head. "I wish I had a hundred like her!"

Hammond shook his heavy head. "You won't get them, I'm afraid. I don't think there *are* any more like her!" He turned, and the two of them moved through the rest of the wards. When the inspection was finished, Hammond gave his approval. "As usual, Miss Dix, you've got things in fine order. I wish the other hospitals were so well organized."

"Thank you, Dr. Hammond," Miss Dix murmured. She stood there, a small woman with an indomitable spirit, and the burly physician saw that something was troubling her. He didn't probe, but finally she said with a marked hesitation, "Dr. Hammond, I'm concerned about some of the patients."

"Oh? Which ones?"

"The men we have in Ward K. I—didn't take you to that ward, but would you come with me now?"

"Certainly."

Hammond followed the woman out of the building, across several sidewalks, and finally stepped inside another of the rectangular, white structures. Glancing around curiously, the surgeon at once realized that something about this ward was very different from the others. Not that it varied in size or shape, for like the rest of the wards it was basically a large room with two rows of beds. But the patients—!

Hammond blinked with surprise. Many of the beds were

133

not occupied by men lying down. Rather, several patients were either sitting on the beds or in chairs, while others were walking around aimlessly. One man came over to stand five feet away, directly in front of Hammond and Miss Dix. He limped badly, but it was his face that caught the surgeon general's attention, for it seemed blank of all expression.

"How are you, Private?" Hammond asked curiously.

But the man stared at him without speaking. Hammond noted the man's long, cadaverous face, with eyes deeply sunken into their sockets. His lips were thin and pale, almost bloodless, and they twitched as he seemed to be whispering. His long fingers fumbled at the buttons on the front of his shirt, and he stared at Hammond with wide-open, unblinking eyes.

Hammond glanced at Miss Dix, then asked more loudly, "Well now, what seems to be the trouble?"

Suddenly the man's mouth opened, and a high-pitched whine emerged. It was a wordless cry that made the hair rise on the back of the physician's neck as he realized that the man was quite mad.

"Now Roger—" Miss Dix moved forward at once, taking the man's arm and turning him around—"there's a good fellow. You just go sit down. Everything's all right."

She coaxed the man back across the room, sat him down on one of the beds, then came back to say, "He's not dangerous, poor man!"

Hammond looked around the room and understood why the chief of nurses had been hesitant to speak of this place. "These men—they're all mental cases?"

"Some of them have physical injuries," Miss Dix said, sadness in her blue-gray eyes. "But yes, their worst injuries seem to be mental. We thought it better to keep them separate from the other men. Not just for their own good, Doctor," she added quickly. "They were bad for morale."

"I can understand that," Hammond responded. He shook his head sadly, then asked, "What happens when they're well enough to be sent home?"

"Why, most of them are taken in by their people. But there are a few who are able enough to be dismissed, but they have no family . . . or their people won't have them."

"It's the asylum for them?"

The word *asylum* caused Dorothea Dix's lips to form a knifelike line, and anger sparkled in her eyes. "Yes! And you know what that's like!"

Hammond knew only too well! In most cases, an asylum was worse than many prisons. They were no more than dark holes where mentally disturbed patients were chained like wild beasts. Unwashed and uncared for, these desperate souls lived their lives out in the horror of great darkness.

"Too bad! Too bad!" Dr. Hammond shook his heavy head, then a question came to him. "I suppose the surgeons are not much help with such as these?"

"Most of them come in to care for them physically," Miss Dix shrugged. "But they don't care about their minds."

"But Miss Dix, there isn't much they can do, is there? We know so little about this sort of problem." Hammond, a compassionate man where broken bodies were concerned, looked over the room, noting the blank faces and staring eyes. "I wouldn't know how to start with men like these!"

Miss Dix was forced to agree. "I know, sir, but we must do what we can. These men are here because they took up arms and fought to keep our Union intact. Just because their wounds are in the mind doesn't make them any less honorable than those wounded in the flesh."

"What is it you want me to do, Miss Dix?"

"Some of the surgeons want to discharge these men at once because we need the beds." Miss Dix was not a woman who begged, but now she was appealing with her whole heart. "But to do that would be a terrible injustice to these poor souls. Will you do what you can, Dr. Hammond, to let me keep this one ward for this kind of problem?"

Hammond nodded firmly. "Yes, I'll see to it." He looked over the men once more, then turned to go. When they were outside, he said, "Do any of them ever recover?"

135

"Oh yes, some of them."

"How do you account for it?"

"I can't, really." Miss Dix thought about his question as they walked along, and finally said, "I think all we can do is to be kind—and wait. They're locked inside some sort of grim prison. The only thing they seem to respond to is kindness."

After Miss Dix had said good-bye to Dr. Hammond, she sat at her desk for some time staring at the wall blankly. The pressures of her task were tremendous, and her nerves were strained. She thought of the men in Ward K, searching for some way to help them. It was so hopeless! So few of them ever came out of the darkness that clouded their benighted minds.

She was thankful for Dr. Hammond's willingness to help, and that made her feel a little better. Then she thought about her response to his question regarding the men's recovery: *The only thing they seem to respond to is kindness.*

Long she sat there, struggling with the problem. Then, suddenly, something came to her. She was not an impulsive woman, but the idea persisted with such force that she finally rose and moved out of her office, going to find Grace Swenson. "Nurse Swenson, come to my office please."

Grace looked up in surprise, but made no comment. She followed the superintendent through the halls, and when they were inside the small office she took the seat Miss Dix offered her.

"I have something to ask you."

"Yes?"

Miss Dix plunged at once into the problem of the men in Ward K and ended by saying, "It's a thankless service, I'm afraid. So few of them ever recover. But I think you could be of help to some of them."

Grace agreed instantly. "I'll do what I can, Miss Dix."

"I'm so shorthanded," Miss Dix warned. "It will have to be extra duty, I'm afraid. I'll take you off of Ward C, but it will still be more work. And you'll have to be strict with the male nurses. Some of them aren't much! They know these men can't report them, so they mistreat the patients."

"How do they do that?"

"Steal their food or the whiskey used for treatment, let them go dirty, become careless about changing dressings— there are far too many ways." Miss Dix gave the young woman a direct glance. "You can't be soft on them or your patients will suffer."

"I'll do the best I can, Miss Dix."

Pleasure came into Dorothea's thin face, and she took a deep breath. "I was hoping you would, Grace." It was the first time she'd called Grace by her given name, for she was not given to informality. "I'll see that your supervisors are informed. When would you like to begin?"

"I'll start first thing in the morning," Grace said.

Miss Dix hesitated, then said gently, "You won't be able to do much with your religious convictions, I'm afraid. They're all too far gone to understand you."

But the superintendent's words didn't seem to trouble the young woman. "God is able to minister to a troubled mind as well as to a maimed body," she said softly, then rose and left the room.

Miss Dix—who was not considered a praying woman— stared at the door, then whispered, "God be with her!"

"Are you going to be nursin' *loonies?*"

It was breakfast time at the Johnson house, and Willie had listened with increasing interest as Grace spoke of her new assignment at the hospital. He blurted out his question, his eyes big as half-dollars.

"Willie, that's no way to talk!" Ida Johnson rebuked her son sharply, but there was doubt in her own expression. Turning back to face Grace, she said, "I never thought about such a thing—men losing their minds from the war."

Grace sipped her coffee thoughtfully before answering. "It's not too surprising when thee thinks about it. People go insane over less than what these men have gone through."

137

"Are they dangerous, Grace?" Lettie asked breathlessly.

"Oh, not at all, Lettie!" Grace spoke up quickly. "Most of them are wounded so badly they couldn't hurt anyone."

"I'd be afraid to stick my nose in the door," Mrs. Johnson announced, shaking her head. "There's something about a person losing his mind that's worse than losing an arm or a leg."

"I agree with thee, Mrs. Johnson," Grace said. "But the Scripture enjoins us to comfort the feebleminded, doesn't it?" She glanced at the old clock on the mantle, then exclaimed, "I've got to hurry. Do you mind if I don't help thee with the dishes, Mrs. Johnson?"

"No, Lettie can help."

Grace grabbed her coat, put her hat on, and raced out the door just as Ryan Callihan arrived in his cab. Grace scrambled up on the seat with him, greeting him cheerfully. As he drove along she inquired about his family. He had a grandson in the Army of the Potomac and another in the Union navy under Farragut. When he finished his report, she spoke of her new assignment, and Callihan stared at her in astonishment. "Faith! Is it crazy men ye'll be nursin'?"

Grace was discouraged at the response from the Johnsons and from her old friend, but she shook it off. "They're God's children, and I'm thankful he's allowing me to help them."

Callihan shook his head, mystified by all of this. He had become very fond of Grace, despite her efforts to wean him from the bottle. His sharp blue eyes cut around more than once to watch her as she sat beside him, and finally when he stopped in front of Armory Square Hospital, he took her arm just as she prepared to step down.

"Lassie, you be on your guard!"

Grace patted his hand, gnarled with arthritis, and smiled fondly into his seamed face. "God will take care of me, Friend Callihan, and thee stay away from that saloon today!"

She stepped to the ground, waved at him, then turned and entered the hospital. She went at once to her locker, a wooden closet she shared with Ada Clower, and found the older woman putting on an apron. Ada was forty-two years old and built along the lines of a garden rake. She had been married twice, but widowed that same number of times. Grace had heard one of Ada's patients mutter, "Her husbands must have soured to death! She'd curdle milk with that face of hers!"

But Ada was capable enough, if somewhat bitter. "I heard you wuz goin' to Ward K," she grunted as she tied her bonnet in place, giving the strings a firm yank. She peered at Grace, then shook her head. "None of the rest of us would do it. Did you know that when you told Miss Dix you'd take the job?"

"No, but it's all right, Ada. I don't mind."

"Humph!" Ada sniffed, then nodded sharply. "Ain't no picnic, waitin' on crazy men!"

Grace shook her head, saying cheerfully, "God is in Ward K, just as he's in the other wards." Turning away from the other nurse, she made her way down the hall, left the main building, and followed the raised wooden sidewalks that led to Ward K.

When she stepped inside, she stopped instantly, assaulted by the foul air. *The waste cans haven't been changed lately,* she thought, and when she moved to the first bed, she discovered that the helpless man was lying in his own filth. Anger swept through her like a fire, but she let nothing show on her face. "Now then, let's get you cleaned up," she said cheerfully.

The patient was a middle-aged man with a full crop of salt-and-pepper whiskers. He stared up at her with frightened eyes and began to flop about on the bed, crying out, "I'm all right! I'm all right!" His eyes were bright with fever, and when she touched him, she knew that it was dangerously high. Quickly she cleaned him and changed the dressing on his stomach, then put him down on the clean sheets, which she had expertly changed.

Placing her hand on his head, she stood there praying silently, and presently the wild eyes grew more calm. "I'm all right," he muttered over and over, until he finally seemed to go to sleep.

Grace left the ward at once. She prayed for a quiet spirit, but it took all the power she could summon to keep from letting her anger spill over. Going at once to the mess room, she saw Nurse Sawyer eating breakfast. Going to her, she asked directly, "Who is the night nurse in charge of Ward K?"

"Why, Jesse Ormstead," Nurse Sawyer said with surprise. She pointed at a group of the male nurses who were drinking coffee at a table near the wall. "He's the one with the brown beard."

Grace nodded, then walked to the table. The men looked up, and one of them winked at the others, saying something that made them laugh. Ignoring their behavior, Grace spoke firmly. "Jesse Ormstead, come with me."

Ormstead was a sharp-faced man with a brown scraggly beard and a pair of sharp, hard brown eyes. He looked up at Grace, leaned back indolently, then said, "Why, you must be the new nurse in Ward K, I reckon."

"That's correct."

"Well, you hustle on down to the ward," Ormstead said with a sneer in his tone. "I'll be along directly, soon as I finish this coffee." He winked at the men and settled back in his chair.

Grace's expression never altered, but she knew that if she allowed the man to get by with his insolence, she would never be able to maintain order in the ward. She stood there watching him, and it came to her what she must do.

"I understand Gen. McClellan is in need of fifty thousand new men for his army," she remarked pleasantly.

"Little Mac always needs men." Ormstead shrugged. "What's that got to do with me?"

Grace smiled easily. "It has this to do with thee, Jesse—" Grace's voice took on a steely edge as she pinned the man with her eyes. "Thee will be one of those men if thee does not come with me right now. I can see that thee is a sloppy man, afraid of work. But thee will work . . . or thee will go to face the Rebels!"

"Hey! Now wait just—"

"Either come with me right now and do the work you left undone, or I will go at once to Dr. William Hammond, the surgeon general. When I tell him what a poor excuse for a nurse you are, he will have thee transferred this morning to the infantry. Make up thy mind, Jesse, which it shall be."

Ormstead had always been a bully—it had served him well with other nurses—and he fell back on that now. His face grew red with anger and he rose to his feet ominously. "I'll see you in Hades before—"

"Fine!" Grace whirled and walked purposefully away. She had no idea if she could carry out her threat, but she was hoping that Ormstead would think so.

One of the men with Ormstead whispered, "That Gen. Hammond, he's a hard nut, Jesse! And that female looks like she means business! You better eat crow—and fast!"

Ormstead looked wildly after Grace, then dropped his coffee cup on the table. "Nurse!" he called out, and when she exited without a backward look, he grew pale and scurried after her.

Nurse Sawyer laughed and said to an assistant surgeon sitting across from her, "I think Ormstead's met his match! He's an arrogant fellow, and I hope Grace works him until he drops!"

Her words were almost prophetic, for after Ormstead's abject apology and promise to reform, Grace forced him to work for four hours. She saw to it that he emptied all the pails, then mopped the floor.

While he was working, she moved around the ward, meeting the patients. Some of them were badly wounded, and she spoke with them calmly, changing dressings and feeding them when the breakfast was sent in from the kitchen.

Despite her resolution to keep a warm pleasant expression, there was something chilling about the work. It was, she recognized, the blankness in the patients' eyes that made it so. Most of the time they made no reply at all to her chatter. Some of them spoke only obscenities, others rattled off words with no meaning at all.

Grace spoke to them all the same, noting that some seemed fairly normal. But when she mentioned this to Miss Dix, who came to visit her just before noon, Miss Dix said, "Yes, some of them seem very normal—but those same men in five minutes might be raving or they might go into that dreadful silence, just staring at the walls with poor mad eyes."

The two women talked for fifteen minutes, and then Miss Dix asked, "Have you met John Smith yet?"

"No, I haven't. Which one is he?"

"The tall one, standing by the window."

Grace had noticed the man, for he was, to say the least, eye-catching. He was very tall, with darkly handsome features, and he seemed to have no serious wound. In fact, compared to the others in the ward, he seemed quite healthy.

"You'll be surprised when you talk to him, Nurse Swenson," Miss Dix said, watching the tall man. "He's the mystery man of our hospital."

"Mystery man?" Grace asked, her curiosity quickened.

"He's been here for nearly a month, but in all that time he's never spoken once. He had some serious wounds, but they've healed—or almost so. But the mystery is that we can't find out who he is."

"What does thee mean by that?" Grace asked, puzzled.

"Just what I said," Miss Dix shrugged. "We can't find out his name. He can't speak—or won't—and there was nothing on him to identify him when he was brought in from the battlefield."

"But surely some of his fellow soldiers—!"

"We don't know which unit he was with. The battle scattered the troops terribly, and though we've tried, nobody has been able to identify him. We gave him the name John Smith to make bookkeeping easier."

"How strange!"

"Yes, it is. But many men were taken prisoner in the battle—or simply blown to bits. Others were buried in unmarked graves, so there are many whose identification has been lost. It's not really so surprising that we haven't been able to identify Mr. Smith as of yet."

"What will happen to him?"

"If he doesn't get better, I suppose we'll have to put him in an institution."

"The insane asylum?"

"Yes."

Grace looked again across the big room. The sunlight came in through the high windows, falling in a tapering bar across the face of the man who stood there. "What a terrible thing!" she whispered.

"War is terrible," Miss Dix said with pain in her voice and in her eyes. "Do the best you can for these men," she said, then left the room.

Grace moved about the room, stopping to speak to first one, then another, and finally came to stand beside John Smith.

"Well, Mr. Smith, you're looking very well."

For one moment she didn't think the man heard her, but then he turned and looked at her. He had the darkest eyes she'd ever seen, so black it was almost impossible to see the pupils. He regarded her carefully, but said nothing, and when she saw that he was not going to speak, she said cheerfully, "Well, now, my name is Nurse Swenson, Mr. Smith. I'm going to take care of you for a while."

The black eyes did not change, and finally Grace grew uncomfortable. She had the strange feeling that somewhere behind the blank stare that this tall man laid on her was a mind screaming and clawing to get out.

Sadly, she had no idea how to set that part of him free, but as she went about her work that day, it was John Smith who occupied her thoughts the most. When she left that evening, she was still thinking of him, troubled more by his opaque black eyes than by any of the other patients.

And when she lay down beside Lettie that night, the last prayer she prayed was for life to come into those dark, suffering eyes.

CHAPTER ELEVEN
The Awakening

★

From the first, Ward K had a special place in Grace's heart. Perhaps it was similar to the inexplicable love a mother or father has for an afflicted child born in the midst of healthy children—but however it came about, she found herself spending more and more energy and time in that ward.

Certainly it was not because she saw more progress in Ward K than in other wards. On the contrary, she saw much less! The physical cures of the patients were about the same as those in the rest of the hospital, but only rarely did she see any of the men come out of the fog that shrouded their minds.

As winter came on, with October coming in like a lion with icy breezes, she found herself paying a price for her long hours. She began to lose weight and could not sleep. Miss Dix came to notice this and asked her to have tea in her office. This was fairly common, for the superintendent liked to keep personal contact with her nurses. When Grace arrived, Miss Dix indicated one of the chairs and began to pour the tea from a brass tea kettle, which was singing a merry little tune.

"Now, tell me all your problems," Miss Dix said when they were sipping the tea. A thin smile touched her lips, and she shrugged. "Not that I can solve any of them—but it does one good to let them be said once in a while."

Grace returned her smile. As she waited for an answer, the older woman noticed there was a thinness in her young associate's face that had not been there in the fall, a hollowing of her cheeks and a more deep-set look in her eyes. Her color was not as good, and she seemed honed down to a thin fine edge.

"I have no complaints," Grace said. She paused and sipped the tea from her cup, then added, "Whenever I get tired or upset, I think of some of our poor patients. Those without legs or arms. It makes my problems seem so small."

"Yes, I do the same." The older woman leaned back in her chair and closed her eyes for a moment. "They keep coming in, don't they? Sometimes I think there'll never be any end to it."

The two women sat there, enjoying the quiet moment. Such times were rare, for the hospital ran night and day, and new casualties kept arriving. Finally Miss Dix asked, "How are conditions in Ward K? I understand you built a fire under Jesse Ormstead."

"Does thee know everything that goes on in this hospital?" Grace asked, surprise in her tone. Then she laughed shortly and nodded. "Jesse is my heavenly sandpaper, I think. He is the most worthless man I've ever known—and that's saying a great deal! He's lazy, shiftless, dirty, and a thief."

"Why don't you let me get rid of him?"

"Oh no, don't do that." Grace looked down at her hands, studied them carefully, then looked up with a strange smile. "I think God has given me Jesse to keep me mindful of how often I've displeased him. Just when I'm ready to hit him with a broom, I remember some of the times in my life when I must have caused God as much trouble as Jesse causes me."

"Well, that's one way of looking at it, I suppose. But if he gives you too many problems, just let me know."

Humor came to light Grace's fine eyes. "I think he's quite afraid of me," she mused. "He's convinced that I can have

146

him put in the front lines of the army at any moment. He'll do anything in the world to escape service in the army."

Miss Dix nodded with satisfaction, pleased that Grace was able to handle her own problems. "How is our Mr. Smith?" she asked, sipping her tea. "Any sign of improvement?"

Distress came to Grace's expression, and she shook her head sadly. "I'm afraid not. His physical wounds have healed, but he still hasn't said a word."

"Too bad! Such a fine-looking man," Miss Dix said regretfully. "We still haven't been able to find out a thing about him."

"I think so much about his family," Grace murmured. "Somewhere he must have a mother and father who are grieving over him."

"Or a wife and children," Miss Dix put in, then she glanced sharply toward Grace, thinking of why she had invited her for tea. "Grace, you're not looking well. Aren't you sleeping well?"

"Oh, I'm fine," Grace said quickly, but she flushed slightly under the scrutiny of the superintendent. "Thee must not worry about me, Miss Dix. Thee has too much of a burden as it is."

"You won't be able to help your patients at all if you fall ill," Miss Dix stated. "I've seen this before—always with my best nurses. They wear themselves out caring for their patients, and then they're flat on their backs and I'm left with no one to take their places. The better the nurse," she added thoughtfully, "the more likely this is to happen." Setting her cup down firmly, she said, "Take more time off, Grace. You can only do so much, and I think you've passed the point of good judgment."

Grace started to protest, but one look at Miss Dix and she knew that there was no use. "I'll be more careful," she nodded. "But thee must take heed of thy own advice. What would happen to the program if thee were taken ill?"

It was a thought that Dorothea Dix had pondered often, for she knew that if nurses were in short supply, there was literally no one to replace her. She held the entire structure on her frail shoulders, and if she were to leave for any length of time, the good that she had wrought in the system might well be lost.

"Both of us must be careful," she admitted, then stood up, signifying that the tea party was over.

Grace was slightly depressed by the discussion, but knew that what Miss Dix had spoken was good counsel. She knew her own body, and it was telling her to slow down. She was honest enough to admit that she worked such long hours to take her mind off of her own problems, for when she went to bed early she would think for hours of the past—dwelling sometimes on her father until the loneliness became so painful that she could not bear it.

She thought as well of Clyde Dortch, which shamed her in some mysterious fashion. She felt a guilt over such thoughts and prayed much to not have hard feelings toward her sister and brother-in-law. Still, despite her efforts to bury the bitterness of the past, she would find herself thinking harsh and vengeful thoughts—some of which shocked her. *Oh, God—don't let me have this bitterness!* she would cry, and for a time things would be better.

But losing Clyde had cut her deeper than she supposed. This revelation came when she discovered that she was fantasizing over what might have been. Without purposing it, she would construct a dream of herself as Clyde's wife, with a family of children. She was the heroine of these dreams, and they always ended the same—and when she snapped out of it, she would be flooded with a new wave of bitterness toward Clyde and Prudence. Then she would have to begin wearily to seek forgiveness from God for such thoughts.

As she walked down the hall toward Ward K, Grace thought about her future. Though it didn't seem like it now, someday the war would be over. *What will I do then? Where can I go?* These thoughts depressed her, and she attempted to shake them off. *No sense letting my mood bring the men down,* she thought, and as she entered, she shook off her blackness and began to go from bed to bed, examining the dressings and giving words of encouragement.

One of the patients, Aaron Bent, a tall, fierce-eyed man from Michigan, had showed some promise. He had spells of such deep depression that he seemed to die inside, but they faded away and he could have passed for normal during these periods. Now he was sitting at one of the tables used for writing and playing games, staring at a sheet of paper.

"Writing your family, Aaron?" Grace asked as she came to stand by him.

"I reckon." Bent looked up at her and shook his head. "I ain't much on my letters, Miss Grace."

"Would you like me to look at it for thee?"

"Sure would." Bent handed her the letter, then sat back and studied her as Grace read what he had written.

Alf sed he heard that you and hardy was a runing to gether all the time and he thot he wod gust quit having any thing more to doo with you for he thot it was no more yuse. I think you made a bad chois to turn off as nise a feler as Alf dyer and let that orney, thevin, drunkerd, card-playing Hardy Simons come to Sea you. He aint nothin but a theef and a lopyeard, pigen toed helon. He is too orney for the devil. I will Shute him as shore as i Sea him.

The letter was signed, "All my love, Aaron," which almost brought a smile to Grace's lips. Ignoring the terrible spelling, she asked with a straight face, "I take it thee doesn't care for Hardy Simons?"

"No, I hate his guts," the soldier said with a shake of his head. "He's a dead man if he don't leave my sister alone."

"But—" Grace struggled to find something to say, but nothing seemed appropriate. "Perhaps your sister loves him."

Aaron Bent gave Grace a hard, unbelieving stare. "Ain't

no sister of mine goin' to marry up with a no-account skunk like that! She kin just find some other man to love."

"But, Aaron, a woman can't—she can't just switch off love!"

"Why can't she?"

Though Grace felt she was getting in over her head, she tried valiantly to explain. "Well, when we love somebody, we can't just *stop* loving them, can we—even if they're not what they should be? What if God stopped loving us just because we didn't behave right."

Aaron shook his head firmly. "God never told nobody to be stupid."

That comment caused Grace to stare at the tall man speechlessly, and he nodded firmly. "Shore he didn't. And any woman who marries up with Hardy Simons is gonna have a terrible life. He'll drink and steal and lie and beat her, and she'll have to raise all the kids by herself. So only a stupid woman would ask fer thet kind of life, ain't it so?"

Grace found her face glowing slightly with a blush. She said, "I—I can't answer that, Aaron."

Bent's lean face was serious, and he nodded emphatically. "Don't you be marryin' up with no trash, Miss Grace," he said firmly. A thought came to him, and he added, "I'd marry up with you myself, but I already got me a woman."

"That's . . . nice of thee, Aaron." Grace summoned a smile. "I know thy woman will be glad to have thee home again. And thee has improved so much, it won't be long now."

Bent looked down at the floor, his face growing sad. "I'm most afraid to go home. When these fits take me, I ain't fit to live with my family."

Grace suddenly felt the Holy Ghost move on her heart, more powerfully than she had ever felt it before!

Speak the Word to him—and he will be made whole.

The message came as plainly as if it had been painted on a huge sign, and a joy filled Grace, for she knew that God was about to do something for the man who sat beside her.

"Aaron," she said quietly, "God wants to take your fears away. . . ."

Twenty minutes later, Aaron Bent called on God, asked for salvation, and was filled with the Holy Ghost and with peace. He had sat there listening as Grace had read to him from the Scriptures, then had told him how God had given her peace. When she'd given Aaron the gospel and asked him to pray, he'd said at once, "I need God, Miss Grace!" He'd bowed his head and, with tears running down his face, had called on God as simply as a little child.

Finally he lifted his head, his eyes wide with wonder, and exclaimed, "Miss Grace . . . it's all gone! All that heavy weight I been carrying! It's just gone!"

"Thank God!" Grace was weeping, too, and she noticed that a few of the patients were watching and listening avidly. Glancing around, she saw that the tall soldier who'd never spoken was leaning against the wall, watching them. Grace smiled at him, but there was no change in the stolid countenance. She turned back to Aaron and rejoiced with him. Finally she said, "Now, Aaron, let me ask thee to do something."

"Yes, Miss Grace?"

"Tell people what God has done for thee," Grace said. "Follow Jesus. Learn to love him more. I will teach thee to pray and to read the Bible, but thee is a new creature, and it will help thee to tell people."

"Why, shore I will!" Bent exploded. He glanced around the room and said, "Some of these pore fellas can't understand much, but I'll shore tell 'em what God's done for me!"

He rose at once, saying, "Hey, Cyrus, lemme tell you what jest happened."

Grace sat at the table, unable to contain her tears. This was the first real breakthrough in Ward K, and her heart overflowed with thanks to God. Doubt had come to her many times, and the devil had whispered to her that all her efforts were in vain. Now she knew that wasn't true, and the power of the gospel was at work all around her!

Getting to her feet, she wiped the tears from her face and moved around the room, speaking to the men—and the blank looks in most of their faces didn't discourage her at all! When she came to John Smith, she smiled brightly, saying, "John, you're going to be set free! Jesus Christ is able, and I'm going to pray harder than ever for you!"

She left the ward, going at once to share her good news with Miss Dix and others. Some would doubt and scoff, but Grace was strong in the power of the Lord and cared not one pin what they thought or said! Had she not seen today the power of God displayed in her ward? And what God could do once, he could do again!

The stove made popping noises as the wood burned. There were two stoves, one close to where he stood and another like it down at the other end of the room.

Everything was white and clean. Two rows of beds ran the length of the room, their heads touching the walls. Some of the beds were empty, but others held men who wore white shirts of some kind and lay still.

Looking down he saw that he was wearing a dark blue shirt. He wondered why he wasn't wearing a white shirt like the men in the bed. His pants were light blue, and he had on black boots.

Something was warm in his hands, and he looked down. He stared at the brown cup filled with black hot liquid, not understanding what it was.

Then a voice came to him, and he was suddenly afraid. He didn't know why, though, and that made the fear worse. He looked at the table to his right and saw a man wearing the same kind of clothing he had on. He was a small man with bushy hair and wide-staring eyes. He was looking up at the ceiling and saying in a shrill whisper, "George Washington, George Washington, George Washington—!"

The staring eyes turned in his direction and he wanted to run out of the room—but what would be there waiting for him? He looked around, and the sight of a nearby blank-faced man walking slowly back and forth and wringing his hands brought more fear.

It was better in the dark—there were no blank-faced men there. He closed his eyes, trying to go back into the warm darkness where there was nothing to frighten him. The darkness began to close in and he felt himself slipping back. It was like a huge pool that was creeping up his body, and he knew that it would cover his chest, then his head—and there would be nothing then but the void . . .

But he wrenched his eyelids open with a physical effort, for he suddenly remembered that there were terrible things in the darkness, too! He couldn't remember them clearly, but shadows and phantoms danced across his brain, and he began to tremble.

A noise came to him, and he looked to his left where one of the men dressed in blue was squatting on the floor and flapping his arms like a chicken. He was making odd noises and advancing steadily. Again he wanted to run, but that would have meant leaving the room.

He closed his eyes and heard something hit the floor.

"Hey, Smith, you spilled your coffee!"

He opened his eyes to find a man standing in front of him. The man was small, but his eyes were filled with anger.

"I got more to do than clean up your mess!" The man pulled a rag from his pocket and tossed it at him. "Wipe that up! What'd you do that for?"

"I don't know."

The man's jaw sagged and his eyes flew open wide. He grunted sharply, then reached out and grabbed the patient's arm. "Hey—what'd you say?"

"I—don't know—"

Jesse Ormstead could not believe his ears. His mouth clicked shut, and he whispered, "You all right, Smith?"

"Yes, I'm all right."

Ormstead dropped Smith's arm, wheeled, and dashed out of the room.

Smith began to be afraid again. *I did something wrong,* he

thought, and he closed his eyes trying to slip back into the darkness. His hands trembled, and he discovered he held the rag the man had given him. He stared at the pool of black liquid at his feet, then stooped down. He mopped it up, then stood up, the cup and rag in his hand, wondering helplessly what to do with them.

He heard a man's voice arguing loudly and looked down the room to see the man who'd given him the rag come in with a woman behind him.

"You'll see!" Jesse Ormstead was saying as he burst through the door. "He talked just as plain as you or me! Come on and I'll show you!"

Grace had been in the next ward when Ormstead had come bursting in, speaking so excitedly that she'd had to ask twice what he was babbling about. When she understood, she whirled and followed the orderly, her mind reeling with what she'd heard.

"Now, come on, Smith," Ormstead coaxed. "Say something!"

His relentless demand frightened Smith, who looked down at the cup in his hand in confusion.

"Let me try, Jesse." Grace moved forward and took the cup and rag from the man's loose grasp. When he looked up at her, she saw the fear in his eyes. Quietly she said, "Don't be afraid, John. Nobody's going to hurt you." Encouraged by the way he looked at her, she said, "I'm Nurse Swenson. Do you know me?"

Nurse Swenson? Yes, I know her . . . she takes care of me—
"Yes, I . . . I know you."

"See? Didn't I tell you?" Jesse Ormstead crowed. He looked around at the men who were watching as if he'd done something wonderful. "See, he can talk good as me!"

Grace wanted to get Smith away from the other patients. "Jesse, you stay here. I'm going to take the patient to see Miss Dix."

Ormstead grew sullen. "It wuz me who made him talk. You tell her that!"

"I'll tell her, Jesse." Grace smiled at Smith, saying, "Come along with me, will you, John?"

She turned and Smith followed her obediently. He glanced at the man who'd been saying "George Washington" and at the man who'd been scrambling across the floor toward him, and he was glad to be leaving.

As soon as they were outside, Grace put her hand lightly on the patient's arm, saying, "I want you to meet a very nice lady, John." She hesitated, then asked, "Are you afraid?"

He turned his eyes toward her. "Yes," he whispered quietly.

"You mustn't be afraid," Grace said, tightening her grip. "I won't leave you alone."

"All right."

Grace nodded, and the two made their way to the main building and, by a stroke of good fortune, found Miss Dix in and able to see them. When they entered the office, Grace saw surprise cross Miss Dix's face. "What's this, Nurse Swenson?" she demanded, rising to her feet.

"I wanted you to meet John Smith," Grace said, her face slightly pale.

Miss Dix stared at the tall man, then at Grace. "What is it?" she asked carefully.

"John, this is Miss Dix."

Miss Dix blinked, then at a nod from Grace said, a little breathlessly, "How are you, John?"

Smith looked quickly at Grace for assurance, then nodded. "I'm all right . . . Miss Dix."

Dorothea Dix gasped, then a smile spread across her face. "I can see you are!" She motioned at the chairs, saying, "Sit down, both of you." She came to stand in front of her desk and look down at them. Carefully she said, "It's good to see you so much better, John. You've been very sick."

Both women were watching the patient intently. He seemed to be in a daze, and when he spoke it was in a slightly husky whisper, as though his voice was rusty from disuse.

"What's wrong with me?"

At the sight of the tall strong man sitting there, looking so lost and helpless, a wave of pity rushed through Grace. Tears stung her eyes, and without thinking, she leaned over and put her hand over his, which were tightly clenched. "You've been injured, John. Do you remember anything about it?"

The broad brow creased with effort, but finally Smith shook his head. "No, nurse."

Miss Dix said quickly, "Well, it'll come back to you, I'm sure—" She broke off suddenly as something occurred to her. "You should know, though, that we weren't able to discover your real name. So we just called you John Smith. Perhaps you can tell us your real name now."

The two women waited, and when the man said nothing, they exchanged glances. "Just your name?" Grace said encouragingly.

But John Smith had closed his eyes and dropped his head. His hands were clenched so tightly together that the veins stood out like cords. He began to tremble, and Grace at once said, "John, don't worry about it! Don't be afraid!"

"But—I can't remember!" The dark eyes opened, and fear pooled in them as he cried out, "I can't remember my name!" He suddenly grasped Grace's hand, his iron grip hurting her. "Why don't I know who I am? What's *wrong* with me?"

Grace ignored the pain in her hand, saying very quietly, "Thee needs time, John. It'll be all right. Thee *will* remember. I promise you."

Smith stared at her, then slowly nodded and relaxed his grip. He slumped in his chair, seemingly exhausted.

Miss Dix's eyes narrowed, and she said quickly, "Nurse Swenson, why don't you take John for a walk. I'll have Nurse Miller take over your duties for a while."

Grace caught her meaning at once and nodded. "I think that would be nice. Come along, John. We'll get you a warm coat and we can go for a walk outside."

"All right." The tall man rose obediently and followed Grace out of the room.

Miss Dix stood at the window, thinking hard. Finally she saw the pair come out of a side door. They were both wearing blue coats, and the dark hair of the tall man made a striking contrast with the blonde locks of the woman. Miss Dix watched them as they walked slowly along and disappeared around the corner.

Dorothea Dix did not sit down for a long time, but gazed out at the rows of white buildings, thinking of what she had just seen. Finally she took a deep breath, then said aloud, "Well, we need a miracle once in awhile around here!"

Then she sat down at her desk and began writing in a small, cramped script.

CHAPTER TWELVE
"Thee Has a Man of Thy Own!"

★

Winter swept over Washington suddenly, bringing freezing rain, sleet, and driving snow, and the city struggled to free itself from the mountains of snow that were dumped on it from leaden skies. Nobody except the vendors of firewood and the excited children enjoyed it after the first fluffy drifts were transformed into sheets of ice.

On the second day of November Grace was sitting in a large oak rocking chair, knitting gray yarn into a large sock and watching the snow fall in slanting lines out of a buttermilk sky. Beside her in another rocker, his long legs stretched out, John Smith gazed through half-shut eyes at the large flakes, which were building a crystal mound on the outside of the window.

"This is nice, isn't it, John?"

"Yes, it is."

Grace was accustomed to her companion's brief answers. For the past two weeks she had spent a large part of every day with him, robbing other patients of her service. She had the implied consent of Miss Dix, who had said at the beginning of all this, "He needs you right now more than the others do, Grace. He has a chance to recover, but somebody must stay with him and lead him out of the darkness."

159

Grace had taken Miss Dix at her word, and not a day had passed but that she had spent hours with the mostly silent patient. Some of the other nurses had complained, as well as one or two of the patients, but Grace chose to ignore them. She was engrossed with the man known to her as John Smith—and it was more than a casual interest. She believed in what the Quakers called the Inner Light—a divine guidance, a word from God giving directions for living.

She had tried once to explain this part of her life to Lettie Johnson, but had made no headway at all. Lettie had listened carefully, but had finally demanded, "But if it's all in your head, Grace, how do you know it's not just what *you* are thinking?"

Grace had been unable to answer Lettie's question, for that *was* a problem. Sometimes her own thoughts were so intermingled with the things God was speaking, that she made mistakes. But this time, in the matter of John Smith, she knew as surely as she knew she was alive that God was using her to minister to his beclouded mind.

She had to restrain herself, however, for the temptation was strong to push him, to *force* him to remember his past. Early in their time together she had learned that this was counterproductive, for the more she attempted to pressure him, the more confused he grew until he withdrew into complete silence.

Now as they sat together on the small enclosed porch that looked out on the front of Armory Square Hospital, she spoke infrequently, and he sometimes offered a comment of his own. This in itself was progress, for two weeks earlier, he would sit for hours without volunteering a word.

Now Grace looked out the window at the snow. "It reminds me of home. In Pennsylvania, where I grew up, we have deep snows like this. Sometimes we go for rides in my father's sleigh. I always liked that so much." Her eyes grew dreamy and she stopped knitting as she went on in her quiet voice. "Riding in a sleigh is so *different* from riding in a wagon. Thee just glides over the snow, and there's no bumping . . . just a hissing sound. Thee can hear the bells jingling and the sound of the horses' hooves plopping into the snow."

Smith turned to look at her, then shook his head. "That sounds like fun. I've never done anything like that—at least I don't think so."

Never ridden in a sleigh? Where could thee have come from where thee has never gone for a sleigh ride? Grace wanted to pursue this, but feared that if she did, he'd grow moody and silent. Instead she merely said, "Well, maybe thee can visit my home and I'll take thee for thy first sleigh ride."

John Smith's lean face was smooth, and he nodded with some eagerness. "I'd like that, Miss Grace." He hesitated, then shook his head. "But I doubt it'll ever happen."

"Oh, perhaps it will," Grace said quickly. She started to speak, but a sudden fit of coughing overcame her. Her body was racked by the harsh spasm, and Smith watched her with some alarm.

"I don't like the sound of that cough," he said uneasily.

"Oh, it's just a cough, John."

But he leaned forward and looked into her face closely. "I don't think so. You've had it for almost a week. It's the same kind of cough that Davie and Sim and Dexter had."

Those three had developed a fever, which then went into pneumonia, and when Grace saw the concern on John's lean face, she knew he was unhappy. It was a good sign—and a bad one, she had come to understand. It was good that he'd come to trust her, but not so good in that he'd become dependent on her.

"Now, thee mustn't worry about me, John," she said with a smile, overcoming the need to cough by a monumental effort. "I'm well enough."

He was not satisfied and turned to look out the window at the white landscape. It was this sudden tendency to turn his mind inward that troubled Grace, for she knew it was not good for him. She felt weak and tired, and she longed to go

161

home to bed—but somehow she felt that she could not leave him.

She went to the mess hall with him for dinner and, while she ate almost nothing, she was glad to see that he ate well. She watched him, studying his face while he gave his attention to his food. He had a strong jaw, determined and a little pugnacious, and the deep-set eyes glowed with intelligence. His mouth was a wide slash, and his long English nose gave him a slight aristocratic air. His raven black hair had a slight curl and was long enough to curl up over his coat collar; the black eyebrows formed a shelf over dark eyes.

He is good-looking, Grace thought, *but he has no idea of such a thing.*

He turned suddenly and met her eyes, and she felt her face redden as she dropped her gaze. "You haven't eaten two bites, Miss Grace," he said. "You have to eat."

"I had a snack earlier," Grace evaded his eyes, then said, "Thee has a good appetite, John. I think you've gained five pounds the last few weeks."

"I'm fit enough."

Grace glanced at him quickly, for there was a note in his tone that she recognized: a nonchalance that hid despair and depression. "Are you finished?" she asked. When he nodded, the two of them left and made their way back to the porch. "It's chilly out here," Grace said, "but let's sit and talk for a while before I go home."

He threw himself into a chair, and there was tightness in his lips as he stared out at the night sky. "You'd better go now," he muttered. "Not much fun talking to a man who has nothing to say."

"Oh, don't speak like that!" He really *was* despondent. Grace set herself to cheer him up. "You know how much I enjoy talking with you." She glanced out the window at the glittering stars that had come out. "Look, the sky's cleared," she said. "Maybe it won't snow any more."

"Maybe not."

Ignoring his short reply, she leaned forward, peered out

the window, and exclaimed, "Look at that star, John! It's so bright! I wonder which one it is?"

Glancing at the skies, Smith said, "That's Sirius, the Dog Star."

"Really? I don't know the name of any stars. I don't think most people do."

His answer had been casual, but he suddenly straightened his back and looked at Grace, his brows raised. "I can name most of those out there. I wonder how I came to know them."

A slight thrill ran through Grace, but she suppressed it, saying with a tone of mild interest, "Maybe thee was a sailor, John. They know the stars, don't they?"

He considered that, then shook his head. "No, I wasn't a sailor."

"No?"

"No. I don't know the names of the sails on ships. A sailor would know all those, wouldn't he?"

"Yes, I suppose so." She shivered in the cold. "People of all sorts study the stars."

"You mean like astrologers?" The thought caused him to smile. "Maybe I can tell your fortune or whatever it is they do."

"No, that's nonsense, John."

"Is it now?" He turned to her, interest making his eyes glow. "I seem to think that people guide their lives by the stars."

"Some do, but they're foolish." Grace thought for a moment, then said, "God made the stars, just as he made us. We're to learn about ourselves from God's Word, not from the stars."

Smith's lips tensed, and he said, "You read the Bible all the time, Grace. Is there anything in there about me? Will it tell me who I am?"

"In a way, yes, it will." Grace spoke very carefully, for he had never shown any interest in the spiritual side of his life.

"All of us need to know three things, John, about ourselves."

"What three things?" he asked, his curiosity aroused.

"All of us need to know where we came from, who we really are, and where we're going."

"I need that second one, at least," Smith said, irony in his voice. "I'd settle for that—just to know who I am."

"No, it wouldn't be enough, John," Grace shook her head. "The world is full of people who can give thee their names, but they don't really know who they are."

"I don't understand."

"They just live without God, as the animals do—and that's not enough."

He studied her face, intrigued by the smooth lines of her cheek. "Guess I don't understand any of it. I don't know where I came from, I don't know who I am, and I sure don't know where I'm going!"

Grace felt sympathy for him rising with her and reached out to touch his hand. "Neither do millions of people, John. And the false religions of the world have no answer. Only the Christian knows his beginning, for Christianity has the only answer. 'In the beginning God created the heavens and the earth.' And he made man, so that's where you came from. And only the Christian knows where he is going. The other religions say when man dies, he becomes less than a human, but Jesus said he himself would come back and that he would take us to live in a place prepared for us. That's the answer to the third question."

"Which leaves number two," Smith said evenly. "Who am I? Does Jesus answer that?"

"Yes, he does, John. Just before he died for our sins, he prayed, 'And now I am no more in the world, but these are in the world, and I come to thee. Holy Father, keep through thine own name those whom thou hast given me, that they may be one, as we are.' Isn't that marvelous, John? Jesus, the Son of God, prayed that we may be so joined to him that throughout all eternity we'll be *one* with him and the Father!"

Smith stared at the young woman, noting the light in her eyes and the joy in her face. But he finally shook his head, saying, "It's too much for me to take in, Grace. All I want to know is my *name!*"

Grace knew he was in despair, and quickly she said, "Don't let fear come to thee! God will help thee."

She sat there for fifteen minutes, then rose, saying, "I must go home, John—" But she had risen too rapidly, and a wave of dizziness caused her to weave.

"Miss Grace!" Smith reached out and steadied her. "What's wrong?"

Grace was so overcome with dizziness that she clung to him. He put his arms around her, and she yielded to his strength. Finally she drew back, laughing ruefully, "I just got a little giddy, John. I'm fine now."

"You shouldn't go all the way home in the dark and in this weather!"

"I'll be all right," Grace insisted and forced herself to smile. "I'll see thee in the morning."

She left the hospital, but when she finally got into a cab, she was feeling much worse. She began to cough, and her chest was racked with pain. She stumbled out of the cab, paid her fare, and, by the time she got into bed, was aware that she had a fever.

I can't be sick, she thought, but her head whirled. She began to sweat, and sometime later she awakened Lettie, who got up at once. "You're shaking, Grace!" she said in alarm. "I'll get Mama."

Grace protested, but Lettie was gone. She returned with Mrs. Johnson, who took one look and shook her head. "It's the ague," she announced. "I've got some medicine left over from when I had it last month."

"I can't be sick!" Grace protested feverishly. "I've got to be at the hospital at seven in the morning."

"No, you have not! You'll be down a week, if not longer.

I'll have Dr. McGuire come in tomorrow, but he'll not be telling me anything about the ague!"

And the next day it was as Ida Johnson had so firmly said: Dr. McGuire came, announced that Grace had the ague, prescribed the medicine that Mrs. Johnson had already started pouring down her patient's throat, and commanded her to stay in bed until she'd had no fever for twenty-four hours.

Grace's protests made no dent at all in Mrs. Johnson. She was kept in bed for five days despite her protests. She did persuade Lettie to carry a letter to Miss Dix, and she got one in return that was brief and to the point: *Stay in bed until you get well. You won't help matters by returning to duty too soon. I hope your recovery is swift.*

The days dragged by interminably for Grace. She knew there was no alternative but to rest, yet she fretted and longed for the day when she could get out of the house. For the first two days, she almost drove Mrs. Johnson to distraction with her pleas to be allowed to get up, but that stopped abruptly when her landlady finally asked her impatiently, "Aren't you Quakers supposed to be patient? I always heard you'd go to church and sit around waiting for hours for God to speak. Is that right?"

"Well, yes it is—"

"Then why don't you *act* like a Quaker?" Mrs. Johnson demanded. "You've got to stay in this house for a week. Why do you have to keep fretting and fussing and driving me crazy? I wish you'd show a little of that famous Quaker patience with *me!*"

The admonition struck home, and Grace lay quietly in bed from that time on. She became so docile that her landlady said with amazement, "I declare, I wish Lettie and Willie would pay as much attention to me as you do, Grace!"

And so time moved slowly, but Grace had learned her lesson. She began to practice the art of silence. Which meant that she lay in bed, thinking of God, praying, and asking God to make his will known to her. As she did so, peace washed over her. It was a strange sort of peace, for she had no idea what would happen in the future, but she realized she didn't need to know. She only needed to know the one who was in control.

Finally, the day came when she went for twenty-four hours without a trace of fever, and the next morning she got up and dressed. She was too weak to do anything more that day and the next, but on the following morning, she dressed, put on her heavy coat, and Ryan Callihan took her to the hospital. He'd been to see her twice while she was ill, and now he protested vehemently that she had no business getting out so soon.

But Grace only smiled, saying, "I'm well, Ryan. God will take care of me."

"That's as may be," the old man retorted as he pulled up in front of the hospital. "But I'm staying here to take you home, and no arguments."

"I won't stay long this morning, Ryan," Grace said. "Only an hour, perhaps."

"I'll be waitin' fer ye," he said grimly. He leaped down and helped her to the ground. She needed his help, for she was weaker than she had thought. Finally, he left her inside the door, saying, "Remember, I'll be waitin' right outside."

"Yes, I'll remember."

Grace went at once to Miss Dix's office and was greeted many times as she made her way down the halls. Miss Dix stared at her with surprise, then rose to come and greet her. "You're so thin!" she exclaimed. "And what in the world are you doing here? You'll have a relapse, Grace! You should know better!"

Grace took the chair she was offered, saying rather breathlessly, "Don't scold me, Miss Dix!" She smiled and pleaded, "I just couldn't stay away any longer."

Miss Dix stood rigidly before the young woman. "You're in no condition to work," she announced. "Look at you, trembling like a reed!"

"I'll be better soon!"

"Yes, in about a month," Miss Dix nodded. "You're on a thirty-day leave as of this day. Go home and do nothing but eat and sleep. You were falling down with overwork, and this sickness has hit you hard." And then her voice softened and she smiled. "I must be hard with you now, my dear, for your own good."

Grace pleaded, but Miss Dix was adamant. At the end of fifteen minutes, the superintendent said, "I'll call a cab for you."

"No, I have one waiting. But, please, I must visit a little."

"Well, make it a *very* little. Then go home to bed!"

Grace agreed and left Miss Dix's office. She was very tired, but went at once to Ward K. She had thought about all the patients, but it was John Smith who'd been foremost in her prayers. As she entered, she saw him standing with his shoulder against the wall. He looked tired, and there was defeat in the sagging shoulders.

She greeted all the men, then came to him. She was exhausted by now and spoke with an effort. "Hello, John."

"Hello." He stared at her, then shook his head, "You look weak. Why are you out in weather like this?"

"I—wanted to see thee, John."

He stared at her, then said somewhat bitterly, "Well, it's a good thing you came this morning."

She knew then that something was wrong. "What's the matter?"

"You don't know?"

"No. What is it?"

"I'm leaving here today."

"Leaving?" Grace tried to think but was so weary she could make nothing out of it. "Where is thee going?"

"To the devil, I suppose!" The answer came sharply from tense lips, but Smith saw how it hurt her and shook his head, saying in a gentler tone, "Sorry. Didn't mean to speak that way."

"Why is thee leaving?" Grace asked quietly.

"I've been asked to leave." He shrugged. "They say they need the space, and I'm able enough physically."

"But—where will thee go? I'll speak to Miss Dix—"

"No need of that. She was the one who told me I'd have to leave. It's not her choice," Smith said. "She told me she fought for me, but she has her superiors, and the order is for all able-bodied men to be discharged at once."

Grace stood there, filled with confusion. She was very tired, and her head ached, but even at that moment, she was aware that all this was not unknown to God. She whispered, "John, help me sit down . . . just for a little while."

He blinked with surprise, then shrugged. "Not much privacy around here."

"Take me to the porch, the one in front."

"All right."

He took her arm and was shocked at how weak she was. He walked slowly, and finally they reached the small enclosed porch. "Nobody here," he announced, "but it's cold as the North Pole."

"Just let me sit down . . ."

John helped her into one of the rockers, then stood to one side where he could watch her. She was very pale and thin, and when she closed her eyes, he saw that her eyes had grown sunken, giving her a distinctly unhealthy appearance. She put her head back, and he saw that her skin was very pale; she had lost the bloom of health that had always seemed so much a part of her.

As he watched her, he thought of how he missed her. The other men had missed her, too, but only as a source of physical care. He had not needed that, but he'd desperately needed that other thing she'd brought: the lively presence that had meant hope to him . . . the only hope he'd had.

Now he watched her. Though her eyes were closed, he was aware she was not asleep. Her lips were moving slightly, and he knew that she was in a realm of which he was totally ignorant. Despite the strength of her face, there was a

169

gentleness and a fragility such as he had not encountered in his new world.

Finally her eyelids fluttered, and then she was looking at him. Something about her expression was so changed that he stared at her, wondering what was in her mind.

"John, has thee been signed out?"

"Oh yes. They just wanted to keep me here to feed me at noon."

Grace nodded slowly. "Get thy kit together." When he stared at her uncomprehendingly, she smiled. "Thee is going with me. God has told me so."

John Smith was rocked by this as he had been by nothing since coming out of the coma. "God told you to do this?"

"Yes," Grace said firmly. "Now, pack thy things."

Smith stared at her, wanting to argue, but the strength of her gaze was such that he could not. "I'm already packed up," he said with a shrug. "They gave me ten dollars and told me to pack this morning after breakfast."

"Go now and get thy things."

He left at once, and Grace sat in the rocker, staring out the window. The snow had turned to ice, and it reflected glints of light as the sun struck it. When John returned, Grace rose and he took her arm. They left the balcony, and he led her through the corridor to the front door. When they stepped outside, Ryan Callihan spotted them at once. He spoke to the horses, and when he pulled the cab up, he said, "Put her inside, Soldier. I'll see her safe home."

"He's going with us, Ryan," Grace said. She looked up at the long step and tried to get in, but could not. Suddenly strong arms lifted her and she was lightly placed inside as easily as if she'd been a baby. She gasped and had one fleeting thought: *Clyde Dortch would never have been able to do such a thing!*

Then John was inside the coach, and she heard Ryan say, "Hup, Babe—Butch!" and the cab jerked forward.

John Smith looked out the window, watching as the low buildings of Armory Square Hospital were left behind.

Turning to her, he asked, "Where are we going?"

Grace took a deep breath and moved to meet his gaze. A smile touched her lips then, and she said, "Pennsylvania, John—to my home."

The steel-clad hooves of the team clicked against the icy streets, making a sharp sound on the stillness of the early morning air. The forms of ice-capped buildings flashed by, but though Grace was looking out the window, she saw none of them. She was thinking of Pennsylvania. And of the man beside her.

A smile curved her lips, and she thought, *Well, Grace Swenson, thee has a man of thy own. Now see what thee will do with him!*

CHAPTER THIRTEEN
A Sleigh Ride

★

Clyde Dortch was not in a happy mood. He snapped at Prudence as she set his breakfast out, and she blinked with resentment. "What's the matter with you, honey?" she asked petulantly. "Thee has been as touchy as a hornet lately."

Dortch scowled at her as he cut his fried eggs with the edge of his fork. He speared a large segment of one, stuffed it into his mouth, and chewed it. "I don't like it, Prue," he said after swallowing. "Why'd she have to bring that fellow home?"

"Why, he's been sick, Clyde," Prudence answered. "He didn't have any place to go when the hospital turned him out—not with him not knowing who his family is or anything."

Dortch glared at her as if she had lost her mind. "Does thee believe that fairy tale?" he demanded. "I don't. He's a bummer looking for a place where he won't have to work."

Prudence had started to sip her coffee, but his statement caused her to pause with the cup half lifted. "Thee doesn't really think that!"

"I'm not a fool—and that's what I'd be if I swallowed his cock-and-bull story. There's nothing wrong with him. He's strong as a workhorse." He chewed viciously on a piece of bacon, swallowed, then pointed at Prudence with his fork, punctuating each word with a jab. "Mark my words, he'll wind up marrying her, and we'll be out on our ear, Prudence!"

This had never occurred to Prudence, and the shock such a thought caused her ran over her face. She was not a thoughtful young woman. Since coming back home, she had been happy with her new husband and her new life. Now she grew frightened, for Clyde's face was dark with anger, and what he had said shook her.

"Grace would never do that to us," she whispered.

"No? Maybe *she* wouldn't," Dortch retorted, "but Smith would, in a second!"

Silence fell on the room as the two of them thought of what might lie ahead. Dortch was shaken, for he had fallen into the easy life of the farm at once. With two hired hands to do the work, he was freed from most of it. There was enough money for his needs, he had a handsome wife, and the future looked rosy.

Now all that was being threatened, and he had become an angry man since the arrival of his sister-in-law and her tall, silent guest. He had kept a smiling face when the pair were around, going to great trouble to welcome Grace back home, but his first glimpse of John Smith had set off a warning inside him. Being the kind of man he was—one who knew how to manipulate women—he suspected all other men of the same sort of behavior. As soon as Grace had introduced Smith, Dortch had thought, *He's after the farm! He'll marry Grace, and even if he lets us stay, I'll wind up doing all the work while he sits around and eats the cream!*

Dortch had not changed his mind since that first moment. Rather, he had fallen into a moody state, though he'd been careful not to show it to Grace. He'd had two weeks to think about it and had watched the pair carefully. Now he shook his head, an angry light in his brown eyes as he said, "We've got to do something about it, Prue."

"Do something? What can we do?" Prudence was upset, for she felt that her husband was a shrewd man, and if he was concerned, then something surely was afoot. "It's Grace's farm. . . . Oh, I don't see how Pa could give it to her and leave me out in the cold!"

Dortch didn't point out that their own reckless behavior might have had something to do with that. Instead he said, "We've got to get her to see the truth about that fellow Smith."

"She won't listen to us."

"Maybe not, but she listens to other people—like Jacob Wirt, for example." Wirt was an elderly man, a Quaker minister who had been Amos Swenson's best friend. He was in his eighties now, but Grace loved and revered him as she did no other man, now that her father was gone. "We'll have to let Wirt know that Grace is about to be foolish."

Prudence nodded slowly. "If anyone could do it, he'd be the one. Grace dotes on the old man." She thought of it and asked finally, "But he's a sharp one, no matter if he is old. How will we get him on our side?"

"I'm going to see him today," Dortch said at once. "I've been thinking about it, how to get the old man to talk to Grace." Dortch was a scheming man and had indeed been carefully plotting his move. "What I'll do is go see him, and I'll tell him we're worried about Grace. I'll say, 'She's been very sick, and this man has taken up with her. You know Grace, how kind she is, and he's taking advantage of her, so Prudence and I think you should have a talk with her.' That's what I'll say, and I'll bet he'll do it. He's always been jealous of Grace, like she was his only chick!"

Prudence nodded thoughtfully. "It ought to work, but I don't know." Her eyes narrowed and she shook her head. "That man is so handsome! Grace is still mad, if you ask me, because you took me instead of her. Now she's got a chance at a big, fine-looking man like that—"

Always sensitive to any reference to his lack of height, Dortch snapped angrily, "We'll see about that! I'll just cut that fellow down to size!" He rose and yanked his coat and hat from the rack, starting for the door.

175

"Clyde, you haven't finished your breakfast!"

"Save it for that 'big handsome man' upstairs!" Dortch left the room, slamming the door so hard the glass rattled. He saddled his horse quickly, then left the farm, spurring the stallion into a dead run.

"John, let's have that sleigh ride thee never had. It's going to be a fine evening for it."

John paused in the act of hefting an axe and looked at Grace. She was sitting on a sawbuck watching him split wood, and he thought how much change two weeks of rest and good food had made in her appearance. When they'd arrived at the farm, he'd had to carry her into the house, she'd been so exhausted by the long train ride. He'd been afraid she might have a relapse, but getting home had seemed to infuse new life into her. She had gotten up the next day, eaten the food that Prudence cooked, and talked animatedly. The following day she had sat on the porch, watching the hands put up a new fence. From that time on she had improved rapidly, so that now as he glanced at her, he was amazed at how well she looked.

She was wearing a dark blue wool dress, with a pair of sturdy black boots peeping out from underneath the skirt. A wine-colored scarf was knotted around her throat, and a blue-and-white wool knitted cap perched on her head. Her fine blonde hair escaped, blowing with the slight breeze, and he was glad to see the rich color in her face and the liveliness in her sparkling blue eyes.

Suddenly he was aware that he was staring at her, and he quickly turned his attention to the wood. "I'd like a sleigh ride," he said, then set a round section of the beech upright. Lifting the axe, he brought it down with a sharp, hard blow that divided the wood neatly in two. He split the two halves into quarters, and then tossed the sections on the top of a pile almost as high as his belt.

"Thee splits wood better than any man I ever saw," Grace remarked. "It looks so easy when you do it!"

"I must have had a lot of practice," he remarked. He smiled at her, his teeth very white against his dark skin. "Maybe I worked in a woodyard."

Grace smiled, glad that he had reached the point where he could talk about his cloudy past without becoming depressed and moody. "I don't think so. Thee doesn't look like a woodcutter."

"Oh?" he asked, lifting one eyebrow quizzically. "What do I look like? A lawyer?"

"No, not a lawyer." Grace's tone was light, and she shook her head, adding, "Thee looks too honest for that."

"You don't like lawyers? First time I ever heard you speak against anyone."

"They're caught in a devious trade," Grace said quickly. "Besides, thee is too—" She broke off, suddenly embarrassed.

"I'm too what?" he demanded.

Grace had been about to say, "Thee is too fine-looking to be a lawyer," but changed it to, "Thee is too much an outdoorsman to be a lawyer." Color tinged her cheeks at the statement she'd almost made, but as she watched him place another section of beech upright, she thought, *He is fine-looking. More than any man I've ever seen.*

He was wearing the same light blue trousers he'd worn in the hospital, and the exercise had caused him to take off the heavy woolen coat, which had belonged to her father. John's coal-black hair glistened as the red rays of the afternoon sun touched it, and the powerful muscles of his back, arms, and chest were clearly defined through the thin cotton shirt he wore. He split the log, tossed the sections on the pile, then grinned at her.

"I'm tired of this. Let's go look at the new colt."

"All right."

"Not too tired?"

"Oh, no!" Grace rose quickly, and the two of them left the backyard, following a path that led down to the barn. As they walked along, he remarked, "You're much better. I was worried about you."

Grace was pleased with his remark. "Good. I've worried about thee enough, John. It's only fair thee should worry a little about me."

He glanced at her, liking it that she was able to tease him. Still he said, "I really was worried. You were pretty weak."

She thought of how he'd had to carry her off the train like a child and put her into the buggy he'd rented for the trip to the farm. He had taken care of her all the way on that trip. It had been the first time she'd been so zealously cared for, and the memory of it had stayed with her. "I'd never have made that trip without thy care, John."

Her remark brought color to his cheeks. "Well, maybe I was just looking out for myself," he muttered. "I didn't have any other place to go."

"No, that wasn't it." Grace spoke firmly, shaking her head slightly. She dropped her hand to pet the massive head of Rip, the shaggy sheepdog, who nuzzled her. "Get away, Rip," she protested. She walked along silently, then said, "Thee is a very kind man."

Her praise disturbed him. He shook his head, saying, "Don't know about that, Grace. I am a very grateful one, though."

She glanced at him quickly and felt sure he'd been waiting for this chance to speak with her. "I'm grateful that God has let me help thee, John."

"You have helped me, Grace," he said slowly. He had thought about this for days, and now in the quietness of the afternoon, he spoke out what had been building in his mind. "I've never told you, but the first time I began to wake up was when you prayed for Aaron Bent."

"I never knew that!"

"It was like a faint echo, I guess you might say." Smith tried to find words, then shook his head. "It's hard to say how it was, Grace. The best I can put it is that it was like I was locked in a black box with no light and no sound. And then I heard this voice. Your voice, and you were praying for Aaron."

"Thee didn't show it."

"No, but it was the beginning. After that, I began to be aware of things. Mostly of you."

As they reached the corral, the leggy colt lifted his head from underneath his mother to stare at them. Smith called out, "Come here, little fellow." As the colt staggered across the rough ground, he added, "It was you praying for me and reading the Bible for me that brought me out of that darkness."

Grace watched as the colt reached a spot five feet away and stared at them, wild-eyed and ready to bolt. "I didn't think thee heard me."

Smith reached into his pocket and came out with a lump of brown sugar. He held it out, and the colt advanced nervously. He licked the sugar, tentatively at first, then with greater pleasure. When it was gone, John reached out to touch his head. The colt snorted, leaped back, and bolted in a wild stagger back to his mother.

"I heard you, Grace." He wiped his hand on the top rail, then turned to her. "And then when you came to the hospital, still sick, I was about as low as a man can get." Shaking his head, he said slowly, "If you hadn't come when you did . . ."

When he didn't finish, Grace said gently, "I think God knew we needed each other, John."

They stood there, watching the colt, laughing at his antics. John gave Grace some sugar, and she enticed the foal to come to her, enjoying the rough texture of his tongue on her palm.

Finally he said, "Better not do too much. I still want to go on that sleigh ride."

"So do I!"

After supper that night, John went to hitch the team to the sled, and Prudence, still thinking of what Clyde had said, tried to talk with her sister. "Thee doesn't know much about him, does thee, Grace?"

"He doesn't know much about himself."

"Fellow like that, why, he might be anything," Clyde spoke up. "No telling what kind of man he is. Could be a bank robber."

"No, he's not that," Grace said instantly, then seeing the two glance at her, she defended her statement. "He's not that sort at all."

Prudence remarked innocently, "I've wondered about his wife and children."

Grace was startled. "How does thee know he's married?"

"A fine-looking man like that?" Prudence snorted. "Of course he's married!"

"Even if he isn't," Clyde added, "he could never marry any woman as he is. He could never be sure—nor the woman, either—that he wasn't committing bigamy." He was watching Grace's face and saw that his remark had troubled her. He said, "I saw Jacob Wirt today, Grace. He wants to see you."

"I've missed him," Grace said, glad to have the subject changed. "I'll go see him this week." She heard the sound of the horses outside and got up to put on her coat. "There's John with the sleigh."

"Don't stay out too long, Grace," Prudence called as Grace left the room. "It's too cold out there for you."

But Grace only waved and left the house. She climbed into the leather seat, and John said, "Better pull that blanket over your feet. It's sharp out tonight."

When he had seen to wrapping her carefully in the blanket, he spoke to the horses, and they stepped out at once. As they left the yard and turned toward the open country that lay east of the farm, he said, "You were right, Grace. This is much different than a buggy ride!"

A huge silver moon shed its beams over the snow, which gave back a glistening reflection. The sleigh traveled easily over the hard-packed crystals, making a sibilant sound.

There was no rocking, and John said, "It's almost like flying isn't it?"

"Yes. I've always loved it. My father took us all for rides like this, almost every night. He loved it, too."

They spoke quietly as John drove the horses at a slow trot, and finally they reached the small lake that glittered under the pale moonlight. Stopping the horses, he tied the reins and leaned back to admire the view. "So quiet! I didn't know a place could be so quiet!"

Grace swept her eyes over the view. "I've missed this."

They sat quietly, letting the stillness sink into their spirits. Perhaps it was this silence that finally prompted John to say, "I didn't want to say anything until I was sure, but things are coming to me, to my mind."

"You're beginning to remember your past?" she asked at once.

"Well, not exactly—"

She saw his hesitancy, then asked, "Can thee tell me what it's like?"

He pushed his hat back, then said slowly, "It's like being in a large room with all sorts of objects. I see them and know what they're for, but I don't know what they have to do with me." He frowned, for he felt he was doing a bad job of explaining. He shook his head and remained silent.

"Does thee remember anything for certain?"

"Faces." He nodded. "All kinds of faces. People I don't know, but who seem to know me. And sometimes it's . . . well, like *scenes* in a play. I seem to be in the play, and I'm doing things. Simple things, usually, like eating a meal with someone. Sometimes doing something that I don't understand, but with people I ought to know—and don't."

A great sympathy welled up in Grace. She turned to him and put her hands on his, unconscious that she'd done so. "It'll come back, John," she whispered. "God will help thee!"

He sat there, and it was a few moments before he began to respond to her. They talked quietly, watching the moonlight on the snow and the lake. The air was still, but cold, and when Grace began to shiver, he said, "You're getting cold! I should have brought another blanket!"

"When we came here when I was a child, we all huddled under the blankets together," she recalled with a smile.

"Well, I guess we can do that." John pulled the blanket over them, then put his arm around her shoulders and drew her close. It gave Grace a peculiar feeling, being held close this way, but John had done it so naturally that she moved against him without restraint.

"That better?"

"Yes, it is."

They sat there, huddled together under the blanket, sharing their warmth. Suddenly he said, "I just remembered something—a line of poetry, I think."

"What is it?"

"'Two are better than one, because they have a good reward for their labor,'" he quoted. "Don't know what that is."

"It's from the Bible, John, from the fourth chapter of Ecclesiastes." She could feel the warmth of his arm on her shoulder, and she whispered, "I'm glad thee told me that!"

He turned to face her, blinking with surprise. "I remember more of it," he said and spoke again. "'For if they fall, the one will lift up his fellow; but woe to him that is alone when he falleth; for he hath no other to help him up.'"

"That's such a beautiful verse!" Grace whispered, gazing out at the lake. "I've always loved it so."

John smiled and went on. "'Again, if two lie together, then they have heat: but how can one be warm alone?'"

Grace smiled and looked up at him. They were very close, closer than either of them had realized. He could feel the firmness of her shoulders under his arm, and the curves of her body pressed against his side. Her eyes were enormous under the light of the moon, and the rich curve of her lips made her suddenly very lovely.

She was looking up at him, and without intending to do

so, he lowered his head, letting his lips fall on hers. She didn't move, and the softness of her lips was sweet under his. He had no thought, all was impulse, and he let his lips linger on hers, savoring the moment.

Grace was shocked, but there was something in her that had longed for such gentleness. John was not demanding, and the caress brought her some sort of fulfillment deep within, a fulfillment she had not even been aware she needed.

She had always been a lonely child—and an even lonelier young woman. Now as John held her firmly, she was only conscious that somehow this was something she had longed for—and it was sweeter than she could ever have imagined.

Then she pulled back, and when John saw tears glistening in her eyes, he was stricken. "Grace—!" he whispered. "I'm sorry!"

She put her hand on his lips. "No, thee must not be sorry," she said. "It was my fault."

"I—I've just been so lonely, Grace," he said after a long silence. He moved away from her. "I wouldn't hurt you for anything in the world." And then he tried to smile as he gave his only excuse. "You looked so beautiful, so lovely, I . . . I just couldn't help it!"

His words were like ointment to her spirit. Grace had heard so many other young women telling what their lovers had said, yet she had been forced to remain silent—for there were no lovers speaking to her. Now she had felt the caress of a man's lips and heard his tender words—and she was happy.

"We're both lonely, John," she said quietly. "I think we're entitled to one mistake."

Mistake. The word stung, though he did his best not to show it. He knew he and Grace could never be more than friends, not while he had no memory of his life before the hospital. Yet, as he gazed down at her in the moonlight, he suddenly realized that his feelings for this strong, devout, beautiful woman went much deeper than mere friendship.

But if she considered their kiss a mistake, then it would be best for him to keep his feelings to himself. She had done so much for him, he didn't want to impose on her tender heart with protestations of a love she did not want.

He nodded, then took the reins and spoke to the horses. They rode back and soon were talking easily. But when he lifted her out of the sleigh, they both knew that something was different. They could never be the same again, for the kiss and the moment had stirred things deep within both of them—things that would not easily be forgotten.

CHAPTER FOURTEEN
An Unexpected Visitor

★

At the same time that Grace Swenson was engaged in her own private battle to redeem the soldier she knew as John Smith from his bondage, the war rolled on. After Lee and Jackson had wrecked John Pope at Second Manassas, President Lincoln was in despair, thanks to the military genius of Robert E. Lee.

Four classic victories—the Seven Days', Second Manassas, Fredericksburg, and Chancellorsville—all confirmed Lee as the most gifted general of the American Civil War. He was the greatest living war asset of the Confederacy. No other general in that conflict, and few others in military history, ever displayed such a wide-ranging talent for making bricks without straw. When it came to turning retreat into advance, vulnerability into sudden dazzling promise, Robert E. Lee stood alone.

Under Lee's hand, the Army of Northern Virginia became a master weapon, one that marched into military legend with its commander. Never in the darkest days of the war did Lee even once lose the personal devotion of his army's rank and file.

This, then, was the adversary whom Lincoln faced, and the president was hard put to find a general to stand against Lee. After the debacle of Second Manassas, he put McClellan in charge again, for though the small commander had no killer instinct, he was the best general alive at putting heart into defeated men and getting them whipped into shape for another campaign. He met the defeated troops of Gen. Pope and molded the broken Army of the Potomac into a fine striking force.

Unfortunately, Lincoln did not replace McClellan with a fighting general. He had one, though he did not realize it: one Ulysses S. Grant, who in the end would be the hammer that would bring down the Confederacy. But Grant was fighting at Vicksburg right then, and Lincoln thought he had no choice but to let McClellan lead the Army of the Potomac. Even if he *had* tried to replace McClellan, it would have caused a rebellion, for the troops admired Little Mac to a fault.

So it was that when Lee led the tattered Army of Northern Virginia into Maryland, it was McClellan he faced at Antietam. McClellan outnumbered his adversary by something like two to one and should have steamrollered Lee's thin ranks. But Little Mac once again failed to send his men into the fury of battle. Instead of ordering an overall assault, he sent men in by small units, thus giving Lee time to shift his divisions from spot to spot on that bloody field, stemming the Union tide.

Nothing reveals Lee's superiority over McClellan more than the fact that the Union commander had in his hand that which should have guaranteed Lee's destruction. For on September 13, two Federal soldiers from Indiana found some cigars wrapped in paper on the site of Lee's encampment—a paper that proved to be a missing copy of Special Order 191, which gave Lee's exact movements!

And even with *this* advantage McClellan could not acheive a decisive win!

When the battle took place on Wednesday, September 17, McClellan failed miserably. The battle was bitter, and it cost the lives of more men than any other day of the war—

12,500 Union soldiers and 13,000 Confederates killed or wounded.

Amazingly, after the battle, McClellan still had a chance to destroy the Confederate forces, for Lee's battered army was helpless. But Little Mac was so dominated by fear of Robert E. Lee that he let the Army of Northern Virginia slip away, taking its wounded. As a result, although the North won the battle at Antietam, it lost an invaluable opportunity for possibly speeding the end of the entire conflict.

Still, Antietam was enough of a success to accomplish one thing. Lincoln had been waiting for a Union victory to take a far-reaching step: to proclaim all slaves in the country free men. This he did by means of the Emancipation Proclamation.

Even so, Lincoln was through with McClellan. The absolute final straw for the exasperated president came the day after the battle, when McClellan refused to obey a direct order from Lincoln to attack Lee. In early November 1862, McClellan was relieved of his command, and Maj. Gen. Ambrose E. Burnside took over the Army of the Potomac.

In one way this was a desperate move on the part of Abraham Lincoln, but the president had reason to be desperate. The North was ready to quit—at least many of its citizens were. Even after the battle of Antietam, the Confederacy had sound reasons for optimism. The South was united in its goal: to keep the unprincipled and wholly ruthless foe at bay. There was no such unifying emotion in the North, where feelings were split over the war. The Peace party was booming its drums, and it seemed likely that England would declare its support of the Confederacy.

Truthfully, the North was worn down with war-weariness. Twice in the eighteen months since Sumter, the Union had succumbed to the siren call "On to Richmond!" Both attempts had been defeated in battle. Now the road to Richmond was blocked again by Lee's army, which, if not fought there, would invade the North again under its daring commander.

So the president appointed Burnside, who would begin a new Union assault against the South—and the appointment sent echoes through the entire North, changing the destinies of countless thousands.

Throw a stone into a quiet lake, and its ripples move in circles evenly out to the edges of the shore. But if you drop two stones, the ripples intersect into a more complicated pattern. Throw in a handful of sand, and all is confusion. The stone of Burnside's appointment was merely one factor in a series of days that further complicated the war, but it was the factor that sent a ripple that carried all the way to a small farm in Pennsylvania where Burke Rocklin, known as John Smith, had just begun his painful climb out of the black pit of amnesia. Slowly, he seemed to be gaining ground, so that he felt he could see faint glimmers of light and hope.

Then came the ripple that threw all into confusion—and it came in the form of Col. Harold Drecker. A man with a vision, Drecker was a moderately successful manufacturer of furniture who lived, not for his tables and chairs, but for a dream of military glory. At the age of forty-three, he had seen his chance for this glory and after Antietam had begun to raise a regiment. He had mortgaged his factory to the hilt, left his brother-in-law to run it, and started out to form the Merton Blue Devils. He had bought the flashiest uniform money could purchase, a sword with a golden handle, and a fine war-horse. Spending his money lavishly on bounties, he had managed to fill the ranks of his company to about 50-percent strength. When enlistments had dropped off, he had used every means at his command to get his men.

One of these methods was to call back to active duty soldiers who had not served out their enlistments for one reason or another. Some of the soldiers Drecker sought out were those who had been mustered out before their time had expired—others were those who had been wounded, but had since recovered.

It was almost an accident that Col. Drecker got one particular name—one of his lieutenants had the brilliant idea of going through the list of wounded men who had been released from the hospital. Among these was the name of one John Smith.

"He's able-bodied, Colonel," the young lieutenant said as he went over the list with Drecker. "But I couldn't find out his rank or his former outfit."

Drecker said instantly, "We'll have him, Lt. Little! Where is he?"

"Apparently living on a farm not far from here, over by Rogers."

"Ah! I'll be in Rogers next week for a rally." Drecker beamed. "I'll stop by and bring the fellow back with me."

Lt. Bob Little was dubious. He had never served in the army; his current rank he held by virtue of being the nephew of Col. Drecker. He was a slight young man with a smooth face and a pair of mild blue eyes. "Don't know about that, sir," he protested. "Do you have the authority to bring men like that back into service?"

"Yes, indeed, from Secretary Stanton himself! I'll get him, Bob, don't worry! You can have him in your company if he looks like a good one."

And so it was that chance and happenstance sent Col. Harold Drecker to Grace Swenson's small Pennsylvania farm. Of such small things life is constructed, and no man is able to know or explain why these things happen—or fail to happen!

As December approached, it seemed it would reverse the biting cold blasts of November and bring relief to Pennsylvania. With each passing day, snow began to melt slowly under the sun's rays, and by contrast the breeze seemed to grow almost warm and balmy.

Though Grace was as strong as she'd ever been, she had requested—and received—permission from Miss Dix to extend her stay for another month. Miss Dix had not asked the reason, for she had read all she needed to know in Grace's letter. *Come back when you can give your full heart to the work,* she had written, and Grace had been quick to tell John that she was not going back until spring.

As for himself, John was happy. He was fully recovered physically and spent his days working on the farm and his evenings inside the snug house, reading or talking to Grace. He had become fascinated by the Bible and asked endless questions of her. Many of them she could not answer, so the two of them had gone three times for study with Jacob Wirt. The old scholar had welcomed them, and Grace knew that he was examining John Smith carefully. She trusted Wirt implicitly and waited impatiently for his judgment of the young man.

It came one evening when another guest had taken John upstairs to show him some samples of fine early furniture. Wirt leaned back and put his wise old eyes on Grace. "Well, thee isn't asking me what I think of the young man?"

"Oh, thee knows I want so much for thee to like him!"

"Why?"

"Because . . . the Lord is doing a work in him—and he is using me as part of it."

"Ah? Thee sees him as a convert? Thee is a holy young woman!" Grace knew Wirt was laughing at her and she blushed visibly—which only drew a broad smile from Wirt. "Has thee noticed he is a handsome fellow?" he inquired.

"Why, I believe most would say so."

"Most? What does thee say, Grace? And let thy answer be yea or nay."

Grace met Wirt's eyes and nodded. "Yes, he is handsome."

"He seems very strong."

"He—is very strong." The flush on her cheeks and neck grew richer, for she had thought, *What if he asks me how I know John is strong?*

"Ah. And he is intelligent, very much so." Wirt studied the girl, thinking back over the years he had known her—all her life, actually. He had grieved over her aborted marriage, for he had told an intimate friend that of all the young women in their community, Grace Swenson was likely to make the best wife. But he knew he had to make himself plain to Grace, so he said, "What is his view of God? He listens much, but says little."

"I think he is a seeker, Jacob."

"I sense that in him." Wirt grew silent, his sharp chin settling on his thin chest.

Finally Grace grew impatient. "What does thee think of him?"

Wirt lifted his eyes. "He is outside of my experience, Grace—as he is outside of thine. We have no way of knowing what sort of man he really is. He's like a babe, with no past—and yet he *does* have a past, one that I cannot help but believe will one day catch up with him." He paused, then added gently, "Thee knows all these things. Be careful, my daughter. I think thee could be in grave danger."

Grace understood the old man's gentle warning perfectly and was aware that she would get no approval from him. But she was shocked at his next statement. "Thy brother-in-law thinks John Smith is a deceiver. He asked me to warn you to have nothing to do with him."

Grace was indignant. "He had no right to come to thee!"

Wirt smiled and shrugged his shoulders. "He is afraid for himself and his wife."

Grace fell silent. She was painfully aware of the resentment in Clyde and Prudence, but she refused to speak of it, even to Wirt. Still, she knew the old man wanted some reassurance from her, and she gave it. Reaching out, she took his hand in hers, smiled and nodded. "I will be as wise as possible. Thee must pray much for me. I am a trouble to thee, Jacob."

"Never! Thee is the apple of my eye!"

On the way back to the farm Grace noticed that John was unusually quiet. When they entered the house, he said, "Before you go to bed, I want to show you something, Grace." Reaching into his inner coat pocket, he drew out an envelope and handed it to her. "This came yesterday," he said evenly.

Grace took the envelope with a puzzled look, took out the single sheet of paper, and scanned it. It was written in a woman's hand and was very brief:

> My dear Mr. Smith:
>
> I have just returned from a visit with Miss Dorothea Dix, superintendent of nurses at the Armory Square Hospital. My purpose was to try and find my husband, Matthew. He has been missing since the second battle of Bull Run. I have made every inquiry, including many with the Confederate war prisons, all to no avail.
>
> Miss Dix related your history, and I write this letter to inquire if your memory has returned. If it has, you will of course be restored to your people. If you are still suffering from a loss of memory, I will simply give you a description of my husband. He is tall, several inches over six feet, and on the lean side. He has black hair and dark eyes. He is thirty-five years of age.
>
> My two sons and my daughter I have not told of this possibility. I write with little hope, but if this fits your description and you would like to meet me, I can be reached at the address at the bottom of this letter.
>
> Mrs. Leota Richards

Something caused a constriction to grip Grace's throat, and she swallowed hard before she looked up to say, "Does thee think she may be right?"

"No way to tell." John's face was tense, and he shook his head with a negative expression. "I fit the description pretty well, but so must a thousand other men."

"What will thee do?"

"Already done it," John answered. "I wrote back, saying I'd meet her."

"Oh." Grace felt a pang of disappointment, for she had

assumed that he'd talk it over with her before acting on it. Then she said quickly, "Yes, thee must see her."

"I knew you'd think so." His brow suddenly wrinkled and a strange look came into his eyes. "What if I am her husband? With three children I can't even remember? And there must be other family—parents, brothers—"

"Thee must not worry," Grace said at once. "God will give you the truth of it."

"I guess Mrs. Richards will do that," John said tightly. He suddenly took her hands, saying, "I'm always trouble for you, aren't I, Grace?"

"How could you be trouble?" she protested. The warmth and strength of his hands made her nervous. Withdrawing her own hands, she said, "Go to bed. Read the Gospel of John. It's God's best prescription for a troubled heart."

But the Gospel, for once, failed to calm her own spirits. She read for a long time, but when she put the Bible down and blew out the lamp, sleep would not come. The letter had shaken her world, and she tossed for what seemed like a long time. Finally she drifted off, but slept only fitfully.

Three days later an answer came. Grace herself picked it up from the post office, and it lay like lead in her purse all the way back to the farm. She found John splitting rails for a fence, and as soon as he saw her face he asked, "What's wrong?"

"Thee has an answer from . . . the woman who wrote."

He put the maul down, took the envelope, and stared at it. Then he looked up and said wistfully, "I'd like to burn this without opening it."

"No, thee must not do that."

"I suppose not." He opened the envelope, ran his eyes over the page, then looked up. "She's coming here, Grace."

That surprised Grace. "Here? I thought she'd ask thee to come to her."

He handed her the letter. "Her family lives in Gettysburg. She'll take the train there, then come here."

"When—when will she come?" Grace asked.

"Next week." John folded the paper and put it in his pocket. He stared down at the ground steadily, then expelled his breath. "For some reason this scares me. You'd think I'd be happy as a lark, wouldn't you?"

"It's a very difficult thing." Grace shook her head, adding, "Anyone would be nervous, I think." She tried to smile, saying, "Just think, thee may be with thy family soon."

But he was gloomy and only shook his head. "Guess I'd better finish splitting these rails."

It didn't take long for Clyde to notice how quiet the tall man had become. He finally asked Grace, "What's wrong with him? He's not getting mental, is he? Going crazy?"

"Of course not, Clyde. He just has a heavy load."

The following day, that load grew much heavier.

John had gone into the woods to chop firewood, and when he returned, he found he had a visitor.

"This is John Smith," Grace said as he entered the house. "And this is Col. Harold Drecker, John."

"Glad to see you, Mr. Smith," the officer smiled. "Or is it *Private* Smith?"

John stared at the man. Drecker was wearing a spotless uniform of light blue trousers and a long, dark-blue coat with two rows of polished brass buttons. Shoulder-strap insignia bore the eagles that marked his rank. A high-crowned hat with the right brim pinned up and sporting a black ostrich feather lay on the floor next to his chair. A gilt-handled saber dangled from his left side.

"What can I do for you, Colonel?" John asked.

Col. Drecker smiled heartily. "Why, I've come to do something for you, Smith!" He spoke quickly, like a salesman, and had a habit of stabbing the air with his forefinger for emphasis. He did so now as he continued. "I'm planning to field the most distinguished regiment in the Army of the Potomac! I suppose you've heard that Gen. Burnside has been placed in charge?"

"Yes, I've read that in the paper."

"Well, sir, I've known the general for a long time, and he's been most enthusiastic about my efforts. In fact, he's promised me that the Merton Blue Devils—that's what my regiment is named—will be at the forefront of the fighting!" Drecker beamed with pleasure, and for the next fifteen minutes he spoke rapidly about what a glorious future lay ahead for the fortunate soldiers who would be under his command. They would, he asserted boldly, whip Bobby Lee and Stonewall Jackson, then march straight into Richmond!

"The only thing I fear is that Burnside will do the job before the Blue Devils can get into action!"

"I doubt you have to worry about that, Colonel," John said dryly. "But what brings you to see me?"

"Why, I thought I'd made myself plain," Drecker said with surprise. "I'm filling the places still available in the ranks of the Blue Devils, and you're being given a chance to join with me in driving the Rebels back to Richmond."

His proposal caught both his listeners off guard. Grace said, "Mr. Smith was invalided out on a medical discharge, Colonel."

But Drecker had thought that out. "Not really, Miss Swenson. His record shows that he was wounded and sent to Armory Square Hospital, and the record there clearly indicates that his wounds were healed and that he was discharged with a clean bill of health."

"But did thee not know of his—mental problems?"

"Oh, there was a note, I believe," Drecker muttered with a shrug, then spoke with energy, "but we must not give in to our fears. Many men break under the strain of battle, but they recover." He put his rather close-set brown eyes on the tall man, examined him critically, then nodded. "You seem very fit, Smith. How do you feel?"

"I'm all right, Colonel." There was no point, John saw at once, in arguing with this man.

"Of course you are!"

"But I have some—personal problems that I have to take care of, so I'm afraid I won't be going with your regiment."

Col. Drecker lost his smile, and a hard glint appeared in

his eyes. He was no longer the amiable recruiter. "You misunderstand me, Smith," he snapped harshly. "You *are* going with my regiment." He pulled a paper from his pocket, extended it, and continued as John read it, "You are not being enlisted, for you are already a soldier of the Union army. That paper will inform you of your status—that you and the others named there are under my command. And you will notice that it's signed by Secretary Stanton himself!"

John read the order, then slowly handed it back to the officer. "I have no choice, it seems."

Drecker, now that he had his man, grew congenial again. "Oh, you'll have time to get your business done," he said with a nod, slipping the paper back into his pocket. "The regiment is forming now. I want you to take a week, Smith. Report to my headquarters on the first of December." He turned, picked up his hat, and placed it firmly on his head. "Good to have you in my regiment, my boy! I'll see you in a week."

Drecker left the house, and when the sound of his horse's rapid hoofbeats faded, Grace stared at John speechlessly. He caught her eyes, then shrugged. "Well, I don't have to worry about my future, do I? At least not until the war's over."

"Oh, John!" Grace whispered. "There must be something we can do."

"I don't think there is. If I don't go, I could be shot for desertion. I know that much about the army." Seeing the stricken expression on her face, he grew more gentle, stepping closer to her and reaching down to take her hand. "Don't let this give you trouble," he said. "I'm just one man. All over the country men are being scooped up to fight this war."

Grace felt the pressure of his hand and could think of no reply. The two of them stood there, touching—and yet so far apart! Finally, he said heavily, "You've done all you can for me, and I'll always be grateful." That sounded heavy and pompous to him, and he found a smile. "Why, I'd never have known what a sleigh ride is like if it hadn't been for you!"

"I—I was hoping . . ." Her voice trailed off.

He waited for her to finish, but she turned her head away. "Tell you what, Grace," he said quickly. "Let's have a fine week! Go fishing through the ice, go for a sleigh ride every night—oh, do all the things we've done together."

"All right, John," Grace answered, and she forced herself to smile. "We'll have the best week we ever had!"

CHAPTER FIFTEEN
"A Wife Ought to Know"

★

Fair skies and mild weather blessed the land that week—John's last week on the farm. The old men and women could not remember a milder winter, and people were beginning to wonder if they would have a white Christmas. Grace and John spent the early part of the week driving the sleigh all over the county. She took him to every spot that had been a pleasure for her, and in the evenings they walked under the bright moon or spent the time in the parlor together.

It was a quiet time, a time when they both stored up memories. They didn't speak of the future, almost as though they'd made a covenant to ignore it.

On Sunday they went to meeting, and again John was impressed with the Quaker style of worship. "Whatever kind of church I went to," he told Grace once, "it wasn't like this one. I know that!"

"I think there are many ways of worshiping God, John," she'd said quietly. "The name on the sign outside the meeting place isn't as important as the condition of our hearts."

On that last Sunday, it had been Grace among the ministers who'd risen after a long time of waiting for a word. Her face was still, though somewhat pale, and as she spoke a light seemed to flow out of her eyes. She spoke of the love of God, and her simple words moved John tremendously. After the service, while they were on the way back to the farm, he said, "I wish I knew God like you do, Grace."

"Thee must find thy own way, John," she answered at once. "But God longs for your heart. He made thee to have fellowship with him, and thee will never be complete until thee is safe in his arms."

He sat quietly, holding the reins loosely, a puzzled look on his face. "That's a strange way to put it," he said finally. "I thought it was we who were seeking God."

"No man or woman seeks God by nature. We're too wicked for that. But God has been seeking his people ever since they fell. In the Garden he called Adam after the Fall, and he's been calling us all to come home ever since."

He stole a look at her face, wondering at the glow of joy that suffused it. He shook his head, saying, "I don't think everyone has your capacity for love, Grace. Nobody that I know has."

She parted her lips to protest, but then saw that he was looking downcast. "Thee must not give up, John. If thy heart is willing, God will find you."

They spoke no more along those lines, and that night she read from the parts of the Bible that stressed God's call for man to repent. He listened carefully and asked questions. When it was time to retire, he said, "Whatever happens after this week, Grace, I can't ever say that I haven't heard the gospel, can I?" His eyes grew sober and he spoke of what they had been avoiding all week. "We'll know something after tomorrow, I guess."

"Don't take counsel of your fears, John." She knew he had been dreading the arrival of the woman who might hold the key to his past. "We will pray, and God will give us the truth."

He studied her, then nodded. "Guess I'll have to go on your faith until I get some of my own."

Grace lifted her smile to him. "That's part of what being a Christian really is, John. Learning to take from others that which we lack."

Grace never knew how much John slept that night, but she didn't sleep a wink. When they met at the breakfast table, she noted that his eyes were red-rimmed and his features stiff with fatigue. He had shaven closely and put on his best coat, but he only picked at his food.

Clyde and Prudence were already at the table when John sat down. Neither of those two knew about the crisis, for by common consent Grace and John had agreed to keep it from them. Clyde noted John's nervousness, though, and commented, "What's wrong, John? Lost your appetite?"

"Oh, not very hungry, I guess."

Grace ate little as well, and after the meal she excused herself. John had informed her that he intended to go to town alone and meet the woman. She had agreed, knowing that it would not be wise to let Clyde and Prudence meet her.

But at nine o'clock, a knock at her bedroom door interrupted her as she was reading her Bible. She closed her Bible and went to the door. There stood John, looking rather sheepish.

"Grace, would you go to town with me?" he asked abruptly.

"Why . . . I suppose so, John. Is thee ready now?"

"Yes, let's go."

Grace put on her heavy coat and bonnet, then went down and got into the buggy with him. She drew up a blanket—thinking suddenly of the time she'd shared it with him on their sleigh ride. When he saw she was settled, he said, "Hup!" The matched grays lunged forward, and soon they were on the road leading to town.

After a period of awkward silence, John laughed aloud, rather ruefully, saying, "I guess you think I'm the world's worst coward."

"Why—!"

"Oh, don't mind saying it, Grace," he said, turning to face her, and she saw that he was embarrassed. "Well, I tell you right out, I'd rather be thrown into a den of rattlesnakes than meet this woman!"

"But, John—why?"

He struggled with his thoughts, then shrugged helplessly. "Hard to say." He studied the landscape, letting the horses find their own pace. There was a fineness in his face that Grace had always admired. It was more than just handsome features, it was a clean decency that she appreciated and respected.

He turned and met her eyes, then smiled. "Crazy isn't it? I've been crying like a baby for weeks, wanting to know who I am. And now that the chance has come . . . I'm trembling!"

"Perhaps the sight of one you—of one you love—" Grace stumbled over the phrase, then recovered. "Well, it might make thee remember."

He shook his head doubtfully. "It's possible, I guess. I've been seeing more faces, sometimes in dreams, sometimes in my mind when I'm awake. I'm sure they're people I must have known. One of them came to me last night. It was a woman, and she was beautiful—older than you are, Grace, but with the same kind of gentleness."

"What did she look like, John?"

"She had auburn hair, with some gray in it. And the most striking eyes I've ever seen," he marveled. "If I were a painter, I could paint her picture!"

"Maybe thy mother?"

"Could be. I wish I knew. The thing is, these things are coming back more often—and a lot clearer. If I just had *time—!*"

Grace longed to help him, but could find no words. Finally she asked, "Why did thee want me to come with thee, John? You aren't really so afraid to meet a mere woman."

He grinned wryly. "Oh, I don't know . . . just for company, I guess." He fell silent, then added, "I needed you. That's all I can say, Grace."

His simple words warmed her, and she thought, *If I never*

have more than this—I can hold it and remember it all my life!

Aloud she asked, "Does thee want me there when she comes?"

"Yes!"

"She may find it strange."

"We'll tell her you're my keeper," he said, grinning. "Maybe she'll think I'm a lunatic out of the asylum for a little break. That should send her back in a hurry. She won't want a madman for a husband."

Grace saw that he was speaking lightly to cover the apprehension inside and helped him by joining in the frivolous talk.

They got to town an hour before the train was due, and John drove to the town's only hotel and reserved a room. When the clerk asked what name, he hesitated, then said, "Mrs. Leota Richards."

"Very well, sir."

When he had signed the register, John led Grace out of the lobby and they went to a cafe. He ordered coffee for himself and cocoa for Grace. They sat there for half an hour, speaking about everything in the world but the matter that had brought them to town. Finally he rose abruptly, "Let's walk around, Grace."

"All right."

They walked back and forth, looking in the windows of the few stores along the street, and finally the sound of a distant whistle drew their attention.

"There it is!" he said, expelling his breath. "Let's go get it over with."

They walked toward the station, then stood on the platform until the engine pulled alongside, gusting great clouds of steam. The brakes ground until the train stopped, and then the conductor stepped down and began to assist people to make the long step to the ground.

There were only six passengers who got off, and of those, only one seemed to be the one they sought.

"I think that must be her, John," Grace said, nodding toward a woman who had stopped and was looking around.

John nodded, set his jaw, and said, "Come along, Grace." He took her arm so tightly that it hurt, and the two of them approached the woman. She was short and rather heavy— not really fat, but full figured. She turned to them instantly, and Grace saw that she was not particularly attractive. She had a pair of sharp black eyes and a narrow nose that gave her a predatory look. Her lips were firm, but were set in a close-mouthed expression.

"Mrs. Leota Richards?"

"Yes." The woman said no more, though both Grace and John expected her to show some sort of emotion. She studied the pair before her and then said, "Is there a place for me to stay?"

"Why—yes," John said hastily. "Which is your bag? I've taken a room for you at the hotel."

"The black one."

John took the bag and nodded toward the buildings that marked the town. "It's this way." He realized suddenly that the woman was staring at Grace and said hastily, "This is Miss Grace Swenson. She was one of the nurses at the hospital who took care of me."

"I see. And do you live here, Miss Swenson?"

"No, I live on a farm about ten miles from town, Mrs. Richards." Grace felt the gaze of the woman's piercing eyes and added quickly, "When John had to leave the hospital, he had no place to go, so he came to stay with my family."

"Very kind of you."

An awkward silence fell and, after a few steps, John asked inanely, "Did—did you have a good trip?"

"Yes. It was very comfortable."

Grace saw that John's brow was covered with perspiration despite the cool air and knew that he was somewhat desperate. *He expected the woman to identify him at once—and she says nothing! What kind of a woman can she be?*

Somehow they got to the hotel, Grace filling the silence

with small talk about the weather. But when they finally reached the woman's room, John asked, "Can we talk?"

"Certainly. Come inside." Mrs. Richards stepped into the room, but gave Grace a forbidding look. "If you don't mind, Miss Swenson, I'd like to speak privately."

"Why, of course!"

John gave her a rather desperate glance, but nodded. "Wait in the restaurant, Grace."

Grace nodded and, when the door shut, John turned to face the woman. She was pulling off her coat calmly. "It's rather cold in this room, isn't it?"

Ignoring her remark, he demanded, "Well—?"

But she forestalled his demand, saying, "Sit down, please. I want to hear your story."

John hesitated, then surrendered. He sat down and began to speak. The woman listened to him, not taking her eyes from his face. He could not tell one thing about what was going on inside her heart, for she let nothing show in her features.

Finally he finished, saying, "So I have no idea of my past, none at all."

"You don't recognize me?"

"N-no, I don't!"

She sat quietly in her chair, then said evenly, "Your name is Matthew Richards. You're my husband."

A great emptiness suddenly swept through John, and he felt as powerless to speak as if he'd been struck in the pit of his stomach. She watched his face grow pale, then asked, "Don't you remember me at all, Matt?"

"I . . . don't think so."

Mrs. Richards studied him carefully. "It's a strange thing. It must be terrible for you." She began to speak, telling him of his family and of his past. After a time she rose and came to stand beside him. "We'll be very patient, Matt," she said. Then she asked, "Do you need to go back to the place you've been living, or can we catch the next train home?"

He licked his lips, then shook his head. "I don't know. I'm

205

confused." He felt short of breath and somehow was terribly afraid, more so than he'd been since he'd come back from the darkness that had swallowed him.

Suddenly he knew that he *had* to get away! Just for a few minutes! "Look, I'll leave you here to rest up," he babbled desperately. "I—I need some time alone. You understand." He made a dive at the door and left her, saying, "I'll be back soon!"

He stumbled down the stairs and found Grace seated in the lobby. "Come on!" he cried hoarsely. "Let's get out of here!"

Grace rose at once and the two of them left the hotel. He said, "Get in the buggy," then helped her in and climbed in the seat beside her. He whipped the horses up, and they snorted at that unexpected treatment, bolting forward and splashing mud on a large man, who turned and cursed them roundly as they went flying down the street.

When they were clear of the town, John let the horses run until they slowed of their own will. He sat there, his face pale, saying nothing. Grace remained silent.

The bustle of the town faded, and soon they were plodding along the muddy road, surrounded by the quietness of the countryside. The trees were naked and bare, and the raw earth of plowed fields peeped through breaks in the snow.

On and on they drove, and Grace thought, *It's a good thing I'm a Quaker and accustomed to silence! It must have been dreadful for him!*

Finally he took a deep breath and turned to her. "Sorry to act like this, Grace," he muttered. "I just had to get away for a few minutes."

"It's all right," Grace murmured. "What did she tell thee, John?"

"She says I'm Matthew Richards, her husband."

Grace had been prepared for this, for she had sensed that he would not have reacted so violently had the woman said otherwise—and yet she was stunned by the pain that shot through her to hear him say the words. "Tell me about it, John," she said, forcing her voice to be steady and calm.

He spoke quickly, but jerkily, as he recounted the meeting, ending by saying moodily, "She's absolutely certain I'm her husband."

Grace had listened carefully, but somehow she was troubled. "John, I need some time to pray."

"Why, of course!" John was surprised, but said no more. He allowed the horses to pick their way down the muddy road for half an hour, sitting silently beside Grace as she sought the Lord. Then she turned and said firmly, "Go back to the hotel."

"What?"

"Go back to the hotel."

He stared at her, then nodded. "I guess I've got to face up to this thing."

"God has given me a word."

"What?" Confusion caused him to blink. He had heard the expression several times among the Quakers but had never understood it. "What does that mean?"

"It means that God has spoken to me."

"About me, and about—her?"

"Yes. Turn the buggy around."

He stared at her, then shrugged. "All right, Grace."

She said nothing as they made their return trip, and he was too depressed to make conversation. When they got back to the hotel, she said, "Let's go to her room."

He tied the horses, and the two of them climbed the stairs. When he tapped on the door, it opened almost at once. Mrs. Richards had a half-smile on her face, but it died when she saw Grace.

Grace stepped inside, practically forcing herself past the woman. John stepped in after her, and the woman closed the door and turned to face them.

Grace met the woman's gaze squarely and spoke with quiet confidence. "Mrs. Richards, I do not think this man is thy husband!"

John's mouth dropped open and he took a sharp breath. He was watching the woman's face and saw quick anger come to her sharp eyes.

"Are you telling me I don't know my own husband?" Mrs. Richards demanded shrilly.

"I think thee does know thy *own* husband, but thee is deceiving this man. He is not thy husband."

"Get out of here! Matthew, get this woman out of my room!"

"I'd sort of like to hear what she has to say," John remarked. He turned to Grace and studied her carefully. "What makes you so sure I'm not married to her?"

Grace didn't answer his question. Instead she faced the woman and said evenly, "How long does thee say this man has been thy husband?"

"Twelve years!"

"And how many children has thee had by him?"

"Three! Do you think I could make a mistake about a man I've been married to for that long?"

"If thee will answer one simple question, I will admit he is thy husband."

Mrs. Richards glared at Grace suspiciously. "What question?"

"The purple birthmark on thy husband's side, is it shaped like an egg or like a cat's paw?"

A dead silence fell on the room. Mrs. Richards stared at Grace, then at the man beside her. Defiantly she said, "Like a cat's paw!"

John's face broke out in a broad smile, and he said, "Well, it's been nice to meet you, Mrs. Richards. You can catch the next train to Gettysburg at six this evening." He put his hat on and took Grace's arm firmly.

He paused long enough to speak to Mrs. Richards. "The birthmark is shaped like a star, and it's on my back, not my side."

Mrs. Richard's face had lost all color. She glared at Grace, then hissed, "You'd know all about that, wouldn't you? I

knew you were after him from the minute I set eyes on you!"
She began to curse them both as they walked from the room,
and they could hear her as they marched down the stairs.

He helped her into the buggy, barely pausing as he took
up the reins and slapped the horses into action. When they
were safely out of town, John turned and took her hands in
one of his. "Grace, how did you know? And why in the
world did she ever come and make such a claim?"

"I suspected when we met her," Grace said quietly. "No
woman who loved her husband could be so cool when she
saw him after thinking he might be dead. Either she was
lying or she had never loved thee."

Relief showed in his face and he laughed out loud. "Who
could help loving me?" he demanded. "And why did she try
such a crazy thing?"

"I think she took a chance that thee would never remember anything. She wants a husband so badly that she did all
this to get one."

He abruptly threw his arms around her and hugged her.
"Oh, Grace! I feel like I've been let out of jail!"

She lay crushed against his chest, unable to keep the grin
from her own features. Finally she pushed him away and
admonished him with a tremulous smile, "Don't be so
conceited."

But he didn't release her immediately. He kept his arms
around her for one moment longer, then let her go. "My
good angel, Grace," he whispered gently. Then he said
quietly, "I knew that woman wasn't my wife."

"Really, John? How did thee know that?"

He reached out and stroked her cheek. "Because," he said
slowly, "I didn't feel about her . . . as I do about you."

Swift color filled Grace's face, and her heart constricted
painfully. Could he possibly mean . . . ? "Thee—thee
shouldn't speak so!" Her voice was unsteady and breathless.

John Smith shook his head, pulled the horses to a stop,
and dropped the reins. Reaching out, he put his arms around

her and drew her close. Grace's eyes grew alarmed and she cried out, "John—!"

But he ignored her protest. His eyes were fixed on her face and filled with a tender determination. "I love thee, Grace Swenson!" He whispered, then pulled her into his embrace, kissing her thoroughly.

His touch stirred impulses in Grace that she hadn't known were within her, and she felt as though her heart would burst with the joy that swept through her at his words. A small part of her mind scolded her, telling her she should push him away . . . but she ignored it blissfully.

Finally he released her, but he held her gaze, letting her see for herself the intensity of his love for her. He reached up to touch her face gently, and when he spoke his voice was strong and deep. "I don't know who I am or where I'm going, but I know one thing full well. And that is that I love thee, Grace. For now, that is enough."

Three days later, Grace stood beside John at the depot. The conductor called out, "All aboard!" and he turned and held her in a tight embrace.

"John—!" she whispered, holding him fiercely.

He kissed her, then said, "Don't forget, I love thee!" He had said it that way often the past three days, which had stirred both happiness and sorrow in her. Happiness that they had discovered such a wondrous love; sadness that they both knew the future was blank and they could make no plans.

But now as he tore himself from her and climbed the steps of the train, she felt a pang of loneliness such as she'd never known. As the train lurched and left the station, she caught a glimpse of his face and waved.

He loves me! she thought and, as she turned and walked away, she bit her lips to keep them steady. *I love thee, too—and I'll never love another!*

As she climbed into the buggy and started her homeward journey, the train whistle sounded—a lonesome, haunting wail that echoed plaintively on the stillness of the air.

CHAPTER SIXTEEN
Into the Valley of Death

★

The battle of Fredericksburg should never have been fought.

The Army of the Potomac was shoved into the suicidal attempt by a man who had endeavored to refuse the command of the army and who had to be directly *ordered* to assume that post by the president.

Maj. Gen. Ambrose E. Burnside was a man with incredible whiskers, who moved from disaster to disaster with an uncomprehending and wholly unimaginative dignity. He had wooed a Kentucky girl and taken her to the altar, only to be flabbergasted when she returned a firm *no* to the officiating minister's climactic question. (The same girl later became engaged to an Ohio lawyer who had heard about Burnside's experience. When the wedding date arrived, this man displayed to her a revolver and a marriage license, telling her that she could choose one or the other. This time she went through with the ceremony.)

Burnside quickly won the admiration of the soldiers, for he showed a great concern for their well-being, always poking his nose into mess shacks, sampling the food, and checking on supplies. In a way, this revealed his tragic flaw, for he needed to be studying strategy and tactics in order to meet Robert E. Lee, not tasting soup!

The first plan he made was sound, and his first move

caught Lee by surprise. He did not advance directly on Lee, as that general expected, but headed southeast, arriving on the Rappahannock River, just across from Fredericksburg. This left Lee out of position, with half his army at Culpepper and the other half under Jackson in the Shenandoah Valley.

For two precious days, the road to Richmond lay wide open to the Federal army—the first and last time this happened during the Civil War!

Sadly, the pontoon bridges that Burnside had ordered from the War Department did not arrive on time, so the unique chance passed. Burnside's army waited on the north bank of the Rappahannock, looking across the river to the heights above Fredericksburg as they gradually filled with the infantry and artillery of Lee's frantically redeployed army.

Burnside had ample heavy artillery to keep the Confederates from securing the line of the south bank, but he failed to use it. His pontoon bridges had to be built under fire, and Union blood was shed by this tragic oversight. On December 11, after three wasted weeks had given Lee time to lodge the Army of Northern Virginia, the situation was hopeless for the Northern troops.

On December 10 a woman crept down to the bank of the Rappahannock and called across to the gray pickets that the Yankees had drawn a large issue of cooked rations—always a sign that action was at hand.

That night there was a party given by the officers of a New England regiment in a riverside hut. Some twenty men who had no illusions about the kind of reception they were going to get when they crossed the river met to sing songs and drink whiskey punch. The hut rocked with cheers and the glasses went bottoms up, and later as they marched up to the river they heard the high soft voice of a contraband camp servant lifted in the song "Jordan Water, Rise over Me."

The next day, the engineers put the pontoon bridge across the river, but only at a high price. Confederate sharpshooters, taking refuge in the buildings of Fredericksburg, picked them off as easily as if they were shooting squirrels. Burnside finally ordered the town destroyed by artillery, after which he sent infantry across by boat to drive the sharpshooters back.

The fight was rough while it lasted. The Twentieth Massachusetts Regiment lost ninety-seven officers and men in gaining fifty yards. In the end the town was secured, and men remembered afterward that a strange golden dusk lay upon the plain and the surrounding hills, as if a belated Indian-summer evening had come bewildered out of peacetime autumn into wartime winter. A newspaper correspondent wrote: "Towering between us and the western sky, which was still showing its faded scarlet lining, was the huge somber pillar of grimy smoke that marked the burning of Fredericksburg. Ascending to a vast height, it bore away northward shaped like a plume bowed in the wind."

When darkness was complete, Lee ordered Jackson to bring his two nearest divisions to Longstreet's support. He was pleased, though he could not quite believe that *any* general would attack him in his present position! He thought of the position of the Union army and of his own position—the strongest he had ever held in his military career. He called for a light, and when an aide brought a lantern, he studied the map on which he had placed the positions of both armies.

The Confederate army, seventy-eight thousand men, was in a formidable line on the high ground west of the Fredericksburg plain. The ground was only forty or fifty feet above the plain, but that made it exactly right—high enough to offer an impregnable defensive line, but not high enough to scare the Federals and keep them from attacking. Directly west of the town rose a ridge called Marye's Heights. To the north, slightly higher hills slanted off to the river. To the south, the high ground pulled farther and father away from the river.

Lee studied the map and thought about the men who would lead: For the union it would be Maj. William B. Franklin leading the left wing and Gen. Joe Hooker leading the right wing; for the Confederacy, Gen. Longstreet would defend the left and Stonewall Jackson the right.

Lee smiled, put up his map, and went to bed. *The South never had to worry less about a battle than this one,* he thought happily.

The next morning Lee and Longstreet stood looking down on the snow-pocked plain where the blue host was massing. The two men made a contrast indeed. Lee was tall and handsome, with a short-clipped iron-gray beard. Beneath the brim of a sand-colored planter's hat, his quick brown eyes had a youthfulness that disguised the fact that he would be fifty-six years old in one month.

His companion was a burly, shaggy man, six feet tall and of Dutch extraction. Except for Lee himself, no commander in the Confederate army was more admired and loved by his men. This was based on their knowledge of his concern for their well-being in and out of combat. They called him Old Pete and sometimes The Dutchman.

The two men looked up as the third-ranking member of the army triumvirate came riding up. It was Jackson, but a Jackson quite unlike the Stonewall they were accustomed to. No officer in the army paid less heed to his dress than Stonewall Jackson. But now, gone were the mangy cadet cap and the homespun uniform worn threadbare. Instead he wore a new cap bound with gold braid and had more braid looped on the cuffs and sleeves of a brand-new uniform.

One of the men called out, "Lookee thar, Old Jack will be afraid for his clothes and will not get down to work."

Jackson got off his horse, muttering that the uniform was "a gift of my friend Stuart," and asked permission to attack.

Lee smiled, for Jackson seldom asked for anything else. "No, Gen. Jackson. Let those people wear themselves out on our guns."

Old Pete baited him, saying, "Jackson, don't all those multitudes of Federals frighten you?"

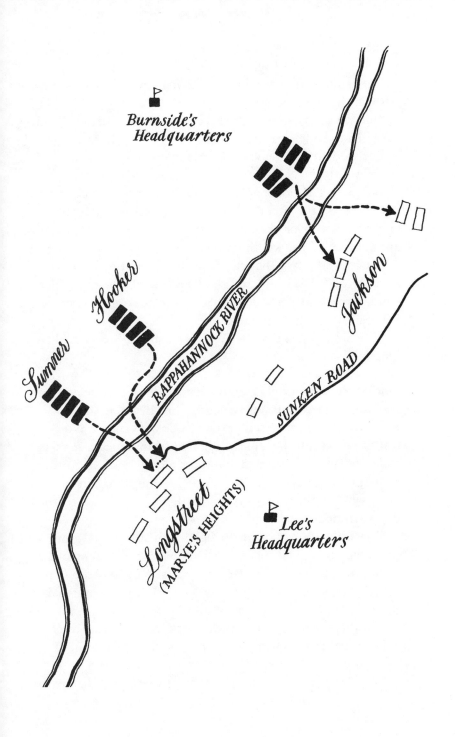

Burnside's
Headquarters

Hooker

Sumner

RAPPAHANNOCK RIVER

Jackson

SUNKEN ROAD

Longstreet
(MARYE'S HEIGHTS)

Lee's
Headquarters

Jackson glared at Longstreet. "We shall see very soon whether I shall not frighten *them!*"

Longstreet winked at Lee. "But what are you going to *do* with all those Yankees, Jackson?"

"Sir, we will give them the bayonet," Jackson snapped and turned and rode away.

Lee studied the masses of blue soldiers below and said, "I am afraid they will break your line, General."

Longstreet shook his head. "General, if you put every man now on the other side of the Potomac in that field to approach me over that same line, and give me plenty of ammunition, I will kill them before they reach my line!"

Lee looked down the lines at muskets that bristled from a sunken road that wandered the length of the heights, then studied the heavy artillery aimed at the open plain that the Federals would have to cross.

"I believe you are right, Gen. Longstreet," he remarked quietly.

One of the blue dots of color that made up the army that Lee looked down on was the coat worn by John Smith.

He had been mustered in only three days earlier. No one had inquired into his ability. He had been issued a musket and uniform and rushed by train along with the other members of the Merton Blue Devils to join Franklin's division, which was drawn up for battle on the banks of the Rappahannock.

Now as he looked up at the heights bristling with guns, a cold feeling gripped him. The lieutenant of his company, a young man named Robert Little, was staring at those same guns. Little swallowed hard, then said, "Cheer up, men! We won't have any trouble gettin' in!"

A burly private glared at the lieutenant and snarled resentfully, "Getting in? Them Rebs *want* us to get in. It's getting *out* that won't be so easy!"

Col. Drecker came striding up, his face pale but filled with excitement. "Don't worry, men!" he called out. "We'll be going in soon!"

The Merton Blue Devils were held as reserves, however, and all day long they watched as masses of men marched into the fury of battle. When the order to charge came to each of the other regiments, the soldiers would surge forward—but none of them even got close to the wall of fire that belched from the guns of the defenders. Every attack "broke in blood"—failing because the men were too badly shot up to press on—and the Federals fell back, leaving the stretch of open ground thick-strewn with corpses and writhing men whose cries could be heard above the clatter of musketry.

Sunset did not slow the tempo of the fighting. A fifth major assault on Marye's Heights had been repulsed, and from behind the sunken wall the Confederates taunted the warmly clad Federals coming toward them in a tangle-footed huddle, "Come on, Bluebelly! Bring them boots and blankets! Bring 'em hyar!" And they did bring them, up to within fifty yards of the flame-stitched wall. There the forward edge of the charge was frayed and broken, the survivors crawling or running to regain the protection of lower ground.

At three o'clock Col. Drecker came to say, "All right men, fix bayonets! We will advance!"

John looked at the man next to him and said grimly, "That's a foolish order! Not a man of ours has gotten closer than fifty yards to the Rebel lines all day!"

Then the call came, and the Blue Devils moved forward. John kept in rank as they crossed the low ground, and soon men began to fall.

"Come on, men!" Drecker screamed, waving his sword. "Your colonel will lead you!" He plunged forward, heading straight for the sunken road where bodies from five previous charges covered the ground. Shells began to burst in their ranks, blowing men to bits. One man not ten yards in front of Smith fell, his leg all but severed. Three men jumped to pick him up, but Drecker was there, screaming, "Forward! Leave him there!"

By the time they had reached the top of the incline and faced the concentrated fire of the Confederates, half of the regiment had either been killed or wounded. The slaughter continued, but Drecker plunged ahead. He turned and screamed, "Come on! Follow me! We'll show—!"

A shell removed his head neatly, and his body slowly toppled to the ground.

The brigade stopped at once, but they were pinned down. To go back, Smith saw, was as dangerous as to go on. He threw himself into a shallow depression and dug deeper with his bayonet. Others were doing the same, and when darkness fell, he lay down and waited for morning. He thought about crawling back to his own lines, but sharpshooters were firing at everything that moved. He saw four men cut down as they tried to make it back, and finally he gave up.

He lay there, his legs twitching and his mouth as dry as dust. At last the need for water drove him to crawl five yards to get the canteen of a dead private. He tipped the canteen back and drank thirstily.

Crawling back to his hole, he huddled down, facing the enemy line. For hours he lay there, until he finally drifted off into a fitful slumber. He was awakened abruptly by a sharp pain in his shoulder. At once he came awake, reaching for his musket—but saw that it was held by a ragged Confederate who was grinning at him.

"End of the war for you, Bluebelly," the Rebel said with a nod. "Now, you shuck out of them nice boots and that warm coat. You kin have mine if you want."

The wolf-lean Confederate held a .44 aimed directly at his heart, so Smith said, "I guess you got the best of the argument, Reb." He removed his boots and coat, sat down as ordered, then put on the poor bits of leather the soldier had been wearing, and slipped into the thin coat. He shivered as he got to his feet, and his captor nodded, "Nice boots you Yankees bring us. I 'preciate it. Now, get going!"

As John plodded along toward the enemy lines, he knew the war was over for him. The wind cut through him like a knife, and he was exhausted by the time he'd been quick-marched five miles back of the lines and placed with a large group of captured Federals.

The lieutenant in charge formed them in lines and said, "I don't reckon you fellers will be killin' any more Southern boys now, will you?"

"Where'll we be held?" one of the captives asked.

"Libby Prison." The lieutenant looked at them with pity. "You'll be wishing you got killed before you've been there long! Now, march!"

As Smith slogged along the road, his feet began to freeze. The bits of leather fell off, and soon his raw feet were leaving bloodstains in the mud. The cold seemed to get worse, touching his lungs with a tongue of fire when he inhaled. He reached the point when he could go no farther and was about to fall, when the command came to halt.

"You men lie down. In the morning you'll be fed, then you'll march to the station. From there you'll be took to Richmond, to Libby Prison."

John no longer cared. He took the vile-smelling blanket from a private who was handing them out, wrapped it around himself, and fell to the ground. His last thought before he slipped away was of Grace, and he prayed simply, *Lord, let me see her again!*

Three days later he was a prisoner in Libby Prison.

He also had pneumonia, which he had developed from being exposed to the icy roads of Virginia and from lying on an open flatcar in freezing weather for two days.

When he was carried into Libby Prison, he was barely conscious enough to feel the rough hands of the soldiers who carried him, but he heard the voice of the doctor well enough when he said, "Another pneumonia case? Well, he'll die in a week, like the rest of them."

But the patient was too far gone to care. It didn't seem to matter very much, so he slipped away, welcomed once again into a stark black hole that closed around him silently.

PART THREE
The Prisoner and
the Bride

CHAPTER SEVENTEEN
Captain Clay Finds a Man

★

"Melora, come and see!"

Melora Yancy looked up from the rough-backed hogs, who were grunting and squealing as she tossed ears of corn into the trough. Her seventeen-year-old sister Rose was running toward her, hair flying. The girl didn't wait to reach Melora but cried out, "It's Mister Clay, Melora—he's comin' in a funny looking wagon!"

At once Melora tossed the rest of the corn into the pen, then threw the basket aside and ran lightly to meet her sister. Her face had paled slightly, but she said nothing, listening as Rose urged her to hurry. When they came out of the grove, Melora saw at once the closed wagon Clay was driving.

He saw her and lifted his hand in a wave. Melora's father, Buford Yancy, appeared in the doorway, had his look, then came to stand beside the two girls. Josh, Martha, and Toby were standing back shyly, watching as Clay pulled the wagon to a halt in front of the cabin.

"Hello," Clay said. He jumped down and tied the team to a slick hitching post. Turning, he faced them, and Melora's heart skipped a beat, for he was not smiling.

"Is one of the boys kilt, Clay?" Buford asked carefully. He was a tall man with green eyes and was remarkably active for his age.

"No!" Clay said quickly. "Bob took a bullet in his leg, but it's not bad."

Melora released her breath. With brothers in the Confederate army, all of their family lived under a shadow of constant dread. "Bring him inside, Clay," she said. "Rose, go fix a bed for him."

Clay stepped to the back of the ambulance, saying, "He did fine, Buford, real fine!" Opening the canvas flap, he found eighteen-year-old Bob Yancy propping himself up, and he gave him a hand. "Easy there," he cautioned.

Bob blinked owlishly in the bright noon sunlight, then grinned sheepishly at his father. "Didn't duck fast like you told me to, Pa," he said cheerfully. He put his leg down, and the pain drew a grimace from him.

Clay nodded at Buford. "Get his other side. That leg's pretty tender."

The two men picked young Yancy up, ignoring his protests that he wasn't a baby. They carried him inside, put him on a cot beside a window, then as the two women hustled around fixing a quick meal, Clay sat back and let the wounded man tell his story. Clay deliberately kept his eyes off Melora, though only with an effort. He was intensely aware of her presence, and when she came to put a plate of stew and glass of milk before him, he looked up at her, saying, "You're looking well."

Melora nodded, but studied his face. "You look tired."

"He ort to be!" Bob Yancy spoke up. He was enjoying being the center of attention. The younger children had drawn as close to him as possible, their eyes wide with worshipful adoration. Bob waved a chicken leg and grinned. "Ain't none of you noticed nothing about him?"

Only then did Melora notice the bars on Clay's shoulders. "Why, Clay—!" she exclaimed. "You're a captain!"

Clay shrugged disdainfully. "It's just a brevet promotion," he said.

"Whut's thet, Clay?" Buford demanded.

"It means he does the job of a captain but only draws a

224

lieutenant's pay," Bob said, grinning. Then he gave Clay a look of admiration. "When them Yankees came boiling across the river right at us, we got caught with one shoe off," he explained. "Capt. Simon of G Company, he went down at the first volley, and Maj. Franklin, he hollered, 'Clay, you're promoted to captain!'"

"Well, when Capt. Simon was wounded, Col. Benton promoted me to take his place. Wasn't very smart of the colonel," Clay broke in. "Some of the other men have more seniority."

"Aw, everybody in the regiment knows you're the best soldier in the bunch, Clay—I mean, *Captain Rocklin!*" Bob ate his meal and made light of his own wound. He talked with animation, and the rest of the family—including his father—listened intently.

Clay got up and helped Melora with the dishes, then said, "I'd better feed and water the horses."

"I'll help you." Melora took off her apron, and the two went outside. Clay unhitched the horses and took them to the corral, saying, "We'll let them roll a little after they eat." He fed them from a sack of grain he'd brought, then turned them out. He turned to her, smiled, and said, "Let's go look at your pigs."

She smiled, too, for he always teased her about the hogs the Yancys were raising. He slanted a grin at her. "I'll bet you've got some favorites, haven't you?"

"Now don't scold me, Mister Clay!" she retorted, laughing, and led him to the hog pen, pointing out the different animals' beauty. Actually it had been Clay who had persuaded Buford to raise corn and feed out hogs instead of raising cotton. *"We can't eat cotton, Buford,"* he'd said bluntly. *"It won't be worth a dollar a bale next year, with the blockade cutting us off from England—but bacon will be sky high!"*

After looking at the hogs, they walked along the edge of the woods beside the small stream until they came at last to a large pool, where they stopped and looked at the rippling water.

It was in these peaceful surroundings that he began to talk about the battle, and she listened quietly. Finally she asked, "Are you all right, Clay?"

He turned to look at her and was struck by the picture she made. Her hair fell over her shoulders, framing her face. Her eyes shone emerald green, and her clear complexion gave her face an almost translucent appearance. Clay thought her the loveliest woman he had ever seen, and he rested his gaze on her, knowing that she was asking about more than his reaction to the battle.

"You mean about losing Ellen?" he asked quietly. He had always been honest with her, and now he was no different. "I feel bad about it, Melora," he said quietly, his eyes moody and tinged with sadness. "I should have been able to help her more."

"You mustn't feel like that, Clay!" Melora spoke firmly. "You stayed with her and were faithful to her for years, and that was more than any other man would have done. And at the last, she found God." She reached out to lay a gentle hand on his arm. "Let her go, Clay," she said quietly.

He studied her countenance, then slowly nodded. "I'll have to learn, I guess. I made such a mess of the first part of my life, maybe I'm afraid of doing it again."

Melora took his hand and led him along the stream, and there was nothing artful or seductive in her gesture. She was, he thought, not the kind of woman to practice such things. He was constantly amazed that she was as guileless and sweet as she had been the first time he'd met her, when she was but a child.

They walked for an hour, talking of small things, then he said, "I've got to get back, Melora. I just didn't want Bob in the hospital. He'll be out of action for quite a while, and he'll be happier here."

"Is your regiment leaving again right away?"

Clay shook his head. "I doubt it. We whipped the Yankees

so badly they'll do what they always do: run back to Washington and lick their wounds. Lincoln will probably get McClellan to pull them into shape."

"And then what?" Melora asked quietly.

"Then they'll hit us again." A weariness came to Clay's shoulders, and he shook his head sadly. "There's so *many* of them! They lost twelve thousand men at Fredericksburg, but there's ten times that many in the North ready to fill the ranks." He shook his head in a hopeless gesture. "But who's going to fill Bob's shoes? Nobody! We'll be stretched a little thinner, and we'll have to fight harder." He paused for a moment, seemingly deep in thought. Melora didn't push him. Finally he went on quietly. "But there will be an end to all of this, Melora. The South doesn't have a chance unless the Peace party in the North gets its way and calls off the war."

They returned to the corral, and Clay hitched up the horses. "I'll be back to see Bob," he said with a smile. "Which means, I guess, that I'll be back to see you."

"I'll be here, Clay," she whispered. He held her eyes for a brief moment, then nodded and went into the house to say his good-byes. Within minutes he was climbing back into the seat of the wagon and driving out of the yard. Melora stood and watched him go, sending a prayer up for his safety.

By late afternoon Clay arrived at the camp where the Richmond Grays were stationed. He turned the ambulance over to a teamster at the quartermaster's stables, then made his way to headquarters.

Only about half of the regiment had returned to Richmond, the rest being left on the Rappahannock to keep an eye on Burnside's beaten army. Clay worked with the headquarters staff on reports for two hours, then said, "I'm going to the hospital to see Capt. Dewitt, Sergeant. You can finish these reports, I think."

He made his way into Richmond, where he found his old

friend Capt. Taylor Dewitt in Chimborazo Hospital—and in a bad humor!

"Clay! You've got to get me out of this place!" Taylor protested at once. He'd been hit in the side and in the neck by bursting fragments from a shell and was sitting in bed, his thin, handsome face twisted with displeasure.

One of the nurses, a tall, angular woman, turned from her position three beds away and came to stand over the patient. "You are worse than any child, Captain!" she snapped. "Now if you don't lie down and rest, I have ways of handling you!"

Dewitt blustered, but did as the nurse said. When she left, he grumbled and complained, but Clay was relieved. "I'm glad to see you're all right, Taylor. When I saw you go down, it made me—" Clay broke off and shook his head, thinking of the moment. "It's one thing to think about death, but it's something else to see your friends go down."

Dewitt nodded slowly. "Yes, and we lost some fine friends on this one, Clay. You'll have to write some letters to their people—and you'll have to train some new men. . . ."

For half an hour the two friends talked, then Clay rose. "I've got to go. Anything I can get you?"

"Send me some cigars. Good ones."

Clay left the hospital and returned to the camp. For the next week he was buried in work, for Col. Benton, who knew he was going to be gone most of the time, had told him, "Clay, you'll just have to fill in. Make all the decisions you can, and hold off the rest until I get back."

It was late on Monday afternoon when Clay looked up from the drill field where he was helping train new recruits and saw a buggy pull up bearing a short civilian.

"Clay—!" The man waved, and Clay recognized the Rocklin family physician, Dr. Kermit Maxwell. He said, "Take over, Lieutenant," and walked quickly to the buggy. At once he asked, "Is someone sick, Dr. Maxwell?"

"No. Can you get loose for the rest of the day?"

Clay blinked at the suddenness of the request. "Why . . . I think so. What's wrong?"

"Get yourself loose," Maxwell grunted. He was a short, heavy man of eighty-two, with a round red face and a pair of sharp blue eyes. He had no bedside manner to speak of, but had been setting bones, birthing babies, and patching up Rocklins for nearly sixty years. In addition, he was a stubborn man, Clay knew, and when he saw that he'd get no more information, he called the lieutenant over, gave him instructions, then got into the buggy.

They left the camp, and Clay waited for Maxwell to explain his abrupt actions, but Maxwell talked about the war and then filled Clay in on what had been happening in Richmond. The doctor seemed to know everyone and was a careful judge of people, so his commentary was rough and colorful.

Clay asked about his father, and Maxwell shook his head. "I wish I could give you better news, Clay, but your father is in bad shape. I've done all I know. You might want to send him to one of the big hospitals."

"No, he'd hate that." Clay shook his head. He said no more, but it brought a heaviness to him, for he'd learned to love his father. It had taken years, but he'd won his father's love and respect in the fullest measure. Now, he knew, he didn't have much time to spend with Thomas—and the war took most of it away.

Maxwell drove through the city to the James River, pulling up the team in front of Libby Prison. He got down, then said to Clay, "It's pretty hard to find a doctor who'll treat the Yankee prisoners. I've been helping out some." He spat an amber stream of tobacco juice that splattered on bricks, then grunted, "Come along."

Clay was mystified, but he followed the doctor without comment. Originally, Libby Prison had been the warehouse of Libby and Sons ship chandlers, so it was situated on the James River at the corner of Twentieth and Cary streets. It was a large four-story building that was used primarily for housing injured Union officers.

Once they were inside, Maxwell muttered, "You boys shot up so many Bluebellies, there's no place to put them. We had to put some enlisted men in here with the officers."

"Back again, Dr. Maxwell?" A smallish sergeant with a wiry mustache greeted the two men with surprise, but made no objection when Maxwell mentioned he wanted to make the rounds again. "Guess it's OK." He nodded and led them to a large room packed with beds so close that there was hardly room to walk.

Maxwell was greeted by several of the patients and stopped to look at a few. He was a gruff old fellow, but Clay noted how the Yankee prisoners followed him with their eyes. He kept close to the doctor, puzzled, but saying little. One of the prisoners blinked at him, then whispered, "You just wait, Captain! We'll be back."

Clay smiled and reached into his pocket. He'd put a sack of candy there, a present for the niece of one of his sergeants. "I guess you will, soldier. Here, have a treat from the Richmond Grays."

The soldier was surprised, but took the sack. "That'll go pretty good, Captain." He smiled. "Thankee!"

Clay moved to where Maxwell was standing, bent over a still form. As he approached, the bulky physician suddenly moved aside and motioned for Clay to look.

The light was dim, and Clay, after giving Maxwell a quizzical glance, stepped to the cot and bent over the man. The patient had his face turned away and Clay could tell little, but then Maxwell reached down and turned the man's head so that the light from the barred window across the room fell full on the lean face.

Clay sucked in his breath, gasping audibly. He blinked and leaned closer, studying the still features, then turned to face Maxwell, his face gone pale.

"Burke!" he whispered. "It's Burke!"

Maxwell demanded, "Are you sure, Clay?"

"Sure? You think I don't know my own brother!"

"Come on, let's get out of here."

"But—!"

"I said let's go!"

Clay grew angry and would have argued, but Maxwell gripped his arm, whispering, "Come on, you blasted fool!" And Clay suddenly understood his urgency. He nodded, not speaking until they were outside.

When they were in the buggy, Maxwell said, "I wanted you to see him without knowing who he was."

Clay was staring at the grimy old building, trying to shake off the confusion that had sent his mind reeling. "He's alive! Alive, Doc!"

"Yes—and wearing a Union uniform!" Maxwell said sharply. "It's a touchy thing, Clay. If he is Burke, he'll be shot for desertion." He studied the face of his companion, then shrugged. "Let's get out of here. We've got to figure something out."

"How sick is he?" Clay asked after they had driven a few blocks without speaking.

"Very bad," Maxwell grunted. "If he doesn't get better care, he's not going to make it."

"We've got to get him out!"

"Yes, but *how?*"

They drove along the streets of Richmond for an hour, then went inside a cafe, where they got a table by the back wall. Clay drank tea and Maxwell drank beer as they went over and over the thing.

"We've got to hear Burke's side of it," Clay said at last. "There's got to be an answer. And we've got to get him out of that place before he dies."

"The warden's name is D. K. Templeton, and he's a tough one," Maxwell said. "He's not going to let anybody out of Libby. We've got to find somebody with clout, Clay!"

Clay blinked abruptly, a thought forming in his mind. He was a systematic thinker and said nothing for a few minutes. The talk from the other patrons hummed softly as he sat

231

there loosely, then he stirred his shoulders. "You're right, Doc. We'll have to have someone on our side with influence, and I think I know just the man."

Maxwell stared fixedly at Clay, then muttered, "He'd better be someone with clout. Is this man a good friend of yours?"

"No," Clay said thoughtfully, "He isn't. But I've got a friend who's a good friend of his *best* friend."

Maxwell was skeptical by nature and a cynic by reason of a long life of observing the failures of human beings. He gulped down the last swallow of his beer, wiped his mouth, and muttered heavily, "I wouldn't bet a dime on it, Clay, but if it's the best you've got—why have at it!"

Jefferson Davis was the president of the Confederate States of America, but he was a husband as well. Despite the power of one office, he was as vulnerable as most men are when their wives decide that something must take place.

Davis, sitting in his study at his home, knew at once that his wife Varina was plotting something. As soon as she had entered the room accompanied by her little friend, Mrs. Raimey Rocklin, the signs were obvious. His wife was a beautiful woman and a romantic, Davis well knew. She had been captivated by Raimey, whose beauty was not in the least marred by the fact that she was blind. And when the dashing Dent Rocklin had begun to pursue the girl, Varina Davis had been thrilled. Truth be told, the Rocklin-Reed courtship seemed to have captured the imagination of all of Richmond—but no one seemed more pleased when they had finally married than the first lady of the Confederacy.

Davis himself was fond of Raimey and was fascinated by her courage and ability. He found a slight smile crossing his austere features as he watched the two women coming toward him. "Well, what are you two plotting? Last week you talked me into having a charity ball for the widows of our Confederacy. What now?"

"Sit down, dear," Varina Davis said. "I want you to hear what Mrs. Rocklin has to say, and I know you'll help her."

Davis sighed, but sat down. "All right, Mrs. Rocklin, what is this terrible problem?"

But if he was not serious at first, he became so very quickly. He was besieged by requests for leniency, and as soon as Raimey had laid the matter of Burke Rocklin before him, he knew he must be very careful indeed!

He studied the beautiful face of the blind young woman, his mind darting to and fro, in fine lawyer fashion. Finally he said, "Let me see if I understand this matter. This Federal captive is your husband's uncle? And the brother of Capt. Clay Rocklin of the Richmond Grays? And he was believed to have been killed in action at Second Manassas? But—how could that be?"

Raimey said quickly, "My father-in-law, Capt. Rocklin, identified the body, but only by a ring on the dead man's finger because he was—too mutilated to be identified by his face."

"And now this man eveyone thought was dead turns up as a prisoner wearing a Union uniform. That's a serious offense, Mrs. Rocklin. If he really *is* Burke Rocklin, it would mean his death."

"Oh, we know that, sir," Raimey said quickly. "But we believe there must be some explanation. All we want is to give him the chance to defend himself."

"Every man must have that chance, of course."

"I *knew* you'd agree!" Varina Davis beamed at her husband, who stared at her with a confused look. Mrs. Davis lifted her eyebrows. "You do understand, sir, that the man is dying?"

"Well, that's unfortunate, but—"

"Surely you must see that we can't let him die like this? He must be nursed back to health so that he may clear his name!"

"I'm sure the doctors will do their best."

"No, sir, I know you will want to do more than that."

Mrs. Davis smiled fondly at her husband. "What I would like to see is for you to parole this man into the custody of his people."

Davis thought quickly. "That would be Mr. Thomas Rocklin, I believe."

"Yes, solid supporters of your administration!" Varina smiled. This made a difference as she had known it would, and she quickly stepped up her attack. "There's no danger of the man escaping. He's completely helpless. After he recovers, a thorough investigation can be made, of course. I know you my dear, and I know you are too compassionate a president to sacrifice one of our brave men or let him die unjustly accused."

Ten minutes later Raimey stepped outside, where she was greeted by Clay. "Well," he demanded, "did you get it?"

"Yes!" Raimey held out the slip of paper, and Clay threw his arms around her and lifted her off her feet.

"What a woman!" he cried, and he hugged her hard.

"Careful!" Raimey laughed. "Don't hug me too tightly." He released his grip at once, and she grasped his hand. "Does the prospect of being a grandfather make you feel old?"

"It makes me feel wonderful!" he answered. Raimey nodded fondly, and they moved to his carriage, talking excitedly of what had just happened.

He took her home, and when she asked what his plan was, he shook his head. "I'm taking Burke home in the morning."

"Your parents . . . how will you tell them?"

"I'll tell them that God has given Burke back to us, and we'll have to pray that we find the truth so that we can keep him!"

The next day at one o'clock in the afternoon Clay pulled up in front of the big house, sweating from nerves. He'd had no trouble getting Burke released—not with the name of Jefferson Davis on the order! But all the way home, as he'd driven the same ambulance he'd used to deliver Bob Yancy to his family, he'd been praying for a way to break the news to his parents.

His father was in poor condition, and a sudden shock could be—well, it could be serious. As for his mother, she was the stronger of the two, but this was such a shocking thing!

Finally he gave the matter to God, and when he stepped down from the seat of the ambulance, he greeted the handsome black man who came to meet him, saying, "Highboy, I'm going to speak to my parents. Hold that team right there until I get back. Don't let anybody go inside the wagon."

"Yas, Marse Clay!"

Clay found his parents in the parlor, his father reading and his mother sewing. They were very surprised, and Thomas asked at once, "Have you bad news, Son?"

"No, Father," Clay said, thinking that it was the same reception he'd gotten at the Yancys. "It's good news, but you must be very calm."

"What is it, Clay?"

Clay studied his mother carefully, thankful for her strength. He said slowly, "You both know that mistakes are made in battles and afterwards. That sometimes men are reported killed . . . and later they turn up alive."

Thomas and Susanna stared at him in disbelief. Thomas looked very frail, and now he licked his dry lips. "Son—?"

"Is it Burke?" Susanna asked when her husband could not finish.

"Yes. He's alive." He came to them as they rose to their feet, their eyes filled with amazement. "Wait, there's more."

They listened as he related carefully how Burke had been found and warned them, "He's very ill and may die. We've got to be ready for that. And even if he lives, he's under a cloud of suspicion. He'll have to have a trial and prove his innocence."

Susanna listened to Clay, and then she went to her husband. Putting her arms around him, she whispered, "God has given our son back, Tom!"

Clay looked apprehensively at his father and was amazed to see a strength in Thomas Rocklin's face that he had never seen there before. He had been a weak man in his youth, but now he said firmly, "God didn't send my son back to die, Susanna. He'll live! I believe it with all my heart!"

The three of them held each other, and then Thomas drew back. "Go bring your brother in, Clay." When Clay quickly left the room, Thomas turned to his wife. "Susanna, I've not been a strong man in the past, but I swear to you—I'll die before I let our boy go!"

Susanna Rocklin had waited for this moment for years! Now she moved to her husband, folded her arms around him, and whispered, "I'm so proud of you, Tom!"

They kissed, stood silent for a brief moment, then moved out to see the son they had given up for dead.

CHAPTER EIGHTEEN
"I Remember You!"

For three days Burke lingered between life and death in the master bedroom at Gracefield. Sometimes he would throw himself wildly about on the bed and had to be restrained. In his delirium he cried out, but usually his nurses could make little of his incoherent babblings.

At other times he would sink into a coma, his lank body so still that the only sign of life was a faint, ragged breathing. More than once Thomas and Susanna came to peer at his sallow face, fearing that he had slipped away.

Strangely enough it was Thomas who never lost faith. For years it had been Susanna who had been the strength of Gracefield, but during those long hours and days when their son lay gasping for breath, it was the father who stood against the grim specter of death that lurked in the room.

Dorrie, the brown slave who had ruled Gracefield with her mistress for years, spoke of this to her husband. Zander, at the age of sixty-two, looked the same as he did when he'd become the body servant of Thomas Rocklin years earlier— except that he was now white-haired and slightly overweight. On this day he had come into the kitchen to sit down on a high stool beside his wife, who was making biscuits.

"I'se scared Marse Burke ain't goin' ta make it," he muttered, shaking his head sadly.

Dorrie glared at him, snapping, "Whut you know 'bout it? You started doctorin' folks?"

Her remark angered Zander. He pushed his lips out in a mulish, angry fashion, snapping, "I knows what I knows, don't I? And I tells you dis, woman, if Marse Thomas don't watch out, he's goin' ta kill his ownself takin' care of that boy!"

His remark caught at Dorrie, bringing a thoughtful look into her brown eyes. She picked up a rolling pin and began flattening the lump of dough thoughtfully. She rolled it out, picked up an empty jar, and began cutting circles in the mass. When Zander reached over, picked up a fragment of the remains, and stuffed it into his mouth, she said out of habit, "Leave that alone." After a moment, she sat down beside Zander and said slowly, "It's de first time dat man's ever showed backbone, ain't it now?"

Zander chewed thoughtfully on a mouthful of dough, reached for another, then nodded. "Reckon so." A look of pride came to his eyes, and he said softly, "Marse Thomas— he's got to be a right good man in his last days. Miz Susanna, she's plumb proud of him fo' de first time."

Dorrie said in a low tone, "If he kill himself takin' care of dat boy . . . well, there's worse ways fo' a man to die."

They sat together, these two who had no interest in the war—at least not in its political implications. Abraham Lincoln could issue a dozen papers declaring them free, but they were so bound to the Rocklins that they would die before abandoning them. It was true that there was much cruelty in slavery, but the love and devotion shared between these slaves and the Rocklins went beyond institutions, and as they thought of their future, they never once thought of anything but being part of the house of Rocklin.

Nearby in the sick man's room, the subjects of their conversation were sitting quietly, watching Burke's pale face.

"His fever's gone down," Susanna said. She stood beside her son, her hand resting lightly on his broad forehead. Her eyes dwelt on the wan features, then she looked across at her husband.

"Thomas, go get some rest," she begged. "You have to save your strength."

Thomas was slumped in a small sofa, watching the pair. His flesh had fallen away from his bones, made slack by the sickness that had come to him months ago. Only traces of his good looks remained now, and his once-proud eyes had faded and were sunken into cavernous sockets. His hands were skeleton thin and trembled where they lay loosely clasped in his lap.

But a light came to brighten his eyes, and he shook his head. "I'm all right, Susanna. But you need to get some sleep."

Susanna went to him, sat down beside him, and took his hand. "I'll go presently," she said quietly.

Her gesture pleased him, and he turned to examine her. He was so weak that his voice was a mere whisper as he said, "You're still the best-looking woman I know."

Tears came to her eyes, and she blinked them away. "You must want something, paying compliments like that! What is it now?"

He smiled at her, then looked back at Burke. "He's better. He's going to make it."

"Yes. God is good."

They sat together, closer in spirit, they both knew, than they had been since their youth. The future looked grim indeed, for the war cast its gloom over the entire land. But Susanna was thankful, for she knew that her husband had become a man she could be proud of—something many women never had! They spoke softly, letting the long silences run on, content to be together, and each of them prayed for this broken son and for the other members of their family.

Once after a long silence, Thomas turned to face her, and she saw tears in his eyes. He was not a crying man, she knew, and she whispered, "What is it, Tom?"

"I feel that we're going to see God do a mighty work with Burke," he said, nodding. "Just now, Susanna, God dropped that into my spirit. It was as if he said, 'You will see this son redeemed.'" Wonder was on his face, for it was the first time he'd ever had such a thing happen. "Can it be God speaking to an old reprobate like me, Susanna?"

"You are God's own child, Tom," she said at once, and a great love rushed inside her spirit, so that she reached for him and pulled his head close to her breast so that he could not see her tears. "I'm so proud of you, my dear!" she whispered.

Susanna was alone with Burke when he regained consciousness. She had finally persuaded Thomas to go to his room and rest, and she had gone for a quick meal, which Dorrie had prepared.

"Lemme sit wif him," Dorrie urged. "You done wore yo'self out."

Susanna smiled tiredly, but shook her head. "No, you've got everything else to take care of, Dorrie. I'll be fine." She patted Dorrie's shoulder fondly, then returned to the sick man's side.

Her bones ached from the long vigil, but after she checked Burke, she curled up on the narrow couch that occupied space along the wall. Her eyelids drooped, and for five minutes she fought sleep, but soon succumbed.

She awoke with a start and sat up. Her muscles were so stiff that she knew she'd been asleep for some time—but something had awakened her. . . . She looked at Burke, alarm running along her nerves. Standing quickly, she went to him at once. Picking up a cloth, she dipped it into the basin of water on the nightstand, wrung it out, then began to clean his face.

As soon as the cloth touched his face, his eyes opened and Susanna cried out, "Burke!" When he stared at her unblinkingly, she placed her hand on his cheek, pleading, "Do you know me, Son?"

Burke's eyes were clear, but she could see only a faint response. He tried to speak, but only a croak emerged. "Water—!"

Susanna quickly poured cool water from the pitcher into a glass, then helped him raise his head. As she placed the water to his lips, he gulped thirstily, bumping the glass in his eagerness so that the water ran down onto his chest.

"Careful," Susanna said. "Drink more slowly." She held his head until he'd finished the glass, then nodded. "You can have more soon." Replacing the glass, she bent over him with a tremulous smile. "You've been very sick," she said. "How do you feel?"

Burke blinked at her, then began to struggle into a sitting position. She helped him, placing a pillow behind his back. He licked his lips, then nodded. "I feel better, but I'm so thirsty."

Susanna filled the glass and handed it to him. "You've had pneumonia, Burke. And a very high fever."

He took the glass and drank it more slowly. "That tastes good," he whispered. He handed the glass back, and the act seemed to have tired him. He rested his head on the pillow for a moment, closing his eyes.

Susanna asked, "Will you be all right for a minute? I want to get Tom."

His brow wrinkled, but he nodded and she left the room. She went to her bedroom and awakened Thomas. He blinked as she told him the good news, then he got out of bed hurriedly. Pulling on an old robe and a pair of slippers, he accompanied her down the stairs. When he entered the room where Burke sat upright against the pillows, his eyes brightened and he went at once to the bedside.

"Burke, my son," he said, his voice husky with emotion, "I was never so happy!" He bent over and put his arms around Burke, holding him close, then drew back and cleared his throat. "Now—," he said, striving for a normal voice. "Do you feel like talking?"

Burke was confused. He had only vague memories of the

241

past, dreams mixing with some sort of foggy reality. He felt terribly weak, and the two people who stood looking down at him made his confusion worse.

"I—guess so," he muttered. Looking around the room, he saw nothing that looked familiar. "Where am I?" he asked.

"You're home, Burke. You're at Gracefield." Susanna had been watching Burke's eyes, and the vacant expression troubled her. She said quickly, "You've been so sick it's confused you."

Thomas nodded. "You don't need to talk much, Son, but just tell us where you've been. We thought you were killed at Manassas." His son's dark eyes turned to gaze at him, and the expression in them somehow filled him with apprehension. "What is it, Burke? What's happened to you?"

Burke felt as though his head was spinning, and he tried desperately to find some sense in what they were saying. He looked at Thomas silently, then shook his head. "I—I can't remember this place." He licked his lips, then added, "I know I should remember you—but it's all out of focus."

"You—you don't remember me?" Thomas stammered. He turned to exchange glances with Susanna, then shook his head. This was much worse than he thought. He said quickly, "You're just tired, Burke. And a high fever like you've had, why, it can mess up a man's mind."

"Your father's right, Son," Susanna said, nodding gently. "You'll feel better soon."

Your father!

Burke blinked as he took in the words. He stared at the two older people, and then a memory came to him—or an image, at least. He stared at the woman and remembered telling someone how clearly he'd seen her in some kind of a dream. She was the same, and he tried to pull his thoughts together.

"I . . . remember you—!" he said to Susanna. "But . . . I've been in a hospital for a long time."

"A hospital?" Thomas asked, his brow wrinkling as he tried to piece this all together. "Where was this, Burke?"

Burke—that's my name!

"Why, in Washington," he said slowly. And as he lay there, memories came of that time. "I was hurt—but I got well."

"You were in a prison?" Thomas probed.

"No, it was a hospital," Burke answered. He stared hard at the man, then knew he had to tell them the truth. "My wounds healed, but my mind wasn't right. I couldn't remember who I was. Not even my name." He shook his head, adding, "You say I'm your son, but I can't remember you."

A silence fell on the room, and Burke felt sorry for both of them. He was very tired, his eyelids heavy. "I wish—," he said fuzzily, "that I could remember—"

He drifted off, his head falling to one side. Susanna at once laid him down in the bed, then stood staring down at him. "I never heard of such a thing, Tom," she said slowly. "But it explains some things."

"I guess he was mistaken for one of the Yankee soldiers," Thomas said slowly. "And the man we buried—he got hold of Burke's ring before he was killed." He looked down at the pallid face on the pillow. "We've got our son back, Susanna—but not all of him." He shook his thin shoulders in a gesture of determination, then took her hand saying, "God is in this. We'll not doubt, and one day we'll have all of him!"

Burke slept soundly for nearly twenty-four hours. It was a healthy sleep, and he awoke with his mind free from the dark specters of doubt and confusion. Bright sunlight flooded through the window across the room, falling in golden pools on the polished heartpine flooring, and for one fleeting moment he thought, *I've seen this room. . . . I've been in it before now!*

The door opened and a woman entered, her eyes meeting his at once. Again the memory he'd had of her touched his mind, then eluded him.

"You're feeling much better, aren't you?" she said, com-

243

ing to put her hand on his brow. "No fever at all and your eyes are clear." She poured him a drink of water, then when he had finished it, asked, "Are you hungry?"

The question stirred violent hunger pangs, and he blurted out, "I'm starved!"

Susanna laughed at his vehemence. "I'll go fix your breakfast."

"I want to get up," Burke announced.

"Well, it'll be good for you." She produced a robe from the armoire, along with a pair of shoes. Throwing the cover back, she held the robe as he pushed his arms through, then pulled a chair from the wall so that it faced the window. She guided him into it and urged him to sit down, then slipped a pair of house shoes on his feet. "Now, you sit right there until I get back with your breakfast," she commanded.

"I'm weak as dishwater!" he countered. "Don't guess I'll get up and run around the room."

After she left, he sat there staring out the window. Snow covered the broad grounds, reflecting the sun with bright crystal glints. He studied the wide, sweeping circular drive and the huge oaks that lined it, and knew he'd seen it before. It was not a fully formed memory, but a thrill came as he realized that he knew exactly what the outside of the house looked like, though he was inside.

"Looks like I've come home," he mused aloud. He thought of the couple, of their obvious love for him, and shook his head. "I've got little to bring to them. Mostly just a shell."

But when the woman came back with a tray, he covered this feeling as he ate. "You don't need to be a glutton, Burke," Susanna admonished him. "You need lots of small meals, not a lot all at once."

He nodded, then ate more slowly. When he was finished with the eggs, he spread blackberry jam on one of the thick biscuits and ate it in small bites. Then he drank the hot, black coffee, sipping it slowly.

"My name is Burke," he said. "Burke what?"

"Rocklin," Susanna said quietly. "You have a fine family. Your father's name is Thomas, and I'm Susanna."

Burke sat in the warm sunbeams, listening as she gave him the details of his own identity. As she spoke, faint memories tugged at his mind, some of them stronger than others. She was a beautiful woman, he realized, and very strong. Finally she smiled, saying, "Well, that's who you are, Son. Do you remember any of it?"

Burke hesitated, then asked, "My father, he's not well, is he?"

"No, Burke. He started failing about a year ago."

"What is it?"

"His heart." Susanna's lips grew tight and she dropped her eyes for a moment, staring at her hands. Then she lifted them, saying, "I must tell you something, Burke. Your coming home has done more for him than I can tell you. He's been . . . noble!"

Burke could not think of how to answer. "I feel so strange," he said with a shrug. "Like an impostor, I guess." The sound of the door opening came to him, and he turned to see Thomas enter. "Come in, sir," he said at once. "Sit down and help me finish these biscuits."

Thomas came across the room, moving slowly with a sick man's gait. His eyes searched Burke's face, and what he saw brightened his own countenance. "Ah, you're much better," he said with satisfaction. "I think you're out of danger."

Burke waited until his father seated himself in a chair that Susanna moved from the wall, then said at once, "I want to tell you all I can remember about what's happened to me." He began from the time he came out of the coma in Armory Square Hospital, and the older people sat with their eyes riveted on his face. He spoke for a long time, leaving out little of the story. Finally he paused, took a deep breath, then shrugged his shoulders. "Before I was put in the army, I was starting to remember things. I think if I'd been able to stay on the farm with Grace, my memory would have come back in time."

"You owe that young woman a great deal, don't you, Burke?" Susanna asked.

"Just about everything, I guess." A thought came to him, and he blinked. "I've got to let her know I'm alive!"

Thomas said slowly, "That might not be wise . . . not right now."

"Why not, sir?"

"Son, you're out of a Confederate prison on temporary release." Burke listened with shock as his father spoke of the terms of his release. "You'll have to defend yourself as soon as you're able," Thomas said. "I think when the authorities hear the full story, they'll understand. But you were wearing a Yankee uniform, so it might be best if you didn't contact the young woman until this thing is cleared up."

Burke's face was a study in bafflement. "So I could be shot for treason? That's what it amounts to?"

"Oh, it won't come to that, my boy! We have the ear of the president, you see."

"Jefferson Davis."

"Yes, of course! He agreed to your release when one of your relatives went to Mrs. Davis with your story."

Burke listened incredulously as Thomas told him the machinations that had gotten him out of Libby Prison, but when his father finished, he shook his head, doubt clouding his eyes. "I don't think the president will be too sympathetic to a Confederate soldier who fought against the South in the Union army."

Thomas tried to put the best face on Burke's chances, but later when he and Susanna were alone, he was less optimistic. "Burke's got a point," he admitted. "We've got to get on this thing right now. When will Clay be here?"

"He's so busy, Thomas, with the new men and the training. Do you think we should send for him?"

"No." Thomas gave her an adamant look, then said, "I'll go see the president."

"You're not able—!" she began to protest, but a look

from her husband silenced her. She had never seen such determination in his eyes.

"Susanna," he said, his voice stronger than it had been in weeks, "I'll get my son out of this trouble even if I have to die for it!"

The city of Richmond was a microcosm of the larger world. The new nation had not learned very well how to forge cannons or produce gunpowder, but it had a system of gossip equal to that of any nation.

The story of Burke Rocklin was too good to be kept secret, and it was not long before everyone who was anyone had some version of it.

Thomas Rocklin got his first warning that getting Burke set free from the charges against him would not be simple when he spoke to Davis's secretary. "The president is very busy, sir," he was told. "Perhaps you should put your request in writing. Or perhaps you should go through a member of the military staff?"

Thomas did both, but neither accomplished much. He found Clay, and the two of them discovered that while Varina Davis had great influence over her husband, the president was listening to others as well. They finally talked to a member of Davis's cabinet, who said, "Don't use my name, if you please, but I think it fair to tell you that the president is under pressure to see that your son is charged with desertion. You'd better start looking for a good lawyer."

The strain had worn Thomas down, and when they left the office, Clay said, "Sir, you *must* go home!" His father looked ghastly, thin and sallow, and he insisted on taking him home to Gracefield—which Thomas finally agreed to only when Clay promised he would persist in trying to see the president.

One tangible result of the talk about Burke Rocklin was a visit paid to Gracefield by one Belinda King. She had been on a visit to Lynchburg and had received the news by means

247

of a letter from Chad Barnes. He had pursued her with determination since the "death" of Burke Rocklin, and Chad lost no time in letting her know what had happened. In a short letter, he had written:

> You will hear it soon enough, and I would rather you would hear it from me. The man we buried was not Burke Rocklin. He is alive and at Gracefield.

When Belinda read this information, her eyes grew large, and she scanned the rest of the short letter avidly. Barnes related how the president himself had paroled Burke, but there was cynicism in his written remarks concerning Burke's loss of memory:

> The story is that he lost his memory and didn't even *know* he was in the Confederate army. Not only that, but he joined the Union army and fought against our brave fellows at Fredericksburg. Well, I find that a little hard to swallow! There will be a trial or a hearing of some sort, of course. I know you will want to return at once. When you return, I will take you to see Burke myself. What this will do to what we have been feeling I am not sure. It will not change *my* feelings, but you are very romantic. I warn you now, Belinda, I am convinced that Burke Rocklin is an opportunist. He set out to marry you for your money, and it is my belief that somehow when he was captured, he sold out his country to avoid being sent to a prisoner-of-war camp.

Belinda *was* romantic. She knew full well that the trial of Burke Rocklin would be a sensational affair, and she longed to be there. She packed at once, sent a wire to Barnes, and he was there when she stepped off the train.

He kissed her, held her hard, then let her go. "Belinda, I'm going to fight for you. I warn you now, I'll do all I can to prove that Burke Rocklin isn't worthy of you."

This was an exciting statement to Belinda. To have two attractive men fighting for her hand—and in full view of Richmond—was thrilling. She put her hand on Barnes's broad chest and whispered, "I want to do the right thing, Chad."

He studied her, then smiled. "You will, Belinda. Now, let's go see the famous man who's fought in both the blue and the gray!"

CHAPTER NINETEEN
Two Visitors for Burke

⭐

The terrible casualties suffered by the Union army at Fredericksburg sent shock waves throughout the North. The Peace party stepped up its efforts to allow the South to go its own way. President Lincoln knew that they were a formidable power and feared that all the blood shed by the Union would be for nothing. It took all the moral force Lincoln possessed to keep the North from giving up, and in one sense, the winter of 1862 marked the high tide of the Confederacy.

Burnside, agonizing over his losses, withdrew the Army of the Potomac to the north bank of the Rappahannock, still determined to keep the initiative and exploit his impressive numerical superiority over Lee. But all were agreed: Burnside had to go. By January of 1863, his attempt to move upstream and cross the upper Rappahannock behind Lee's left flank foundered in liquid mud, so Burnside told Lincoln he must either have a new staff or Lincoln had to accept his resignation.

Lincoln found that the leadership of the ill-starred Army of the Potomac was only one of his problems, for the Union was suffering setbacks in other areas.

On the Mississippi, Sherman's first drive on Vicksburg had been stopped in its tracks on December 29 at Chickasaw

Bluff. At Chickasaw Bluff, Lt. Gen. John Pemberton, commanding the Vicksburg sector, drove back Sherman, who suffered more than seventeen hundred casualties. Hard-riding Confederate cavalry had captured Grant's supply base at Holly Springs a week earlier, and Grant withdrew to build up a new base at Milliken's Bend, twenty miles north of Vicksburg and on the wrong bank of the river—the west bank.

And so, by the New Year of 1863 it was clear that there would be no more runaway Union victories on the Mississippi, and that the campaign against Vicksburg would be long and hard. Even so, despite pressure from those who believed Grant's drinking was a serious liability, Lincoln refused point-blank to replace him. "I can't spare this man," was his terse comment. *"He* fights."

The news was equally dismaying from central Tennessee. On December 26, Rosecrans marched out of Nashville to attack the Army of Tennessee under Gen. Bragg at Murfreesboro and drive on to Chattanooga, 125 miles to the southeast. But on December 31, 1862, Bragg struck first, staging an uncanny replay of Shiloh by unleashing a storming attack on Rosecrans. As at Shiloh, the attacking Confederates bent the tortured Union army into a horseshoe before its desperate resistance took effect. Repeated Confederate assaults only increased the toll in casualties without winning the battle.

The cost of Murfreesboro was proportionately worse than that of Fredericksburg, as terrible as that had been! Rosecrans, with an army far smaller than Burnside's, lost the same number of men: thirteen thousand. True, Bragg had lost ten thousand and could not find replacements, but the North reeled under the shock of such losses. Bragg was forced to withdraw, and Lincoln claimed a Union victory, but it was a hollow claim.

And so it was that, with the Union war machine stopped dead in its tracks in Tennessee and on the Mississippi, Lincoln shrank from the prospect of choosing a new commander for the Army of the Potomac. Finally forced to do so, he made one of the most extraordinary appointments in modern military history.

To "Fighting Joe Hooker," the most outspoken of Burnside's critics, Lincoln wrote a devastating letter of rebuke— and at the same time appointed Hooker to command the army! Lincoln poured scorn on Hooker's assertions that both the army and the government needed a dictator. "Only those generals who gain successes can set up dictators," wrote Lincoln. And he ended, "Beware of rashness, but with energy and sleepless vigilance go forward and give us victories."

Lincoln had made a poor choice, indeed, as the future would prove. Hooker was a good organizer and made some reforms, but he was far better at blustering than he was at fighting. "My plans are perfect," he announced grandly. "May God have mercy on Gen. Lee, for I will have none!"

And so the two armies and the two nations fell back and waited as 1863 was born. An unusually foul North Virginia winter enforced a virtual two months truce, and both North and South prepared for the bloodbath that spring would bring.

As ever, the North had all the material advantages, and Hooker made admirable use of them. By the last week of April of the New Year, he would build up the Army of the Potomac to a greater-than-ever strength of 130,000 and proclaim that it was "the finest army on the planet!"

Lee would be less sanguine. In February he would send Longstreet's corps to the lower James River to cover Union forces, and by the end of April Longstreet would still not return to join Lee. Thus Lee would have barely sixty thousand effectives to hold Hooker.

Even so, the South was accustomed to long odds. Lee and Jackson had taken on all that the North could throw at them and had sent them running back to Washington. That winter in Richmond, prices were high—but so were the hopes of the Confederacy. Rumors were flying that England would recognize the new nation soon, and it seemed likely that the Peace party in the North would bring such pressure on Lincoln that he would be forced to let the South go its own way.

This resurgence of optimism might have been good for the Southern Confederacy, but it made things difficult for Burke Rocklin.

He had recovered from his physical ailments almost at once. He sat up for three days, eating the heaping meals brought to him by his mother and by Dorrie and sleeping long hours. During his waking hours, his mother sat with him, reading to him and speaking of his past. She did so easily and naturally, and whether it was her constant bringing before him the details of the past, or simply the natural restorative powers of nature, was not clear, but he found himself remembering many things.

The beginning of this recovery came one afternoon when Susanna was musing about an event that took place when Burke had been six years old. It was a simple story about how Burke and Clay had gotten into trouble. As she spoke, Burke listened almost carelessly, until suddenly he was struck by a memory so clear that he exclaimed, "I remember that! Clay was sixteen and I was only six! He took me with him over to the Huger place!"

Susanna blinked with surprise. "You remember that? You were only six years old!"

"I remember it all," Burke said, his eyes wide. "Clay got drunk with Charlie and Devoe Huger. They took me with them when they went into a saloon in Richmond, and Father came in like a storm and hauled us both home. He gave Clay a whipping and I thought he was going to start on me. But he said, 'It's not your fault, Burke,' and I wanted to cry I was so relieved!"

"Burke, that's wonderful! Thank God!"

Burke looked at her, his eyes filled with wonder. "That's what Grace would say," he said finally. "She always said God would give me back my past."

"She sounds like a fine girl," Susanna said quietly. "You think of her a great deal, don't you?"

"Yes," Burke nodded. "She filled my whole world, Mother. I didn't have a past, and she was there to fill my present."

"I'd love to meet her, Son."

Burke brought his mind back to the present. "You're not likely to, I guess," he said slowly. "Looks like I'm headed for the gallows." He shook his head in a disgusted manner and summoned up a smile. "I hate a man who feels sorry for himself!" he exclaimed. He drew his lips together into a firm line, adding, "I've got a lot to be thankful for. I could have been killed at Fredericksburg, or crippled."

They sat there quietly, and then Burke reached over and took his mother's hand. "I've got a fine family," he said. "I used to wonder what it would be like if I got my memory back and found things so bad I couldn't stand it. But I found you and Father—and that's miracle enough for me!"

Susanna felt suddenly that she had her son back—all of him. She lifted her arms and put them around Burke's neck. "Tell your father that, Burke," she whispered.

"I will." He held his mother, then drew back shaking his head. "He doesn't need the trouble I've brought him. When he comes home, you've got to keep him here."

Susanna shook her head. "No, Burke. Your father has had great fears about himself—he's always felt that his brother Stephen was far above him—but now he's shown his family, and himself, that he's a great man. I pray for him every day, but if he dies, he'll die happy, knowing that his family respects and admires him."

Burke had suspected some of this, and nodded slowly. "When he comes back, I'll make it plain how much *I* admire him." He smiled and said, "Now, tell me some more about what a wonderful child I was, perfect in all my ways!" He sat back, listening as she began to speak, and the following day when his father came home, he made it a point to express his thanks. Thomas was exhausted, but when Burke spoke, his eyes grew bright. Finally he held out his thin hand and clasped his son's hand, saying huskily, "It makes me feel so good to hear you say these things, Burke!"

"I mean it, sir!"

Thomas sat slumped in his chair, racked with pain, but warmed by the knowledge that he had won the approval of his sons. "You know, Burke," he said slowly, "I've spent a great deal of time grieving over my youth. I've wasted most of my life."

"Oh, don't say that!"

"It's true enough. I had everything that most men long for and never have: money, position, a good wife. And I didn't know how blessed I was." He lifted his gaze, adding with a smile, "But God has restored to me the years that the locusts had eaten."

Burke looked puzzled. "What's that, sir?"

"It's from the Old Testament, from the book of Joel. God's people disobeyed him, as I remember it, and he sent terrible judgments on them. One of them was a plague of locusts that devoured their crops and brought a famine on the land."

"I seem to remember Grace saying something about that."

"Well, it was terrible, but God said to them, 'If you'll turn back to me, I'll restore to you the years that the locusts have eaten.'"

"How could God do that?" Burke frowned. "When time is gone, it's gone, isn't it?"

Thomas suddenly felt that Burke was a man who was searching after God—and it thrilled him. Clay had been a wild young man, but now he was a fervent Christian. Now Thomas was filled with a longing to see his other son find peace with God, and he wished that Susanna were present to help. But he prayed quickly for the right words and said, "Not always, Son. Oh, the time itself is gone. Time doesn't stay for any man, does it? But God can change things so that the past doesn't control us. Don't you think so?"

"Well, I don't know," Burke said slowly. "If a man gets drunk and sleeps on the railroad track and gets his leg cut off, he'll never have that leg again."

"True enough," Thomas said, nodding. "We have to live with the results of what we do. But when a man gives himself to God, the Lord can fill his life with something new and better. I think that's what the verse means. God was promising to give his people something *better* than what they had." He hesitated, then shook his head. "I'm doing a poor job of explaining," he said.

"No, I can see what you mean." Burke leaned forward, his dark eyes intent. "I've pretty well wasted my life," he stated. "Mother's been telling me about myself. She's always kind, but I can tell I don't have much to be proud of."

"Neither did your brother," Thomas countered. "Not for many years. He ran out on his family, and no one had a good word for him. He even became a slave trader. But since he became a Christian, God has given him something wonderful, and I know he's going to reward him even more for his faithfulness."

Burke shook his head. "Your sons . . . we haven't been much pleasure to you, sir."

Thomas said at once, "I'm not a prophet, Burke, but God's given me an assurance that both my sons will be men of honor and will bring honor to the name of Rocklin."

Burke was filled with doubt. Shaking his head, he said, "Be hard to do that if I'm hanged as a traitor."

"That will never happen, Burke! I'll fight it to my last breath!"

"That's what you mustn't do," Burke said quickly. "You've done all you can, Father."

"No, I haven't." Thomas shook his head, his eyes alive in his pallid face. "When the truth is known, we'll have justice, you'll see!"

Burke saw that his father was tired, and he insisted that he go lie down. "We'll have lots of time to talk later," he said gently. He smiled, then told him how the memory of his trip to the Hugers had come to him. "You can tell me how you took a strap to Clay instead of me!"

Thomas laughed, and when Susanna came into the room an hour later, she was pleased to find them laughing. Later, however, when she and Thomas were alone in their room, he lay down on the bed, fatigue lining his face. "I'm afraid Burke's in for a bad time," he said slowly.

Susanna came over and sat down on the bed beside him. A lock of his hair fell over his forehead, and she pushed it back. His hair was gray, and she suddenly thought of how black and glossy it had been the day they'd been married. *Like Burke's is now,* she thought. "It'll be all right, Tom," she said.

He lay still, his eyes closed, and she could see the tiny veins etched on his eyelids. "It's this war that's turned everything upside down. Everyone is either a sheep or a goat, Susanna. And I can see it in the faces of people—that they think Burke's one of the goats." Bitterness crept into his tone as he added, "Anyone who doesn't believe in the Cause is the enemy."

"That's how it was with Clay," Susanna answered. "He doesn't believe in this war, and if he hadn't joined the army in spite of that, he'd have been pulled apart."

"Yes, but Burke's in worse condition than Clay was. He was wearing a Yankee uniform, and that's the end of it for lots of people. They haven't been around like we have to see what poor shape he's in."

"He's getting better every day."

"Yes, and that's going to make people say, 'See? There never was anything wrong with him in the first place!'" He opened his eyes and said, "I'm going to retain Gaines DeQuincy. He's the best lawyer in the South—and the most expensive. But we can't take any risks with this thing."

"But isn't he in the army?"

"Yes, and that's why I want him. He's a genuine patriot, and if this thing comes to a trial, it'll be a military court.

Won't hurt to have a certified supporter of the Confederacy defending Burke. I'll write him tomorrow."

"I feel so strange, Chad!"

Belinda King had bought a new dress for her trip to Gracefield, a light blue gown that matched her eyes perfectly. Now she touched her new hat nervously, asking, "Do I look all right?"

"Beautiful, as usual." Chad Barnes was amused at Belinda, thinking how typical it was that she thought of her looks even on such an occasion. They had had dinner the evening before, after he'd picked her up at the station. It was only now, as they were turning into the driveway that led to the big house at Gracefield, that the blonde girl showed any sign of nervousness. *As long as she's dressed in the latest style,* Barnes thought with a cynical amusement, *she can face anything.*

Aloud he said, "Are you sure you want to see him?"

"Why, of course I want to see him, Chad!" Belinda turned to Barnes with amazement in her eyes. "After all, we *were* engaged to be married."

"You'll never marry Burke, Belinda," Barnes said firmly. "You were never in love with him, anyway."

"You're just jealous, Chad!"

"I *was* at the time," Barnes admitted. "But not now."

"You don't think I could still be interested in Burke?"

They had reached the curving driveway, and Barnes slowed the horses to a walk. The trees lining the drive were black and bare, stripped of their leaves, and the icy breath of a new cold wave bit at Chad's face. "No, I don't think you are," he said slowly.

"I'm fickle, is that it?"

Barnes was a blunt man, but knew better than to allow Belinda to know he thought exactly that. He'd figured this conversation was coming and knew exactly what to say. He smiled to himself. *I can handle this girl. She's filled her head*

259

with romantic notions, but once we're married, I can change that.

"No, I don't think you're fickle, honey," he said softly. "I think you've grown up. All beautiful girls like to flirt. It was natural enough for you to like seeing Burke and me make fools of ourselves fighting over you. But I think I've seen something in you these last few weeks. You've grown up to be a mature woman and can see now that I'm the man for you."

Belinda was accustomed to hearing compliments on her beauty, but the idea that she was now a mature woman—that tickled her vanity. "Well . . . ," she said slowly, "we *have* grown close, Chad."

"Yes, and it's unthinkable what you'd have to go through if you married Burke. I couldn't bear to see you dragged through the mess that's coming." He didn't miss the fleeting expression of fear in her eyes, and he struck hard. "Burke's going to go down, I'm afraid," he shrugged. "He's a good fellow, but he's dug his own grave."

"You don't think he's a traitor, do you, Chad?"

Barnes hesitated, then said, "Yes, I do, Belinda. And it hurts me. Burke and I . . . well, we've had our differences, but I don't like to see any of my friends turn out like this."

"I—I can't believe Burke would do such a thing!"

"Well, you may be right," Barnes said, shrugging. "I hope you are. But even if Burke didn't sell out, he'll never be able to live in this country."

"What do you mean?"

Barnes stopped the horses, but said before getting out, "Just that, Belinda. Even if Burke is declared innocent, he'll never be admitted to the homes of the people of the South." He drew her gaze, then added, "You'd be in exile, Belinda, if you married Burke. He'll have to leave the country, and I'd hate to see you cut off from your family and friends." He saw that the thought horrified her and knew he'd said enough for now.

He leaped to the ground, helped Belinda down, handed

the lines to a slave, who led the carriage away, then the two of them went up the steps. They were met at the door by Susanna.

"Come in," she said. "I saw you drive up."

The older woman's clear direct gaze disturbed Belinda for some reason. Burke's mother had never been anything but courteous to her, but something in Susanna Rocklin's stately bearing made her uneasy. She said in a rather flustered manner, "I know I should have written you, Mrs. Rocklin, but after Burke—"

"It's all right, Belinda." Susanna turned to Barnes saying, "How are you, Maj. Barnes?"

Now it was Barnes's turn to feel uncomfortable, and he felt totally out of place as he answered, "We shouldn't be intruding on you, Mrs. Rocklin, but Belinda and I wanted to see Burke."

"Yes, I came as soon as I got word he'd come back," Belinda said quickly. "But if he's too sick to see us . . . ?"

"He's feeling much better," Susanna said. "He's in the study now, reading. I'll take you to him."

"Is he—that is, does he remember *anything?*" Belinda asked as they followed Susanna down the hall.

"It's very selective. It's as though his memory is waking up a little at a time. Every day he remembers more, but don't be shocked if he doesn't remember you at first."

Susanna opened the large walnut door, then stepping inside said, "Burke, you have visitors."

Burke got up from his chair at once and laid the book he was reading on the table. He stared at the two visitors, then nodded. "Hello, Belinda."

Belinda's face glowed with surprise. "You remember me?"

"Well, not really," Burke said quickly. "Mother's told me so much about you, and there's a picture of you in my room."

Belinda looked slightly crushed at his explanation, and it was Barnes who asked, "Do you remember me, Burke?"

Burke stared at the big man carefully, noting the hostility

261

in the stiff features. "No, I'm afraid not." He paused then added, "But I probably will. When I meet somebody from my past, it seems to trigger something. I think about them, and usually it sorts itself out."

"You all sit down," Susanna said, "and I'll fix some tea."

"Do you mind if I walk around the grounds while you do that, Mrs. Rocklin?" Barnes asked instantly. He laid a level gaze on Burke, saying in a mocking tone, "I wouldn't want to overburden our patient with too many old 'memories.'"

Susanna stared at him, then nodded. "Perhaps that would be best, Major." She left the room at once, followed by Barnes, who turned to give a cynical smile to Belinda.

Burke watched him close the door, then turned to face Belinda. "Obviously the major thinks I'm a fraud," he remarked.

"Oh, no, he's just—just careful," Belinda said quickly. She was rather confused, for the man who stood before her was greatly changed from the Burke she'd last seen. Then he had been strong and in uniform, but now he was pale and thin and wore a simple pair of brown trousers and a heavy wool shirt.

Catching her glance, Burke smiled slightly. He'd picked up enough from his parents and others to have some idea of what kind of a girl this was. Dorrie had sniffed, *"Dat little ol' gal you wuz gonna marry, she's 'bout as empty-headed as de ol' peacock dat runs round heah!"*

"This must be difficult for you, Miss King," Burke said. "But I want to make it easy on you. Won't you sit down?"

"Thank you, Burke," Belinda said quickly. When she was seated she laughed with embarrassment. "It is hard, isn't it? Not just on me, but even more so on you. Here's a perfectly strange female come to demand that you take up where you left off."

Burke had to admire her straightforward admission. "Let's be honest with each other, Belinda—may I call you that? Well, put your mind at rest. I've got my hands too full of trouble right now to think of anything but saving my neck. I don't think it would be wise for us to build on what was in the past."

This caught Belinda totally by surprise—and hurt her feelings! It was one thing for *her* to break off an engagement, but quite different for someone else to do it! Her eyes brightened with anger, and she flared out, "You just throw me out for all Richmond to laugh at, is that it?"

Burke blinked in surprise at the attack but shook his head quickly. "I thought it would be unfair of me to make any demands on you, Belinda. When I asked you to marry me, things were very different. I don't think it would be best for you to be caught up in my trouble."

"Oh, I see," Belinda said, more calmly. Then she nodded, saying, "That's very noble of you, Burke. Perhaps it might be best. But what will I say? People are already asking about us."

"Tell them that you've decided we acted too hastily, and the engagement is off."

"Well, if you think it's best, I suppose I'll have to do it," Belinda said, secretly relieved, for this was not the romantic, dashing Confederate officer she'd agreed to marry.

"Now, Burke," she said, "tell me everything."

When Barnes came in thirty minutes later, he was taken aback by Belinda's greeting. "Chad, Burke and I have agreed that our engagement was a mistake."

Prepared to fight for Belinda, Barnes was nonplused and could only stammer, "Well—I think that's best for both of you."

"I thought you might find it convenient," Burke said dryly. He was well aware from what his parents had told him that Chad Barnes had been vindictive after the engagement was announced.

Barnes stiffened and his voice took on a hard edge. "I don't care for what you're suggesting, Burke."

"You want to marry Belinda. From what I've been told, you always have. Now I'm out of the way, so you can pursue her with a good conscience."

Chad Barnes disliked being handed the girl as if she were a prize. He knew that the world would say exactly what Burke Rocklin had just put into words, but it angered him. Rashly he said, "I want to warn you, Burke, I don't think for one moment you're telling the truth. In fact, I think you're a turncoat and a coward!"

Burke stared at Barnes, but did not raise his voice. "I suppose this is where I slap your face and we meet at dawn with pistols?" He smiled and shook his head. "I won't act a fool, even if you do. However, I do think you'd better leave this house." He turned to Belinda, saying, "I regret to have to speak this way in front of you," and then he turned and left the room.

"Come on," Barnes snarled in disgust. "Let's get out of here!"

Belinda was practically towed out of the house, and as soon as they were in the carriage and headed toward the main road, she protested. "Why are you acting like this, Chad? I think Burke was very nice to see we weren't for each other."

But Barnes spoke furiously, "He handed you over to me as if you were a cheap prize he didn't want! I won't take his cavalier attitude, Belinda—and I'd think you'd be insulted!"

Belinda fell silent, but finally asked, "You're not going to fight a duel with him, are you, Chad?"

"No. He's a coward. But I'm going to make it my business to see that he doesn't get by with this trick he's trying to pull."

"What will you do?"

Barnes struck the horses with the buggy whip and took a perverse pleasure as they leaped forward into a run. "I'm going to see that he hangs for treason, Belinda," he said, and there was a smile of satisfaction on his heavy mouth as he thought of the thing. "Mr. Burke Rocklin's always been a little brash—but a rope necktie will take that out of him!"

CHAPTER TWENTY
Desperate Journey

★

"Look at that, Pat," Cotter said, nodding toward the small group of passengers who had descended and were being met by relatives. "What do you make of those two?"

Pat Grissom was a tall, stooped man of fifty who spent most of his time playing checkers with Cotter. He picked up a few dollars transporting freight and sometimes a passenger or two. He looked up from the checkerboard, stared out the window at the two men his friend had indicated, then shook his head. "Never seen 'em before."

Cotter shot his friend a disgusted look, then put his sharp black eyes back on the old man and the Negro, who was collecting his bags. "Might be a fare for you, Pat," he grunted. "But we better be careful. That darkie might be a runaway slave."

"Not likely," Grissom observed. "He wouldn't be traveling by train, would he? He'd be sent along by the Underground Railroad. But I better check it out," he muttered. "I'm a deputy sheriff, you know." In the small town where he lived, the office was mostly ceremonial, but Grissom took it seriously. He watched with narrowed eyes as the tall man in the heavy coat came slowly across the brick pavement to enter the small ticket office.

"Yes, sir. Can I help you?" Grissom said brightly. He

noted that the man was not young, and it was obvious that he was not in good health. Grissom noted the pain-dulled eyes and the slow, tentative movements such as only men who are very tired or sick use.

"Yes, sir," the old man nodded. "Can you direct me to a family named Swenson?"

"Why, you must mean the Amos Swenson place, I reckon," Grissom said with nod. A small alarm went off in his head, and he thought, *Got to have something to do with Sister Grace and that soldier she nursed. Always knew no good would come of that!*

"Yes, that's the name. Is it far?"

Cotter noted that the man had a Southern accent. He looked quickly at the black man, noting that he was well dressed and healthy. "It ain't in town, sir," Cotter said. "You'll need a buggy to get out there. I don't believe I caught your name? You're not related to the Swensons I don't reckon?"

The old man hesitated, aware of the station agent's burning curiosity, then shrugged. "My name is Rocklin, and I'm no relation to the Swensons. Could you tell me where I might rent a rig?"

"Why, I reckon you're in luck, Mr. Rocklin." Cotter nodded toward the man seated at the table. "Pat here can take you out to the Swenson place, couldn't you, Pat?"

Grissom nodded. "Guess I ain't got nothing else in the way," he grunted. "Can take you in the spring wagon—but I got a two-seat carriage that rides better. Fare will be ten dollars, though. Takes half a day of my time."

"Can we start now?"

Grissom eyed the black man, then turned to ask, "He goin', too?"

"Yes."

"All right. I got the carriage outside."

"Is there a place I can get a quick meal in town?"

"Oh, sure," Cotter said, nodding. "See that sign, the little one next to the feed store? That's Ma Stevens's place. She'll feed you real good. Tell her I sent you—Al Cotter."

"Thank you, sir." Thomas turned to Zander, saying, "Put the luggage in the carriage, Zander. I'll bring you something to eat."

"Yas, Marse Rocklin."

Cotter watched as Rocklin moved slowly down the street and disappeared into the cafe. He saw that the black man had put two pieces of luggage into the carriage and had seated himself on one of the bales of cotton by the wayside. A thought came to him, and he filled a coffee cup with black coffee and added sugar and cream. Moving outside, he came to where the black man sat and extended it. "Have some coffee. Makes a man thirsty, them long train rides."

"Thank you, sah." Zander took the cup, sipped it, then smiled with approval. "Dat's mighty fine coffee, sah," he remarked.

"Your name is Zander is it?" Cotter said, leaning against the bale. "Well, Zander, how's your trip been?"

"Oh, fine, sah! Mighty fine!"

"Come far, have you?"

"Well, sah, pretty far—and yet, not so far either."

For the next ten minutes Cotter tried with scant success to pry information out of Zander. But all he received were generalities. *Either this darkie is a fool or he's plenty sharp!* Cotter concluded.

"Your master, he's not too well, is he? Kind of strange he'd be making a hard trip all the way from the South to Pennsylvania, ain't it?" When Zander allowed it was, Cotter asked directly, "Well, I guess you was a slave for quite a while, wasn't you? How's it feel to be free?"

"Free? I belongs to Marse Rocklin," Zander said.

"Ain't you heard, man? President Lincoln freed you. He put it all in a paper. It's called the Emancipation Proclamation. You don't belong to nobody!" Leaning closer to Zander, Cotter said confidentially, "I know you don't want to go back South and be a slave. Maybe I can help you get away from Rocklin." He had no idea how he would do this, but thought it best to test the Negro.

But Zander gave the white man a direct look. "I ain't studyin' no paper, sah. I been wif Marse Rocklin all my life, me and my wife and our chilluns. He been good to us, and I reckon as how I gonna die a Rocklin!"

Cotter stared at the dignified Negro in disbelief. He had read the horror stories of slavery and could not believe that there was another side to it—but though he tried his best, he could not shake Zander's adamant statement that he'd die a Rocklin.

Disgusted, Cotter left Zander and presently saw Rocklin come down the street and take a sack to the slave. "Stubborn ol' slave!" Cotter grunted to Grissom. "Ain't got a lick of sense!" Then he added, "Try to find out what Rocklin's going out to the Swenson place for, Pat."

But Grissom, though he tried valiantly, could not discover anything of this nature. All the way to the Swenson farm, he asked questions, most of which the tall man beside him on the wagon ignored. Finally, in desperation, he asked, "You know the Swensons well, do you?"

The old man did not answer for a long time, so long that Grissom thought he'd chosen to ignore his question. But finally he said, "We have a mutual friend. What is the name of that tree, may I ask?"

It was a rebuff that even a man such as Pat Grissom could not ignore, and he drove the rest of the way in sullen silence.

Grace broke the skim of ice that had formed in the basin, washed her face, then dressed in a pair of heavy wool trousers and a red flannel shirt that had belonged to her father. She put on two pair of wool socks and a pair of thick-soled leather boots, then moved to the kitchen. Clyde and Prudence slept as late as possible—especially in the winter months—so she rekindled the fire in the cook stove, made a quick breakfast, then slipped into a heavy sheepskin coat, pulled on a broad-brimmed hat, and left the house.

Since both of the hands were gone for two weeks, Grace had taken over their chores. She went to the barn, milked the cows, then, after taking the frothy buckets of milk to the house, fed the rest of the stock. Clyde had made a half-hearted offer to rise early and do these chores, but Grace had said, "I like to get up early. You and Prudence might as well sleep."

After the chores were done, she picked up her rifle and made her way across the pasture toward the woods. It was so cold that her lips and eyelids were stiff, but she didn't mind. She loved the cold weather. A large rabbit, startled by her passing, leaped up and made a wild run for the thicket, his feet making a thumping sound on the frozen ground. Grace threw up her rifle and tacked him as he zigzagged frantically, then lowered it. She could have shot him easily, but they'd had plenty of rabbit meat lately.

Entering the deep woods, she made her way along the trail, alert and aware of her surroundings. She loved the woods and knew that she would be miserable in town. The pattern of her life had been tied to the rhythms of the sun, the clouds, the seasons. In towns, men and women organized their lives by clocks, but Grace was always aware of the faint urgings of nature, just as animals are. She always knew when it was time to plant, not by something she'd read in a book, but because some combination of weather and the skies and the earth told her so.

Coming to a frozen brook, she broke the ice, stooped, and dipped the icy water with her hand. It was so cold it hurt her teeth, but she liked the taste of it better than the water that came from the well. Blowing on her hand, she proceeded to a spot she often frequented. A stand of huge oaks stood sentinel over the small brook, and in the summers she came to yank the plump bream and bluegills from a deep pool formed by an S-shaped crook in the stream. Now the stream was frozen, and as Grace leaned back against a massive oak, she wondered about the fish, what they did in winter. How do they eat cut off from the bugs and life by the ice? They were still there she knew, for she'd caught them by breaking the ice and fishing for them with bits of meat.

A quietness lay over the woods, and Grace soaked it up. Overhead the sky was silver-gray, and she knew there would be snow falling very soon. The thought of snow reminded her suddenly of her rides in the sleigh with John Smith—and a shadow came over her face.

He had come into her life suddenly—and had disappeared without warning. She had gone to the post office day after day, yearning for a word from him, but finally had understood that nothing was coming. She had said nothing to Clyde or Prudence, and when others had asked of the tall man who'd filled so much of her life, she'd merely said she'd had no word from him.

She'd grown more silent, had become a recluse in the days that followed. More and more she threw herself into the open, leaving the house early and staying out until dark. After supper, she'd fallen into the habit of going to her room, reading her Bible for long hours, then going to bed for a restless night's sleep.

Jacob Wirt had seen her restlessness. "You are not happy, are you, Grace? Ah, well, God knows our hearts. If the young man is for you, God will bring him back."

But Grace's spirit, which had been filled with the joy of an awakening love, grew still and sad. She sought God, but the heavens were brass, and finally she knew the anguish that comes with a lost love.

Now as she stood braced against the oak, she was attacked by a wave of bitterness. "God, why did thee let him touch my life if thee meant to take him away?"

Her words startled a doe that had come up on Grace's left, and as the animal leaped into the air, Grace instinctively threw up her rifle. The bead was right on the deer's heart, and all she had to do was pull the trigger. She tracked the beautiful, flowing motion of the fleeing deer, but did not fire. Finally as the deer disappeared into the depths of the forest, she lowered the rifle and turned.

For two hours she tramped the cold woods, then returned to the farm. Prudence met her as she came into the kitchen, saying impatiently, "Grace, where has thee been? Thee was supposed to go look at the cattle old man Potter wants to sell."

"Oh, I forgot," Grace said.

"Well, Clyde went to look at them," Prudence said with a shrug. "We talked about you last night . . . what's the matter, Grace?" She gave her sister a strange look, then shook her head. "Thee has got to forget about that man. He's not coming back."

"I know," Grace said quietly. "I'll ride over and see the cattle."

She went to her room and changed her rough clothing for a dress, then stood for a while brushing her hair. Finally she put the brush down and left her bedroom. She had no desire to go look at the cattle and made up her mind to tell Prudence so. When she did, Prudence brightened up. "Well, if thee is not going, Grace, I'll go and meet Clyde."

"And go into town later, I suppose?" Grace ventured, then smiled. "You go on, Prudence. Tell Clyde to make the decision about the cattle. He's got a good eye for stock. I'll hitch the team to the light buggy."

Prudence lost no time in shedding her apron. She rushed off to change and, when she came down, gave Grace a hug. "Now don't wait up for us. We may be late."

"All right. I'll keep something on the stove in case you are hungry."

After Prudence drove away, Grace listlessly performed the household chores. Finally she went into the parlor and sat down. Looking around the room, she saw a hundred reminders of her father, and loneliness came to her. Her thoughts returned to the days she'd spent at Armory Square Hospital, but that brought to her mind the letters she'd received from Miss Dix, asking her to return to duty.

I'll have to write her. It's not fair to let her think I'm coming back. She had tried to force herself to return, but somehow could not face up to it. Now she tried again to analyze what it was that seemed to loom before her like a wall when she thought of returning to Washington. *Is it that I can't stand to be reminded of John? No, because I'm constantly reminded of him right here. What is it, then?* Something came to her mind, and she brushed it aside, but it came again persistently. *Can God be keeping me here for some purpose? What on earth could it be? I'm no good to myself or anyone else—not the way I am!*

She got up and was about to leave the room when she glanced out the window and saw a two-seated carriage emerge from the trees that blanketed the main road. *Why, that's Grissom's carriage,* she thought. *He has no reason to come here.*

But the carriage turned in to their drive, and Grace hurried out to the front porch. Grissom pulled the carriage to a halt, touched the brim of his hat, and said, "Howdy, Miss Grace."

"Hello, Pat," Grace responded. "Cold drive from town."

"Yes, right sharp." He turned to the figure huddled beside him, saying, "Mister Rocklin, we're here."

Grace saw the man beside Grissom lean forward and said something quietly, and Grissom turned to say, "Miss Grace, Mr. Rocklin wants me to wait. Kin I put the team in the barn and grain 'em, let 'em warm up 'fore I start back?"

"Of course, Pat." Then she smiled and said, "Then come inside and warm yourself up, too." She watched as a tall black man stepped out of the backseat and helped Grissom's passenger to the ground. The two of them made their way to the steps, and the passenger took off his hat, revealing a crop of gray hair and a face gray with fatigue. He seemed to be studying Grace's face for a few moments, then he spoke in a low voice.

"My name is Rocklin, Thomas Rocklin. You are Miss Grace Swenson?"

"Yes." Grace saw that the man was trembling and said quickly, "Come in, please. It's very cold."

She held the door open as the black man helped Rocklin up the steps. "Come right in, both of you." As soon as they were inside, she said, "Come into the kitchen. It's warm there, and there's coffee on."

"I want to tell you, Miss Swenson—," Rocklin began, but she interrupted at once.

"Come and thaw out, sir. It's a cold ride from town." She supervised the thing easily, drawing out a chair, seeing that the old man was comfortable, then smiling at the black man. "What is thy name?" she asked.

"Why, it's Zander, ma'am."

"Zander, thee looks cold. Come and stand by the stove while I get something hot to thaw thee out."

Grace quickly poured two cups of coffee, laced them with sugar and thick cream. "Drink this, and I'll heat some soup."

As the woman busied herself with the food, Thomas exchanged glances with Zander, and they both nodded. The gleam in Zander's eyes was a mark of approval, and Thomas relaxed in the chair, soaking up the heat from the stove. He sipped the scalding coffee, almost burning his lips, and when the young woman set two bowls of steaming soup and a roll of fresh bread before him, he realized how hungry he was.

"Would thee ask the blessing on the food, Mr. Rocklin?" Grace asked.

"Why, I certainly will," Thomas nodded. He did so briefly, then said, "Zander, sit down and eat your soup."

Zander looked scandalized. He had never sat at a table in his life with white people. But his master muttered, "Don't be a fool. Sit and eat."

"Yas, suh, Marse Thomas," he said and sat down, eating carefully, keeping his eyes down.

The door opened, and Grissom entered, gratefully taking the steaming cup of coffee that Grace held out to him. He seated himself in a chair, and Thomas noted how he seemed not fully removed from the group, his eyes and ears taking in everything in the room.

Thomas ate most of the bowl of soup, saying nothing. The food warmed him, brightening his eyes and reviving him. He had had a bad time on the trip from town, but now felt stronger. The young woman had sipped coffee, speaking casually of how bad the winter had been and the trouble it had caused with the stock. She was, Thomas realized, skilled at putting people at their ease, and understood that she kept up her speaking to avoid a painful silence.

She's a smart young woman, he thought with approval. *Not many women would have that much tact.*

Finally he was finished, and she said, "Now, let's go to the parlor. It's more comfortable there."

Rocklin cast his eyes at Grissom and nodded. *She knows I've come to talk—and that I want some privacy.* "Thank you for the meal," he said. "It was delicious."

He followed her down a short hall, and when they were in a small room with bookcases on one wall, she said, "Take that chair, Mr. Rocklin." While he sat down with a sigh of comfort, she put two small logs on the fire, then came to sit across from him.

Rocklin said, "I must apologize for thrusting myself on you, Miss Swenson. I asked the driver to wait, because I wasn't sure if I'd be staying."

"Thee is welcome, sir."

"I—hope I will be more welcome, Miss Swenson, when you know my reason for coming." The fire snapped and a spark rose and fell on the stone hearth. Rocklin had tried to anticipate this moment, to plan what he would say—but now that it had come, he found himself in difficulty. "I don't know how to put this to you," he said finally.

"Perhaps I can help thee," Grace said. Her face seemed to be rather pale, Rocklin noticed, and her lips trembled slightly. He was surprised, for she had been so placid until this moment. She hesitated, then asked, "Is it about thy son, Mr. Rocklin?"

Grace had fed the men, curious as to the nature of the visit, but it was not until the old man sat down in the chair that the answer came to her: *He's John's father!* Something about the planes of the older man's face, the way he held himself—and the way it was an echo of how John had sat in that very chair—brought the truth to her.

Thomas stared at her in shock, then nodded. "You're very quick, Miss Grace!"

"He is much like thee," Grace said simply.

"They say so."

Grace licked her lips, then spoke almost in a whisper. "Is he alive, Mr. Rocklin?"

"Oh, yes!" Thomas rapped out at once. "Yes, indeed! I—I guess my visit does seem like a portent of doom."

Grace took a deep breath, her hand on her breast. "I'm very glad," she said simply.

"He's alive, but in terrible trouble. That's why I've come to you."

"Tell me," Grace said quickly, leaning forward. And for the next twenty minutes, she sat still, asking no questions as Rocklin explained how his son had come to be in a Union hospital. He paused to say, "He's spoken of you so much, Miss Grace, that I almost feel I know you."

"But if his memory is back, how can there be trouble?" Grace asked.

Thomas hesitated, then said, "He was captured by Confederate troops, and he was wearing the uniform of a Union soldier. Do you know what that means?"

Grace grasped it at once. "He's suspected of being a traitor?"

"Exactly! And if things don't change, he'll be hanged."

Grace stared at him. "But—he didn't *know* he was a Confederate soldier. And he was *forced* to join the Union army." She spoke rapidly, explaining how Col. Drecker had given him no choice at all.

Thomas listened carefully, then nodded. "That's exactly what Burke told us."

Grace hesitated slightly. "His name is . . . Burke?"

"Yes."

Grace stood up abruptly and began to pace the floor. Her knees were weak, and she clasped her hands tightly together to control the trembling that had come to them. She had always been a calm woman, but this had shaken her, and she had to wait and pray until peace came to her. Finally she came to stand before Thomas. "Thee is not a well man, Mr. Rocklin. Why did thee not send someone else to tell me about . . . about Burke?"

Thomas said simply, "I don't have long to live, Miss Grace. And many of my family and friends told me I was a fool to make such a desperate journey in my condition." He shook his head, but there was a brightness in his dark eyes and a note of triumph in his voice as he added, "I've failed my family so much, but if I could do this *one* thing—if I could save Burke—why, I'd feel my life was not in vain!"

Grace suddenly knew that God was in the room. There was no change in what she saw with her eyes or what she heard. Yet she *knew* that she was being dealt with by the Spirit of the Lord.

"What does thee want me to do, Mr. Rocklin?"

"I want you to come to Richmond with me. Our lawyer says that we have to have records from the Union hospital where Burke was treated, records that bear out what he claims about losing his memory. And he wants you to testify. If we can get those records, and if you will come and testify, Burke has a chance. If not, he will be convicted. And he will die."

Suddenly Grace understood why she had felt unable to go back to Washington. God had been keeping her here so she might do all she could to save Burke!

"I'll go with thee," she said quietly.

Thomas whispered, "Thank God!" He took her hand, kissed it, then asked, "Grace, do you love my son?"

Grace nodded. "Yes, I love him. I'll always love him."

"And I love him, too," the man said, tears glistening in his eyes.

The two sat there in the quiet room, speaking of what must be done, and as they spoke, a great joy came to Grace. *He's alive—and I can help him!* she thought.

The next morning, three passengers boarded the southbound train, and it was Al Cotter who summed up the feeling of the town: "Well, Pat, that'll be the last we see of Sister Grace! She's gone to Richmond, and there ain't no good can ever come out of a thing like that!"

CHAPTER TWENTY-ONE
The Verdict

Gaines Franklin DeQuincy chewed slowly on the stub of his cigar as he stared out the window at the long icicles that hung along the eaves of the courthouse. The icicles glittered like diamonds in the morning sunlight, but the lawyer felt there was something sinister and ominous in their pristine beauty. He rolled the cigar around in his catfish-shaped mouth, thinking, *Pretty enough, but they look like knives. One of them could pierce a man to the heart.*

DeQuincy was a startling combination of cynic and romantic. He kept the romantic side of his nature carefully hidden, however, so that his friends—and his enemies— would have been startled to discover any trace of it in his makeup.

Pretty as a picture, those icicles. But it's a cold sort of beauty—like some women I've known. A bitter memory lifted like a specter out of his past and threw a fleeting shadow across his mind, and he abruptly tossed his cigar into the brass spittoon with an angry gesture.

He wheeled away from the window, turning to face Clay Rocklin and Mrs. Susanna Rocklin, wishing he'd never allowed himself to get involved with Burke Rocklin's trial. He'd accepted the case only after a persistent pleading on the part of Thomas Rocklin. And he'd warned Rocklin plainly, *"I'm not a miracle worker, Mr. Rocklin. Chances are fifty to one against acquittal."*

Now DeQuincy knew that the two in front of him were expecting exactly that—some sort of legal legerdemain—to set Burke Rocklin free.

Susanna's eyes were fixed on DeQuincy. It was the third day of the court-martial, and no visitors were permitted except as witnesses. She'd studied the lawyer each day and had been unimpressed by his appearance. DeQuincy was less than average height and not at all impressive. He wore a scruffy brown beard that covered the lower part of his face, and the only noticeable facet of his appearance was a pair of sharp brown eyes that missed nothing. His uniform was wrinkled, and traces of his breakfast were evident on the lapels of his coat. He spoke in a rather bored tone of voice, and Susanna had no way of knowing that in a courtroom he could lift that voice into a bellow that would rattle the rafters!

"You're not optimistic, are you, Maj. DeQuincy?" she asked.

The lawyer shot her a sudden glance. "No, Mrs. Rocklin. I am not." He pulled a fresh cigar from his pocket, bit off the end, and spit it into the cuspidor. Pulling out a match, he struck it on the surface of the desk, leaving a fresh scarred track on the walnut surface. He got the cigar going, sending clouds of lavender smoke into the air, then tossed the match on the floor. Only then did he put his sharp eyes on the two of them, saying, "It's not a case any lawyer would be hopeful about."

Clay was wearing a fresh uniform and looked very distinguished. "What's going on, Major?" He shook his broad shoulders in a gesture of impatience. "Are the officers prejudiced against my brother?"

"Why, certainly!" DeQuincy stared at Clay as if he had said something rather stupid. "Didn't you know they would be?"

"I thought a prisoner was supposed to get a fair trial." His lips drew together into an angry line. "It can't be very fair if the jury's already made up its mind!"

DeQuincy's crooked lips twisted into a wry grin. "Capt. Rocklin, you don't spend a lot of time in courtrooms, do you?"

"No, I don't!"

"Well, if you did, you'd know that ninety-nine juries out of a hundred have their minds made up about their vote before they're even picked. And in this case, that fact is all but guaranteed."

"Why is that, Major?" Susanna asked quietly.

DeQuincy removed the cigar from his lips, examined it, then replaced it. "Because your son was wearing a Federal uniform." He shrugged. "No matter what other facts may be involved, they're sure about *that* fact, and nothing's going to get it out of their minds."

"I see." Susanna sat there quietly, and DeQuincy admired her calmness. He'd never seen a woman who had her strength, and he wished he had better hopes to offer her.

"Don't give up," he grunted. "It's never over until the verdict is in."

"When will that be, Major?"

DeQuincy looked down at the fresh scar on the desk thoughtfully. Tracing it with his forefinger, he said, "I think tomorrow."

"So soon?" Clay blinked in surprise. "But they haven't heard our witnesses."

"No, but they're officers, and they don't have the freedom of civilians," DeQuincy stated. "They can be pulled out at any moment and sent to the western theater or to some other spot. I've done all I know to slow things down, but I'm guessing they'll end it tomorrow." He looked up as a sergeant opened the door and informed him that the court-martial was about to resume. "Now, you two will have to keep your temper," he warned. "Some of the members of the court are antagonistic. Don't let them make you mad. That's what they want. No matter what happens, just tell the truth as calmly as you can."

Grabbing his briefcase, he left, slamming the door behind him.

Clay stared moodily at the door, then shook his head. "He's not my idea of a great lawyer."

Susanna shook her head. "He doesn't look like much, but he's a fighter, Clay. That's what we need for Burke."

Clay nodded slowly. "That's what father said." He noted the lines of fatigue on his mother's face and put his hand on her arm. "Hard to believe when everything's going against you, isn't it?"

"Anyone can believe when things are right," Susanna said. "Faith is for when things are all wrong." She smiled slightly, adding, "I've been thinking of Abraham. Remember how his one dream in life was to have a son? And then when he had Isaac, God told him to take the boy and sacrifice him?"

"Pretty stiff test, wasn't it?"

"Yes. All he ever wanted, and God told him to let it go." Susanna's eyes grew sombre, and she fell silent. The two of them sat there as time passed, and finally she whispered, "I wonder where your father is?"

Clay knew her thoughts, for he had been wondering the same thing. It had occurred to him that his father might have fallen ill on the way to Pennsylvania—that he might be lying unconscious somewhere and would never bring the woman to testify.

"I don't know, Mother, but he's doing his best. I know that!"

They sat there in the small room, helpless and totally cut off from what was happening down the hall. Their hopes were in the scrubby hands of Gaines DeQuincy—insofar as human help was concerned—and they both felt, as they sat facing their fears, those hands seemed to be very unlikely security.

DeQuincy stared at the officers seated at the long table. They were the enemy! He always thought of the jury as the enemy, even more so than the prosecuting attorney.

"You know the prosecuting attorney is going to go for your throat," he told young lawyers. "You can handle that. But the jury, they're the ones who can send your man to the gallows! So you fight them—but you smile and never treat them rough. Find out who's on your side and who's out to kill your man. Then you work on them!"

He stared at the five officers, then glanced down at the single page in front of him. He always drew up a chart, showing the jury. In this case it was very simple. He had put the members of the court-martial into two categories: friends and enemies. Next to each of the names, he had written a description and some comments:

FRIENDS

Capt. Maynard Wells. Age 25. Good combat record. Sense of humor. Listens to everything. Hard—but fair. Will vote to acquit if he has a chance.

Lt. Powell Carleton. Age 21. Feels out of place with senior officers. Afraid to ask questions because of his youth. (Smile at him often, give him confidence!) Seems meek, but will not kill my man unless he has to. Will acquit if evidence gives him a chance.

ENEMIES

Maj. Carl Lentz. Age 50. Lost an arm at Malvern Hill. Hates Yankees. Would be fair in most circumstances, but he will never be able to forget the charges against Rocklin. At best, a "maybe."

Maj. D. L. Patterson. Age 62. Too old for a combat officer. Has his commission as reward for political favors. Not a bad man, but a political animal. Will not *dare* set Rocklin free for fear people will say he's not a thorough patriot. Will vote to kill my man, no matter *what* I do or what evidence is produced!!! Will vote guilty.

Col. Ransome Hill. Age 55. Never saw a finer looking man—except for Gen. Lee! Tremendous field commander. Will make general sooner or later. But has lost his only two sons in the war, one at Seven Pines and one at Fredericksburg. Lives for nothing but to kill Yankees. He is fair enough as ranking officer of the court, but his eyes are cold when he looks at Burke Rocklin. Will vote guilty.

DeQuincy ran his eyes over the list. *Three to two—at best!* he thought.

"Not very good odds, eh, Major?" Burke Rocklin murmured.

DeQuincy turned, startled, to find his client staring at the sheet. He quickly wadded it up, saying, "Just a game I play, Burke. Doesn't mean a thing."

And then he looked up as Col. Hill said, "The court will hear Capt. Clay Rocklin."

When Clay entered, he turned and gave Burke an encouraging smile, then took the oath in a firm voice and sat down.

"Capt. Rocklin," Col. Hill said promptly, "please tell this court how you identified the body that was buried under the name of Burke Rocklin."

DeQuincy had heard the story several times and saw that the captain made a good impression on the two younger members of the court. When he was finished, Maj. Patterson demanded, "How could you have made such an error, Captain? After all, it was, supposedly, the body of your only brother!"

"Sir, the man I identified was practically destroyed from the waist up," Clay said evenly, staring at the major. "But he was wearing my brother's uniform, and he had my brother's ring on his finger."

Capt. Wells, the young captain, asked with some sympathy, "Captain, did anyone else identify the body?"

"Yes, sir, my son Denton, an officer in the Army of Northern Virginia."

Score one for the home team! DeQuincy said to himself with satisfaction. *We've got Capt. Wells on our side for sure. Now—give it to them again, Capt. Rocklin!*

"Now, Capt. Rocklin," Maj. Lentz piped up. His face was red, and he had the air of a drinking man. "You found your brother in Libby Prison, I believe. What was his condition?"

"Very poor," Clay said instantly. "He seemed unlikely to live."

"Are you a physician, Captain?" This from the prosecuting attorney, a lean captain of thirty named George Willing.

"No, sir," Clay said evenly. "I am not, but Kermit Maxwell is. I believe he's already been before this court?"

The question brought a flush to Willing's cheeks. He had tried hard to shake Maxwell's testimony, to prove that Burke Rocklin had been faking his illness. But the old man had stopped him with a withering look and a few acid words. Willing said quickly, "Just answer the question, Captain!"

"No, sir, I'm not a physician."

The court asked Clay many questions, mostly concerning the matter of the defendant's loss of memory. Clay answered briefly and was not afraid to admit that it was a difficult thing to describe.

The youngest member of the court, Lt. Powell Carleton finally asked, "Captain, you were convinced that the defendant was telling the truth. What made you so certain?"

Clay gave the young man a thin smile. "Two things. One, my brother was *never* an actor. If he was putting on an act, he'd changed completely. And secondly, I tried him out."

"Tried him out?" Col. Lentz asked. He leaned forward, about to put his elbows on the table, then realized that one sleeve was empty. He sat back a little embarrassed, asking, "How did you do that?"

"I'd mention things that never happened as if they *had* happened," Clay said at once. "I'd say, 'We lost that gray stallion you liked so much,' when there'd been no stallion. He *never* remembered those things. And sometimes I'd drop things he ought never to have forgotten, and he almost always remembered them."

285

"What sort of things, Capt. Rocklin?" Lentz demanded.

"My brother could always name the presidents of the United States with the dates they served. I'd say, 'Now when was it that Madison was in office?' and he'd always know. Once when I did that he stared at me and asked, 'How did I know that?'"

Lentz was intrigued by this, and for some time drew Clay out. Finally he nodded, saying, "Thank you, Captain," and leaned back.

George Willing knew that he'd lost points and set out to prove that such things meant nothing. Finally Clay was dismissed, and DeQuincy whispered, *"That* didn't hurt us any!"

"Send in Mrs. Susanna Rocklin," Col. Hill said, and they all rose when Susanna came in. She took the oath in a quiet voice, then sat down.

"Mrs. Rocklin, please tell the court of the 'recovery' of the defendant." The slight difference of tone on the word *recovery* was noticeable to everyone in the room. It was almost tangible evidence that the colonel did not accept that "recovery" as real.

Susanna heard the tone and understood it very well, but let nothing show in her face. She spoke quietly for ten minutes, then waited for the challenge she was certain would come.

And so it did, from the prosecuting attorney. "Mrs. Rocklin, you love your son, don't you?"

"Yes, I do."

"Of course." Capt. Willing nodded. "And I'm sure that we all honor you for it. You'd be an unnatural mother if you didn't!"

"He's out to get her," DeQuincy whispered to Burke.

"Can't you stop him?" Burke demanded.

"Stop him?" DeQuincy turned his sharp black eyes on Burke with amazement. "Bless you, no! I hope he chops her to ribbons!" When he saw the look of indignation that leaped into Burke's eyes, he grabbed Burke's arm, saying,

"He's a hothead, and he's not learned that you don't attack a woman in court—especially not the mother of a soldier in the Army of Northern Virginia! Let him go! He'll be more help to us than ten witnesses."

For the next twenty minutes, Capt. Willing questioned Susanna over and over again about the details of what he termed "the alleged recovery." At one point he grew so abusive that Col. Hill looked at the defense lawyer in disgust, asking, "Maj. DeQuincy, don't you object to the fashion in which Capt. Willing is treating your witness?"

"No, sir," DeQuincy said smoothly. "The captain has no facts, so he's doing all he knows how—he's abusing a helpless woman." DeQuincy enjoyed the sudden reddening of his opponent's face, adding, "I'm sure the *gentlemen* on the court understand what Capt. Willing is doing."

Willing was filled with wrath. "Mrs. Rocklin, you love your son, and you would do *anything* to save his life. Isn't that true?" he shouted.

"No, sir," Susanna answered. "It is *not* true!" Her eyes were bright, and when Willing stopped in shocked surprise, she said, "I took an oath to tell the truth. That oath was to God, and I would not lie to save my son's life!"

"I suppose you'd let him hang?" Willing sneered.

Susanna faced him squarely. "Many mothers have given their sons for the Confederacy, Capt. Willing. I love God, and my son would despise me if I denied my faith to save his life. Isn't that right, Son?"

Burke said clearly, "Yes!"

At once Col. Hill said, "You will not speak to the defendant, Mrs. Rocklin. And you, Mr. Rocklin, will have your turn to speak! Now, are there any more questions from you gentlemen for Mrs. Rocklin?"

"Mrs. Rocklin," Lt. Carleton asked in a subdued tone. "I believe you have relatives who are in the Union army?"

"Yes, Lieutenant," Susanna said, nodding. "My husband's brother Mr. Stephen Rocklin has a son in the Army of the Potomac—Col. Gideon Rocklin. The colonel has two sons in the Union army."

"Well, do you think it possible, since some of your family are in the Union, that your son Burke might have sympathies with the North?"

"No, sir, I cannot think so. My son took an oath to the Confederate States. He was not always a good son, but he was never a liar."

Lt. Carleton seemed to find this answer sufficient. "I have no more questions, Col. Hill."

As soon as Susanna left the room, Col. Hill asked, "Maj. DeQuincy, do you have other witnesses?"

"Yes, sir, I have one. I call Burke Rocklin."

DeQuincy stood up, but moved to the side of the room so that the court had a clear view of the defendant. "Mr. Rocklin, will you please relate your experience to this court. Begin with the Battle of Second Manassas."

Burke nodded and began at once to tell his story. He spoke of the battle, but said, "I was struck down on the battlefield and have no memory of anything that took place between that time and the time I woke up in the Armory Square Hospital in Washington."

"Now, please tell the court of your time in that hospital," DeQuincy said.

Burke spoke carefully, omitting no detail, explaining all he experienced, including the time he'd spent at the Swenson farm.

He makes a fine witness, DeQuincy thought, *but wait until Willing gets at him!*

Finally Burke finished, and DeQuincy thought quickly. Ordinarily he would have drawn the witness out, but he knew nothing could improve on what Burke had said, nor the manner in which he had said it.

"Gentlemen, I have nothing to add to my client's statement. Capt. Willing, your witness."

Willing leaped up, and for the next two hours he slashed at Burke's testimony. Burke kept his head, never losing his temper, and DeQuincy knew it was better for him to stay out of it.

Finally Willing said, "So we have your word, Mr. Rocklin, that all of this happened?"

"Yes, sir."

"Your word? But nothing more?" Willing turned to the court and made a solid speech regarding 'reasonable doubt' and the necessity of facts over hearsay. As he listened, even DeQuincy had to admit to himself it was good stuff. Finally Willing said, "If there were only *one* witness, I would not be so adamant. But you gentlemen know that the most heinous crime in any army is desertion and joining forces with the enemy. By all the *evidence,* this is exactly what Burke Rocklin has done. I know not his reasons, but there is *no* justification for this behavior."

DeQuincy studied the faces of the men on the court and knew he was licked. *Even the younger men can't let him go—not with evidence so piled against him!*

"We will hear the closing arguments after a short recess," Col. Hill announced. The members of the court got up and filed out, and DeQuincy rose and accompanied Burke to the room that was his cell. The lawyer sat down, lit up a fresh cigar, and then looked at his client.

Burke caught the look, then shrugged. "You didn't have much to fight with, Major."

"Now, don't be handing down any verdicts, Burke," the lawyer admonished. "We've still got a chance."

But late that afternoon, when DeQuincy emerged from the courtroom to speak with Clay and Susanna, his face told the story. Even before he could speak, Susanna said, "He was convicted, wasn't he?"

DeQuincy nodded slowly. "If we could only hear from your husband—!"

Clay felt his stomach knot up. "We've got to do something! It can't end like this!"

DeQuincy knew that things *did* end just this way—often—but he only said, "We'll hope for clemency in the sentence. I'll try for life imprisonment instead of execution."

"No!" Susanna said at once. "That's worse than death, to be locked up for life!" She was pale, but her eyes were not defeated. "We will believe God! In the shadow of the gallows, I'll believe God!"

CHAPTER TWENTY-TWO
"Give Love a Chance!"

Melora pulled her horse up in front of the mansion, slipped to the ground, and handed the reins to the servant who came to take them. "Thank you, Moses," she said with a nod. As he took the lines, she asked, "Has your father come back?"

"No, ma'am, he ain't." Moses was the tall son of Dorrie and Zander. His high-planed face was sober, and he shook his head, adding, "Sho' is miserable 'bout Marse Burke!"

As the slave led her horse away, Melora turned and mounted the steps. When a young maid opened the door in answer to her knock, she said, "Hello, Lutie. Is Mrs. Rocklin here?"

"Yassum, Miss Melora. She's in de' parlor wif' Marse Clay. I guess you knows de' way."

"Thank you, Lutie."

Melora went down the long hall to a small room and knocked lightly on the tall double doors. When she heard Susanna's voice bidding her to enter, she opened the door and stepped inside. Clay got up at once and came to her. She put out her hands to him, saying, "I just heard, Clay."

"I knew you'd come," he said. He wanted to take her in his arms, but turned as his mother stood and came to Melora. The two women embraced, and then Susanna said, "You two sit down. I'll go make tea."

She left the room, and Clay summoned a sad ghost of a smile. "How'd you hear about Burke?"

"Tad Greenaway heard about it when he was in Richmond. He knew we'd want to know."

"It'll be in the paper today," Clay muttered. He looked pale and ill, Melora noted. Catching her glance, he shook his head. "It's hit me harder than I thought anything could, Melora."

"Come and sit down," she urged.

"No, I've been sitting here for hours. Is it too cold for you to walk?"

He got his coat and forage cap, helped her on with her heavy coat, and the two of them left the house.

"Your mother will wonder where we are," Melora said.

"No. She'll know," Clay said. He led her to a path at the side of the house, and the two of them walked down the narrow road that led to the summerhouse. The air was very cold, and he asked, "Are you warm enough?"

"Yes. I love cold weather."

They walked for half an hour, past the summerhouse where Clay had lived alone until Ellen had died. As they moved deeper into the woods, Melora thought of all that had happened in the last few months and knew that Clay's thoughts were on this too.

The snow was packed down into hard plates of ice, and they walked carefully to keep from slipping. When they came to a small creek, Clay said, "Let's cross over. The ice will hold us up."

They edged carefully across the ice, grabbing at saplings to pull themselves up on the far bank. Clay went first, then reached back and pulled Melora after him. Her feet slipped, and she grabbed wildly, but he caught her and pulled her to firm footing, holding her close.

She had cried out as her feet flew out from under her, but when his arms closed around her, she held on tightly. Clay pulled her closer, and she looked up quickly. She knew he was going to kiss her and could have pulled away . . . but she did not. She surrendered to the pressure of his arms, and rested against him, lifting her face.

The feel of her in his arms and the sight of her soft lips raised to his were enough for Clay. He held her tightly, and their kiss was wildly sweet. For that one moment, he forgot about Burke and the war and the children. There was only the joy of being with this woman he'd loved for so long and the solace of that love.

Melora clung to him, her hands going up to pull him closer. A tumultuous rush of love rose in her, and she gave herself to him completely, yielding herself to him with a sweet willingness.

Finally Clay lifted his head, but he did not let her go. "Melora, I love you so much!" His voice was husky with emotion.

"I know!" Melora whispered. "I know, my dear!" Reaching up, she cupped his cheek with her hand. "And you're the only man I've ever loved!"

They stood there, clinging to each other, shut off from the world. Finally she took his hand and drew him down a narrow path that followed the creek. They said no more until he drew her to a stop, turned her around, and asked with torment in his fine eyes, "Melora, what are we going to do?"

"We're going to be faithful to God and to each other," Melora said at once.

"But—"

"I know, Clay," she broke in. "I know all that stirs within you, because it's in me, too. We're older, you could get killed in the war—" Her voice broke, and she shook her head. "It's all true, but God knows our hearts, and through him, we'll always have each other. Do you believe that?"

"I only know I want you," Clay said simply. "But with Ellen dead so short a time and with a war to fight—"

"I'll be here, Clay," she said softly. "When the time is right, I'll be here."

He groaned and held her close again. "Oh, Melora! If we

could just run away from here, just you and I! If we could find some place where we could just be together and love each other."

Melora's lips curved in a tender smile, and she let him hold her for a time, then pulled back. "You'd never run away, Clay Rocklin, not in a million years!" Pride was in her eyes, for she knew this man so well. "You'd let yourself be pulled into pieces before you'd run away from your duty!"

Clay peered at her closely and then smiled. "I never knew I was such a noble cuss," he said. "Tell me more."

She talked with him, telling him of her love and the reasons for it, and so took the sting out of Clay's sorrow. By the time they got back to the house, he realized what she had done. Just before they went inside, he took her hand and kissed it. "Came to get the old man out of the grumps, didn't you?"

"You're not an old man!"

"Well, old or young, I am a grateful man," he answered. "You know me pretty well, I guess."

"Clay, let's take what we have and be grateful for it." Melora turned her face upward to him, and Clay knew she was sweet beyond anything he'd ever known. "It's too soon to talk of anything permanent between us, so let's just take every moment we do have and savor it."

She kissed him lightly, then went inside. Clay followed her, and as soon as Susanna saw them, she knew what had happened and was glad. She, too, longed for the day when this son of hers could claim the joy he'd been waiting for.

After Clay left to go back to camp, Susanna and Melora sat for a long time, speaking some—but often sharing the silence in the way fine friends often do. Finally Susanna said, "Melora, you're the daughter-in-law I've always longed for. Has he asked you to marry him?"

"No, it's too soon."

Susanna shook her head, a wistful smile on her face. "It's often too late for love, but never too soon, Melora! I'll pray God will help that foolish son of mine see that!"

A few days had passed since the verdict, and still no word came from Thomas Rocklin. With each passing day, the hopes of the family were dimmed. "He must be sick and unable to speak," Susanna said finally.

Burke had stood before the court for his sentencing and listened as they sentenced him to death—but the judgment had come only after a stormy session in which Lt. Powell Carleton almost managed to get himself court-martialled!

Lt. Carleton literally blew up when he saw that the court was going to hand out the death sentence. He turned pale, then stood up and said, "No! He's not going to hang—sir!"

Col. Hill was taken completely aback—even more so when young Carleton refused to be admonished. A wild session ensued, in which Carleton had cried, "I won't be a part of it! He may be guilty, but I'm not convinced of it. The least we can do is hand down a life sentence so that there's a chance to straighten things out!"

"Straighten things out!" Col. Hill grew incensed. "Are you telling me we're unjust?"

"You're not God, are you, Colonel?" Carleton demanded—and if the other members of the court had not intervened, it is likely that Lt. Carleton would have been Pvt. Carleton and in the guardhouse!

Finally Burke was brought in and the sentence was pronounced by Col. Hill. But Lt. Carleton stood up and stared straight at the colonel, stating flatly, "I want it on record that I oppose this sentence as being overly harsh!"

"Sit *down,* Lieutenant!" Col. Hill almost shouted. He calmed himself, then looked at Burke. "You have been found guilty of treason and this court sentences you to be hanged. You will be taken from this place to a place of confinement, and at dawn on February 14, you will be executed by the provost marshal."

Burke said nothing to the colonel. He only looked at the young lieutenant and smiled. "Thank you, Lieutenant," he said softly, then turned and followed the sergeant out of the court.

George Willing came over to stand beside DeQuincy. The captain had a great admiration for DeQuincy and said with a certain sadness, "Too bad. But there was never any real chance for him, was there, DeQuincy?"

DeQuincy kept his head down as he stuffed his briefcase. Finally he lifted his eyes, which where hot with anger. "Willing—I hate to lose!" he gritted between clenched teeth.

"Why, Gaines, I believe you think the fellow is innocent!"

DeQuincy snatched up the briefcase, and as he stalked toward the door, Willing asked, "Where are you going?"

Maj. Gaines Franklin DeQuincy stopped and turned his head. "I'm going to get drunk," he announced, then did an abrupt about-face and marched out of the courtroom.

Capt. Willing stared after him, then shouted, "Hey! DeQuincy! Wait, blast it all! I'm going to get drunk with you."

Burke was moved from the city jail to the stockade immediately after he was sentenced. He was treated kindly enough and spent most of his time writing. For the first two days he had visitors, but he pulled Clay aside to say, "On the last night, don't let Mother come. Or anybody else."

Clay said, "I'm coming, and that's final."

Burke grinned at his brother. "Just the two of us, then. All right?"

"If you say so."

And so the two days went by, and on the last night, Clay came and the two men sat and talked. Clay marveled at his younger brother's coolness and finally said, "Burke, I couldn't take it like—like you are."

Burke had been sipping coffee, but lowered the cup. He stared at the other man for a long time, then said, "Clay, you were wrong."

"Wrong? About what?"

"About my not being an actor. That's what you told the court." He sipped the coffee, then stared into the cup. "I'm an actor all right. Because I'm scared. Have been ever since this thing blew up." He looked up and caught Clay's look of amazement. "Oh, come on, Clay!" He smiled briefly. "It's like before a battle. Everybody's scared, but no one wants to show it. Isn't that right?"

Clay nodded slowly. "It's the way it happens to me. I get so scared I can't swallow, but of course you can't show that in front of the men."

Burke grew silent, then asked with some difficulty, "It makes a difference, doesn't it, when a man knows God?"

Clay answered carefully. "Christians get scared just like men who don't know God. But—it's a different kind of fear, I think. Before I became a Christian, I was in a few spots that looked like the end, and I was plenty afraid. But after I got saved, why, I was scared, but it wasn't the same."

"Tell me about it, if you can, Clay."

"Well, a lost man doesn't have much hope. He's afraid of two things—death and what comes after. But a Christian, he *knows* he's all right after he dies, so it's just that fear of the unknown that gets him. And I think some of that's built into us, Burke. Self-preservation. Some men get close enough to God so that they lose even that. Men like Stephen, in the Bible, the man who was stoned." Clay's eyes grew thoughtful as he added, "Now *there* was a man for you! Praying for his enemies as they killed him!"

The lamp outside the cell threw yellow bars that fell across the faces of the two men, and as Clay studied Burke, he saw the younger man's fear. "Burke, I've never believed much in shoving people toward God. Always thought God could do the drawing and a man could do the giving up."

The shadow of death lay on Burke, and he looked down into his cup for a long time before finally saying, "I've—wanted to call on God, Clay." He looked up with misery in his dark eyes. "But it seems like such a—a *rotten* thing to do!"

"Calling on God, rotten?" Clay blinked in astonishment. "How could that be?"

"I've never called on him before, never listened to him when I had the chance. Now I'm in trouble and need him. It seems so cheap and insincere, Clay!"

Clay shook his head. "You're making a big mistake, Brother. You're thinking of God as if he were a man. God doesn't act like we do. He's God, and he acts like God."

"I don't see what you mean."

"Well, when somebody hurts you, what do you do? Hurt them back if you can, right? But that's because of what we've become. God didn't make us like that, Burke, sin makes us like that. Adam wasn't like that, not before he fell away from God's grace. He was like God. The Bible says that God said, 'Let us make man in our image.' That really means God made man like himself."

"I haven't seen much of God in people," Burke said quietly.

"Yes, you have." Clay nodded. "You see it in Mother and in Raimey and in Melora. And you saw it in Jeremiah Irons. Isn't that right?"

Clay saw that his words hit Burke hard.

"Yes, I did!" he answered thoughtfully.

"And you saw it in that young woman, Grace Swenson, didn't you? I know you did, Burke."

Again Burke nodded. "You're right, Clay. She was full of God!" Then his lips drew into a harsh line. "But I'm not like them, Clay!"

"They're what Jesus Christ made them, Burke." Clay drove home the words, and for hours the two men talked. For Clay it was like one of the battles he'd taken part in. Sometimes he seemed to forge ahead, winning ground, and then Burke would counterattack, and he'd fall back. It was hard, agonizing work, for he knew he was wrestling for the very soul of his only brother.

More than once Burke cried out, "Leave me alone, Clay! It's no use! I've gone too far!"

But Clay never gave up. He read Scripture after Scripture. He prayed as he'd never prayed before in his life! And all the while he knew that some power was flowing into him, for he found himself quoting verses he didn't even know!

It's Melora and Mother—they're praying for me! he thought with certainty. And that realization encouraged and energized him, helping him as the night wore on and he pressed the matter on Burke.

Burke was holding himself together by will alone. He was terribly afraid, more afraid than he thought a man could be. He wanted to weep and beat the walls with his fists, but he sat in the chair trying to believe what Clay was telling him. "Do you mean that all I have to do is *ask*—and God will save me?"

"If you ask *rightly* you'll be forgiven," Clay answered. When he saw the bewilderment in Burke's eyes, he said quickly, "Many people call on God who don't mean it. They want *something,* but they don't want God himself."

"Well, I want to live," Burke said.

"I think you want more than that," Clay said. "You talked a lot about that preacher woman. I'm thinking if you lived, you would want her. Is that right?"

"Yes!"

"Well, you know you'd never have her as you are, don't you, Burke? And why do you want her? You may think it's because she's a woman and because she cared for you. But I will guarantee you that what drew you to Grace Swenson is the fact that you saw God in her! *That's* what drew you, for there is no greater lover than the Lord. Now, if you could walk out of this cell and go to her, you know what she'd say?"

Burke nodded wearily. "She'd never have a man who didn't love God." He shook his head. "If only I could believe like she does . . . if I could know God the way she does—" He broke off suddenly, blinking in surprise at what he'd just said. Then he turned wondering eyes on his brother, eyes that were beginning to fill with understanding. "Why, maybe I *have* wanted God, Clay! Ever since I met

Grace, I wanted what she had! The peace and the strength . . . the capacity to love and love . . .”

“It’s Jesus, Burke. Grace has Jesus,” Clay said with warmth. “And that’s what you want, I believe you don’t just want to live. I think you really want to live the kind of life that you’ve seen in Grace Swenson.”

Burke sat silently, then said, “I—I guess you’re right. And I think I see what you mean, about asking God to forgive me.”

“Then you must ask him!”

Burke’s eyes and voice filled with anguish. “I don’t know how.”

“Just talk to him, as you’re talking to me. You don’t have to be afraid to ask God for forgiveness,” Clay said gently. “He wants to give it to you even more than you want to receive it. He’s been after all of us all our lives. And if you ask God what he wants in return, why, he’d say, ‘I don’t want anything you have, my son, I just want *you!*’”

Tears came to Burke’s eyes as Clay spoke. He made no attempt to wipe them away as they ran down his cheeks. He leaned forward and whispered, “I can’t imagine why *anyone* would want me, much less, God!”

Clay knew his brother was being convicted by the Holy Spirit. He spoke gently about God’s mercy and finally said, “There’s no secret formula to asking God to save you, Burke. People ask in different ways—the way doesn’t matter to God. It’s what’s in the heart of the one who asks. Your heart is hungry for God, isn’t it?”

“Yes!”

“Then we will pray. As I pray for you, you tell God you’re tired of your old life. Tell him how bad you feel about what you’ve done. Tell him anything that’s in your heart. He’ll listen. And when you’ve told him that, just ask him to pardon you, to forgive all your sins. Claim the protection and redemption of the blood of Jesus, Burke! Claim the blood! God always hears when we claim the blood of his Son!”

Clay dropped his head and began praying. He prayed fervently, his own tears falling down his face, and finally he heard a sound. Opening his eyes, he saw that Burke had fallen to his knees and was pressing his face against the floor, his shoulders shaking with sobs.

At once Clay knelt beside his brother, and the small room was filled with angels—or so it seemed to both men. After a time, Burke lifted his head, and Clay saw that his brother's eyes were free of the fear and anguish that had filled them. Instead, they were filled with peace.

"You're really part of the family now, Burke!" Clay cried, throwing his arms around his brother, and he held him as the two rejoiced.

Finally they sat down, and Burke let his hands fall on the table. "You'll tell Mother?" He laughed, feeling like a child, so full of happiness. "Of course you will!" Then he smiled at Clay, wonder in his eyes. "It's so *different*, Clay!"

"Are you afraid, Burke?"

Burke Rocklin thought hard, then a smile came to his lips. "I've been burdened down so long . . . and now it's all fallen away! I guess I might have a little fear about the thing itself—the hanging—but the awful fear is gone! It's gone, and I feel like I'm free for the first time in my life."

"That's what Jesus does for us all, Burke, he sets us free!"

They sat there talking softly for a long time, and then Burke asked abruptly, "You're in love with Melora, aren't you, Clay?"

"Yes, I am."

Burke leaned forward, his eyes intent. "And you were faithful to Ellen all those hard years?"

"By the grace of God, I was, Burke."

Burke struggled with his thoughts, his brow knitted in a frown. Finally he asked, "Why don't you marry her, Clay?"

Clay had not been expecting such a question. "Why, Ellen's been dead less than a year! People would never understand. Besides, I may not live through this war. Melora would be left alone."

301

"Who cares what people say?" Burke demanded. "It's your life, and Melora's! You know Mother and Father love her dearly!"

"But if I die—!"

"If you die before you marry her, she has nothing. But if you marry now, she'll have *something!* And she deserves it, doesn't she? She's waited for you for a lot of years, years when she could have married a dozen times. It's not fair to her!"

"Burke, I can't—"

"Listen, Brother," Burke spoke earnestly. "It makes a man see some things pretty clearly, being in a spot like I'm in. And what I see is that every one of us ought to give love a chance. My only regret now is that I'll never be able to show Grace how much I love her! But if I could get out of here, I'd marry her in a second, even if I knew it was going to last only a month!"

Clay sat like a man who had been struck in the stomach. Burke's words seemed to beat against him, and he could not move or think clearly.

Burke watched as Clay struggled with himself, and finally there came the moment when his brother seemed to collapse. His face broke and his hands trembled so much that he held them together tightly.

"Maybe it's so, Burke," he whispered. "Maybe it's so!" He gave Burke a look of wonder. "I've been so blind!—So very blind!"

CHAPTER TWENTY-THREE
Witness for the Defense

★

"Wha—!" Col. Ransom Hill struck at the hand that was pulling at him. He'd slept poorly and thought he was having a nightmare.

"Sir, a message from the secretary of war!"

The words drove sleep away from Hill. He sat upright and peered at the lieutenant who had come into his tent. "What's that? The secretary of war?"

"Yes, sir! I thought you'd want to see it at once."

"Light that lamp!" Col. Hill threw the covers back and fumbled on the table for his reading glasses. Settling them on his nose, he took the envelope the lieutenant handed him and slit it with a knife he kept for that purpose. Drawing out a single sheet of paper, he read it carefully. His eyes widened, and he turned to the soldier standing nearby.

"Lieutenant, go find the other members who served on the court-martial for Burke Rocklin. Tell them the court will reconvene at eight o'clock."

"Yes, sir. You mean—*this* morning, sir?"

"Yes, blast your eyes! Get moving!"

When the lieutenant scurried out the door, Hill read the message again carefully, aloud: *"You are hereby ordered to reconvene the court and reconsider your verdict concerning Burke Rocklin. There is new evidence, and President Davis wants you to be certain that it is properly considered.*" It was signed *"James A. Seddon, Secretary of War."*

Although it was only five o'clock, Hill knew that he would sleep no more. He dressed and sat in his tent waiting for reveille. When it came, he got on his horse and rode slowly to the courthouse. He was two hours early, and there was nothing to do but wait.

Finally the doors opened, and he went at once to the courtroom. He took his seat at the table, and the other members of the court came in, sleepy-eyed and puzzled. He waited until the last of them appeared, then said, "We have been ordered to reopen the case of Burke Rocklin."

"By whose authority, sir?" Maj. Patterson asked.

Col. Hill gave him a frosty stare. "President Jefferson Davis."

Patterson's mouth dropped open, then he shut it and swallowed hard. Hill could see the man's mind working. *If Patterson thinks the president wants the man declared innocent, he'll do it like a shot!* He had nothing but contempt for Patterson and was himself determined not to give an inch. Let the secretary of war and the president step inside his courtroom in person, he would not budge!

Burke and Clay were waiting for the sun to come up, but at six they heard steps, running footsteps. The door opened and a lieutenant came in, his eyes open wide. "Burke! It's not what you think—I mean, something's happening!"

"What is it, Fred?" Clay demanded.

"Well, I can't say, Captain," the lieutenant said. "But I got orders to have the prisoner in the courtroom at eight o'clock."

Clay cried out, "Praise God!" He grabbed Burke and nearly lifted him off his feet. "It's got to be good news, Burke!"

"Better get shaved, Burke," the lieutenant said. "I'll be back to get you in half an hour." He grinned nervously. "Wouldn't want to be late for this, would you?"

Burke stared after him, then looked at Clay. "Maybe Father's come back with the papers from the hospital." He began to shave using cold water and then shrugged into his coat. It seemed a matter of minutes until the lieutenant came and led him away. When Burke entered the courtroom, he saw the court assembled. DeQuincy and Willing were standing up, and DeQuincy came to him at once. "Good news, Burke—"

"The court will begin proceedings!" Col. Hill stared at DeQuincy and said, "Major, I understand there is new evidence to be offered?"

"Yes, if it please the court."

"It does *not* please the court, Major," Hill said coldly. "But it seems we have no choice. Present your evidence."

DeQuincy moved to stand before the officers at the table and saw that, for once in his life, he was speaking to a *live* court! All five of the officers were staring at him avidly. "Gentlemen, I regret the inconvenience you've been put to, but the new evidence came at midnight. It took a visit to the president to get the court reconvened, but I think you'll not be hard on us after you hear what we have."

"Bring on the evidence, then, Major," Hill snapped. "It's too early for speeches."

"Of course, Colonel." DeQuincy nodded. "This case rests on one question: Did the defendant actually suffer a loss of memory? Once that is proven, the verdict can be nothing other than for acquittal. And I will admit that the defense was unable to prove this beyond a reasonable doubt before now." DeQuincy was a shrewd man. He knew enough to take the guilt from the shoulders of the court, to allow them to have some room to maneuver.

"Naturally you gentlemen brought in the only possible verdict you could, but let me now present you with some facts." He walked to the table, picked up a sheaf of papers, and brought them back to the court. "If you gentlemen will examine these papers, you'll find clear evidence that the defendant was indeed suffering from a complete loss of memory when he was taken off the battlefield. These are statements from the personnel of Armory Square Hospital—surgeons, nurses, orderlies—all swearing that from the moment the man we know to be Burke Rocklin became conscious, he had no memory at all of his past!"

DeQuincy watched the officers reading the papers with great interest and took the opportunity to turn and wink broadly at Burke.

"How are we to know these are reputable people?" Hill demanded. "We know none of them."

"You'll find a covering letter verifying all these statements. It's signed by one Dr. William Alexander Hammond, who is the surgeon general of the Union army. He is a personal friend of the surgeon general of the Confederate army, who will be happy to testify to this court both as to the validity of the signature and to the character of Dr. Hammond."

"I see," Hill said, nodding slightly. He read on, then exclaimed, "This letter is from Miss Dorothea Dix!"

"Yes, sir. All the world knows that Miss Dix is a woman of unquestionable character. She is willing to come to this court and swear that this man, known to her as John Smith, was in her hospital because he had absolutely no memory of his past."

"Why, this puts quite a different light on things!" Maj. Lentz spoke up. He stared at the documents, then asked, "How were these obtained, may I ask?"

"They were brought by one of the staff who arrived in Richmond last night. Would the court care to hear a personal testimony by this staff member of Armory Square Hospital?"

Col. Hill knew he was whipped. "Why yes, of course!"

"Thank you, Col. Hill." DeQuincy walked to the door, opened it, and said, "Will you come in, please?"

Every eye was on the door as a young woman in a gray dress stepped in. DeQuincy spoke to the officers, hard put to keep the triumph out of his tone. "This is Miss Grace Swenson, the nurse who treated Burke Rocklin when he was taken to the hospital in Washington. And, I believe, the person responsible for bringing him back to health."

Burke was on his feet, staring at Grace—and when she turned to meet his eyes, every man on the court saw his lips form her name. DeQuincy let the moment run on, for he was a man who loved drama, and a quick glance at the court told him that at least part of the officers of the court were the same!

Col. Hill cleared his throat, saying in a gruff tone, "Mr. DeQuincy, please escort your witness to the stand. And Mr. Rocklin," he added in a reproving tone, "you will take your seat, sir!"

Burke didn't mind the order, for he wasn't sure his legs would hold him up much longer anyway. He sat with a thud, amazement and longing warring in his expression.

Grace followed DeQuincy to the stand, then turned and took the oath. When she was seated, DeQuincy said, "Miss Swenson, what are your credentials as a nurse? Tell us about yourself."

"I was trained by Miss Dorothea Dix as a nurse, Maj. DeQuincy. Here are her recommendations. Would thee care to read them?"

At the use of *thee* the officers on the court sharpened their attention. As Grace continued to speak, they grew fascinated by her demeanor and mannerisms. Finally, she paused, and Capt. Wells asked, "You are of the Friends, I take it?"

"Yes, Captain."

"Would you tell us how the man you called John Smith behaved when he first came to you?"

"Of course. He knew nothing, not even his name—"

The officers listened as Grace spoke, and DeQuincy knew they were captivated. And why not? He was fascinated himself!

That woman is something! What a witness! he thought with admiration.

Finally Grace finished, and DeQuincy gave the prosecuting attorney a slight bow. "Do you have questions, Capt. Willing?"

Willing was stubborn, determined, and a poor loser. But what he was not was stupid. He saw at once that his goose was cooked and decided to make the best of it.

"Why, no, Maj. DeQuincy," he said blandly. "If this evidence had been in the hands of the court earlier, I feel certain that there would have been no trial." He turned boldly to Col. Hill and took his political and military future in his hands. "Colonel, the prosecution recommends that the case be dropped."

"Second the motion! Second the motion!" young Lt. Powell Carleton yelped, jumping to his feet, and from Capt. Wells came a rousing "Hear! Hear!"

Col. Hill was not a fool, either. He glanced at Burke, then smiled and said, "Do you gentlemen concur with me that the recommendation of the prosecuting attorney be followed and the case against Burke Rocklin be dropped?" He took only one look at the expressions of consent, then turned to face Burke.

"Mr. Rocklin, you are hereby released from this court. The case against you will be dropped from the records."

Burke heard the words Col. Hill spoke but could make no response. His eyes were fixed on Grace, and everything in him screamed at him to go to her—but he could not seem to move.

It was Gaines Franklin DeQuincy, the incurable romantic, who nudged him roughly in the side and whispered, "Go to her, you young idiot!"

And then he was moving, bolting from his chair, not even noticing pieces of furniture that he pushed aside . . . and she was in his arms. The court pretended to be busy with their papers, but when Burke lowered his head to tenderly kiss the tall young woman, a cheer went up from the irrepressible Lt. Powell Carleton.

DeQuincy stood there, a silly grin on his face, watching as the couple recovered their senses enough to walk through the door—though neither one released his or her hold on the other. Willing came over to his opponent and said, "Let's go get drunk again, Gaines! And after the war, I may want you to come to work for my law firm!"

DeQuincy slanted a look at him. "Willing, I *may* permit you to come to work for *my* firm after the war, but if I condescend to do so, you will have to watch your drinking habits!"

Thomas Rocklin died four days after his son was set free. The trip to Pennsylvania and back had been too much for him, but he was totally content. Burke seldom left his father's side, and during the times his father was completely conscious, they talked together, sharing their hearts. It was those times that Burke was to remember all his life. And he knew he would never forget the tears of joy his father shed when he told him of his finding the Lord.

On the final day, Burke awoke from a nap in his chair to find his father's mind clear. He moved his chair until he was next to the bed, and gravely met Thomas's gaze. "Father, you saved my life. How can I ever thank you?"

Thomas was very tired, but the words seemed to bring new life into his eyes. He looked over at his son and whispered, "You will have a son. Name him Thomas. Pour yourself into him!"

It was almost dawn when the family was called to Thomas's bedside. Susanna was holding her husband's hand as Thomas said his farewell to his daughter, Amy, then to her children, Grant, Rachel, and Les. He did the same for Clay's children, then he whispered, "Clay—?"

"Here!" Clay stooped beside the frail form and took his father's hand. "You've been a good father, sir!" he whispered. "These last years—you've held me up when I couldn't find myself!"

Thomas smiled. "I—I'm glad, Son. You've been—a proper son. Look after your mother—" Then he said,

"Burke?" When his youngest boy came to him, the dying man asked, "Where is Grace?"

"Here, Father." Grace dropped to her knees and took the thin hand in hers.

"We did well . . . didn't we, daughter?"

"Thee did it all, Father!"

"Well, well . . ." Thomas closed his eyes, then opened them with an effort. "Marry him—have his children—!"

Grace's eyes filled with tears as her heart overflowed with love. "Yes! I will marry him!"

Pleased, Thomas gazed upon them all, then his body arched. "Susanna—!" he cried out.

"I'm here, Tom."

Thomas looked into her face, smiled beautifully. "You have been my darling—wife!"

Then he took a deep breath, his eyes closed slowly, and his head fell to one side. Susanna brushed his hair back, and for the first time tears came to her eyes.

"Good night, Tom," she whispered, bending over to kiss him. "We'll meet in the morning."

Three days after the funeral of Thomas Rocklin, Clay rode up to the Yancy cabin. He was met, as usual, by the tribe of young Yancys, but when Melora came outside, he said, "Melora, put your coat on. I want to look at the hogs."

Melora looked at him uncertainly. "Why, all right, Clay." She slipped into her coat, and the two of them made their way to the hog pen. Once there, Clay turned quickly, saying, "Seems like this hog pen is the only private place around here."

"What is it?" Melora asked, trying to read his expression but failing. "Is something wrong?"

"No." Clay was watching her in a peculiar way, and Melora demanded, "You didn't come here to look at hogs, Clay Rocklin! Now, what is it?"

Clay said slowly, "That night before we thought Burke was to be hanged, I was with him in his cell—we both thought it was the last night he had." His eyes grew thoughtful, and he spoke of how Burke had gotten saved.

"That's beautiful!" Melora smiled. "You must be very happy."

"Yes, we all are."

When he said no more, Melora asked gently, "Will you tell me what is troubling you, Clay?"

He took her hand, smiling. "I couldn't keep anything from you if I tried, could I? You know me better than I know myself. Well, Burke asked about us, about you and me and our feelings for each other. When I told him I loved you, he—" Clay broke off, and Melora was surprised to see a tinge of red flow into his face. "Well, he told me to do something about it. He said that everyone ought to give love a chance."

Melora stood very still. Her heart seemed to be beating very rapidly, and she had the feeling that if she looked down she could see it beating against her chest.

Clay watched as her eyes searched his. "I'm too old for you, Melora. I've got a family, and when I'm old, you'll still be young and beautiful. I may die in battle, or come home blind or maimed—" He halted uncertainly.

"What are you saying, Clay?"

He took a deep breath, then spoke the words he had despaired of ever being able to speak—the words that filled him with a great joy and wonder: "I'm asking you to marry me, Melora."

Melora stared at him with amazement. She had expected anything but this. Oh, she had been sure it would come some day, but not now, not so soon. "But—what about your family . . . and the community?"

Clay took both her hands in his and drew her close, his eyes never leaving her. "I don't care about anyone but you. My family loves you—and who cares what Sister Smellfungus says?" He slipped his arms about her, and she rested her hands on his firm, strong chest. "So I ask you again, will you have me as your husband, Melora?"

Light seemed to explode within Melora as she answered, "Yes, Clay. I'll have you . . . and you'll have me!"

Their lips met, and they clung to each other desperately. Nothing else mattered, nothing else existed in that moment in time—for they finally had their dreams in their arms.

It was some time later when Clay lifted his head to whisper, "Oh, Melora! I've got the world in my arms!"

CHAPTER TWENTY-FOUR
The Oregon Trail

★

Spring came to Independence, Missouri, early that year. The warm breezes melted the snows, and the first golden buds appeared like tiny hearts.

The wagon train that pulled out of Independence, the first one of the year, was not large—only seventeen wagons—but there was a happy spirit about it that seemed to affect everyone. The train followed the Kansas River for two days, then turned north on the Little Blue. A few days later, the scout lifted his rifle and shouted, "There she is, the Platte—a mile wide and an inch deep!"

A cheer went up from those in the wagons, and they lurched forward anxious to make Fort Kearney off in the distance.

On the seat of the third wagon, Burke Rocklin sat loosely, his eyes searching the horizon.

"Can thee see Oregon, husband?"

Burke turned to Grace, reached out a long arm, and drew her to him. Ignoring her protests, he kissed her thoroughly. When she pulled away, looking around to see who might be watching, he laughed at her.

"You're a married woman, Grace. You can kiss all you please—as long as you're kissing me."

"Has thee no shame?" Grace scolded. She pouted—which

only made him want to kiss her again—and for all her protestations, she had a gleam in her eyes that she could not hide.

"Nope, not a bit," Burke said, shaking his head. "What should I be ashamed of? You've got the most beautiful lips for kissing I've ever seen," he declared. Then he grinned and reached for her again. "As a matter of fact—"

"Burke, thee must stop!"

Grace pushed him away, but then he winked at her, saying, "You won't get rid of me that easy when we make camp!"

"Burke!"

He laughed out loud, saying, "I love to see you blush. Makes you even more delectable."

"Thee talks like a fool!"

"Why, no, I talk like a man in love."

Grace closed her mouth and moved closer to her husband. They had been married two months, and she was enjoying every minute of learning to be a wife. Now she said, "Burke, I feel so—so shameless!" Dropping her eyes she whispered, "Do I make you happy, husband?"

Burke had discovered at once that his new bride had a fear that she would not be a good wife. He had learned that she needed to be told over and over that she was beautiful and desirable and that he adored her. And it was not difficult, for it was all true.

"Thee is the most beautiful and loving wife a man ever had," he said, smiling at her, then drew her close. "Every day I thank God for giving you to me."

"Truly?"

"Truly!"

She sighed and leaned against him with contentment. Finally she asked, "Do you feel lonely?"

"Lonely? Why, no! Not with you here, Grace!"

"I mean, thee is leaving thy home, husband, and all thy people. Will you not miss it?"

He smiled at the way she called him "husband"—it was something she had done often since their marriage, almost as if to reassure herself that he was hers. He touched her face tenderly. "I'll miss my people, Grace," he answered thoughtfully. "But I don't believe in the war. I think the South is going down, and no able-bodied man can live in Virginia and not believe in the Cause." He turned to face her. "Are you afraid, Grace? Of leaving your home? Oregon is a pretty rough place."

Grace took his hand and held it. "No. I'll never be afraid. But what will we do in Oregon?"

"Don't know," Burke admitted cheerfully. "I always wanted to see it, though. We'll just have to wait until we get there and see what happens."

They rolled along, contented and happy. That evening, they joined in the circle of wagons, cooked supper, and listened to the songs that went up from around the fires.

When it grew late, he looked up at the sky and pointed. "Look, there's Orion."

She looked up at the spangled night until she found the star he indicated. She leaned back against his chest, and he held her close. "You smell good, like a woman should," he whispered.

The compliment brought tears to her eyes—what a miracle God had worked in giving her this man to be her love and her companion! "Come, it's time for bed," she said and pulled him to his feet. "We've got to get a good night's rest. It's a long way to Oregon."

"You go on," Burke said. "I'll take care of the chores." She got inside, and he fed the stock, saw that they were well tied, then put out the fire. When he climbed inside the wagon, she drew him down at once.

"Husband," she whispered. "Does thee truly love me?"

"Yes! Truly!"

He kissed her, and she held him tightly.

Overhead Orion and his fellows did their great dance as the moon turned the canvas on the wagon to silver. A coyote yelped soulfully somewhere in the distance. The small stream bubbled over rounded stones, making a friendly sound. And finally—

"And will thee love me forever?"

"Yes, wife—forever!"

GILBERT MORRIS is the author of
many best-selling books, including
the popular House of Winslow series
and the Reno Western Saga.

He spent ten years as a pastor
before becoming professor of
English at Ouachita Baptist
University in Arkansas and earn-
ing a Ph.D. at the University of
Arkansas. Morris has had more than
twenty-five scholarly articles and
two hundred poems published.
Currently, he is writing full-time.

His family includes three grown
children, and he and his wife live in
Baton Rouge, Louisiana.

If you're looking for more captivating historical fiction, you'll find it in these additional titles by Gilbert Morris....

THE APPOMATTOX SAGA
- #1 A Covenant of Love   0-8423-5497-2
- #2 Gate of His Enemies   0-8423-1069-X
- #3 Where Honor Dwells   0-8423-6799-3
- #4 Land of the Shadow   0-8423-5742-4
- #5 Out of the Whirlwind *(New! Spring 1994)*   0-8423-1658-2
- #6 The Shadow of His Wings *(New! Fall 1994)*   0-8423-5987-7

RENO WESTERN SAGA
A Civil War drifter faces the challenges of the frontier, searching for a deeper sense of meaning in his life.
- #1 Reno   0-8423-1058-4
- #2 Rimrock   0-8423-1059-2
- #3 Ride the Wild River   0-8423-5795-5
- #4 Boomtown   0-8423-7789-1

THE WAKEFIELD DYNASTY
This fascinating saga follows the lives of two English families from the time of Henry VIII through four centuries of English history.
- #1 The Sword of Truth *(New! Summer 1994)*   0-8423-6228-2